Burning Moon

A WIL HARDESTY NOVEL

Richard Barre

CAPRA PRESS
MEMORABLE BOOKS SINCE 1969
SANTA BARBARA

A Robert Bason Book
Published by Capra Press
815 De La Vina Street
Santa Barbara, CA 93101
www.caprapress.com

Cover design, book design and illustrations by Frank Goad

LIBRARY OF CONGRESS CATALOGING-IN-PUBLICATION DATA

Barre, Richard.
Burning moon : a Wil Hardesty novel / by Richard Barre.
p. cm.
ISBN 1-59266-011-8 -- ISBN 1-59266-012-6 (numbered) -- ISBN
1-59266-013-4 (lettered)
1. Hardesty, Wil (Fictitious character)--Fiction. 2. Private
investigators--California--Fiction. 3. Vietnamese Americans--Fiction.
4. California--Fiction. 5. Gangs--Fiction. I. Title.
PS3552.A73253 B87 2003
2002014285

Edition: 10 9 8 7 6 5 4 3 2 1

First Edition: May 2003

For Sonny (Son Van Nguyen)

Who came far to make it home

Again
It seems we meet

In the spaces
In between

−GLEN PHILLIPS

Acknowledgments

Thanks to all who sheltered a grateful writer from the storm: Shelly Lowenkopf for his guidance, Son Van Nguyen for his translations and inspiration, Robert Bason for his faith, Frank Goad for his design and friendship, Harry Sims for his eagle eye, Audrey Moore for her boundless optimism, the Santa Barbara Library System for being there, and one very patient wife for more than words can express.

San Miguel Island, Months Earlier

*U*NTIL THE SQUALL ROLLED OVER THEM *like something out of a disaster flick, things aboard* Harmony *had been more or less confined to the fight. The same one that had started almost from the time they'd left the harbor: Wen's mother, her habit of calling about a hundred times a day, then dropping by unexpectedly—so that whenever he came home, SHE was there. Which meant, of course, no* lam tinh, *even what little it had come down to these days.*

Then there was Wen's rag on Jimmy's old man, Vinh. Attempting—according to Wen—to intimidate his future daughter-in-law into naming the baby when it came after Vinh's first wife, Giang, the dead one from Vietnam. Not even Jimmy's mother, as Wen put it.

Next issue was Jimmy's insistence that shaving their newborn's head was a useless, archaic tradition. Custom or no custom, nobody was going to do that to his kid; this was America. Which really went over big with mama-san, who spoke about four words of English, generally when she needed something and nobody else was around who chattered in Vietnamese.

Then there was Jimmy's Uncle Luc.

His name, of course, sent it spinning off into the usual flaming row. Which was the way the whole thing seemed lately, Wen not missing a beat with her comeback—regular tennis match with razor blades imbedded in the balls.

That is, until the wind shut them both up with its own screaming.

Now Wen's eyes were pullet eggs, face the pallor of her knuckles holding tight against the boat's pitch as wave after wave slammed the hull. Jolts that fanned through vertebrae and muscle and bone like current spikes, Jimmy trying to anticipate them as he would a composite-court opponent, bend but don't break, thinking definitely not a place you'd choose even in the best of weather, let alone this. Wind-lashed rain forcing them to shout now just to be heard.

"I SAID THIS IS NOTHING. I KNOW WHAT I'M DOING."

Forget the mainland, Jimmy added to himself, not even lights showing, twenty-five-mile visibility down to zip in no time. Extreme but, well, bonding, too, their own little world: pumps and diesel engine humming, the interior lights glowing red and orange.

They'd be fine.

Harmony *had been through worse.*

He felt her eyes on him, the heat in them finally gone. As he had before all the tension between them, he winked at her and saw her expression shift, the beginnings of a smile. Trust replacing fear, at least wanting to.

What the hell, they'd ride it out.

Because that's what you did.

In that instant the wheelhouse was bathed in white, Wen raising a hand to it, a choked-off "Oh-my-God." And the sound: even through the wind, there was no mistaking the engines.

Everything around them seemed alien now, bled of color. The searchlight's brilliance striking the rain and spray gave it the appearance of a beast raging to get at them.

"Jiiiimmmy..."

"I SEE it."

"What are we going to do?"

"I don't know. If you'd—"

A wave roller-coastered them, Wen screaming with the lurch, grabbing at him, and for a moment they lost the beam. Then it found them, but from a forward angle, as if the more powerful craft were herding them, cutting off escape.

Jimmy was conscious of his sweat and, for a moment, contemplated a run, even as he knew it was suicide. At least by not running they stood a chance.

"WHO ARE THEY? WHAT DO THEY WANT?"

"They want to talk, Wen, to me. All right?"

Not that it was Wen he was angry at, not by now. It was himself, the risk he'd exposed her to, the child inside her. And like that Jimmy flashed on the ultrasound again, the heartbeat, the doctor's telling them it was a girl. All his senses magnified, life forever tuned to a different frequency.

Now this—despite Wen's insistence on coming along, insisting it was a chance they needed to work things out. Great fucking work, Jimmy thought, only a genius. He wished he could take it back, the stuff with her, with them out there. But of course that was impossible; it was far too late for that.

The beam came from dead ahead now, in spite of his running the boat as hard as he dared, near flank against the surge.

No place to run.

Nowhere to hide.

Jimmy took his hand off the wheel, brushed it against the .357 Rossi in the flap pocket of his anorak, felt the magnum's heft even as he tried to smile reassuringly. Then he spun the wheel over and headed back toward San Miguel.

Santa Barbara Channel, Present

THE BOAT WAS A DRAGNETTER OUT OF AVILA, crew of four, on the prowl for anything the nets would bring up. In particular, flounder, rockfish, lingcod, snapper, cabezon—halibut if they were lucky; toilets, pipe, and rusted junk if they weren't—the weather solid gold even if the hauls so far were thin.

Roy Portis, the trawler's skipper, took a sip of the New Orleans with chicory he'd brewed, watched the booms dip and strain with the net's weight, the crew dozing before it got crazy. Out here was the place to be, all right—burnished swells, riffle breeze, basking sun. San Miguel broad off, larger Santa Rosa coming up, Santa Cruz off the starboard bow, their clawed topography standing out against the wall of gray.

Three dolphins rolled off the port beam.

It was a nice life when it paid, a cold bitch when it didn't, like this year. Still, it beat being stuck behind a desk where breeze was meted out by an air conditioner and what you gathered mostly was years. Easy to be philosophical on a day like this, he thought: Even the seagulls looked good—starched white gliders against a blue-glaze sky—those that weren't folded up and picking their teeth along with the crew.

Portis gave a thought to noting that one in the journal he'd been keeping for his creative writing course, then decided he was just too comfortable to move. Besides, he'd remember—

A shudder, a hesitation...

A noticeable loss of way, even though the engines hadn't seemed to falter.

He heard the shouts, saw what was happening, jerked back inside to lever it into neutral, then reverse. Until the bend and creak of the booms had eased.

Shit—if he'd been any slower...

Bobby and the others already were checking the lines, which he could see still strained.

"More slack, Skip. Winches are frozen."

Portis eased off further, tried to picture what was down there. Damn near anything, of course, that came with the dragger's lot. His luck, too, shaving a corner off the marine sanctuary, those arbitrary dotted lines the Park Service bureaucrats drew around the islands like moats around their castles.

And his options: tear the net trying to wrench loose and there went the haul, the score he needed; disable the booms, there went the season; lose both and kiss the boat good-bye. Already he was in too deep with the bank; might as well radio them to come get her if that went down. One thing was sure: The charts showed nothing to steer clear of, even as he double-checked them.

For a while he maneuvered, circling the spot in search of a release point. Slack, no slack...slack, no slack.

Come on, come on, come on. COME ON.

"I'll go," Bobby finally piped up. "Baby needs a new pair of shoes."

Portis glanced again at the depth finder, squinted out on deck where Cowboy already was zipping him into the wetsuit, strapping on the tank. "Looking at a buck and a quarter, Bob, big rock or reef or something. Go easy down there."

"*Absolutamente.*"

"Pry bar and knife?" he shot back. "Dive watch?"

"Guerrero's got 'em at the rail."

"Air?"

Portis knew the answer, he'd checked it after last time, just wanted to see if Bobby had. It was always the basics.

"Relax, Skip, man knows the drill." Cowboy answering for him.

"Twenty minutes, no chances," Portis said. "You got that?"

He watched Bobby nod, was going to add that he couldn't afford another bath and keep everybody on, even himself, but decided against it; at least for now, this was his problem. Then Bobby was settling his mask and stepping overboard, an upward thumb before disappearing in a kick of fins, a roil of bubbles.

It didn't take long: twelve minutes by Portis's watch before Bobby was breaking the surface. Tossing his mask and pry bar up to Guerrero and Cowboy, giving a whoop and shouting, *"You ain't gonna believe what we're hung up on,"* before they'd even pulled him back in.

2

WIL WHIPPED THE DISK AS FAR AS HE COULD and watched the dog tear after it, this black and white and caramel blur kicking up sand and, at the precise moment, leaping to snap it out of the air. Three girls about fifteen, T-shirts over their suits, applauded as the dog pranced it back, looking at them like, *Average arm, fair hang-time, no wind: What'd you expect?*

Light surf retreated; a line of pelicans bent to the Rincon.

On the four-lane between La Conchita and the beach, traffic sped toward Santa Barbara, the thirty-story bluff above looking harmless in the sun. Belying, of course, the nine houses it had dropped in on a couple of winters before, county-strung tape still in place around the hazards that had once housed friends.

Progress, Wil thought: lawsuits inching through the courts while the lawyers dodged and weaved, the politicians opted out, and property values headed south.

Great work, guys, always the right thing.

By then Matt was standing over the Frisbee and looking up at him.

Wil picked it up, angled one high and inland so that at zenith it would shear off toward the surf. Except Matt had seen that one before. Braking as the Frisbee broke, he put on a burst parallel to the surf line, jumping to save the throw before it kamikazed into a breaker.

"All right, Matty."

Faint clapping from the girls moving off toward Mussel Shoals, the little pipeline-connected petroleum island with its palm trees and white-rock skirt. Which left the beach pretty much to him and Matt, four-thirty and the families heading home for barbecue and watermelon, maybe a stop at *El Mercado* where Fiesta vendors already were selling tacos, tamales, and roasted corn. No charge for the aromas that had you chewing your sleeve while waiting to order.

That time of year in Santa Barbara.

Whirling skirts and stamping feet; dark eyes coy behind patterned fans; five- and six-year-olds looking like rainbow come-ons in their adult-applied makeup. Adding to the surreality: blurred nights that began and ended with tequila shooters, holding onto bar rails as the Fiesta revelry seduced like the bright shards in a kaleidoscope. Finding meaning in your tabletop that had eluded you at the start of the evening, and none whatever in the morning after. His ex-specialty.

Just ask Lisa.

Ex-specialty, ex-wife.

"Fine-looking dog..."

Wil turned, caught the man who had come up on them. Lost in reverie, he hadn't followed Matt's raised ears and alert-status posture. He did his own scan, saw nothing untoward: nothing you banked on.

"That's Matt," Wil said, seeing the dog relax at the sound of his name. "Matty's Australian. Aren't you, Matt?"

"Long way from home," the man said in a familiar accent.

Vietnamese from his appearance as well: prominent cheekbones, narrow chin and wide-spaced features, late forties from eyes that looked as if they'd seen beyond the light. Five-nine and solid in the way a hiker might be rather than a lifter—a leanness that spoke of hard work and long hours.

He wore cargo pants close to the end of the line and a faded blue polo shirt, *Island Seafoods* over the pocket. Worn Sperrys without socks, military-style web belt, bifocaled sunglasses he removed to hang on his placket.

Wil got a whiff of fish market.

"Sorry, I meant the breed," he said. "Australian Shepherd. He's actually from the Central Valley."

The man toed off his shoes, poured sand from them, looked as if he were wondering how to address something. "Bakersfield," he said, finally. "If I'm not incorrect."

Wil stepped up his alert level a notch. Figuring more was coming, he waited.

The man said, "Your neighbor said you might be here. The woman with the tomato plants?"

"So far, so good," Wil answered.

"Sand feels good—something so simple." And when Wil didn't respond, "Central Valley relatives. Farmers who read the newspapers."

Doc Whitney, country music, oil, murder new and old, betrayal, greed, blackmail. A year-plus since Leora Graybill had him come back a final time to take Matt, his pledge to her. The near-parchment hand taking his, piercing eyes momentarily undulled by pain. The feeling that always rose when thinking of his father: their time together in the land's vastness, Valley smells rushing in through the Buick's open windows as they raced the dawn.

Wil shook it off.

"I must speak to you," the man was saying.

Wil waited.

The man said, "It is about my son."

"He would be Vietnamese, too?"

Nod. "Born there. Does it matter?"

"Not so far."

They had begun walking, Matt keeping pace, sandpipers playing tag with the waves. On the roadway, a big-rig brapped into a compression brake as a bottleneck developed.

The man said, "You fought in my country. I read it. Sean Wilson Hardesty?"

Wil looked at him. "Are you always this thorough?"

The man squinted at the horizon. "He was my only son. Now he is gone. Does that answer your question?"

"I assume you're implying that it should."

"I could hardly overlook the fact of your own loss. The article—"

Wil knew the one, a female journalist he'd opened up to and still kicked himself for. "That was a long time ago, Mr...."

"Tien. Vinh Tien." Fumbling in his pockets for a card.

Wil raised a hand to it. "Both my son and the war are history, Mr. Tien, and I allow neither as leverage. Now if you'll—"

"I meant no presumption. Sometimes my English—"

"Your English is fine. But your teachers forgot to tell you not to bullshit a bullshitter. Come on, Matt." As he headed for the access tunnel, Matt glanced at the man as if having picked up on Wil's tone.

Vinh Tien said evenly, "My son's boat was sunk from under him. On board were his wife-to-be and unborn child—my granddaughter." He'd stopped now, feet planted, as though facing down something only he could see. "They were murdered and no one cares. At least you know what happened to your son."

A pelican tucked itself into dive and hit the water; seconds later it surfaced and took off.

"This has gone badly, for which I apologize," Vinh Tien said. "I had intended to have you to my home, to dine with my wife and daughter, look at photographs of my Jimmy. In this way to see into his heart."

A wave overwhelmed the backwash, humped up the beach.

Gulls squabbled over a windfall.

Wil stopped, looked at him. "Jimmy Tien was your son?"

Hope flared; Vinh Tien found the card and held it out, an address and phone number already written in pencil on the back.

Wil took it, scanned the front: thumb smudges, the shirt logo, and a Santa Barbara address.

Vinh Tien bent to Matt and said, "You will bring your friend?"

From his deck, Wil watched the surf break, gold warming its edges as the sun pooled into the ocean. He stroked Matt's fur, sipped lapsang souchong—Lisa's least favorite tea, his stash of *that* totally uncontested in the divorce. As she used to put it, tar steeping in a honeypot.

So far Matt shared no such compunctions.

But then it was early in the relationship.

"You're wondering what Vinh Tien was talking about, aren't you," Wil said to him.

Traffic streamed toward Ventura-L.A./Santa Barbara-San Luis, some showing headlights. The air felt cool with the onset of night. Heavy with dew.

Wil said, "See, it's this way: Once upon a time this nice Japanese girl married a surfer without much going for him. They had a son." Flashing on *Waaatch meee, Daaad,* the never-ending mantra. "Devin Kyle Hardesty...this great kid."

Hearing himself say it as Matt leaned into his thigh.

"So everything's fine until the surfer thinks how swell it would be to teach his son the grand passion at this spot he knows about." Wil gulped the tea, its raw heat doing what he'd intended.

"Bad idea," he said at length. "Very bad idea."

Two coupled freight engines slipped past, the upline S.P. track showing green. In a bit they were lost from view and the signal had returned to red.

"I just thought you ought to hear it from me in case you get too trusting here. Know what I mean?"

Matt sighed audibly.

"So," Wil added. "You ever eaten Vietnamese?"

3

VINH TIEN'S HOUSE was in the neighborhoods west of the airport and north of the freeway, on a street needing a fresh cap of asphalt. Salmon-colored bougainvillea and purple lantana formed a low frontage while mini-lawn ran between clumps of Mexican sage, blue salvia, and ornamental garlic. Parked in the driveway was a white Toyota pickup with the Island Seafoods logo; in front, a ten-year-old red Honda Civic.

As Wil pulled in behind the Civic and got out with Matt, Vinh Tien met them in an open-collar shirt, gray slacks, polished slip-ons, sandal-wood soap where the fish fragrance had been. The aroma of things cooking once they were inside.

"Sea bass," he said, taking Wil's jacket. "House specialty."

Wil handed over two cans of Alpo. "These are for Matt. Would you have a back patio where he could keep us in sight?"

As he was explaining about Matt's recent dislocation, Wil looked inside to see a woman in a batik apron. Beside her stood a younger version, perhaps twenty-two: five-four, about an inch taller than her mother. Black hair cut short and swept boyishly around one ear, eyes more black walnut than almond, black jeans and black DKNY sweatshirt.

Glass of white wine in her hand.

Reminding him both a little and too much of Lisa.

Vinh Tien said, "My wife, Li, my daughter, Mia. Mia is a physics major at the university." Proud-sounding.

"Volleyball was mine, as I remember," Wil lobbed at her, with a smile that went unreturned.

Li Tien said, "We are most glad for your presence. In this house you are welcome."

"*Very,* Mom," Mia Tien corrected her. "We're *very* glad."

"You have a fine home," Wil said in remembered Vietnamese, shaking hands in turn, aware of Vinh Tien's glare at his daughter. Of how easily the picked-up phrase had come to him over two-plus decades…a finch awaiting the opening of its cage.

Li Tien bowed, excused herself to her tasks, Vinh Tien following with the cans. Which allowed Wil to take in a table set for five, napkins matching Li Tien's apron, sliding glass fronting a yard with a fish pond backed by tall bamboo. Inside, the decor was modest: embroideries of small birds, water buffalo on a table beside a couch, stylized painting of an eye framed by convergent gold rays.

Black eyes took his measure over a swallow of wine.

"Points made," Mia Tien said. "With them, anyway."

"But not with you?"

"Volleyball…" It hung there, a spikeball at the top of its arc.

"Kept me out of trouble for a semester."

"But you were there…the war and all."

"I was," Wil said. "That okay with you?"

More wine, a flip of forelock. "If I had a say, which I don't, here's a clue: Hiring somebody like you is a waste of money. Dad's the one who killed my brother. And while you're at it, skip the far chair and place setting. Might get embarrassing if Jimmy showed up with seaweed all over him and found you in it."

Vinh Tien reappeared with a ceramic bowl into which he'd spooned the Alpo, Matt looking first at Wil before pinning on the bowl and starting a wag that enveloped his whole frame.

@

Dinner was as fine as it was tense: pho soup with the long thin loaves Wil remembered from countless Vietnamese cafés, spring rolls, salad with chopped peanuts and hard-boiled egg, the sea bass served with rice and raw vegetables. And afterward, candied ginger and French roast brewed in the press Li Tien poured it from. They spoke of Wil's two tours and Vinh Tien's fishing-village life before the war, toasted the incongruity of violence in a country as beautiful as that, the Tiens' desire to return one day.

Li Tien mostly deferred to her husband, while Mia Tien drank wine, said little, and ate with a fork.

"Daddy was boat people," she interjected after one exchange. "Did he tell you that?"

"That will be enough wine, Mia," her father said. "You have no studies?"

"Fall, winter, spring, and summer."

"I suggest you count your blessings."

Wil swung a look outside, where a sundowner spilling from the canyons rustled the bamboo.

"Yes sir, Captain Vinh, sir."

Mock salute accompanied by the tilt clink of wine into her glass.

"I said that was enough, daughter," Vinh Tien said, grabbing it, spilling it before she could retract the bottle.

Jumping up so it didn't get on her, she said, "You are pathetic, you know that? Isn't losing Jimmy enough for you? How many does it take?"

Beyond the sliding glass, Matt's ears had perked at the sharpness of their voices. By now Vinh Tien was on his feet and Mia was yanking open the front door, slamming it behind her. Wil heard the Civic's engine wound tight, the screech of rubber as she roared away.

"I apologize for my daughter's behavior," Vinh Tien said, righting her chair as Li hurried dishes off the table. "She is too much her father's daughter and this has been hard on her. She was fond of her brother."

Wil noticed Matt still looking from face to face.

"So I gathered. What did she mean by what she said—'How many does it take?'"

Vinh Tien stood. "Bring your coffee and follow me," he said, the phrasing vaguely like the echo of an old order.

❧

It was more den than bedroom: wood-framed futon, walls showcasing Jimmy in boy-to-man stages. Cowboy hat and boots just after arriving in the states, hot wheels and in-lines, skateboards, even a surfboard. An intense kid who ceased smiling in the later photographs, donning Wayfarers and projecting model-like good looks, black hair worn almost to his shoulders.

Movie star potential.

Poker face revealing not so much as a card.

Yet despite these later poses, tennis clearly stoked the younger Jimmy. Singly, with his metal Wilson and trophies beside him as he knelt; paired with partners at the net; team portrait with the teenage Jimmy staring down the lens. Then there were the shots Wil pictured Vinh snapping from the stands: Jimmy lunging, punching a forehand volley, two-handing a baseline backhand. Hair flying at the point of impact.

"That's how he got his nickname," Vinh said. "He was always a fan of Jimmy Connors, that bad-boy thing, his speed and fight. Even before he met Connors once at a match, we were instructed to call him 'Jimmy'."

"And his given name?"

"Tuan," Vinh Tien stated quietly. "After the uncle who raised me." He produced a scrapbook, thumbed past yellowing tennis stories to a section in back, the clippings still new-looking. Thick black borders pasted in.

"This is for you to take," Vinh Tien said. "It is every story about his disappearance that ran. Even the Los Angeles paper."

Wil scanned headlines and subheads, including one detailing the findings of the official inquiry board: ACCIDENT RULED IN BOAT TRAGEDY. He sat forward on the futon-couch.

"When did Jimmy leave home?"

"Three years ago," Vinh Tien answered. "We saw him not often after that. We did not communicate well." As though suddenly out of steam, he pulled the folding chair from a small desk opposite and sat.

A thought struck. "Was he working for you?"

"When he felt like it."

"Doing what?"

Vinh Tien paused as if to measure his response. "My son liked diving. We sell sea urchin to the Japanese, though it has fallen off with their economy. The boat he took was the one we used for urchin, but not just that. We are not so big we can use a boat for one purpose. Our other boat is larger but older, with nets we—"

"What about the day he went out?"

Vinh Tien nodded. "A Sunday. We did not work that day."

"Do you know why he went?"

"Not in all this time. I—" Hand to his temples as though trying to erase an image.

Wil flipped through pages for the time it bought. Pausing at one, he asked, "How far along was Jimmy's girlfriend?"

Release of breath. "Wen? Seven months. It was not a topic we explored with him, if we wished to talk at all."

"How long a trip is it out there—three hours?"

"We allow four. In good conditions."

"Fairly arduous, is my point," Wil said. "Even in optimal conditions."

Vinh Tien looked at him.

Wil framed it for him. "With that weather even a possibility, is San Miguel a trip you'd make if Li were seven months pregnant?"

"It is not." A shake of the head. "Not unless I had no choice. And if you're wondering why Jimmy had the mother of his child with him, I do not know."

"Would her parents?"

"Her mother..." Pause. "If she does, she has said nothing to us about it. But then, we were not on the best of terms with Nguyen Diem."

Wil made a note of the name.

Vinh Tien said, "I have written down where you may contact her. As to your unspoken question, perhaps it was because my son and his girlfriend considered me a harsh and demanding parent, a throwback."

Not seeing the man as using words to hear himself, Wil said, "You said harsh before demanding. Harsh in what way?"

Vinh Tien stared at the opposite wall as though a scene played behind it that excluded not only Wil, but anyone beyond another boat person. "In the way that life is harsh," he began. "*Bui Doi*, they called us. The dust of life."

4

IGHT MONTHS AFTER SAIGON'S FALL—after as many years of war as they, their parents, and grandparents had been alive—Li became pregnant with their first child. Vinh kept on with the farming and fishing that had sustained them through the recent fighting. Then he found work with a relative whose boat still functioned. Mostly they fished the old way, with line and hand net, selling to the new government for a fraction of what they had made before.

That was when the armed cadres began rounding up not only Vinh and most of his village for re-education, but thousands of peasants and city-dwellers who'd merely ridden out the war. This as the new government was turning what agricultural capability remained into hard-line collectives—rice going almost immediately to ration, inflation raging, people disappearing without trace.

For three years, Vinh saw home not at all and Li but once, when she came to visit him and he was able to sneak them to a wooded area for a few hours, Vinh remembering afterward her tears and little else. Certainly not the socialist dogma they were being force-fed like ducks for the table.

The final chapter was his conscription into the new Vietnamese infantry: Report at once to repel the Chinese, who in '78 had sliced open a front when the Viets intervened against Pol Pot's killing fields. Two wars having replaced the old one now, the north-based government only too willing to feed into the grinder anyone from the south. Especially its political recalcitrants.

Instead of reporting, Vinh slipped his column and went home. There he promised Li, two-year-old Jimmy, and newborn Mia that he'd send for them as soon as possible, next morning fighting his way aboard a patched-together hulk bound for Indonesia, so jammed with refugees they were unable to lie down except in shifts.

Barely at sea, troops intercepted them, stole their valuables and half their fuel, ordered them to turn back. Days later it was Thai pirates with M-16s, throwing overboard a man who defied them, spearing him with an oar until he sank in a trailing red cloud. Beating to death another man with their rifle butts, they stole the boat's food and remaining fuel and raped the women, Vinh at least thankful he hadn't brought his family with him.

Adrift, some became sufficiently crazed to drink seawater and died; others became so sick they couldn't stand. Sharks took care of those who perished, and it was at that point Vinh knew he was going to die out there. All of them were. Then the island—tiny and deserted, but lined with coconut palms that, with the giant clams Vinh was able to harvest, kept them alive until another boat arrived and took them to a camp staffed by volunteers who ultimately helped Vinh find sponsorship. Relatives in California, the ones in Bakersfield, helped him get on with a small outfit working the Santa Barbara Channel.

"Three years later, I bought it," Vinh said without emphasis. "By then I was able to sponsor my own family. And in the larger sense, I suppose the experience *has* affected my view of the world. It is a different generation, these children born to so much."

Wil tapped the scrapbook, thought *No shit.*

"Why was this not the accident they said it was?"

"For one thing, there was no distress call—none." Vinh Tien said. Second, the emergency homing device was missing from its rack. A freak wave, or so the Coast Guard thought."

"But you don't believe it."

Vinh Tien's eyes clouded. "My son knew the channel, ask anyone. He was handling boats before he was fourteen."

"Why would someone do him harm?"

"I don't know why. I only know who."

Wil could see him building to it, words to strike from the storm that was his expression. "You're saying you know who's responsible?"

The storm broke. "Someone without conscience who seduced my son with his lifestyle and his promises. A monster."

"I'm sorry, you've lost me."

Looking at his hands as though wondering how they'd become curled into fists, Vinh Tien said, "The monster, Mr. Hardesty, is my brother."

In the telling of it, Luc Tien was younger by two years and everything his older brother was not. The son of a different father, he was a thief almost from birth, stealing equally from those he knew and those he did not. Punishment simply left him unaffected. Leaving home on his thirteenth birthday, Luc entered the employ of a Saigon-based Chinese gangster who taught him numbers, extortion, hijacking, prostitution, the slavery and opium trades.

But it was the war that made him rich.

The war and its black market.

Luc Tien became known to American authorities, but not in a way that threatened to shut him down. He became a procurer, often selling the Americans' own goods back at cheaper prices than the cost to manufacture and reship from the states. Consequently, he was buffered from prosecution not only by his own people, but by American supply sergeants, warrant officers, and G-12s skimming off the percentages he gladly paid.

Fat city, fat times.

The North Viets were a different breed. Targeted as one to make an example of once the city fell, Luc was dragged from the hold of a Manila-bound single-stacker, fingered for the reward by one of his own lieutenants. It took the better part of his fortune just to keep him from the firing squad, his very public apology *quid pro quo* in return for luring from the woodwork profiteers who paid the ultimate price for their trust in the new government's pledge of similar treatment.

This before landing at the same re-education camp as his brother Vinh. Let alone aboard the same hellish refugee boat.

"Luc told the pirates about diamonds one of us was holding in return for some of the stones," Vinh Tien went on. "The man they beat to death? Luc knew him."

"What happened after that?"

"The others wanted to throw Luc overboard. I was forced to defend him, which...*merde,* what is the proper word?"

"Ostracized?"

"Yes—ostracized us both."

"Until you provided them with food."

Nod. "Still, it was touch and go, especially in the camps."

"I can imagine," Wil said. "Where does he live now?"

"On Mountain Drive. My whole home would fit into his garage."

Wil pictured the area: Montecito, the L.A. side of Santa Barbara. *Architectural Digest* fantasies, thick-walled Mediterraneans and Spanish Colonial revivals hunched behind equally thick walls. *Town and Country* photo spreads.

"How does Luc make his money?"

Vinh Tien smiled sourly. "Perhaps I did not speak clearly. The way he's always made it."

"You know that for sure?"

"Am I not his brother?"

"Which means what at this point?"

"Which means nothing," Vinh Tien said. "Less than nothing."

Wil waited as the man drew a breath. "But you do see him."

"No. But Jimmy did."

According to Vinh Tien, Tuan "Jimmy" Tien always had an affinity for his free-living, free-spending uncle. Like a drunk to a morning eye-opener, Jimmy would gravitate to the wealthy enclave where Luc lived the life. There, Jimmy would ride the horses Luc kept for polo matches, storm dirt bikes through the chaparral behind Luc's property, hone his game on the green hard-tru courts Luc invited local pros to practice on and kept immaculate.

"For you, Jimmy," he made sure got back to Vinh and Li Tien in their tract home fifteen miles west and a star system away.

Then there were the parties, the swimming pool, the food, the women—to whom Luc was more than willing to introduce Jimmy.

Prostitutes, refugees working off a debt, China Whiteheads who waited only to trick so they could score—Jimmy had them in spades, his looks and athleticism making him popular not only with them but with Luc's business associates. Viet-*Chings*, Vietnamese, Laotians, Chinese—Jimmy never knew for sure—people who knew a comer when they saw one. Maybe even Hollywood, they told him. *Why, with their contacts...*

"Which made us even stricter and more protective of Mia," Vinh Tien tailed off.

"But you're sure Jimmy went that route?"

"Does the cat digest the mouse it eats?"

Wil shifted on the hard futon. "What about his girlfriend?"

Pause. "I think that's where he met Wen. As to why she was there..." He shrugged.

"I'm listening."

"I went to see my brother," Vinh Tien said after a beat. "I saw the type of girl he favored. Wen was that striking. Even though she was respectful when we met them by chance one time downtown, Jimmy seemed embarrassed. As he should have been."

"He was working for Luc?"

"That was my belief. Jimmy never lacked for money—far more than I could pay him." Vinh Tien paused to war with it again. "Have you any idea how that feels? Competing for your own son and losing him?"

Wil kept his mouth shut, let the man run on.

"As if everything I'd survived for, worked for, was and is a sham. That only money speaks, no matter how you acquire it."

Wil placed the list of contacts Vinh Tien had penciled out on the scrapbook. "All right. I'll go over these and get back to you, let you know if this is something I can reasonably take on."

There was a pause as the meaning set in. "I see. You're telling me you might not."

"There is always that possibility."

Vinh Tien expelled a breath, looked fatigued. "If you're worried about your fee, we have been frugal over the years. And there is the business."

"Mr. Tien, I'm more concerned that you have a reasonable expectation of—"

"Mr. Hardesty," he said, "do you fear my brother? Or do you hesitate for other reasons?"

Wil felt a flush. "How can I put this? Sometimes these things are not a match for either party. I meant nothing more and nothing less."

Vinh Tien attempted a smile, let it go. "Very well. If that's how it is to be."

They left Jimmy's room, got Matt up from the patio, Wil requesting his thanks be conveyed to Mrs. Tien. On the way out, he became aware of sounds from down the hall—muffled but unmistakable: a woman's sobs.

Vinh Tien's eyes were those of a man who's taken one too many shots to the head and to the heart. At the stoop, he turned from Wil and from the spot where the Civic had been and quietly shut the door.

5

N EXT MORNING, WII DROVE TO CARPINTERIA and parked by The Coffee Grinder. He and Matt then looped off a moderately paced four-miler through the quiet streets. After scones and a newspaper highlighting the night-before folkdances, he headed back the five miles to La Conchita and home, Matt's profile like a hood ornament out the window. Showered and shaved, he took his coffee refill onto the deck, opened the scrapbook.

Jimmy Tien had been reported missing in late November, Vinh also reporting his thirty-eight-foot custom rig, *Harmony,* gone from its harbor slip. An employee of the deli there had seen Jimmy leave with a woman carrying a tote bag around seven a.m. That was it for witness accounts—and for Jimmy and Wen, it seemed—despite an extensive search up and down the channel, overflights that further gridded-out the four islands. Immediately following a two-day introduction to winter that arrived from Hawaii like a wet bear, bringing with it downed trees and power lines, flooded intersections and parking lots.

From then until June, there'd been no clues. Island Seafoods reported no cash missing; Vinh's brother, Luc, professed to having no idea about Jimmy and Wen's whereabouts. So did Wen's mother, who lived not far from their Isla Vista apartment among the university students, alternative stores, and, Wil knew from experience, a fair number of immigrants.

He reached down to calm Matt, whining and twitching in his sleep;

Matt sighed deeply, began breathing more evenly.

"Hard night all around," Wil agreed, taking in the sweep of bay before getting back to his articles.

Morning had dawned without fog, pelicans working the mackerel schools from a hazeless sky. Miles beyond the oil rigs, Anacapa Island's craggy grouping stood out; adjacent to it, much-larger Santa Cruz and a piece of Santa Rosa, dwarf mammoth habitat in prehistoric times. Cobalt horizon, finger of smog reaching up from L.A. like a grifter's touch.

Back at it.

Sheriff's Department investigators speculated that Jimmy and Wen had simply gone off to be alone. That was in the first month; beyond it, hope vanished with the news coverage. That is, until the *Susan Marie* out of Avila Bay wrapped a drag net around "something" a hundred and twenty down off San Miguel. Indeed, *Harmony* might never have been found had not the dragger broached the park's six-mile boundary. Instrument malfunction, according to her captain, the matter under review at the time of the report.

No bodies, no signs of foul play, fire, or explosion were found by the divers who inspected and photographed the wreck, the rocks into which she'd wedged. Storm-wave caused; no point seen incurring the cost to bring her up. Findings reviewed, verdict rendered, case closed: yet another day trip that had taken a tragic turn.

Leaving boat-sized questions.

What brought them out in weather that unpredictable? What reason would anyone—Luc Tien by his brother's contention—have to harm them? No way of telling unless—

Phone.

Wil picked it up, punched ON.

"Hardesty."

"You're on the deck, aren't you?" a voice said. "Drinking coffee and eyeing Celia Feyter."

Wil let out a short breath.

"Tell me I'm wrong," Lisa added.

"One out of two's not bad," he answered.

"You're out of coffee? I don't believe it."

"The Feyters moved to Pismo Beach, Leese. Sold it for what they could get."

"Ah. And how is the bluff?"

"No rain, no pain."

"Pretty morning, I bet. At least it looks it from the office."

Something in her pause: Fiesta Week—Dev's favorite time of year—their unspoken agreement not to relive it, reopen their fresh-at-the-time wounds, scarred over in time like the marriage. Now if they even approached the subject it was with this kind of dance-around-it obliqueness.

"You all right?" he asked her.

"Couldn't be better. You?"

"The same. You ready for the list?"

Their standing joke, high ground in the days after the divorce, when they'd run into each other around town. The Howzits.

"How's the business? The folks? Brandon?"

"Still there," she answered. "How's Kari Thayer?"

Wil stroked Matt, who was listening now, head cocked. "As it happens, vacationing in Wisconsin with her son."

"The juvenile delinquent?"

"He's doing better. Besides, they don't call them that anymore. Troubled youth or something."

"I stand corrected." There was another pause before, "Wil, can we meet today, have lunch or something? Staff's off for the parade, so we'd have the office patio to ourselves."

Fiesta Parade: silvered horses, vaqueroed riders, flowered floats, plugged intersections, cordoned streets. "Leese, I can think of better days for parking downtown."

"You'll find a spot," she countered. "Anytime would be good."

"Look, if something is—"

"Feeling sorry for myself is all, not what you think. Another time, if you don't feel like it."

Now Wil paused. "Leese, I didn't say that."

"Must just be me, then, hon. Don't step in the pelican poop."

6

THE NAM SUN JEWELRY EXCHANGE was located in L.A.'s Koreatown, on Normandie, down from 8th. Greasy-spoon breakfast-and-lunch place advertising homemade kim chee next door, dry cleaning franchise down from that, bargain clothing emporium facing the alley that ran between the two stores. Couple of miles from the King-verdict riots that landed the guys who beat a trapped truck driver almost to death a slap on the wrist and lots of shiny new things in the hands of opportunistic shoppers who'd suddenly found them available at no cost.

Plus a shitload of Colts, Glocks, Remingtons, and Berettas from the looted gun outlets and pawnshops squarely in the wrong hands.

Or the right hands, depending on your point of view, Tam Minh thought as he eased the van to a stop in the alleyway across the street.

Through the van's tinted windshield: Trong, the leader; Lang, second in command; Kenny; and Tam-the-new-guy, watched Nam Sun, his wife and daughters getting ready for the morning trade. Finally, at ten minutes to ten, Nam Sun clanked open his accordion grate, broomed the already hot sidewalk, and pronounced the store open by means of the small sign he turned around on its chain in the window.

Trong, riding shotgun, popped the dash with a fist. "All right," he said. "Let's do it."

"With kids in there?" Lang responded.

"He's right." Kenny from the back. "Mother*fuck!* Why today?"

"Their problem, not ours," Trong said. Still, he hesitated, Tam noted.

Lang said, "Why not wait, see if mama-san runs them off to school? Be that much easier."

Kenny nodded. Tam did, too, but not too hard, not wanting to show disrespect to the leader.

"Check it out, dude's looking over here right now," Trong said of Mr. Sun. "I say we hit before he does something dumb."

"I still don't like it." Lang again.

"Good thing you ain't in charge," Trong demeaned him. "It's August, remember? No school."

"Like there's no such thing as summer school. Come on, man, a few minutes..."

"He's *looking*." Trong.

Tam gripped the steering wheel. It was true, Mr. Sun *was* looking their way. Tam was aware of his sweat, his mouth drier than usual. How could that be? The guy was just checking the street, taking a break to case the foot traffic. His reflection on the glass. No way otherwise.

"We go," Trong said. "Tam, you come with us, handle the kids. Tape 'em to something or lock 'em in a closet or something, then help with the gold. Rock and roll."

Tam felt his fear escalate as Kenny tossed him a roll of duct tape.

"Me?" he said. "Who pulls the van up front when you're done?" The frog thing jumping into his voice.

"Can't be helped. Big score, everybody in," Trong came back. Already with his nine out, working the slide and tucking it back in his waistband under the tropical shirt he wore over slacks. Adding now, "When he buzzes me in, you three are right behind: bang-bang. Got it?" Not waiting for a response because this part they'd gone over to where Tam Minh could do it in his sleep.

Except this new thing with the kids.

Through the plate glass window Tam could see their black hair bobbing around the jewelry cases. Helping mama-san set up the displays.

Motherfuck...

7

NOWING HOW JAMMED SANTA BARBARA WOULD BE with vintage cars, drill teams, and castanet-clacking dance clubbers, Wil left Matt sacked out at home and took the back way in. He found a spot not far from Lisa's new office and pulled in ahead of a Caravan whose costumed pre-teens shot him a bird. Two blocks from the crowds lining State Street, he strolled into a Spanish-motif three-story with a sandstone courtyard, took the stairs up the tiled flights, entered an open doorway.

"Lisa?..."

"In here." Looking up from her computer as Wil took note of the Annick Goutal he used to give her.

"Some boss you work for," he said, scoping out her silk tee and Calvins, jade brooch a grandmother had left her. Black hair swept off a neck that still quickened his pulse after twenty-plus years of marriage, three now of divorce.

"The landlord liked us, or Bev he did, anyway." Closing down the spreadsheet she was working on. "Changed your mind, I see."

"Never made it up. I thought tax season was over."

"Gone are those days," she said. "Accounting is like painting the Golden Gate bridge now. Back and forth."

He shrugged. "Keeps you in Acuras."

"A two-year-old Lexus, Wil, leased. And please don't start."

"Me?" He held out the bag he'd brought along, grease stains already spotting the bottom. "The Mercado guy made some earlies for me. Remembering the way you do breakfast."

"That's thoughtful."

"I've always thought so."

"But who listens, right?"

They went downstairs. Under a green metal umbrella and table outside, she teased her *flauta* while Wil finished a second *chimichanga*.

"The guy promised me they don't bite back, if that's what you're concerned about," he said.

"Wil, do you ever wonder where your life is headed? Like maybe you've outsmarted yourself?"

"Unsmarting myself is more my speed."

She shook her head, put down her fork as he canted his head at the building to add, "Leases can be broken, if that's the worry."

"Leases I know about," she said. "Deferred trusts I know about."

Through the opening before his censor could intercept, he said, "Speaking of which, how *is* the boy wonder?" Surprising even himself at how easily it made it past the gates.

"Brandon is someplace we're not going today," she said without looking up.

"Nice weather we're having."

Now the eyes met his. "Wil, you want to talk May-December, we'll talk."

"Kari's thirty-seven," he said flatly. "End of story."

"So is Brandon. *Almost.*"

"And if memory serves, you called me."

"Brandon is *not* the problem here, Wil. Yes he plays baseball, yes he's away a lot and up to here with his shop. But he's not what you think. He has a mind, he has feelings—and he doesn't need me to defend him." She shoved her chair back and stood, sun catching the red in her hair and bouncing it off his libido. "I guess this wasn't such a good idea after all."

"Come on, Leese," he said. "We can do better than this. I can do better." Hands spread to make the point.

"Right—and I always get a pile of stuff done while there's nobody in the office. Thanks for the burrito."

8

TRYING FOR CALM, Tam Minh watched Trong saunter across Normandie—just looking into something nice for his girl—easy does it, no big. Besides, Tam thought, *in* was *in*, the Nam Sun Jewelry Exchange represented a big step up from street strongarms and collecting from the merchants who refused to meet his eyes while handing over their bi-weeklies. And if fate brought the little ones into it, who was Tam to argue? Being *in*, you didn't have to worry about *what*, just *when*.

Like right now.

"Trong's inside," Lang snapped. "Move it."

Chrome S&W .40 in his waistband, lavender shirt open the requisite two buttons; red, black, and green tattoo curling over his right biceps, though Tam couldn't see it, just knew it was there. Like Kenny's dragon was under his striped Hilfiger, coiled in the hollow of his left shoulder blade. And Tam's own, still tender but getting there, over his right nipple: individuality that was important to Tam, important to them all—something to distinguish yourself from the rest as you moved up the ladder, the beauty of their system.

Respectable: like American business was supposed to be.

Bottom line: Look like a street thug, you went down like one.

Except Tam's attempts at distracting himself weren't working. Crossing through a break, he could feel his heart pounding its way out his chest, breath coming in gasps, a voice admonishing him, *You wanted this, now do it.*

Then the three of them were through the still-buzzing security door behind Trong, who had his nine already screwed into Nam Sun's ear as his wife screamed not to hurt her husband and the girls just screamed.

Kenny pulling a sledge hammer out from the duffel bag he'd carried in. Glass shattering and spraying onto their clothes.

"Easy, fool," Lang shouted. *"What'd I tell you."*

Kenny moved to another display case, shortened his arc. Lang produced a pillowcase and began picking rings and pendants out of the glass shards. *"Ow,"* suddenly. Holding up a finger already bloodied. *"Motherfuck."*

"The gold or your brains on the wall," Trong yelled at Nam Sun.

"Please. We have no gold." Mrs. Nam Sun.

"The safe, open the safe. DO IT!"

Lang snapped his fingers, pointed to the wife and daughters, maybe eight and nine. Pretty things reminding Tam of his half-sisters back in Vung Tau—making him wonder how they were doing—before he snapped out of it. *Daughters follow mother.*

Tam reached out and grabbed Mrs. Sun by the wrist.

Which only made the girls scream louder.

He began yanking Mrs. Sun behind the swinging door leading to the back, but she was stronger than expected. Twisting, kicking, holding her free hand out to the screaming girls, she was all Tam could handle. Even then, she managed to break his grip.

Just in time for Lang to bounce his .40 off her skull.

Hands to her head, Mrs. Sun staggered a step and crumpled.

"Now," Lang said, nodding at the girls. "Can you handle *them*?"

Tam just stood there as Nam Sun, seeing his wife fall, renewed his struggle with Trong. Grunting with the effort, his hand caught the barrel of Trong's nine. They began swaying—back and forth until the nine went off, burnt powder adding to the reek of sweat and fury.

Nam Sun let go, grabbed his hand.

"Korean fuck," Trong yelled at him, the gun now in his face. *"Last chance, then we kill them."* Pointing at Tam pulling the girls through the door.

Tam felt his heart double-clutch. *Kill the girls?* Trong's rage was loose now, the dragon they all feared. Tam had seen it before when Trong was beating an 18th Streeter with an aluminum bat, shouting *single, double, triple, home run* each time he connected.

Like then, everything was going wrong.

Tam looked at the girls, the fight in them gone once the door had swung shut. He knelt, pulled them to him so that they had no choice but to focus on him. When they had, he said, "We gotta do this, understand? Don't *want* to—*got* to." He brought the roll of wide gray tape down off his forearm where he'd jammed it, ripped off a piece, began wrapping the older girl's wrists.

"*Noooooo...*" This awful thin wail, while the littler one, more like seven and so pretty despite her tear-streaked face it broke his heart to look at her, heaved up wracking breaths. Reminding him of his stepmother's rabbits when their time came: just giving up.

"I won't let him kill you, I promise," Tam said with sudden resolve. "But you gotta do as I say. All right?"

That's when he heard the pops. Rapid, like an exchange of fire, the girls' eyes as wide as his own. Too many, even if Trong had blasted the Suns three times over.

Which meant the dragon was indeed loose.

Which meant the girls were next.

Crazy fucking Trong.

Tam dropped the tape and, to the older girl, said: "Gotta hide you— right now. You know a place?" Whispering it until she nodded. "I'll say you got away. *Go!*" Closing his eyes like he was six and playing hide-and-seek with his cousins again; wanting the girls to be somewhere he and Trong and the rest couldn't find them. Wanting even more to shut it all out, to open his eyes and just be somewhere else.

Anywhere. Even home.

He opened them; the girls weren't there. No flashes, no doors easing shut: gone. He took a breath, heard the door behind him swing open. He stood to face them, tough it out.

But it wasn't Trong who stood in the doorway.

The man letting the door come to rest on its hinges was tall and leather tan; if Tam had thought about it, he was dressed in clothing too dark for summer. But Tam's eyes still glimpsed what he'd seen when the door opened: the sprawled bodies of Trong, Lang, and Kenny. Dark stains spreading under them.

Tam heard someone moan—Mrs. Sun—Nam Sun's voice trying to calm her. The tall man raised a huge-looking pistol and sighted on the bridge of Tam's nose. "The girls," he said.

As if requesting the time.

"Hiding," Tam managed. "Told them to go hide. When I heard the—"

"Where?"

"I don't know. I didn't look. It's the truth. *Please.*"

The man lowered the gun slightly to scan him with cold eyes.

"How old are you?" he asked.

"Eighteen," Tam said, trying to hold them—viewfinders into the Antarctic. Tears were coming and he could feel a wetness where he shouldn't. "*Seventeen...*"

Tam thought he detected a thaw, but he was too confused to be sure. Because now the man was asking him something in Vietnamese, a fluency he'd never before heard from a Caucasian. Like a window opening on his soul.

"How do you feel about redemption?" the man repeated.

9

KICKING HIMSELF THE FOUR BLOCKS TO THE BONNEVILLE, Wil was unlocking when he figured he might as well stop by an attorney he knew who specialized in marine law. But John Pereira was not behind his arched and nail-studded door, so Wil left his card in the crack and returned to the car. By the time he was easing out, still thinking *What a horseshit performance—three months of not seeing her, then THAT,* a man in a sombrero was waiting for the space.

Free of downtown, the traffic thinned and Wil caught the freeway west to the University of California at Santa Barbara—UCSB—new and older institutional buildings set on a cliff above the ocean and molded around a curve of green-water lagoon. Creek-cut wetlands and airport runway on the mountain side, campanile in the middle, its own surfing point and secluded beaches.

Far too good for students, he'd long-ago concluded.

Bigger now, anyway: which meant the information he wanted was in a different venue than when he'd transferred up pre-Vietnam from UCLA. Still, he found the schedule of classes—anything to do with physics—one on electromagnetism ending, another, a materials lab, concurrent but longer running.

Double-timing it to Physical Sciences, the electromagnetism door-window, he failed to see her, then stepped back as the class rose and filed out. He asked one of the filers where the materials lab was, and this time Mia

Tien was in attendance: Planet Hollywood tee, khaki shorts, black-and-white Simples. She was working with a taller girl with red hair, the experiment they were bent over on a Formica surface near the window.

For a moment, he just watched. In oval metal-rims, brushing back the forelock, this Mia Tien was engaged and animated. Not the dug-in hardcase of last night. He checked his watch: forty-five minutes.

Taking sun-laced paths to the student center as bicycles whipped past, he marveled again at the surroundings, then cruised the bookstore, finding in a sketchy fiction section a marked-down Philip Caputo and a Don Winslow. He bought both, then ran himself out, wondering what he'd have to donate to the library to make room for them.

Fifteen minutes.

She came out holding the door for the red-haired girl, who nodded her thanks before heading up the hall. Mia Tien's eyes widened, dropped to his bag, then came up again. Hurriedly, she tossed the glasses into the backpack on her shoulder.

"Hey, there," Wil said. Unthreatening.

"What are you doing?" Looking around. "How did you find me?" A drawbridge rising shut.

"My work, remember?"

He caught a kid with angular cheekbones and a mustache with aspirations bearing down. Torn jeans and unlaced Reeboks, Hawaiian shirt with blue palm trees. Stepping up beside her, the kid said, "You ready, babe?" A long, portent-filled glance at Wil.

Mia regarded him. "I won't be long, Derek. You in the lot?"

"Till I get tired of it," he said.

"I'll keep that in mind."

Derek was about to turn away when he said, "You need any help with this guy?"

"So now it's Bruce Lee?" Rolling her eyes.

The kid cast another look at Wil's six-two as other students streamed by. Air conditioning pulsed in the ceiling vents, murmur of post-academic chat. "Do I pass?" Wil asked.

"Derek, I can handle it," she said to his glower.

"This time," the kid said. "Late."

"As in too late for any of us?" Wil asked after Derek had slouched his way down the stairs.

"Derek has his moments."

"Babe?..."

"He also has an IQ of 139. What do you want?"

"A moment of your time would be nice."

"There something in it for me?"

Wil reached into his bag, handed her one of the canned teas he'd also bought.

"What joy is mine," she said, a smile half-forming as she popped the tab and took a sip, then led him back into the now-empty lab. Offloading her pack to lean against a countertop. "Well?"

"You said something the other night, Mia. About your father being the one who killed your brother."

"What of it?"

"It got me wondering. Two things, actually: One, I don't think you're as tough as you'd like some people to think—me, for instance. Two, I wanted to see if you actually believed it."

"Why should I tell you anything?"

"Because words mean things," he said. "Start something like that, you finish it."

"Says you." Glancing at the clock.

"Case in point: Did you tell the sheriff that? If you didn't and it's true, you've wasted valuable time your father had to cover his tracks."

Her gaze stayed put, Wil's answer. "He's a bully," she said finally. "A workaholic bully who terrorizes everybody, and my mother just stands for it."

"Meaning what, exactly?"

"They're just so...I don't know—stuck."

"That explains it, all right."

"My brother looked out for me and he was great and I could fucking *talk* to him, and now he's gone. And guess who in effect drove him to my uncle's and told him not to come back."

"Maybe your dad was so scared of losing him he held on too tight, Mia. It happens. And maybe your brother had a little something to do with it."

"He drove Jimmy away. Because of what he is."

"Something else I'm not getting?"

She paused, decided, drew a breath, plunged. "Just for kicks, ask him what side he fought on. Ask to see his pictures. The ones he keeps in the crawl space."

Wil felt a sound rather than heard it: dissolved limestone dripping into a subterranean pool. Hardening. "How about a reason."

"Do black pajamas mean anything to you?"

Just like that.

Wil saw it as bullshit to shock him, tried to read her expression and came up short. "Your father Viet Cong? Sorry, no sale."

"Suit yourself," she delivered with a little flash of triumph. "But you two might even have traded shots."

Welcome to the ruins, he thought. "Mia, you know something? If I were the suspicious type, I'd say you either hate your father beyond all reason or you're trying to run me off because you're afraid of what I'll find. You're too smart for the former. Which leads me to believe you aren't too sure *what* your brother got himself into." Giving it a second to percolate. "We anywhere close here?"

She tilted her head, tried a deep breath without success. "You see anybody who cares what you believe?"

"I happen to. Did you know his girlfriend?"

"Wen? Of course I knew her." Angry swipe at the forelock that had fallen across her face.

"And liked her?"

"She was nice enough. She worked at my uncle's after..."

"After what?"

"Nothing."

File under something. He said, "What was she doing for your uncle?"

"Are you for real? Why do you think Jimmy said it was his baby other than to get her out of there? God knows whose it really was."

Bingo. "Real match made in heaven, huh?"

"What do you know about it?"

"Not enough, obviously. Might be time I had a talk with Uncle Luc."

"Yeah, right." Beyond skeptical.

Wil realized he hadn't opened his tea. Handing it to her before heading for the door, he said, "I'll make you a deal. Cool Bruce Lee's jets with this and I'll get back to you on your uncle."

"Some deal."

"Beats whatever Derek's offering, and you know it."

10

A FTER A SLOW GO PAST A RINCON with mainly kids trying to make something from nothing but still surfing, Wil heard the phone on his way up the stairs. By the time he'd gotten the door open and sidestepped Matt's greeting, the answering machine was taping a message from John Pereira, his marine-law friend.

"Out long-boarding, I assume," the message went. "Must be nice—"

"John...just got in."

"Never lie to an attorney, we're experts."

"Can't pass off a call screening on you, huh?"

"Never," Pereira came back. "What's up?"

Wil told him: Jimmy Tien, no distress calls on the radio, the missing detection finder. The findings in the articles he'd seen.

Pereira said, "I remember it, sort of. Shit happens, right?"

"Jimmy's father swears it was no accident."

"What's he going to say—that he did it?"

No, his daughter took care of that. "He's putting money up, John. What I want to know is whether or not it's a good idea."

"You're asking a lawyer about taking money?"

"Who better?" Hollow-sounding even to himself.

"Or am I sensing somebody looking for an excuse to beg off?"

Am I? Wil thought. *Shadowy figures flashing behind a lattice of green, darkened brass bolting into rifles already old when they drew down on the*

French at Dien Bien Phu. Clink of a mortar round against its tube launcher. Metallic rasp of a bipod under a treasured light machine gun.

He knew guys who'd served and who still hadn't lost their resentment: the country, the ARVN, politicians and profiteers—gooks, period. Guys who refused to talk about it, who'd seen so many friends die they'd simply torched the idea of having friends. Who, if the fires ever did go out, wouldn't know themselves, even if they made it past the cold that set in.

"Want me to write you a note excusing you from school?" Pereira broke in.

"I knew I'd called the right John."

"I'll say this for your edification: Marine law is a different crockpot. None of those landlubber niceties. Some years ago a fishing boat went down off San Nicolas Island. Like a range shell maybe took it out? For months the families of the guys who bought it lobbied for bringing up the hulk and proving it. Finally your favorite uncle agreed, and guess what they ruled despite what they found?"

"Accidental," Wil said.

"Hey, you ever think of going into law, call me."

"Any second now, John."

After hanging up, Wil changed into shorts for a walk with Matt. But instead an old weariness took him and he walked a tea out on the deck, thinking it might restore him. Across the moving line of cars, blue stretched beyond his bay, past the oil rigs and the Channel Islands, Hawaii and the Philippines. To a sweltering Mekong evening in 1972...

He'd been below decks, going over the list of possible hot spots with Rodriguez, when Belcher stuck his head in on the meet.

"Skip wants you both on deck, Mr. H. Possible situation."

They went up—Rodriguez to take over at the stern .50 where they'd gathered.

"What do you make of that," Miller said, field glasses raised.

Wil picked up his duty pair and homed in on this pathetic threesome waving at the Point Marlowe *from the sagging remains of a dock—fishing-skiff access for a dead village Wil remembered from the charts. Small, scared-shitless-looking mother holding a squalling baby, a wide-eyed boy about three clutching her leg. River-and-earth smell reminding him of freshly dug grave.*

"What are they doing out there?"

"You're asking me?" The CO mashing a mosquito into red-black paste,

humidity still rising from the afternoon rain shower that had neither cooled nor freshened. "What makes these people do anything?"

Wil kept scanning. "Frightened of something. The woman keeps checking over her shoulder."

"I'm open to suggestion."

Belcher led off. "I vote getting our butts gone—sir."

"So noted," Miller said. "Rodriguez, Tilson, Ford?"

"The Point Faro ringing any bells here?" Rodriguez.

Nods of affirmation from Tilson and Ford. Sister-ship to their own eighty-two-footer sent over to serve under the Navy, the Faro had been shot up intercepting contraband two weeks prior, VC snipers picking off the ship's XO and a crewman before they could get the hell out of there.

For a moment no one spoke.

Knowing Miller was hearing the same cries he was, Wil said, "She's scared to death and the kids are a mess. Wouldn't take much to swing over and pick 'em up."

"Chief Gunnery Officer Rodriguez?"

"Cheese in a trap, sir, but we can give it a try."

"We got the draft?"

"Sir, yes, sir." Tilson.

Miller was silent a moment, then he nodded, lowered the glasses, headed forward. "All ahead slow, hard'a port, be ready to hit it. One pass, gentlemen. We clear on that?"

"Yes, sir," Wil said, hearing it echo around the ship as he snagged his M-16, checked the breech and safety. Braced himself at his assigned position.

"Just pray you're right," Miller said, mounting the bridge, Rodriguez muttering "Semper Paratus" to no one in particular.

Right before all hell broke loose.

Wil had time to see the mortar round intended for them fall short, the mother and her children vanish in a bloom of muck, small-arms fire erupt from the undergrowth, Rodriguez cut loose with the fifty as their own mortar opened up. He was aware of spraying the undergrowth on full auto, green chaff, the flash of return fire, explosions turning the river inside out. Then, as the boat was completing its arc, the feeling of being lanced by white-hot wire as the bullets struck and seized his breath, spun him over into the dirty wake. Brown light and filtered sounds, no air, Rodriguez hauling him aboard about the time Wil had *packed it in, Miller shouting "Go, go, go, go!" as the crew laid covering fire across a thirty-degree swath.*

And, as he was passing out, of a body lying on the red-streaked deck beside him, a neat round hole cored in Tilson's forehead.

✪

Matt licking his hand, the pop of tires in his drive, brought him out of it. Dutifully, Matt barked at the man getting out of the white pickup.

"May I come up?" Vinh Tien asked.

"Why not? It's open."

Wil waited for the sound of steps, the kitchen door opening and closing. Then Vinh Tien was on the deck, Matt sniffing him before lying back down, his eyes tight on the visitor.

"He remembers me."

Wil didn't answer.

"May I sit?"

Wil slid him over a deck chair.

Vinh Tien took it, sat regarding the ocean. "My daughter told me what she said to you."

"Life's full of surprises," Wil answered. But it was empty and flip and he felt nothing looking at the man. "For what it's worth," he said, "I was expecting you."

"I was going to tell you last night," Vinh Tien said. "Even though I feared your reaction. My wife made me promise. She said it would be worse if you found out later." He cleared his throat. "Of course, she was right."

Wil stroked Matt's ears. A small plane dipped in over the beach and buzzed north over the point.

Vinh Tien said, "Will you at least listen?"

✪

Vinh Tien's village was sixty miles south of the DMZ, the arbitrary buffer between north and south that degenerated into a free-fire zone. Always a good student, Vinh was away at the Catholic school, where they trained those who would become doctors, the day the rangers came to question his people about the weapons. AK-47s an informant said they were stockpiling for the Cong.

"We have no weapons," they replied.

"You do," the rangers insisted.

"You have been fed tales. We do not."

Back and forth until there was no going back. Until eighty of his people—Vinh's mother and the uncle who'd raised him included—were herded to a pen meant for livestock and given a final chance to reveal the cache before a nervous ARVN short-circuited and the rest joined in. Among the massacred: Giang Minh Huong, Vinh's childhood sweetheart whom he'd married that spring.

When they had both turned seventeen.

Vinh heard about it from a boy who'd been wood-gathering and was drawn to the shots; no one else alive had seen it firsthand. Because as the rangers fled with their overheated M-16s, the American fighter planes called in due to "fierce resistance," napalmed the rest into a pyre that rose three hundred feet into the summer sky.

Squatting later in the still-warm crematorium, Vinh Tien had slashed his palms, pressed the ash into the wounds, vowed revenge. For five years—October '71 through April '75—he lived the Cong's Spartan life. Dispatching in a cold rage whatever enemies he and his comrades-in-arms could infiltrate, isolate, destroy.

Americans? Yes, Americans—who by their complicity had turned his heart to charcoal.

Then it was over and he went back to his village, or what was left of it, a few families trying not to starve. And there was Giang's cousin Li, who'd been away at school as well. And it must have been fated, because they were married next fall, almost to the day that Vinh's wife, mother, and uncle were massacred in the pens.

❀

"You know the rest," he told Wil. "The new government, their distrust because we were South. Even those who had bled for them."

Wil said nothing.

"When I learned of your service there, I knew I must speak with caution. That is not generally my way."

Wil nodded, Mia's words a broken record: *You two might even have traded shots*. Playing to the image of a red-spattered ship's deck, a shipmate and friend cooling in a jungle's steaming heart.

Vinh Tien's eyes stayed on the horizon. As though reading Wil's thoughts, he said, "Do you not think what it cost to ask an old enemy for help?" He drew a long breath. "How would you have felt? I apologize for last night, for deceiving you. But not for what I once thought was right."

The evening Amtrak air-horned a warning and clacked off south.

"None of it matters. My son matters. Can you see that?"

"I think so," Wil said.

"We expatriates sometimes think of each other as *Viet Kieu*, after our poem about a young seeker adrift in a hostile land. But this is not a hostile land. It is a good one."

He paused to pet Matt.

"Perhaps someone smarter than I can tabulate what we owe, those of us who fought. I only know this country gave me a chance to begin again." He rose to leave. "War kills the dead but once, Mr. Hardesty, they have that advantage over us. I am sorry you cannot help with my Jimmy. He was a good son."

Vinh Tien's hand was turning the knob, when Wil said, "Mr. Tien, Matt and I were wondering. Do you know the taste of lapsang souchong?"

11

THE NEXT DAY WAS FRIDAY, the day before *Desfile de Los Niños*, the kids' parade down State Street that Devin always got a kick out of. Wil left the house at nine-thirty, figuring ten would be about right to find Luc Tien at home—the dragon in his lair, as Vinh had put it. He nosed the Bonneville out onto 101, felt her hesitate before the surge.

Running on borrowed time.

Like some people he knew.

The morning itself was beautiful, the pressure dome holding: eighty-eight due for later. Off shore, the islands stood out in etched relief: ridges in sunlight, canyons looking as if they'd been raked with a garden claw. Anacapa's graceful arch, if you knew where to look.

His deck scope had brought it in over yet another lapsang, Wil wanting the tea's boost to carry over from the night before: Vinh Tien opening up from a perspective Wil had never thought to hear, Wil reciprocating in kind. Not the bads—those remained a censored letter, the cuts saying more than the remaining passages. This was more about the commonality of heat and travail, irrationality and chaos, humanity and hope. A walk in the mine field, but a start.

Of what, who knew?

Wil glanced again at the map Vinh provided, then at the Rincon's morning glass-off. Not even the kids were out. On the right, summer had left the backbone of mountains a dust green flecked with sandstone—

dried-up seedpods and wildflowers, scented air and backlit grasses the rewards of getting out into the August chaparral, the walkable creek beds. He made a note to do more of that, the obvious ever elusive. Like the miles of blue flowers spilling from the dividers. Until a day like this when you swung your gaze and wondered where they'd come from and what else you'd been missing.

He passed Santa Claus Lane—holdover from a more innocent era—then left the freeway, up and past Montecito's country-urban commerce. Through foothills showing hints of terra-cotta behind high hedges and onto Mountain Drive…which marked a steeper rise, and where he pulled over to check the map again.

Peppery hints rose in the stillness: warm eucalyptus, dust rising from his tires, the dry bright edge to an indrawn breath. He found it, then—a pinkish-buff Santa Fe slab-side behind a matching wall tight to the flank of the hill—parking where new blacktop led up through cacti and succulents, finely-crushed white, red, and pink rock. Squawk-box with a button built into the barred iron gate.

When a male voice answered, he told it Wil Hardesty wanted to see Luc Tien about his nephew.

Pause. "What *about* his nephew?"

"Maybe you should ask him."

"Don't hold your breath."

But in just under ten minutes, a beefy Asian man approached the gate in a white golf cart. White polo shirt over a ham neck, black shorts over tree-trunk thighs, short hair shaved on the sides. *Robb* embroidered on the shirt.

"You got ID?" he asked.

Wil showed him his investigator's and driver's.

The big head tilted, photo to face. "Local, huh? You packing?"

Wil did a turn with his arms out; still, Robb patted him down once he'd cracked the gate. They rode in silence past specimen *cholla,* barrel and Bishop's Hat, ocotillo and opuntia, some good-sized *palo verde,* other spikey things that eluded him. Not a blade of grass, just the colored rock, a giant Indian sand painting.

Two men resembling Robb were hosing down three gray-flake GMC Yukons backed from their garage bays. More men were stationed around the perimeter. The cart stopped then and Robb nodded to a taller man coming out of the house: black-rimmed sunglasses and the same black shorts, *Sonny* on his white polo, longish hair banded off into a nub. Looking Wil over, he nodded at Robb, who left in the cart.

"Your lucky day," he said, leading Wil through the house, a tiled airy space with Santa Fe-style furniture and fabrics. Navajo rugs in glass frames, Monument Valley and Grand Canyon scenes lit by recessed spots, bent-iron chandelier, expansive glass doors opening out on a parallel universe.

"That way," Sonny said.

After the cool of the house, the sun had a push. Then the flagstones gave way to a dark-bottomed swimming pool fed by a series of terraced spillways. Model-bodied women in thong bottoms lay around the fringe; as Wil passed, they shot looks at him before settling back. Pale Asian men in wraparounds also regarded him—looking embarrassed without their holsters.

But maybe it was just him.

Sonny had walked beyond them to a group of gardeners working the floral periphery. Wil let his gaze return to the men around the pool sighting in on him, wondering which was Luc Tien and how it might start.

"Mr. Hardesty..."

One of the gardeners had raised up beside a plaque that read, HE WHO PLANTS A GARDEN PLANTS HAPPINESS. Untucked blue chambray with the sleeves rolled up, knee pads, roundish sunglasses pushed up into damp black hair. Even white teeth in a face that reminded Wil of the actor who played in *The Lover*, that blade-steel quality, his smile now looking as if a contingent of *Sunset* editors had arrived to give him a landscaping award. He wiped sweat off his face and neck with a navy-and-white kerchief.

Then he said, "So you want to talk about Jimmy..."

"You ever in your life see two brothers so different?"

Luc Tien was holding out a dog-eared photo as a houseboy dressed like Sonny only in long pants left them limeade in thick Mexican glasses.

"Not lately," Wil said.

Luc Tien placed the photo back in the album, back in its drawer. "Different fathers. Mine was French, a Legionnaire who came and went— what happens when your mother's a whore."

He slid the drawer shut.

"Vinh didn't mention that? You have to forgive my brother. He's closed-minded about some things."

Wil sipped the tart drink. They were on sectionals with bright pillows scattered for effect. Luc Tien still glowed from his work. Which had led to a discourse about the entire landscaping scheme, some of the names spinning him off into their botanical histories, Wil trying to get a take on the man consistent with Vinh Tien's observations and coming nowhere close.

Not even.

"You can take the Vietnamese gardener out of the soil," Luc Tien was saying as he worked dirt out from under a nail. "Never the soil from the gardener. I cultivate orchids out back, if you appreciate such things."

"Thanks. Another time."

"A passion of mine, indulged by an interest in Asian-backed films. I won't bore you, but through circumstances, a talent company fell to me. At the urging of my investors I accepted modest roles before moving into production and distribution. Not the way my brother did it, of course. Or would have you believe."

"I assumed not."

"You can put that in the bank." He paused to drink. "Jimmy, who you came here to ask about and for which you get a pass this time since I was expecting it, was a particular bone between us. As Vinh is ever willing to point out."

He took a cigarette from an embossed leather box on the table, offered one to Wil, lit up as Wil was shaking it off. Jetting smoke at the ceiling, he said, "Vinh is lucky I don't sue him. Did he let on where he acquired the money to leave Vietnam? No, I didn't think so. Well, guess who?"

"He mentioned giant clams. Among other things."

Luc Tien waved his free hand as though dismissing the subject. "The whole thing with Jimmy has been so depressing. A young couple with everything to live for, their unborn child?" He wiped his face with the kerchief. "Jimmy always was more son than nephew."

Wil said, "I was told he met his fiancé here."

Luc Tien smiled until it dropped away. "Wen worked for me, yes. Until Jimmy took a fancy to her, and that ended that."

"Ended what?"

Limeade, an intake of smoke. "Nothing and no one you'd find interesting."

"Like the others around your pool?"

"Invited guests and their companions, Mr. Hardesty. Here to enjoy our magnificent climate."

"Mr. Tien," Wil said, deciding to cut to it. "Have you any reason to believe what happened to Jimmy and Wen was anything other than an accident?"

"No. Have you?" Blue exhale.

"What did Jimmy do in return for your hospitality?"

Luc Tien rolled ash in an onyx dish. "Are you truly interested? Or is this my brother again?"

"What I find is what I find. Vinh is aware of that."

"Poor Vinh." The headshake again. "Jimmy loved it here. From an early age, he chose to assist with my horses, to help around the property. Later on it was to drive me places and keep me on course. The boy had an agile mind. He was wasted on my brother."

"Did you pay him?"

"Of course I paid him—as I would pay anyone who rendered me a service. Even you." Grinning more broadly as he said it, the blade's tip showing through. He took a long inhale, let the smoke aura. "And now I believe your pass is ending."

As Luc Tien rose, Sonny appeared behind him.

"I have to admit it, I'm curious," Wil said. "Why cactus?"

Luc Tien regarded him as though deciding, then walked him to a slate wall down which water trickled into a pool. Wil saw half a dozen painted wood figures rising from the water—winged females in gold tiaras and colorful dress. Arms outstretched, their bases were anchored beneath the surface.

"*Roi Nuoc*," Luc Tien said. "Water puppets, very Vietnamese. As you may have noticed, about the only thing here that is." The kerchief appeared to wipe his smile back on. "Floods were a problem back when the art of puppet plays was introduced. But my people are ingenious. Their answer? Incorporate the floods into the performance."

He signaled to Sonny, who came forward, eyes on Wil, who met them.

As Wil was being ushered out, Luc Tien said, "If it's not pouring rain in my country, the sun's steaming it out of the ground. Go tell my brother to get a life, Mr. Hardesty. You'll be doing him a favor."

12

For once deciding to take his own advice, Wil changed into trail runners, fed Matt, tied a bandanna around the dog's neck. Then he drove them to the base of the mountains, the Rattlesnake Canyon trailhead he and Devin used to hike. For a while they crunched along to afternoon insect hum, birds in the underbrush, the scent of fennel. Foxtail and manzanita in the dry parts, watercress and bay when they'd cross what remained of the creek.

Hawks swept off the ridgelines, joyrode the thermals. As if it were understood up here, the few hikers they met smiled back, their own dogs taking the obligatory interest in Matt before the rustles and scurries proved too much.

Two miles in, they emerged at a bird's-eye view of the islands through his field glasses. Despite the day and their surroundings, Wil's thoughts went to Jimmy and Wen as the November cold became their cold, the blackness their blackness forty miles out by San Miguel. Then to the brothers Tien, their sad dance with one another—a dozen questions forming around each—until he left the sea for the road below, stopping the glasses at a curve down from where he'd left the Bonneville.

Focusing on what appeared to be two men.

Shadow figures at their distance.

Wil braced the glasses against a boulder. One man appeared to be smoking as he leaned against a blue-gray car hood; the other was looking up the mountainside through his own field glasses.

Looking at Wil...

Which was absurd, of course. The looker could be pinned on anything in his general direction and it would appear the same. Still...

For a while, neither he nor the occupants altered their stance, even as cars passed below on the narrow road. Then the man with the field glasses broke it off, said something to the smoking man before they got in and drove away.

Nothing, Wil thought—*birdwatchers.*

The trails and wetlands were full of them.

And the way Matt frolicked when they resumed the hike and how Wil's own mood lifted just watching him, it was as if the two men and the blue-gray car were no more than thin clouds: there one minute, cresting a far ridge the next.

13

IT MIGHT HAVE BEEN HIS PREOCCUPATION WITH LUC TIEN, the whole brother thing with Vinh, but it wasn't until after their morning walk, Matt running gulls, that Wil became aware of it: phone just off on the nightstand, the Winslow and the Caputo reverse stacked, line of dust where the TV had been repositioned slightly off line.

Yellow to orange.

Wil checked the places where he kept his rebuilt service .45 and the Colt Mustang .380 purchased last year for backup. They were undisturbed. Same with files, closets, drawers, though neatness in these areas had a way of deferring to expediency.

He fixed oatmeal, took it out on the deck.

If somebody were on his case, why? As far as Jimmy and Wen, he was in barely deep enough to matter. And to whom—Luc? Wil hadn't exactly made the man nervous; more to the contrary, a confidence bordering on arrogance. Not that Luc had opened up about much.

So, who? Why?

Questions 2, answers 0.

Post-cleanup, he and Matt drove the twelve miles to Santa Barbara, exiting at the Bird Lagoon, hotspot for watercolorists, except in September when the algae count rose and the fish followed suit. They passed bladers and joggers, sand courts with diggers and spikers already out, the gauntlet of palms and hotels, a showpiece park with a carousel.

And, approaching their turn, the harbored sailboat masts angling back the ten a.m. sun.

Wil eyed them, anything but in the mood. American Riviera, the travel touts called it, all the red tile and bougainvillea you could eat. Or maybe it was just the way he felt when some sonofabitch had been inside his house.

Their turn became a street lined with older mixed-front buildings—counterpoint to the arches and art walks that defined the town to visitors—up another block and a half to a cluster with its own small lot. Working space with bay doors adjoining a take out/sit-down eatery: Island Seafoods on the low sign.

He let Matt out on his leash and they checked the restaurant first. Couple of employees doing prep, unset tables, grills and hoods reminding him of the place his parents had tried making a go of in the sixties. Topsiders they'd called it before his mother's blood level took it and his old man across the yellow line and into a lorry full of Pendleton Marines.

They tried the market side, where a man and two women in aprons were dressing fish and arranging it on ice. Collectively, a fresher version of the aroma he'd picked up on Vinh Tien.

Vinh came forward now in hopsack jeans and a beige polo, nodding and wiping his hands on a towel so they could shake.

"Some operation," Wil said, spotting Li Tien at one of the sinks as he and Vinh took a table.

"Some work," Vinh Tien allowed, Matt alongside taking great interest in the hand extended him. "There is coffee, should you wish."

"Thanks, we had some." He watched Vinh's eyes roam: trademark, Wil knew from experience, of someone in the food business, that nonstop radar. "I went to see your brother."

He described it: Luc's manner, his equally confident denials. Then, "A question, though: Had you told him about me?"

Vinh Tien's eyes came back. "My brother and I speak only when necessary and only through someone. I do not recall the last time. The investigation, I suppose."

Metallic sounds from the kitchen, wet mop on clay floor tile.

Wil said, "Well, he knew I was coming."

"Not from me, he didn't."

Immediate and nothing to indicate it wasn't true.

"Beyond the Coast Guard, were there other government agencies involved?"

"Locally, the sheriff and the Harbor Patrol. I recall no others."

Wil reviewed his contacts at each: Sheriff's, a couple; harbormaster, none. Vinh Tien picked at a scrape on the back of his wrist.

"So," he asked. "What will you do next?"

Wil thought about it. "Wen's mother, I imagine."

A look resembling indigestion crossed Vinh's face. "Then I wish you luck," he said, nodding at a man extending a portable phone to him from behind a counter. "And no small measure of fortitude."

Isla Vista clung remoralike to UCSB's western flank. A creatively coded amalgam of apartment buildings, frat houses, and multiplexes, its commerce was a toss of food co-ops, pizza parlors, sound stores, and coffee hangouts. The county-patrolled turf nonetheless had become a haven for a burgeoning number of Vietnamese immigrants—sober individuals who kept largely to themselves while attempting to decipher the culture: the parties that flared like wildfires; the bottle-jammed Dumpsters; the BMWs, Integras, and Celicas driven by students who seemed intent on down-dressing the most impoverished of them.

Wil was struck again by how little it had changed since the early seventies when he was there. Apart from the names above the hangouts, I.V. was as constant as a myth: bastion of the counter-culture, keeper of the flame if you believed what was tacked onto the phone poles, kiosks, and message boards. Flutters du jour.

It did, however, boast his favorite name for a street.

Sabado Tarde—Saturday afternoon—that sweet sadness marking the divide between Friday and Monday, the feeling that always accompanied his college reflections. Life as Saturday afternoon: Frisbee and beach volleyball, surfing runs upcoast to then-undiscovered Jalama, backcountry overnights with Lisa when they were getting started and the sap was running high.

Things you never fully appreciated until they'd flown.

Wil just missed a cyclist in a peace T-shirt and got fingered in return. Checking Wen's mother's address again, he pulled over next to a small house behind a double overhead of myoporum. Cyclone-fenced dirt yard with kids playing, sandpile in the corner, toys scattered throughout. He rapped the screen door, was met by a young Vietnamese woman with a baby in one arm.

"Mrs. Diem?" The baby staring at him with huge dark eyes.

"Which one?"

"Nguyen Diem?" Obviously not her.

The woman disappeared; in a moment, one in her mid-to-late forties approached the door dressed in a shift that might once have been spotless and on which she was wiping her hands. Wide nose set in a face that looked as if dashed hopes and hard work had been friends since childhood.

"*Heh?...*" Looking suspiciously at him.

Wil handed her his card at which she glanced briefly before giving it to the younger woman, the baby now with a finger in its mouth. For all he could tell, the child hadn't blinked since he'd arrived.

"You detective?" the young woman asked.

"Private investigator," he said, one eye on the baby, who had begun to squirm. "I'm hoping to ask her some questions about her daughter." Noting that even as the younger woman was translating, Nguyen Diem was shaking her head emphatically.

"No more questions," the younger woman said. "Daughter gone. All finished."

Wil nodded, started to explain, addressed the younger woman instead. "Please tell her that I feel her loss. That I am trying to find out what happened to her daughter." Pausing while the younger woman went through it and Nguyen Diem said something too mumbled to follow.

"She want to know why you do this," the younger woman said.

"Please tell her my only wish is to help."

Diem rapid-fired back, swung her eyes accusingly to Wil as it was translated.

"She say you work for uncle."

"No, that's—"

Another staccato burst, the younger woman shifting the baby to the other arm as it began to fuss.

"Government, then. No good, either one. She say you go now."

"Vinh Tien hired me," Wil tried again. "Jimmy's father, her baby's grandfather."

But it had gone too far.

"No, no, no. No more talk. You go 'way." Retreating past a mantel on which a line of stuffed animals sat propped, beyond where Wil could make her out through the screen.

"Animals for her unborn grandchild," the young woman told him, wiping drool from the baby's chin. "Mrs. Diem very sad since Wen is gone. Most lonesome. She and Wen come here from Shanghai."

"Mrs. Diem is Chinese?"

"Chinese born in Vietnam. Viet-Ching—no good life. China no good, either."

"Can you help me, Ms...?"

The younger woman's eyes widened. *"Me? I know nothing. Mrs. Diem—"*

"All right, okay. They lived nearby, didn't they—Wen and Jimmy?"

"That way." Indicating the general direction. "Rented right after—six, seven months now. Many students, not many places." The baby growing increasingly fussy.

"Did Wen—"

"No more. You go now."

The baby's fussings had turned into little cries that matched the ones coming from the house and from a kid behind him in the sandpile. In a minute they'd all be doing it.

"Look, I just want to—"

As the door behind the screen banged shut, Wil turned to face the rising howls in the yard.

14

THE APARTMENT JIMMY AND WEN HAD OCCUPIED was a triplex up one street and over two. As Wil pulled in beside a white Jetta and a red Amigo on the lawn, or what passed for one, he could see sunning themselves on the balcony two girls and a boy in sunglasses that depersonalized an already vacant face.

"That's David's spot you're parked in," the kid said as Wil called up to him, one of the girls blinking open before closing her eyes again.

"Couple of questions," he said. "That is, if you're 217B."

"David's not gonna like that."

"How about it?"

The kid looked down. "That a dog in the car?"

"My driver," Wil smiled until he saw it didn't register. "Would you remember the previous tenants, a Vietnamese couple?"

"You must be kidding, man. I.V.'s crawling with 'em."

"Kenny, be nice," one of the girls said sleepily.

"Oh, yeah, I forgot."

Wil felt like bouncing him off his Amigo, but instead said, "Kenny, the sooner you help me, the sooner I'm gone."

Kenny took a hit from the Coors can beside him, settled back onto his lounge.

"Jimmy and Wen," Wil said, gritting his teeth. "Young couple, nice looking, mid-twenties?"

"That's young?" the other girl said without glancing up.

The one who'd looked his way rose and stepped to the railing. Bikini top and shorts, blonde hair, even tan, navel stud. Sea-blue eyes looking down at him.

"You a cop or something?"

"Nope. Interested party."

She shrugged. "It's no big hush-up. We rented this after they were gone. The landlord gave us the place cheap because he didn't want to rent to any more...um—"

Deciding not to go there after all.

"They leave anything behind?" Wil asked. "Things the landlord or the authorities might have missed?"

"Why? They criminals or something?"

"Ask him if there's a reward," Kenny said.

"Shut up," she said to him without force. Then to Wil, "The usual: bags and stuff, things you might toss in soup. Dust, and like a lot of it."

"Not too neat," the other girl added.

"Anybody else around know them?" Wil feeling his neck getting stiff from looking up. "Neighbors?"

"Nobody in the plex, and we've been here longest." She tried a thought on for size, looked unsure of the fit. "You might try the people next door. Nobody's real permanent around here."

"Thanks, I'll do that." Rubbing his neck. "What's your name?"

"None of his business," Kenny mumbled.

"Amber. What's yours?"

"*Asshole,*" Kenny coughed into his fist.

"Don't mind Kenny," Amber said. "He's just mad his check's late, and David's gone for the weekend. You want to come up, have a beer or something?"

"Another life, maybe." Wil said as the other girl levered up to watch him go.

"What?..."

"I said it's bright. Take care of those eyes."

The only resident who could even place Jimmy and Wen was an Hispanic woman across the street with cats in the living room. Seven or eight of them. She recalled the couple as polite, always greeting her by name— Mrs. Flores—when they'd pass her house, and seeming tense just before they didn't come back.

"*Los pobres,*" she said, crossing herself as a tortoiseshell curled its tail around her leg and looked up at him. "They were nice, well behaved. Not like those party-brats he's got in there now. God forbid they should pick up a book."

"You know the landlord?"

She rolled her eyes. "Hindu dentist or something, drives up from L.A. in his Caddy. Always comes and asks me what his tenants are doing. Like I'm his spy or something."

"Did he mention finding anything after the authorities finished up?"

"Not to me he didn't. Never even cleaned the place before those kids moved in. Let alone after."

Wil bent to a gray shorthair, who sniffed his hand. "You said they seemed tense?"

She thought about that. "I'd never heard them say a cross word till then. But they snapped at each other. Cantinflas has been known to bite, by the way. Not me, but visitors."

"Any idea what it might have been about?" Pulling in his hand.

She lowered her glasses at him. "Does the sheriff know you're asking these questions?" Not challenging so much as *our little secret.*

"Not these specific ones, no," he answered.

"But they do know *of* you?"

"My license, remember?"

She looked at his card again, then up and down the street. Wil thought he spotted a flash of blue-gray metal, but by the time he'd raised his hand to the glare, it was gone.

"Well," Mrs. Flores was saying. "It has been a number of months. Who knows what it might have been about?"

The tortoiseshell landed in his lap; she lifted it to her, cradled it.

"Feeding this crew must be something else," he said.

"Are you kidding? You have any idea what I pay for Little Friskies? You don't *want* to know."

"I can only imagine." Pulling a twenty from his wallet, folding it lengthwise so it stayed flat, extending it.

She eyed the bill. "Wait a minute. I'm not violating any rules here, am I? Privacy or anything?"

"No, ma'am. Just helping out."

She took it, tucked it under her. Wil shifted positions while a clock embedded in a scene showing kittens in a fur hat marked the seconds.

"I think it had to do with whoever was after them," she said.

"After them..."

"Well, maybe not after *them*, I don't really know that. More like some threat." Frowning at the recollection. "Seemed like they were turning on each other because they didn't know what to do, or each had a different idea about it. Body language, a backward glance—they'll tell you things if you let 'em."

"They were scared," Wil said.

Mrs. Flores touched noses with the purring tortoiseshell. "There it is. Something had 'em going."

15

RECROSSING THE STREET, Wil saw no red Amigo in front of the triplex and no sign of Kenny. The only one left on the balcony was the blonde who'd spoken to him.

Amber.

"They went to get some food," she said as he approached. "And the offer still stands."

"How about my card in your jamb instead."

At the sound of Wil's voice, Matt stuck his nose out the half-cracked window and yipped a welcome that sounded more like talking than barking.

"Yeah?" she said. "What for?"

"So that if you think or hear of anything or if something turns up, you'll be able to call me."

He left the card, started again for the Bonneville.

"Be that way," she said, rolling over on her lounge and releasing her straps.

Sabado tarde.

Wil let Matt lick his ear, then backed out with an upward glance. He was heading west toward the spot where the road and the houses ended and an undeveloped section led to a beach where he could run Matt a little, when he made the tail for real.

Blue-gray Buick, late model, block and a half back of them.

Sun glinting off the windshield as it paused at the stop.

Wil waited until the Buick had crossed the intersection then made a leisurely turn into an alley he knew came out on the street just up. Out of sight, he gunned it, spun the wheel, circled in time to see the Buick hesitate before nosing into where he'd turned.

He gave them a second, headed in.

And there they were, halfway through, heads in clipped conversation: woman driving, auburn hair cropped at the neckline, beefy-looking bald man riding shotgun, Wil at least half right from the other day at Rattlesnake. He saw the woman's eyes brush the rearview, saw her alert her partner, the partner start to swivel before checking his door mirror instead. Then her brakes flashed at the alley's narrow mouth, and she hit it.

Through her dust, Wil did the same. Riding the brake with his left foot, the gas with his right, he kicked the Bonneville's big engine, felt the lean, the car's heavy suspension fighting it. He threw a glance at Matt now braced against the door and backed off slightly while trying to keep the Buick in sight.

Blink and lose them.

Braking where the driver had, he whipped a right and accelerated, saw her appearing momentarily confused as to which street was out. The Buick swerved wide, left sparks at the street's crown and almost clipped a parked 4Runner that Wil left-footed for, scattering the same quartet of cyclists the Buick had swerved to avoid. That's when *he* lost it, spinning out, stalling, taking Matt, despite his four-legged brace, sideways into the dash.

❧

By the time he saw to the four girls while a bike-sympathetic crowd lit into him, one writing down his license, it was nearly four, the Buick long gone. The good news was Matt was fine—supervising the scene from his window seat and drawing the interest of the cyclists and even some from the crowd.

Mr. Oil-on-troubled-waters.

Curled on the front seat now as Wil took the slow lane home.

The Buick said agency of some sort, yet at the same time rental. Which could mean nearly anyone. So who were they? More to the point, why him? He stopped in Carpinteria for a double espresso, Milk-Bones for Matt. Then he slipped down 101 past Bates Road and the Rincon, the advance guard already lining up for the *chubasco*...the one the radio was reporting, about to sucker-punch the Mexican coast and already landing curdly clouds up north. Air you could feel in your chest.

He switched to the oldies station out of Ventura, caught *Wiiiild horses...couldn't drag me away*. Waiting out a pulse of oncoming traffic, he swung in past La Conchita's lone gas station/burger joint and the streets dead-ending in the taped-off homes, the '95 slide, the bluffs. Onto his street and to a dead stop, nearly sliding Matt off the seat again.

Wiiiild, wiiiild horses—

Wil lost the Stones, stared at the blue-gray car parked in his drive, at the two heads turning to look at him as he eased in and cut the engine. Waiting as the two stepped out and came together at the Buick's trunk.

He let Matt out his side, told him to stay, started toward them.

Five-sevenish yet dwarfed by the bald man's six-three bulk, the woman was café con leche to his sun-reddened white, dark-eyed to his pale gray. She wore gabardine slacks nipped in on a crunch-fed waist, blue oxford shirt with the tip of a pen showing. Light makeup on a face doing its best to look stern. Not that her utilitarian haircut hurt the effort. Or the trident logo embossed into the grip of her Beretta nine.

The man had the look and size of ex-cop or military, hard tending toward girth, webs around the eyes and nose. Up close, his head had a fringe of almost-shaved gray, a sheen that made it look waxed. Khakis and a short-sleeved white shirt that displayed thick forearms, the mark of a near-successful tattoo removal peeking out from under one sleeve.

Like the woman, he had a Beretta clipped to his belt.

"Your dog under control there?" Voice like a deeper version of Andy Devine's. Matt alternately whining and growling, but staying.

"That depends," Wil said.

The man rested a hand on the Beretta. "Do him and you a favor and put him someplace."

"Fuck yourself. He lives here."

"For the present."

Matt let out a yip that threatened to escalate if Wil didn't renew the command. The woman said, "Mr. Hardesty, I'm Special Agent Lorenz—

Treasury Department: Alcohol, Tobacco, and Firearms." Flipping open her ATF badge to *Inez A. Lorenz*. "That's Special Agent Maccafee. I think we can move beyond this, don't you?"

"Meaning you're finished tossing my house?"

"We would deny that," the man said, his pale eyes still locked on Wil's.

"Why am I not surprised?"

The man looked at Matt, thumbed open the snap restraining his nine, back up at Wil. *Your move...*

"He have a badge?" Wil asked Lorenz. "Or is that your job, too."

The man's face broke an expression reminiscent of a Sheriff's captain Wil knew—someone who, if it were up to him, would light a cigar as Wil sank into the La Brea Tar Pits. At a look from Lorenz, Maccafee badged him, slapped it shut with a pop, jammed it into his pocket.

Lorenz said, "Are we cool now, Mr. Hardesty?"

Up close, she appeared about the same age as Kari Thayer—mid-to-late thirties—the thought of Kari, whom he'd been with on and off for a year, given the turbulence with her son and ex-husband, spilling over favorably into his appraisal. Still, it was the same old tired act. Laughable except for how practiced she and Maccafee were at it.

That was the intellectualization; the reality was he was pissed.

"Cool with what, Lorenz? You showing up here after I nearly make the news?"

"We pick the time, we pick the place," Maccafee said.

"Waco comes to mind," Wil fired back.

"Here and now, friend. You say the word."

"That somewhere in your manual, too?"

Lorenz dropped to one knee and called to Matt, who came to her after a brief look at Wil.

"Some watchdog," Maccafee said. "Remind me to bring a bone next time."

"And what next time would that be, Agent Maccafee?"

"Jesus, Inez," Maccafee said without looking at her. "We gonna do this in the driveway, or what?"

16

THEY SAT ON THE DECK, BREEZE RISING OFF THE WATER. "You want to tell me about my house?" Wil asked, his burner still on simmer.

Lorenz responded before Maccafee could. "Looks inviting, Mr. Hardesty. Maybe you could show us around after we talk." Maccafee smiling the smile.

"I figured as much. And now?"

"We felt it was time you knew who you were dealing with," Lorenz said.

"I wasn't aware I was *dealing* with anyone."

"Luc Tuan Tien," she said.

"Excuse me?"

"The man whose property we observed you entering yesterday."

Wil swung his glance to Maccafee. "In your capacity as..."

"You wouldn't want to take a walk, would you, Inez?" he said. "Give Seinfeld and me some quality time alone?"

Lorenz said, "All right, Mac. To answer your question, Mr. Hardesty, in our surveillance of Luc Tien. You see, I'm trying to be straight with you."

"Arresting use of the term. Tell me, was it you who tossed my bedroom? If it was, take Polaroids next time."

Her smile was after a fashion. "Naturally, we were curious about you, so we ran your plate. Yours is quite a history, isn't it?"

"Sorry," he said, "I don't spend a lot of time with it."

"Can't blame you there," Maccafee taunted. "You might still have your wife and son."

Wil calculated the distance to the big man's nose, felt a fist curl in on itself. But Maccafee wasn't through.

"The name Brandon Smith mean anything to you—younger guy, good looking, owns his own body shop? Seen in your ex's company?"

Baiting him, Wil told himself, jail time for nailing an ATF, a similar effect on his license. Just to get leverage on him? It made no sense. Maybe if he knew something, but that was it, he didn't. Which only made him more intrigued as to why they'd gone to the trouble.

"Mac..." Lorenz warned.

But Maccafee had his notebook out and was running down an entry. "Feel free to update," he said to Wil. "Body count attributed to Shawn Wilson Hardesty: L.A., Hawaii, Bakersfield, *La Conchita?*" Blinking to drive it home. "That one must have endeared you to the neighbors."

Six years ago, the shoot-out in the tunnel.

"Something else, aren't you, Maccafee?"

"Precisely my point. What's a Dumpster jockey like you doing showing up in a federal investigation?"

"Investigation of what?" Wil said.

Lorenz reached down, put a hand on Matt, one-paw-on-the-other intent on their interaction, but pleased by the attention. "Mr. Hardesty," she said, "what do you know about Asian gangs?"

Wil read her, decided it was up-and-up. "About what I've read—home invasions, carjacks, extortion. Mostly their own because the victims don't trust our authority figures, imagine that."

Maccafee snorted; Lorenz tapped the arm of her chair.

"That is one level, yes. Some years ago in New York, our agency became involved in the breakup of a gang known as Born to Kill. Money laundering, drugs, robbery, slavery, murder—you might have heard of it."

"Can't say I have."

"Vietnamese," she said. "Young with nothing to lose. Castoffs from their own country who banded together once they were here. *Viet Kieu* they consider themselves. Which, if you know the culture, means—"

"Strangers in a strange land," he said. "I've run across the term."

"Three guesses where," Maccafee said as Lorenz kept on.

"Some were illegals. Others bounced off the foster parent program and into collaboration with a man who attempted to mold them into a kind of crime family. At first within their urban environment, then nationwide." Her hand stroked Matt's fur. "That was a first."

Maccafee said, "Giving pause not only to the established tongs, for whom they showed zero respect, but to law enforcement in general."

"As usual and unfortunately," Lorenz added, with a glance at her partner, "we were late reacting. And difficulty coordinating is a given."

"Agency wars," Wil put in.

Maccafee looked off; Lorenz didn't.

"Right enough. Too often the gangs have nothing on us. But that's another story. The fact is, we caught a break. We scored an informant who proved instrumental in bringing down the lead people. You see, it's not as easy as rounding up whomever we suspect. Our own limitations—"

"Rules of law, you mean."

"To be argumentative. Actually, I was referring to the code of silence among the victims."

Wil drank from his bottled water. "But now another group has formed to fill the vacuum."

"That is where we were going, yes," she said after a glance at her partner. "Except that—"

"These aren't your average thugs," Maccafee put in. "At least the ones we're after."

"A wild guess," Wil threw in. "Worse than baddies number one."

"And their pretenders, of which there have been a number. Plus, they've formed alliances I won't mention."

"Always the way, isn't it?"

Maccafee stared at Wil as he might a pinned bug. "They're particularly effective in setting examples. One who owned an interstate trucking firm wasn't buying the pitch. So they cored out his eyes with a grapefruit spoon—after they'd gutted his wife in front of him." He ran a hand over his pink scalp, rubbed his hands together. "You ever read Dante?"

"Enough to get the reference," Wil said, beginning to appreciate the man's directness, if not his style.

"Every day these guys find new levels. Meantime, what Special Agent

Lorenz is trying politely to say because she's had more schooling than I have, is that we've had our losses. Enrique Camerena mean anything to you?"

DEA, the agent tortured to death by Mexican drug lords: Wil knew it from not only the papers, but from a friend who'd known him. "Yes," he said.

"Well, hot damn," Maccafee said. "Think Camerena with brains behind it." He went to lean on the rail as Lorenz regarded Wil.

"Mac at one time was paired with an agent, a good man who knew his job. Indications were he'd been burned with a gas torch and fed to pigs." She straightened in her chair. "I hedge because from the remains it was hard to tell. Any of this sticking to the wall, Mr. Hardesty?"

17

I N THE COOL THEY'D MOVED TO THE LIVING ROOM, Lorenz making a show over Wil's signed print of *Moonrise over Hernandez, New Mexico* while Maccafee went back to his horizon.

Great window for seeing your dead, Wil thought.

"Rising Dragon," Maccafee said without turning from it. "That's what they call themselves."

"*Viet Kieu* homage to the old country." Lorenz.

Wil thought of all the dragon memorabilia shipped home. Prevalent as the time-warp documentaries that still ran on the cable channels. "Defiant comes to mind," he said.

Lorenz opened her attaché. "Like other gangs, Rising Dragon members are identifiable by their tattoos." She fanned out shots of more or less the same rendering: a dragon rearing back on itself, claws poised to seize so the jaws could rip and tear.

Some were poorly done with inks that bled through the design; others showed an almost photographic skill. Higher-ups versus foot soldiers, Wil assumed.

"And you think Luc Tien is involved?"

"Now there's a brilliant observation."

"Enough, Mac, I mean it," she said to him, a sword through silk.

"Right. You gonna be much longer? Because I'll be in the car."

Still without a look back, Maccafee clumped down the stairs; Wil could hear his feet on the gravel, car door closed, the radio punched up.

"So, what kind of trouble?" he asked Lorenz.

"Excuse me?"

"That got him demoted."

"I don't know what you're talking about," she said.

"Yeah, I can tell."

"Mac's a legend in this business. Name it, he's done it."

Wil shifted on the couch. "You're also clearly his superior and a lot younger. Which either makes you the best ATF's got, or somewhere along the line our man stumbled."

She didn't respond.

"Moot point," he said, tired of it all. "You plan to let me in on what you want?"

Hesitation, then, "You're working for the brother—Vinh Tien. Jimmy Tien's father."

"Did I say that?"

"Vinh Tien's contesting of the investigation is documented. Via him, you have access."

"The operative term is had. That was made clear yesterday."

"Which puts you a leg up on us."

"So get a warrant," Wil said. "Take him down."

"In time." She looked at Matt snoozing next to his bowl. "Great dog. Where'd you get him?"

"Friend of mine who died," he said. "You'd have liked her."

"Can't have too many friends, can we?"

And suddenly there it was, the piece configuring itself to the space, so apparent that he kicked himself for not already having seen it. It was the reason they'd tailed him to Rattlesnake, through Jimmy's old neighborhood, why they were here.

We scored an informant. Fed MO in spades.

"Jimmy was working for you, wasn't he?" Wil said.

She broke a smile. "Mac bet you wouldn't see it."

"And you went with me?" he said. "I must be slipping."

"Don't get all pumped up. I'm a fan of long shots."

Be careful around this one, a little voice told him. He said, "Was it your idea to have Maccafee try and get me to nail him?"

"Let's just say we work as a team."

Damned careful. "So how'd you leverage Jimmy?"

She went to stand where Maccafee had, rolled her right shoulder. "Not without difficulty, and for too brief a time. You always have sunsets this beautiful?"

He said, "It's the weather down south. Problem with the shoulder?"

"*Chica* with a knife I thought I could talk her out of. Rookie mistake."

"What about Jimmy?"

She shrugged. "A good enough kid, but not our main thrust right now." A flight of pelicans crossed the horizon, razor sharp in silhouette. "Are you thinking his uncle had him killed? Is that why you were out there at the house?"

"Lady, so far I don't know jack, and I'm getting real tired of it."

She turned from the window, herself an etching. "Luc Tien is our target, that must be apparent. And trust me, he's easily capable of killing the kid. Which would tend to put us on the same side now, wouldn't it?"

"Not as yet it wouldn't."

Her bottom lip formed a line against her teeth. "Information—dots we can connect, that's what we need. Things you can learn that we can't."

"In other words, you want me to do your work for you."

"What I want is to bring down a very bad man."

"Lady, that's you. Which doesn't mean it's me. And how far do you think I'd get when it became known I was anybody's conduit."

"Now I see. Except where it suits your purposes."

"We all have our failings, Agent Lorenz."

"I am sorry to hear you say that."

"Big news, if it hasn't dawned," Wil said. "My scope's a tad more limited."

She shuffled the tattoo photos before scooping them into the attaché. "Just where I was headed," she said. "What if we could help you with your case? Finding out what happened to Jimmy?"

"Interesting thought. And Wen."

"Surely we're past these word games."

"You'll tell me how, of course."

"As thoughts occur. But I'm equally certain you'll think of ways." Smiling as she stood. "Goodnight, Mr. Hardesty." Extending her hand from the lamplight. "Agent Maccafee and I will be in touch."

18

THE FUNERAL FOR KAN WAH YEE promised to be one of San Francisco's events of the year, second only to the Chinese lunar holiday. All morning the flower shops had run their deliveries: funeral home and grave site, mom-and-pop establishments up and down Grant, the banners and decorated lampposts, the wreathed shop windows looking like something out of the twenties and thirties, the great tong funerals of that era. Traffic-control officers at the key intersections braced themselves—Broadway-Columbus, California-Grant near Old St. Mary's, where a second memorial service was even now being held. Someplace the politicos could pay their respects in more familiar surroundings.

Besides, the granite foundation stones had come from China.

"Lung cancer," they'd whisper somberly, reminding themselves to have their secretaries schedule checkups.

"All that opium," they'd wink and grin to each other, though you had to be careful with this crowd. Never could tell what was going to upset whom these days, even the casual attempt at humor. Though even old man Yee would have gotten a kick out of that one, they'd agree later in the bars. And how about some of these squint hardcases: faces like they hadn't shit in weeks.

From his spot in Portsmouth Square, Detective Sergeant Arthur Loh of San Francisco's Asian Organized Crime Task Force pictured it, and happily so. He'd take outdoor duty anytime. His luck of the draw: the official civic unveiling of the Kan Wah Yee bust and plaque concurrent with the Old St. Mary's service, the hearse and limousines waiting for the slow parade down Grant. Yee's privately commissioned flower-strewn bust not only befitting Chinatown's no-shit, honest-to-Buddha godfather, but already sending a message to mah-jongg players everywhere.

Kan Wah Yee lives. Through us.

Meaning Yee's Gateway Arch Benevolent Association, of course; they were on the plaque as sponsors. Understood and underlying, however, was the real sponsor—Po Sang, the West Coast's most powerful and influential tong. Be mindful, you pretenders, you dividers, you independents inclined to fancy that our grip has loosened, the plaque told them. We are here as this bust is here, part of your city.

Stone-faced and no less merciful.

Even the ones fresh off the boat understood that.

Looking around, Loh nodded to Detective Sergeant Terry Leong, a fellow Forcer there for the same reason he was: to see which among his mug-shot collection showed up, get a sense of the emerging power structure. Loh lit a stogie against the wind, the fog already rolling in off Russian Hill. Hundred-and-five degrees in Sacramento but overcoat weather here in The City. Making him yearn for the beaches of Orange County where he'd grown up.

Arthur Loh trailed smoke, raised his eyes to the Transamerica Building, the pyramid's top already in shroud, Coit Tower becoming a ghost. Back down to the flowers, then, the uniformed school kids who'd just finished singing *This Land Is Your Land, This Land Is My Land* to polite applause. Spotting then three new arrivals he knew by name: William and Raymond Chang plus their Hong Kong money guy, Benny Lum. Here to pay respects and show solidarity, doubtless. Limo arrivals from the Washington Street side in their two-thousand-dollar suits.

Answering the question about who would inherit the earth.

Not the meek, Arthur thought, that was sure.

Not in this town.

He saw Terry Leong shoot a knowing glance his way, begin easing his way through the crowd and out—where Arthur Loh was headed in a minute. Spell-the-wife time: watch the Niners play somebody in a meaningless pre-season game, the father-son thing with Junior while Valerie recharged at her French-cooking class. Picturing her with flour on her nose, her big glasses taking it all in, Arthur Loh smiled. And almost missed the three young men in knee-length raincoats moving toward the front.

Moving in on the Changs and Benny Lum...

Shit!

Loh searched for Terry Leong but saw only crowd: respectful looks and low tones, something he would never comprehend. This spectacled grandfatherly assassin who for generations had struck terror into his own people. To the point where handing over the protection money was all but second nature to them. Factored in. And they show up to venerate him because here and there he gave some back?

Kan Wah Yee good for business, they'd tell him.

When they'd tell him anything.

Classic.

Loh began elbowing his way forward, at the same time reaching under his jacket to free his double-action Browning. He noted that the crowd was parting more readily for the wedge of black-coated newcomers. As if they radiated a chemical presence.

For a moment they, the Changs, and Benny Lum were lost from view. Then it started: automatic-pistol bursts, firecracker loud against the concrete. Screams, shouts, cries, pandemonium, Loh hollering at the crowd to get down, that he was a cop. *Down, down, down, goddamnit!*

Gripping the Browning tighter, he raised it in a two-handed grip, thinking *Not on my watch, you fucks...* waiting for the panickers to drop and give him visual access. Which is exactly what happened: this sudden, gaping field of fire.

Just not as expected.

There were the Changs, all right, face down with a bloody Benny Lum between them, at least one Chang bodyguard sprawled on the steps. One of the raincoats had a foot to the stone face of Kan Wah Yee, toppling the bust as the other two edged away in a flanking action. Expecting him, Loh suddenly realized. Realizing also that he'd probably been the one to alert them with his cop shouts.

Whatever, both their weapons—Ingrams from here—were pointed his way, his gun only now coming down to find a target. Because that was *it*, what you did, took your chances, picked one and prayed. It was just Arthur Loh's bad fortune that he was up against Slim and None.

19

THE MAN WHO'D HAD SUCH A FRUITFUL CONVERSATION with the young Vietnamese gangster Tam Minh at the Nam Sun Jewelry Exchange before seeing him off to Honolulu, where a contact would reroute the kid for a C-note, emerged from the twenty-four-hour office center more convinced than ever about the future of electronic banking. Hell, the convenience alone. Not to mention the effect thirty bucks worth of computer time just had on his Swiss account, his field report compiled, coded, and sent in the moments prior.

Amazing the technology taken for granted these days.

As for Tam, the farther away Tam got the more likely he was to be having second thoughts. Rarely did his type stay away; it was all they knew. For a moment the man contemplated calling back his contact to finish what he probably should have at the store, nip the inevitable in the bud, the Buddist model of responsibility for a life saved in reverse.

Finally he convinced himself the choice was Tam's, that Tam might prove the exception. That here was the scorpion in a hundred who might defy his nature and not sting the frog giving him a ride across the river.

Or was it simply the dulling effects of time?

Something a man in his business had to watch out for.

He slipped into a coffee place not far from his hotel, ordered a Sumatra, laced it with half-and-half, settled at an outside table to watch the beachwalk finale. Sunday skaters and joggers, cyclists and cruisers, mumblers and amblers. And sure enough, here one came, asking for change before deciding he'd made a mistake: looking back over his shoulder to make sure the whatever-it-was he'd seen in those eyes wasn't coming after him.

By now, however, sun on the water, "Travelin' Man" on the shop's tinny speaker, the man's thoughts had gone to things more generic in nature. Specifically, what it felt like to be back.

Surreal was his strongest impression. Squint and there it was, 1967 again—surf sounds, Rick's easy delivery, laughter and the sound of movement—summer, ephemeral and timeless. Even with eyes wide, it looked the same: same funk and salt-tinged seediness, glitz and superficiality, beach-taffy innocence and margarita-in-a-can-in-a-bag edge. The body-worship thing that to this extent flourished only here.

Trying to recall the last time he'd been on the beachwalk brought a jumble of events and faces, a swirl of dates…before the cell phone's twitter chased them back inside like foxes to the lair.

"Yes?…"

"We read your report with interest," the voice began. "Particularly your debriefing of the gang member."

"I thought you'd like that one," he said.

"He is, I trust, no longer a member."

"Not the last time I checked."

"Good," the voice went on. "And you were pleased with the compensation?"

"Covers the bills, plus some left over," the man answered, eyeing a tiara'd redhead flashing by in pink-and-purple organdy, wind-whipped Mylar balloons trailing behind her.

Only here.

"You are well?" the voice interrupted.

"Well enough to deposit the check, if that's what you mean."

Silence, the voice obviously awaiting more.

"You can't be serious," he added. "My health is the reason for this call?"

"Only in the sense that your services are highly valued. Are you in position to take down a landline number?"

That was more like it. Pencil and napkin. "Fire away."

After the man took down the number, he moved to a single pay phone within sight of his coffee. Two rings, standard procedure, the same voice saying, "You've seen the news?"

"And if I had, what would it have been," the man said, already guessing retaliation—blood and vengeance until one side called it off. Not that it mattered to him. They went down, they stayed down, a simplicity that defied complication.

"The Changs and Benny Lum are dead. Plus their bodyguards and a policeman."

"And I should care about this for what reason?" The man's eyes tracking a blonde in platform sandals, feather necklace, neon-green shorts and halter. Black-and-white Lhasa apso on a braided leash.

The voice said, "We wish to extend your contract. This time to go beyond the dragon's claws to its brain."

"The magic word: contract. You have a name?"

The voice spelled it out, the name not sounding like the one the little gangster had finally spilled and which he had yet to pass along. But who was he to argue; the ones doing the grunt work rarely had the whole dope. That was the idea, no straight path back. Which might or might not make everything else the kid spilled suspect. And so much for that investment.

Now the voice was relaying the name and address of a San Francisco hotel, telling him, "Your room is in the name LeBlanc. Call this number when you're set up, and we will forward the most current information. Is that understood?"

"I believe I'm up to it," he said. "And speaking of my fee..."

The voice paused, quoted a number, at which point the man let a knot of shirtless skateboarders clack past, their baggies low enough to reveal the requisite band of boxer short, however *that* got started.

"Double it," the man said into the receiver. Removing the hand he'd cupped over his ear.

"That is—"

"The deal," he said. "It's up to you."

There was a pause. "First I must speak with—"

"When I reach zero, I will assume you are unable to afford me. Five...four...three...two—"

"Very well." Steamed-sounding, but at the same time resigned.

The man smiled. "Half in the intermediary account now, the other half as before. The usual on top for expenses."

Another pause. "When may I tell my superiors you might begin?"

"How soon can you hang up?"

Dial tone.

After it cut in, the man replaced the receiver and walked to his table, intending to watch the sun begin its descent, take at least that pleasure before resuming. But the warm light had left the water, the Sumatra and the steel chair both were cold, and a twilight breeze already was kicking sand and papers along the beachwalk, thinning the parade to an athletic few.

The man swore once in Thai—always the most expressive, he'd found—tossed the Sumatra into a bus tray and, leaning back, punched up a number on his cell phone.

20

SEVEN-THIRTY MONDAY, fog and overcast making a last stand before the offshores mustered to run them out, Wil called one of his two friends at the Santa Barbara County Sheriff's. Two hours and fifteen minutes later, Frank Lin, detective, a stocky man with a passion for body-building Wil had known since beach volleyball days, appeared at the window in plain clothes: chinos, blue shirt, knit tie, Rockports.

He looked like a taller version of Jackie Chan, that same twinkle. He said something to the duty deputy, then, in his county car, followed Wil to the IHOP not far from the squat office building that was their head-quarters.

"Oh boy," he said, looking over the menu.

"Anything up to five bucks," Wil said.

"Coffee included?"

"Nope—over and above. Bust a gut."

They'd been served and were eating when Wil gradually steered toward longer and longer lapses. Face in the balance, he knew from experience, this little dance he and Lin, whose grandfather had made the Long March in 1949, did on occasion. Had it been Lin doing the asking, Wil's role would have fallen to him.

As it was, Wil was the one having to wait.

"The Tien thing," Lin said finally.

"Farthest thing from my mind," Wil answered. "Shine your holster?"

"I'll settle for the strawberry jam."

Wil passed it.

Lin said, "I got Rudy to give me his impressions of it, too."

Chief of Detectives Rudolfo Yanez's name appeared in some of the Tien articles Wil had read: Lieutenant Yanez of the well-documented profile, the silver-saddled Arabian during Old Spanish Days. Fiesta Rudy some called him, though not within earshot.

Wil let his expression ask it for him.

Lin said, "The kid's old man got the prelim started—nothing more than you already know. Nothing to justify a full-scale."

"And the unofficial version?"

"Nothing that can't be explained the way the Coast Guard did."

"Bad weather doesn't explain why they were out there, Frank."

"Neither can anyone else, apparently."

Around trips from the waitress, Wil mentioned Mrs. Flores, her theory that Jimmy and Wen were scared about something. Lin spread strawberry on a buckwheat, shoved in a piece of bacon after it.

"The neighborhood snoopsister," he said. "Nobody else we talked to bore that out."

"So your guys interviewed her?"

"Cats and students. Quite a philosophizer, our Mrs. Flores."

Wil let it go. "What about the daughter—Mia?"

"Piece of work," Lin said. "Not much of a corroborator for the parents."

"For whom, then? The uncle?"

"Him and everything else." Lin refilling his mug from the carafe. "The old man, of course, went on and on, a real hard-on for his brother. Nothing that matched up, though."

"Any chance I could see the interview?"

Lin smiled around a bite. "Next question?"

"What about Luc Tien?"

"Not much there but a big house. Guy rolled out the red carpet—photos of him with the kid, him on movie sets. You aware he was once billed as the Asian Cary Grant?"

"No." True as far as it went.

"Overseas, anyway. He tried a few of those kung-fu blow-em-ups, but no dice. Impressive photo collection, though."

Wil worked a thread. "Does he have a record?"

"Nothing much. A traffic beef that got settled out of court."

He heard Lorenz and Maccafee again, their take on the man: a hold-out's eyes cored out with a spoon. "Your team believed what he told them?"

"No reason not to."

"How about Yanez?"

"So far as I know. You have reason to think otherwise?"

Remembering his breakfast, Wil forked in a bite with apple glaze. "Nothing concrete."

Lin regarded him, grinned. "But we'll be first in line if that changes, won't we. I could tell Rudy that and be safe."

"Frank, when have I ever—"

It was waved off. "Sell the patron-saint-of-lost-causes routine some-place else. I know you, remember?"

Wil leaned forward. "Something's wrong about it, Frank. Don't ask what because I don't know. It's more a feeling."

Lin set down his fork, unpeeled a toothpick and started working it around, letting his eyes play on Wil's movements. "All right," he said. "But doors tend to jam when they're abused."

"Thanks. I owe you one."

"Speaking of causes lost and otherwise, how's Lisa doing?"

"She seemed fine the last time I saw her." Sipping coffee to trim the hedge.

"Which was when?"

"Couple days ago," Wil said. "Why?"

"Andrea and I saw her coming out of a store with her boyfriend—the one who looks like you about twenty years ago?"

"Thanks a lot."

"Didn't look like a lady in love to me. Andrea either. More frayed around the edges, we felt."

Wil said something about her working too hard, stress from the move, her responsibilities...trying to avoid Lin's look, the one that said he knew Lisa almost as well as he knew Wil. At which point the waitress returned to ask if there'd be anything else as Lin nodded to Wil and slid his way out of the booth grinning, final wave and exit.

Sitting there, the words about Lisa replaying as the waitress took the check, he watched Lin start the black-and-white Crown Victoria, cock a finger at him through the window, then gun it back along the frontage road toward his office.

From the Bonneville, Wil called John Pereira to see whether the marine lawyer had been able to secure a copy of the Coast Guard report. But Pereira was in court, so Wil left a message that he'd called and why. Still waiting, the secretary told him; try tomorrow when their source was due back from Las Vegas.

Wil hung up, started the car, drove west.

At UCSB, with the help of a clerk who went so far as to let him know Mia Tien had no classes Monday, he took a seat outside and watched the marine layer break up. The dripping branches and the Campanile were dark with newly released sunlight; fog steamed off the tower, its carillon chiming first ten-of, then the hour, as bicycles and backpacks ebbed and flowed around it.

The air smelled of wet pines and lagoon.

Fall, winter, spring, and summer, Mia'd said.

A tick from leaving to check the Tien house and Island Seafoods, Wil instead tried the student center, then the bookstore, finally the library, where he spied her at a table on the Lit floor. Black jeans, white shirt rolled to the elbows, hemp-weave V-neck. Staring out the window. Snapping out of it when he pulled over a chair to regard him as she might a Kleenex that had found its way into the wash.

"Not this again," she said.

"You want to go somewhere and talk?"

"Sure, that's why I'm up here. Keep it down, will you?"

Wil followed her glance to the faces turned their way. "And I had you figured for the Physics floor."

"Will you be quiet?"

"Is it so Derek won't look here? Just a guess, you understand."

"Maybe I don't want to be found, period."

"Our deal, remember? I said I'd get back to you?"

Her eyes rose from her book. "You're telling me you saw my uncle?"

"I'm here, aren't I?"

The eyes widened. "You got into the compound?"

"Inside the living sand painting? I sure did."

"Bull." But wavering. "How did you manage that?"

"The usual," he said. "Shot my way in."

"Don't act any dumber than you have to."

Still, she looked impressed, Wil thought.

"Could you and your friend please keep silent or go elsewhere?" a female voice said, not in the interrogative—a slight girl with books on a cart she was wheeling. "People are trying to study."

"I begged her to return my Dead Kennedys," Wil said with a pleading look. "Now she wants her Garbage back, the one that's just out and worth at least three Kennedys and a Fish Worship? Is that fair?"

The girl said, "I'm sure I don't know about that, sir. But I will have to ask you both to leave."

"We understand. You're only doing your job."

"I don't believe this," Mia said.

"Come on," Wil asided to her. "Throwing ourselves off the bluff is the only honorable thing left."

21

"SO WHAT *ABOUT MY UNCLE?*" Mia asked after they'd trekked through coyote brush and fennel, warming air spiced with licorice, eucalyptus, and kelp. Sixty feet down the embankment, swells broke toward the beaches that stretched to either side. Except for a quartet of surfers trying to get a handle on the cutback move below, they were alone, the surfers hitting it high and late, Wil observed as they seated themselves on a rock, the sun by now dancing on the water.

He said, "You figured Uncle Luc wouldn't let me in if you told him I was coming?"

Mia looked away.

"Probably got curious to see who his brother had hired and crossed you up. That sound about right?"

"I wouldn't know," she said.

"You didn't think my talking with him would help?"

"It's family business." Still without meeting his eyes. "No one else's but ours."

He got a closer look at what she'd been reading in the library and had brought along. For a moment he watched the surfers, then, "How about I tell you about your uncle if you tell me about the book."

"God, are you always this way?" Gripping it even tighter.

"Which way is that?"

"Just *into* everything."

"Kind of looks that way, doesn't it?"

She sighed, held up *The Tale of Kieu,* the epic poem Vinh had cited to him, the Vietnamese girl trying to cope with hardship and displacement in alien surroundings.

"Trying to better understand my parents, okay?" she said, laying it title-down beside her. Defensive.

"Fine by me," Wil said.

"Now what about my uncle?"

One of the surfers tried a cutback move, hesitated coming out and got rolled, his board spat upward on its leash. Wil thought about the meeting with Luc Tien and focused on impressions.

"Your uncle, let's see," he said. "Not a great forthcomer, not much regard for your old man, not one to get on the wrong side of. Beyond that, a genuine success story. The dream in every shade."

"That's it?" she asked.

"Not quite. He probably won't be going back to Vietnam anytime soon."

Mia shaded her eyes against the glare, her gesture reminiscent of Vinh Tien's on the beach. "You got squat, didn't you?"

"He didn't confess, if that's what you mean."

"Even though you gave him every opportunity, I suppose. The great private eye."

Wil regarded a forming swell, the surfers buzzing and pointing that way. "What can I say? Some days are better than others."

"It wouldn't be you or anything. *Oh, no.*"

He said, "This is the way it works, Mia. Assuming what we suspect is even what happened, there's a reason things are the way they are. You want accountability, I'm for it. But it might help if you included yourself in there."

"What are you talking about?"

"For openers? Your shuck and jive when I asked what Wen did at your uncle's place. You said she worked there after 'something.' What, I'm left to wonder."

Her gaze left him, settled on the surfers. The first wave in the set arrived, two of the four going for it only to stall and get flipped by the second. As the ones who'd waited caught the best wave in the set and rode it around the point, she said, "You know how to do that?"

"What? You're at UCSB and you've never surfed?"

"Right. Like I've had the time."

"Next time I go out, I'll let you know. You'd look good out there."

"You must be kidding." Her look trying to find the answer in his face.

"Give you a break from Derek."

"What is this thing you have with him?"

"I might ask you the same. Do you even own a bathing suit?"

"That's hardly the issue."

"No, I guess it isn't," he said. "But if you want me to get up to speed here, Mia, give me a push."

A beat passed until she said, "I told you, it's nobody's business."

"Your father doesn't feel that way."

"His thing," she said. "Not mine."

"Then have a nice day."

He stood up to go, started walking away, heard, "If I say something, are you going to run and tell him?"

"Depends on what it is," he answered, coming back. "Not unless I have to."

She took a breath, rubbed her forehead, kept her eyes on a lone seagull riding a draft. "All right," she said. "Wen and her mom came ashore unregistered. They had forged papers. Some people got onto her. They were going to throw Wen in jail, use it against my uncle, I don't know. There's still a chance they could deport Wen's mom if she doesn't cooperate."

"Came ashore how? Cooperate with whom?"

"The government, who else? Whoever handles their dirty work." Reaching for some stones she began to lob toward the cliff. "The rest I have no idea about."

"Did your brother?"

"He never said, but I think so. Anytime I brought it up, Jimmy would get all bothered."

Wil went quiet. Suddenly it made sense what had turned Jimmy into Lorenz and Maccafee's informant, giving Luc Tien a possible motive to kill his own nephew if he'd found out.

Assuming Lorenz's appraisal was accurate.

"What are you thinking," she asked him.

"Just trying to connect some dots."

"Back to that." Rubbing her palms on her jeans.

"Mia, did you ever think of sharing things like this with your old man? That he might be more than you give him credit for?"

"You think that's what we do? Share things?"

"Nah," he said, shoving off. Up to here with the back and forth. "What would be the point when you're doing so well by yourself?"

Arms around herself as though chilled, she said, "Bitter, bitchy Mia, the girl with no shadow." Calling after him down the trail. "Hey, just for grins, which part of *this* did you want me to share with him? The part about me not knowing anything or the part about you coming up with nothing."

22

BEFORE WIL LEFT THE UNIVERSITY, he put in a call to Frank Lin at the Sheriff's Department, caught him as he was leaving for lunch, opening with, "I don't believe it. You're even able to *think* about food?"

"Hey, in this business you're either ready or you're not."

"Nobody could ever say you weren't, Frank."

"Taken in the spirit it was intended," Lin said. "What's up?"

Something present in Lin's tone, an underlay. "Just wondering if I could persuade you to check out what Luc Tien said about Wen's employment there. That is, assuming it was asked."

There was a pause, Lin saying then, "Suppose I could, will you be home in a couple of hours?"

"Blackened snapper in it if you'll check before then."

It was meant to be lighthearted, but Lin's reaction was immediate. "Son of a bitch. Play volleyball with a guy, hang with him and his wife, and you're on his pad? I don't think so."

Wil gave it a second, then, "Mea culpa, Frank, my big mouth. But you can't believe I meant it like that."

Deep breath. "No, I suppose not. You ever had to send five kids off to a foster home after Mom's new boyfriend beat her face in? One held on to me so hard I still have the marks on my arm. Gets you in the lychees, if you know what I mean."

"I can only imagine." Wil catching Lin's early lunch in full context: body and workout bags coming up, some rope to loosen the kids' hold on him. "Later on the request," he said.

"Well, hell," Lin came back. "Hang on a second."

Wil could hear the sound of pages being flipped, papers shuffled, then: "Okay—housekeeper, part-time. T's crossed and I's dotted."

"Tax forms?"

"Uncle offered to produce them, unusual with these types. Mostly it's under the table. What keeps them rich, I suppose."

"Anything in her status?"

"As in illegal?"

"As in anything." Knowing it sounded transparent, but having to ask; waiting out the pause that followed.

Lin said, "Why am I getting this nagging feeling relative to full and enthusiastic reciprocity?"

"Thinking out loud is all," Wil answered. "Grasping at straws."

Another pause, Lin obviously processing it. "Like I said before, some things actually *are* what they seem. Wouldn't be the first boat that bought it out there."

"*If* that's what happened."

"Run that by me again?..."

"Nothing, Frank, mumbling to myself. Have a better afternoon, will you, and thanks."

Wil thinking as he hung up that Maccafee and Lorenz hadn't let the locals into the loop after all. Assuming Mia had it right about Wen's status. *Interesting...*

Luc Tien replaced the white odontoglossum he'd just repotted between the red and the deep purple cattleyas, thinking great flag colors here— why didn't somebody just step up at the U.N., rename some of those worthless countries continually changing for the worse, half the populace turned to bone meal by the other.

The Orchid Republic—now there was an idea.

Grabbing another pot and a handful of osmunda, he tamped in the hapuu-loam-ground-bark mix plus a pinch of his secret ingredient. Setting the lady's slipper in on top—yellow with a maroon pouch, according to the catalog—he tamped in more mix, was starting on another when Sonny opened the greenhouse door and let himself in.

"Can't it wait?" Luc said to him. "You know why I come out here."

"I do, *Anh hai*. But we thought it best."

"We..."

"Dao Hong and myself. He's here."

Luc glanced beyond him and caught a dark shape smoking with its back to the frosted glass. Dao Hong, one of the Bay Area *dai lows* and a comer: ambitious, ruthless, loyal. And, unlike many of them, efficient.

Most recent and obvious example: three old-line tong inheritors, two bodyguards, and a cop. Bloody Sunday, the San Francisco papers were calling it. Give him a hundred like Dao and he'd have whole countries sending peace emissaries.

Luc checked his watch. "What about our friends outside the gate?"

"No sign," Sonny answered. "Hong came in with the groceries."

"And now?"

"He wants to pay his respects. Let you know the loose ends have been attended to."

"The shooters, Sonny. I'll generate the drama around here."

"Yes, *Anh hai*."

Luc sighed, removed his gloves. "Show him in," he said. "Have what's-her-name, the new girl, bring tea."

Sonny backed away and left the greenhouse, returning with a painfully thin man in his late twenties: ink-black pompadour, pocked skin, sunken cheeks, wispy Fu Manchu mustache. Black silk tee over black drape pants, sunglasses dangling from hands clasped in front of him, the cigarette respectfully gone.

Killer's heat behind his drooped lids.

"Look at me," Luc said to him in Vietnamese.

The eyes raised, blinked, slid off, came back.

"Man to man because you did a man's work," Luc went on. "You know that, don't you?"

"For you, *Anh hai*."

Luc bowed, playing to him in a way no acting coach would indulge.

"Dao Hong, your legacy is already being written. Hundreds will become dragons because of yesterday."

As he'd expected, Dao Hong could say nothing.

"Today our people know the dragon has teeth. Today they walk in the valley of their enemies. Sit with me, I wish to hear more." Gesturing at one of the chairs he kept in the greenhouse for such occasions, taking the other himself. Saying nothing for a bit, so the young man would get a sense of who he was with and where. Almost hearing Dao recount the honor to rapt lieutenants back home.

There was a tap at the door and a girl about seventeen entered: long hair worn up and wisping, low halter over painted-on shorts. She smiled at Dao, set down the tea and poured it, smiled again and bowed to him, then the others, and eased out. Thinking Dao might explode on the spot, Luc said, "You like that one? She's yours for as long as you're here. Sonny?..."

"It is done, *Anh hai*."

"Good. And now to business." Folding his hands under his chin and looking Dao Hong straight in the eyes, comrades in arms, he said, "Sonny tells me you have information regarding disposition of the Thai gunmen you so wisely hired."

Dao found his voice. "The Delta Mendota, *Anh hai*."

The canal that brought water to Southern California; water with a Thai flavor, it would seem. "Go on," Luc said, pleased.

"Heavy chain, split body cavities, no chance anyone saw it. The catfish eat well this day."

Luc raised a finger to his lips. "Be careful, my fine young dragon, you'll make my orchids jealous."

Sonny's face broke a smile.

Nothing from Dao Hong.

"A joke," Luc told him. "Something you will understand in time."

Dao made an attempt, but his smile was more that of a deaf-mute thrust on stage and told to light up the place.

Luc sighed. "Never mind. Have you everything you need for the moment?"

"Yes, *Anh hai*. Thanks to you."

"Then be welcome here. Sonny will give you spending money for later.

BURNING MOON

You'll be leaving us when?"

Their guest looked at Sonny, who said, "We thought tomorrow, *Anh hai.*"

Luc thought a moment. "I disagree: a few days to let our people do their work. And I'm certain our esteemed *dai low* will find things to do here." Giving the kid a knowing wink, which was wasted because he wasn't even looking.

After Sonny led Dao Hong out bowing, Luc returned to his bench, the work almost secondary as he conjured ways to use the young man's talents. Regional, at least; the kid was a slasher. Which brought to mind his own brush with the *tay son vo si,* the martial arts mandated by his Chinese tutors after he'd left village life for Saigon. The sand and blood in his mouth as the gongs signaled the mostly predictable ends to his matches— that is, until he'd learned to exploit weaknesses and bend rules, lay on his own pain, which at least got him tossed victorious.

Forever ago.

Reliving the fat faces pressing in on him, their muted squeals as the city pulsed outside, Luc had stopped work altogether, was gripping a bamboo stake so hard he'd snapped it, when Sonny poked his head back in.

"Sorry to bother you again, *Anh hai.*"

Luc covered by pretending he'd taken a piece in the thumb. "What is it now?" Shaking the thumb as if it pained him.

"The phone," Sonny said. "Your niece."

"What does she want?"

Sonny looked chastised, as if he had asked for money and been rebuffed.

"She said you'd know, *Anh hai.*"

23

NOTHING: the hollow resonance of a slug slipped into a vending machine. *Nada*: what Wil had come up with by dropping in on the harbormaster after Mia Tien. Chatting with the Coasties aboard the eighty-two snugged to the pier, his old Point-class amazingly still in service. Reminding him of gray paint and Mekong heat, spent casings and red-streaked decks.

Nowhere: exactly where he stood with Jimmy Tien, Mia's final salvo the truth, Wil comprehending that all too well.

It felt no better to lay it off on Vinh Tien.

"But you're going to stay with it?" Vinh had said, following a pause in which fish-market sounds came through the earpiece.

"I told you I would, and I will," he came back. "I just wanted you to be part of the decision."

"You're concerned about the money."

"*Your* money—you knowing how it's being spent."

Vinh Tien paused, as if he were working up to it. "Do you know what it's like just to function, Mr. Hardesty? Getting up in the morning, bantering with customers, ringing up purchases? Losing track because I'm wondering, always wondering." Muted voices, echo-y hum. "This is my life now."

Which made Wil feel even shittier.

After hanging up, he ran water over his face, changed clothes for the trail; while he and Matt snacked, he re-read the postcard Kari Thayer had sent from Ephram, Wisconsin, a picture of a sailboat on Green Bay:

Wil—

Great weather, pretty islands and coves, Brian's lapping it up. He's in LOVE with the girl next door. They go sailing all day while I swat mosquitoes with the paperbacks you gave me. Do I know how to vacation or what?

Kari.

He got out the field glasses and a sweatshirt, put them in his backpack with a bottle of water, a flashlight, Power Bars and Milk-Bones, his notebook and the small-frame Colt, then locked up. Five o'clock when he and Matt backed out and headed for the foothills.

The trail was one he knew from college days, when he and Lisa trekked the ridges up behind Mountain Drive. To thermal pools where they'd skinny-dip and drink Zin, enjoy a little pot when it wasn't fire season. Halcyon days. Not that time and dwindling county budgets had improved the trail. Little more than a deer path then, it had been widened into firebreak duty, then let go. Green light to the chaparral.

Its main advantage, Wil reaffirmed when they'd set out, was that few saw it as an easy walk, weaving and twisting as it did through toyon and ceanothus, red willow interwoven with poison oak and elderberry. Plus it offered a spot where he could overlook Luc's property and Mountain Drive below.

As he settled them under scrub oak, a throw of dead leaves beneath, Matt seemed puzzled, whining as if to say, *What?*... After a bit, he trooped off to case the surroundings, reappearing then to see if Wil had regained his senses. Six-twenty now, an hour till dark. Pulling out the field glasses, Wil scanned for blue-gray, the locale good for a mile in either direction before he lost the road.

Nothing—a *positive* nothing, for once—Lorenz and Maccafee's surveillance either sporadic, shut down for the day, or called off, that the least likely scenario. He took a breath, filled up on still-warm oak, hay-dry ground cover, damp shadows deepening in the crevices and higher canyons. In his notebook, he made columns for various data and observances: time, who-what, comments. Through the glasses he could see Luc's lit-perimeter walkers; corner of the pool and waterfall, empty now of loungers; Robb tooling around in the golf cart. But after an hour, he'd seen nothing of substance and little traffic on Mountain Drive.

Typical stakeout, he thought—forget anything happening when you first arrived. Only when your attention wandered, your guard slipped or it welcomed distraction, that's when things happened.

Bringing down the glasses but maintaining visual contact, he got out the sweatshirt and put it on, gave Matt a Milk-Bone. Which made *him* hungry. Headlights were appearing now, but none even slowed by Sand-Painting House. A Power Bar later, at seven-fifteen, casually dressed figures appeared on the upper patio, workers in white. Smoke rose in the barbecue pit in the lower area, the garden Luc was tending the day Wil was there.

Less than a week and already feeling like two.

By eight-thirty, the natural light was gone. He was about to pack it in when headlights rounded the east-bound approach: a squat coupe, that hatchback look they'd all assumed. Fifty yards from the gate, it pulled over and stopped, as though trying to decide. Seconds passed, the driver's foot still riding the brakes, twin red blooms. Then the coupe went for it, the occupant getting out to say something into the two-way, enter a code on the keypad, wait while the gate was swung wide.

Wil saw Mia Tien get back into her Honda, drive to where Robb stood at the ported guard station, saw her get out and enter the house without so much as a look at him. He watched Robb get into the Civic, swing it into the multi-bay garage, the taillights lost from view as the door rolled down in sections.

By then it was so dark Wil couldn't see his notebook without the flash.

24

IRST LIGHT after hacking his way through impenetrable undergrowth, the dream close to matching his and Matt's return trip, Wil let his thoughts coalesce around an early beach run and a lapsang brewed almost black. First up: What to do about Mia's visit to Uncle Luc, somewhat out of character unless he'd missed something. In for a sheep, in for a lamb, he'd decided to stick around and see if anything came of it. But by midnight, the Civic was still in Luc's garage, and apart from a brief appearance on the patio followed by a figure that had to be Luc detaching itself and going inside with her, that tied it for one evening.

Wil's guessing-game thoughts on the drop-in ranged from innocent to any number of sinister things. Ergo, Plan A: Talk to the kid before letting her father into the loop, enough pain there without adding to it. Or was that jumping the gun on *her*?

Which led to Plan B: Lorenz and Maccafee—about the only other means of penetrating the nothing-nowhere fog—find a way to use them as they'd intended to use him. That avenue of approach: ferret out what they had in mind, sniff around the bear trap, hijack the bait.

Only not just yet.

Of course, there was always Plan C: Bang on the gates until Luc *had* to do something about him, and in the doing, inadvertently reveal a piece of the puzzle. Not this guy, Wil agreed with himself, more like tipping everybody off as to how empty Wil's hand was of trump. Plan C rejected until he'd exhausted everything else.

Wil was watching a school of dolphins roll their way toward the Rincon when John Pereira called regarding the *Harmony* findings. They'd gotten them in, he was welcome to peruse the report, but on initial blush nothing presented itself as either unusual, untrod by the investigators, or unseemly.

"Just the view from here, you understand," he said.

"Thanks, John. I'll swing by later and pick it up."

"You making any progress?"

"Don't ask, don't tell."

"It's possible I missed something between the lines."

"Lawyers write the lines."

"Great mood you're in," Pereira said before hanging up.

As he cradled the phone, Matt was looking at him.

Wagging his tail and pawing the air.

"That mean you liked last night?" Wil said to him. "Huh?"

Matt came closer; Wil knelt to remove a burr he'd missed earlier, got a lick for it. He'd changed clothes and was about out the door when he looked back and caught Matt's expression, his still-lifted paw.

"Okay, Orphan Annie," Wil said to him, for which he got an immediate rush to the door. "But save the look, okay? We might need it."

By Fernald Point the day began to look promising, the ocean more green than slate. Traffic was even light. At UCSB, Wil snapped on Matt's leash, but it was unnecessary, Matt heeling despite the kinesis of hurriers and cyclists, Wil mentally thanking Leora for the training she'd given him. They were early for the materials lab, so he checked classrooms through their door slots, spotting Mia not at all and no empty chairs. Finally spotting familiar hair in Advanced Quantum Theory.

He and Matt parked themselves until the class ended and Mia's lab partner exited. Immediately her eyes went to the bandanna Wil had draped around Matt's neck. Up to Wil, then.

"Australian shepherd, isn't he?"

Such a good idea bringing Matt.

"He is," Wil said, nodding. "You know the breed?"

"A little," she said. "What's his name?"

Wil told her, pausing so she could pet Matt, smooth his ears as he pinned her with a look that said, *You and me for all time, kid.*

"You're Mia's friend," he said as if suddenly placing her.

"I might be." Her guard coming up. "Why?"

"Wil Hardesty—outside the lab?" Extending her his card. "I really need to talk to her. Did I get the wrong class?"

She looked at him before answering, at his card again, then, "She's not in this one."

"Boy," Wil said, "I must have the days crossed. Now what, Matt?" Getting just the right look back, Milk-Bone coming up.

"You're the guy working for her folks?"

"Not to the point I tell them everything." *Mr. Intrigue.*

"Why the interest?" she asked, rising to it. "Are you worried about her?"

"For heaven's sake, don't tell her that. You know how she is."

The girl checked her watch, said, "Look, I'm Jordan. I have to run, but I guess it's okay to tell you I'm worried, too. She just isn't herself lately. Like majorly distracted."

"Derek?"

"*Oh, God, no.* He's just to jerk her folks around. Such a dork."

"If not him, then, any idea?"

She brushed back red hair from a march of freckles. "Promise you won't tell her I told you?"

"If that's what you want."

She hesitated, then, "It's unlike her to skip, let alone ask me to cover for her. And she's never, I mean never, missed a lab, and that's two in a row. Her folks are so strict. That's why I asked you not to say anything."

"This afternoon's lab—she called you about it?"

Nod. "Late yesterday. She said she didn't know when she was coming back, that she had something to do and she'd pay me for covering. Bullcrap, I told her, friends don't do that. We're not kids anymore. You either want to be here or make room for somebody who does." Flush reflecting the thought and muting her freckles. "Sorry, but that's just the way it is."

Blowing Matt a kiss, she headed off down the hall.

❧

Wil picked up the findings report from John Pereira's receptionist, who was about out the door, then continued on the Mia thing at home, Jordan's comments making him increasingly uneasy.

It's unlike her to miss classes...

Her folks are so strict...

Late yesterday...

Which would have been after Mia talked to him, the nothing conversation. Way to go, Hardesty, he thought, drive the wedge right in there.

Family business, she'd said...*butt out.*

Still seeing her red Civic hesitate before entering Luc's gate, he remembered an unfinished piece of business he *could* do something about. "Wil?" Lisa said when his call found her. "I'm in the middle of something. Later okay?"

"Just wanted to know if you were all right," he said.

Pause. "All right referring to what?"

He let go a breath. "Frank said he and Andrea saw you downtown. He said you looked a little frayed—his word. Put together with the way you were the other day and—"

"You came up with what?" Strangely lacking the usual fire when he'd crossed a line with her, real or imagined. Distracted...if he hadn't seen her handle eight things at once and give each its due...

"No more than you would for me," he said.

"Well, I'm fine."

"That's good to know."

"Is it?"

"And where is *that* coming from?"

"Nowhere, Wil," she said, tired-sounding. "Thanks for taking the time." There was another pause, then, "Wil, I mean that."

25

L UC TIEN SNAPPED OFF THE LOW-PROFILE HDTV, the satellite dish bringing in, among its zillion options, the stations out of San Francisco. He stuck his head out, spotted Robb lounging in front of a baseball game. "Sonny around?" he asked him.

"Checking the market, *Anh hai.*"

"Sonny trades stocks?"

"E-trade," Robb responded. "He's been showing me in his spare time."

Luc shook his head at the thought. "Well, you're both braver than I am. Get him and come in here."

"Right away, *Anh hai.*"

As Robb went for Sonny, Luc put together finishing thoughts. He was looking into the enclosed terrarium that formed one wall when they appeared in his office, seating themselves as he continued to stare at the jungle, its miniature temples, ruins, and ponds.

"Change of plans," he said, turning toward them. "Guess whose pock-marked face I saw on television with a phone number under it?"

"*Fuck,*" Sonny exclaimed. "Already?"

Luc nodded. "It was to be expected, just not this soon." He thought a moment. "Where is our dragon?"

"Getting a massage," Sonny answered, mouthing a silent *Dao Hong* to Robb's expression. "He was looking pretty spent."

"Knowing what's-her-name, that's not surprising."

Robb said, "I wouldn't mind having some of that my—"

"Did I ask for your opinion?" Luc snapped.

"Sorry, *Anh hai*. Not thinking."

Luc let a look suffice for displeasure. "All right, listen up. This is what I've decided." Enjoying them leaning forward into his words, the power and respect that went along. Small in light of the risks that were his, but small things made an endeavor worthy. Even the most minor role carried its own weight, heart, pearlescence, let alone the part of the underdog. An underdog with fangs.

"Dao Hong's coup with the Po Sang is being handled by a San Francisco police detective named Terrence Leong," Luc went on. Checking the pad on which he'd written it, he spelled it for them, watching them do the same on pads they'd brought. "What I want you to do is contact our lawyers up there, tell them to be ready. Is that understood?"

Sonny nodded, then Robb. "Yes, *Anh hai*."

"I want them to surrender Dao to this Leong detective tonight. I'll brief him on what to say, where he's been, the people we have to vouch for him. To the police and the legal system, Dao Hong will act concerned and cooperative, but vehement regarding his noninvolvement. As far as Dao is concerned, Rising Dragon is myth—a straw man created by the Po Sang to shift attention from its own power struggle."

Nods again, this time in unison.

"His will be the stance I conveyed to our lawyers—Vietnamese are the innocent scapegoats of Chinese-American racism, of lingering resentment from the war. If Dao Hong is not released immediately, civil rights charges will be filed with the United States Attorney."

Neither man spoke. Luc went on.

"San Francisco already is preparing leaflets, Little Saigon also." As an afterthought adding, "Why do you two think I open my home to the politicians, give them money? Smiles when I would as soon cut their throats?"

Continued silence.

Luc tapped the terrarium, where a tree frog was being stalked by a snake, the snake jerking back at the sound. "Because to succeed on this scale, we need what? Benefactors—those who comprehend goodwill relative to economic markets and voter blocs." Trying to keep it simple, a point of pride with him, each point a pearl.

"Money and power, yin and yang. Have I made myself clear?"

"Clear, *Anh hai*," Robb said.

"And what face will we show the Po Sang?" Sonny.

Luc smiled; buttoning the pockets of his silk shirt, he smoothed the material. "Not mine, if that is what you mean, not yet. Dao Hong will afford them our usual opportunity to sue for peace, the percentages I have laid out through our contacts. And they will agree. Why? Because they have much to lose and we have little." Pausing for effect. "And because the Po Sang know the next incident will make this last look like something out of *Mulan*."

Respectful silence, exchanged glances, Luc only then getting it.

"You did see the film, the animated story of...no, I suppose not." His two lieutenants looking at each other as if they'd inadvertently touched knees.

"Never mind," Luc said with a sigh, a glance back at the snake, green legs disappearing. "Just bring the man to me on your way out."

26

THE MAN WAS DREAMING OF FIRE.

Oily orange-black clouds, a storm rolling with apocalyptic speed toward where he stood rooted, feet seized by the jungle and his own horror at what he'd unleashed. Hell itself: billowing now—dwarfing the doomed silhouettes in its path, men not nearly fast enough to outpace it, their attempts consumed in mid-stride. Dead men running.

Almost on him now.

Searing his eyes and skin, its roar like—

Drenched, he jerked awake, pegging the sound finally as static on the hotel's radio alarm. He snapped it off, sat on the edge of the bed, head bent almost to his knees, talking himself down with *just a dream, just a dream, just a dream.* The same one on and off for twenty years, the break-out as fresh as if he'd started the fire last night. Never imagining his captors had stashed napalm beneath their prison quarters in case they were discovered. Reduce all trace to ash should the need arise.

Even as it played out, the man knew it was a dream. Still, he was helpless to shift from the overdrive threatening to jam his heart like an engine drained of oil. Once going so far as to connect himself to a heart monitor, one with a memory: finally catching one of the nightmares in progress, the doctor's eyes going wide when he saw the printout later. *The fuck was that?...*

But pills didn't help; they merely slowed his reflexes to a near-defenseless state while creating a need for more pills and a fear of sleep. Only repro-gramming, hypnosis, one of the shrinks he saw for it told him. A snow-ball's chance in hell.

For a long time the man stood in the shower, let it take his thoughts to waterfalls, streams, islands, rain forests. Blues and greens. Finally he toweled dry, shaved, walked over and parted the curtains to the night: San Francisco in full blaze, Bay Bridge its conduit of fire. Soundless puls-ing light rising to a sheared skyline.

Cracking open the courtesy bar, he sipped single malt until things sorted themselves, until he could close his eyes and taste ginger and frangipani, rain and passion fruit. He called room service, ordered up whatever the special was, then dialed again.

"Yes?" a voice answered.

"I'm here," he said. "You have something for me?"

"We were expecting this call sooner. Where were you?"

"Setting up. More recently sleeping, or attempting to."

"Ah yes," the voice allowed. "There is that, isn't there?"

"You plan to talk all night, or what?"

"Why? You won't sleep again, I know you," the voice said. "Our man appeared at the Hall of Justice an hour ago. He was taken into custody by a detective named Leong, L-e-o-n-g. Four lawyers were with him. Their names are—"

"Is this important?"

"The lead is, a criminal defense attorney named Sanger, S-a-n-g-e-r. Evetta Sanger. A black of some talent."

He made note as the voice went on.

"The Sanger woman drives a Range Rover, white with tinted windows, vanity plate #1GUN. We have arranged to have one exactly like it at your disposal."

"When?"

"Soon after four this morning a parking stub will be slipped under your door. Present it at the hotel's parking garage. Are you familiar with the Hall of Justice?"

"No," he said.

"A map of its location will be included, with the route you are to take. We anticipate no more than a twelve-hour hold in light of the political pressure."

When I see it happen. "You know for a fact this Dao Hong is your man."

"One of our sources puts him with the gunmen," the voice said. "We expect his release to be the occasion for a press conference. While Evetta Sanger and her legal team are berating the police for their rush to judgment, Dao Hong will be hustled out the employee's entrance on a side street."

The man checked his watch: just past midnight.

"And you know this how?"

"Sanger's driver. He is scheduled to pick up Hong and take him to a prearranged spot. Only you will be behind the wheel."

"Where will the driver be?" the man inquired.

"Far away. Spending his money."

"I swear you must be psychic."

The voice cleared its throat. "The rest of your payment will be in your account at the first news report, followed by a call to confirm your clearance." There was the sound of something swallowed. "Now, if there is nothing else..."

"What time is the press conference?"

"We don't have that information yet. If it is not included in the drop, stay by the phone. As soon as we know, you will know. As for the rest of the evening, there's a TV film festival running *Bullitt* in twenty minutes. I thought you might appreciate the—"

"Thanks," the man interrupted. "I've seen it."

"As you wish."

The line went dead as dinner arrived, and he ate slowly with the news on. Which became mug shots showing a pocked and sullen face with dead-looking eyes, the man's curiosity about this Dao Hong becoming speculation on an earlier comment the voice had made about him. Specifically, how much of this dragon was teeth and how much was brain.

27

PAST TWO A.M., NO MOON TO SPEAK OF, Matt took off after a possum or raccoon or something, finally wandering back and flopping down in the leaves with a long sigh. Translation: *Is this is the best you can do with your life?*

Wil put down his field glasses, kneaded his eyes, stretched. Leashing Matt to prevent a rematch with whatever-it-was, he raised the glasses and ran them over the compound. Guards moved among the cactus shapes, Wil guessing rheostat or some kind of timer to diminish the lighting the later it got. Robb was in the guard shack; Wil could see the glow of a TV or computer screen. Other than that, the scene was as arresting as a chiaroscuro on velvet.

Mia had appeared the same time as last night; her Civic was still in the garage. Except for a figure Wil thought might be her, wisps of cigarette smoke and a pinpoint of red, he'd seen no trace — no sign of Luc, either. Earlier in the day, there'd been a grocery van, a pool-maintenance truck, cleaning service a half-hour later. In between the last two, Sonny left in one of the Yukons, back with grocery bags an hour later, two-plus more until Mia pulled in.

No sign of Lorenz or Maccafee.

More than welcome considering Mia's involvement.

Whatever it amounted to.

Stretching periodically and drifting, second- and third-guess speculations about what she was doing down there, he kept watch. Matt stirred and Wil let his hand drift there, already wondering what he'd done for companionship BD: Before Dog. The only thing Matt wasn't long on was talking back. The listening and the understanding parts he had down pat.

Nice life, Hardesty. Maybe get out more?

Thinking about that, he missed Kari, and, in a less definable way, Lisa, their history having pared itself down to select moments, one in particular due to the context. They'd hit the backcountry for some thermal-pool time, Devin only four but game. Coming up on one, they'd encountered a naked couple deep in the throes, obviously enjoying themselves. He'd tried fielding Dev's singsong questions as they wide-berthed the pair, but Lisa had to step in and save him: answering but not really, tiptoeing across a glacier. And later, *au naturel* at a farther-in hot spring, Dev's suddenly aware looks, he and Lisa taking refuge later in Chuck E. Cheese's noisy but welcome distractions.

Distractions...

Wil realized he'd lowered the glasses, raised them in time to catch Mia striding toward the garage, the door rising, the Civic driving out, no lights until well past the main gate, almost to a curve and then through it. He checked his watch—almost four—and calculated the duration as close to a shift, whatever meaning that held. The point was that he was a good thirty minutes from the Bonneville even if he and Matt ran it.

Noting the time in his log, he broke out a treat for Matt, sandwich and a hit of thermos coffee for himself, then settled back in to finish his own shift.

@

Four a.m., a muted *Bullitt* long since replaced by *The Getaway*, the man heard a sound and saw a manila envelope slid under the door. By that time, he had a grip on his HK Special Ops .45, safety off and the hammer back.

Resisting the urge to scan through the fisheye, yank open the door, he brought the envelope to the writing table and opened it. Inside were Dao Hong's mug shot, two maps—a small-scale of the Hall of Justice and a large-scale of San Francisco—route instructions and destination. Paper-clipped to these was a parking claim ticket and a smaller envelope containing business cards plus a chauffeur's license with space for a photo above the name Carson Lowell Sage. Included also was a letter on Evetta Sanger's stationary authorizing Carson Lowell Sage to pick up her client Dao Hong and others in his service on the specific date.

The only thing missing was the time.

The next hour he spent laminating a blurry photo of himself in glasses into the license and analyzing the maps for alternatives, backups to get where he needed on his own terms. At five, he claimed the Range Rover from a *Penthouse*-reading attendant and drove to the Hall, a tired-looking L-shaped seven-story looking up at the freeway. Circling until he had its lay, the main entrance on Bryant, the Harriet Street side where he'd be waiting, the man pulled into a yellow zone to let his senses take over. Closing his eyes, he imagined it—angles, video cameras, possible pedestrian traffic—everything going perfectly. Then everything faulty-wrong: construction impediments, stalls, media crush, demonstrators, police roust. Thinking as a quarterback might, changing the call at the line of scrimmage once he'd seen the defense. Sizing up the courtroom before the trial so as to achieve total focus on the matter at hand.

Control and calm.

Calm and control.

Thirty minutes later he reached into the satchel he'd brought and pulled out four stacked traffic cones, setting them in place opposite the employee door. By the time he'd scanned in an oldies station, scrunched into the leather seats that smelled so good, he felt ready. So much so that he was back at the hotel, stretched out and actually nodding off, when the phone rang at seven.

"Everything is in order?"

"With the envelope? Yes," he said.

"Excellent."

"Where'd you find the Rover?"

"Airport," the voice answered. "Long-term parking, where you are to return it. Our people will find it and switch plates."

"And the press conference?"

"Eleven a.m. Hong and perhaps two others. Repeat to confirm."

He did, controlled and calm enough to have envisioned it. Which didn't prevent him from allowing a moment to pass, as if there might be a sticking point.

"Our arrangement was for Hong only," he said. "You are prepared for more?"

No pause. "Already you're being paid twice what we anticipated. But yes, I have adjusted your deposit."

"Good man."

There was a chuckle; then, out of left field, "Is that what I am? So little is what it seems." Leaving him to wonder which of the two, *good* or *man*, the voice was talking about.

28

WIL FINALLY GOT OFF THE HILL AT TEN, figuring tradeoff: Mia—
assuming he could find her since she hadn't reappeared at
Luc's—versus some heatup in the activities below. So far there'd
been little evidence of the latter; Robb emerging for the morning papers was
about it. Two guys blowing down the pool area and the driveways.

The trouble was, you never knew.

On the other hand, breaking from it was a chance for him to clean up,
to sleep before figuring out his next move. Prominent among the alternatives: more of same. Matt was only too glad to hop in the front seat, curl
up by the surfboard slot Wil had cut in when he'd bought the car. Which
left him his thoughts on Mia, assuming she was playing the game he had
deduced for her: leave family after dinner, go to Luc's, return before Vinh
and Li got up to find daughter still in bed.

Resting up for the rigors of academic life.

Considering he'd pulled the same stunt about a hundred years ago, it
was a thought, anyway. And sure enough, as he made the turn onto her
street, there was the Civic on the right side of the drive.

No Island Seafoods pickup on the left.

Wil parked, stood on the stoop with Matt and rang the bell.

"Mia Tien, come on down."

Getting Matt into the act with a couple of coaxed barks.

Ornamental garlic wafted pungent; butterflies worked the lantana. A flock of starlings morphed from a ragged circle into a dumbbell before reforming and darting off over the treetops.

Finally, from inside: "I'm sleeping. Go away."

"Not when we're awake," Wil called.

"Go away."

"How do I know it's really you?"

"What do you *want?*"

"You really want to discuss your evenings this way?"

Hesitation, Wil saying into it, "Neighbors looking. Still here."

The door was pulled open a chain's width to mussed black hair, bleary eyes, one hand clutching a mauve robe.

"Look, I'm really tired," she said.

"I don't doubt it."

She just looked at him.

He said, "Hey, you've had more sleep than I have, so either we do this here or down at the store. With or without you."

She slid back the chain, opened the door, stepped back to let them in, Wil looking around at the living room, immaculate as before. "You won't be sorry," he told her.

"God, you're annoying."

"You haven't seen annoying yet."

"If you say so. Now what do you *want?*"

"Answers. You and Uncle Luc from eight to four in the morning. The deal in twenty words or less."

Something in her eyes flared and died. "Go to hell," she said and turned away.

Wil eased onto the couch, thinking she was indeed a piece of work: Holly Pfeiffer territory, a girl he knew from another case, hardened shell over an unset center. He said, "I figured you might say that, so I've come up with a theory. You want to hear it?"

"Would that matter?"

"No," he said. "Think your dad would?"

"I'm not a minor. My father has no leverage over me."

"Not surprising, the way you feel about him."

"What makes you think you know how I feel about anything?"

Wil rubbed tired eyes, then his whole face. "Here's my theory. You take

Uncle Luc up on some offer he made to come work for him, dig into Jimmy on the side, end-run the lamebrain daddy was dumb enough to hire. Ballpark?"

She let herself lean into the Lazy-Boy, tilted her head at the ceiling. "All right, he pays me to do things. Hostess and computer work. It's a way to make money. Be independent for a change."

"Like your brother was..."

Whatever she was about to fire back faded.

He added, "Probably kick in on home expenses, too, with daddy's blessing. And if you see anybody else buying it, let me know because even Matt can see through that."

By then she was up and facing the glass, the bamboo trembling with light. Just wanting her to see it if nothing else, anything to make a dent, he said, "Come on, Mia. How do you think your uncle acquired all that?"

"My uncle invested wisely. Not like my father."

"So have other people. Yet Luc has armed security twenty-four-seven and walls two feet thick."

"So what? That's his business."

"Just like something in *you* says he had something to do with what happened to Jimmy or you wouldn't be there."

She stood looking out: porcelain hard, hands deep in her pockets. "You're wrong," she said, "all wrong. And you're going to ruin everything."

"Look me in the eyes and say it."

"My uncle is helping pay for my education."

"Nice try."

"Fuck you," she said, turning. "If you're going to tell my father, go ahead. I don't care."

Lord. "Given their relationship, you think your education is all Luc has in mind? He's not manipulating a situation to stick it to somebody? You're not a pawn in that?"

"You are sick. I don't—"

"Mia, either Luc isn't what you think he is, or he is. Either way is no-win. And if he's what some other people think he is..." Pausing to let that sink in.

"What other people?"

"People whose business it is to know, take my word," Wil said. "You'll at least think about it?"

Her nod was barely perceptible.

"Look," he said with a breath, "I understand that you're trying to help, but—"

"You understand jack." Looking away from him. "Just leave, will you? *Please?*"

As he closed the door behind him, all of it echoing, a crazed darkened sound chamber, Wil flashed on what he'd seen on the freeway on the way over. Grazed by a truck, a hawk had fallen between lanes and lay flapping as the cars came at it. Instant decision time: Swerve to give it a merciful death? Let nature take its course? Risk his life to save it? Checking for an exit sign about the time he saw an explosion of feathers in the rearview.

The way he felt then was the way he felt now: *Give me a clue.*

29

WEDNESDAY MORNING, after a trip to Ventura for plugs, oil, and air filters for the Bonneville, Wil was washing it in the drive when the phone rang on the seat where he'd set it.

"Hardesty," he answered.

"You feeling any more like that beer?"

For a moment, nothing, no match to the voice; then it dawned. "Amber?"

"For a second there it sounded like you didn't remember me."

"How could I not?" he said, shutting off the hose and wiping his hands on the drying towel. "What's up?"

"You told me to call—like, if something turned up. But if you don't care..."

"Wait a second. You found something?"

"I'm calling aren't I? Now, are you coming or what?"

She hung up.

Why not? Wil thought. *Stranger things.*

He finished the car, then drove to Isla Vista. *Sabado Tarde*, the street where Jimmy and Wen had lived, looked still asleep; in front of the triplex, only the white Jetta was on the lawn, so he pulled in behind it and parked.

A blonde head lifted on the balcony.

"It's open," Amber called down. "Come on up."

Wil entered to worn carpeting, gypsum needing paint, a stairwell lit by strips of dimpled yellow glass. Upstairs was a living room/ divider/counter arrangement, couch and worn leatherette chairs, expensive-looking stereo components up on pine shelving, a dying fern. Down the hall, he caught hollow-core doors, one revealing a sink embedded in Formica.

"I thought you'd never get here," Amber said, sliding open the glass door to the balcony.

"No roommates?" Pretending to look around instead of at her swim suit, the little it held back.

"France, Spain, and Thailand respectively." Shrug and a resigned sigh; the blonde hair and those eyes. "Thanks to their dads, that is. Mine split—no idea where he is."

"Working on your tan, I see."

"You really think so?" Thumbing down her elastic waistband to expose the line. "Not much else going this summer."

Wil took a barstool, faced her. "You said you found something?"

She worked a loose smile. "I've been keeping that beer cold. Why don't you pop one while I lose the Dark Tropic."

"Pass, thanks."

"You might as well," she said. "I have to shower anyway."

And like that she'd unfastened her top and was twirling-untwirling it in her hand. Her breasts stood alert, her stomach was smooth and tan and flat around the silver navel stud, which seemed to be winking at him. The smile was now equal parts come-on.

"Unless you need one, too," she added.

Wil took in a breath, blew it out. "Amber, you have a body a blind man could spot at midnight. But that's not why I came here."

"Already?" she said coyly.

He chalked one up for her. "I'll be outside if you genuinely have something. Meantime, thanks for the show."

"Such a stick-in-the-mud, our private eye. I had no idea."

"I'm sure."

"You really don't want me?" Bordering on amazement.

Wil looked at his watch, pointed to the kitchen clock behind her. "Fifteen minutes. If you're not outside with whatever, it's been unreal."

Fourteen minutes after he'd leaned against the Bonneville, Matt curled up inside, she came out in cargo shorts, white Jennifer top, wet hair finger-combed back. Even more stunning, if that were possible.

"What are you, homo?" she said.

"Don't worry, it's nothing personal." Then he saw what she had and was handing him: what looked to be a compact disk case, no liner notes or markings. Just the disk in its holder.

Wil turned it in his hands. "A CD?"

"Moron Kenny tried to play it—he found it stuffed in the couch after we'd moved in. Five in and hit Shuffle Play, that's Kenny. I put it in my computer, but I couldn't read what came up."

A data disk, purchased blank to lay down information.

"Words or numbers?" he asked, beginning to feel a race beyond Amber.

"Words, a ton of accent marks." Reaching in to pet Matt, who licked her hand. "For a while I forgot about it. Then I found your card."

"Thanks, Amber, I owe you one."

"Told you so. Probably not when Kenny's back though. He's kind of unstable sometimes."

"I wonder why," Wil said, feeling a sudden pang of sympathy for Kenny as he started the Bonneville.

As with yesterday, Mia's Civic was alone in the drive. This time, Wil simply leaned on the doorbell until she appeared, yawning.

"Tell me it's a nightmare," she said blearily.

"Your laptop have a CD port?" he asked.

"I don't believe this."

"Does it?"

"Why should you care? Of course it does."

"This," he said, holding up the labelless disk in its case.

"You woke me up for a fucking CD?"

Wil said, "I woke you up because you know the language better than I do."

He watched her expression change as she took it from him, turned it over, angled it to the sunlight.

"Where did you get this?"

Something in the way she said it, tiredness gone like mist from an atomizer. "Why?" he said.

"This." A tiny crown about the size of a baby's fingernail molded into the case, the lower right rear corner. "My uncle special-orders them from a place in Singapore—for their capacity. The disk has a similar mark around the hole." Taking it out and turning it over to show him. "Now where did you get it?"

"Jimmy and Wen's old place. The tenants found it stuck in the couch," he said. "The laptop?"

In moments she had on jeans and the DKNY sweatshirt and they were at the kitchen table, Wil handing her the instant coffee he'd found and microwaved, Matt between them on the floor. She slid the disk into her laptop port, hit some keys. Then it was up and they were looking at metered lines and breaks, the squiggles, tents, and hooks characteristic of the language Wil had seen printed when he was in Vietnam.

For what seemed a long time, Mia said nothing, just scrolled, the kitchen smelling faintly of the coffee.

"Is it what I think it is?" he asked finally.

But tears were welling, tracking her cheeks until she stopped swiping at them and raised a hand to her face. Wil set a box of tissues from the drain board beside her, leashed Matt and took him around the block. Finally, he knocked and let himself back in.

She was still at the kitchen table. Staring at the screen.

"Wen had a talent," she said as he sat back down, Matt regarding her with concern. "Now and then Jimmy would read me one of her poems. A couple of them were on here. They're what set me off."

"I'm sorry," Wil said.

"Fuck it," she said angrily, "it's just such a waste." Brushing at hair that had fallen forward. Sniffing and wiping her eyes.

"Mia, I need to know. Are there numbers or data, that sort of thing mixed in or at the end?"

She shook her head.

"Names or contacts? Payment records? Addresses?"

"What are you implying?"

"From Luc's business."

"No. Nothing like that."

Damnit. "Any clues in the poems?"

She glared at him before answering. Then, "You don't quit, do you? You want a sample, okay, you got it. This is what it was like being her." Eyes flashing as she began translating:

They come for me, and I close my eyes
But it is no use.
I feel their stares, their claws for hands,
Their breath in heated ragged gasps
Pause.
And so I cry to you,
My guardian heart
Land of the white water bud, the jade black earth
The burning tallow moon

They sat with it, neither of them speaking. Then she said, "Not that my old man gives a rip, but my mom—are you going to show her?"

"No," Wil said. "And maybe you shouldn't either, not right now."

"Which means what?"

"Down the line when they're better able to handle it," he said. Then, "I'm assuming you copied the file."

"How do you know that?" Searching his face.

"Because it's what I'd have done."

"*Great,*" she said. "Is there anything you don't know?"

All he needed, that tone again; despite himself, he said, "No, but don't tell Luc that. He's right where I want him. Or should I say we?"

For a moment she stared at him. Then she shoved back her chair, spilling coffee on the table, swiping at it before giving up. "Get out," she said, an octave higher than normal. "Leave our family alone. Leave *me* alone."

He heard her bedroom door slam.

Giving pride its inning, Wil took his time snapping the disk back in its case, tossing it in the glove box, starting the car, reconnecting with the freeway. Stopping at The Coffee Grinder helped not at all. Not after he'd arrived home to the note from Kari that concluded a surfacey description of their vacation week with:

Wil—I've been thinking a lot about us since the last card. Brian's made progress, you should see him. I'm not much for handwriting on the wall, but maybe it's telling me something. There, I said it. Which doesn't mean you and I couldn't steal one now and then long distance. Probably best anyway—absence making the heart grow fonder, all that. Anything to add?

Kari.

Nothing to add, he balled up the note and winged it off *Moonrise in Hernandez, New Mexico.*

30

A T TEN-TWENTY, the man pulled the Range Rover out of the hotel's underground lot and hung a left onto Market. Thinking things had changed so much since the last time he'd seen San Francisco that he barely knew it, he turned south on 4th, made a left onto Harrison, looped in around the Hall of Justice, the Bryant Street entrance.

Nice and slow, so as to hit all the lights.

And there they were: the media. Singly and in bunches, smoking and swilling coffee or jockeying for position near the bank of microphones with the city seal attached. Some were augmenting their equipment from vans with their station logos, others were getting their lights in place, their run-throughs down. Note-scanning and anticipation, while their support staff and a number of uniformed SFPD kept their eyes on the men and women looping a tight circle and carrying placards: JUSTICE FOR DAO HONG; NO JUSTICE, NO PEACE; and his personal favorite, NO MORE WAR ON VIETNAM. Thinking, as he sized things up from a red that the more things change the more they stayed the same.

He took the next fifteen minutes to come at it from other angles, noting pretty much what he had expected: cars jammed into the lot within the building's L, the crowd growing, traffic heavying as it slowed for the spectacle, his orange cones still in place.

Nobody hanging around the employee's entrance.

Pulling up on Harriet, the man harvested the cones and the space, turned on the oldies station, adjusted his navy blazer to the correct drape, leaned back into "Fun, Fun, Fun," those tight Beach Boys harmonies. Followed by *Hot damn, summer in the city*—

A tap on the smoked glass brought him upright, a uniformed female when he levered it down, ten-till by his watch. "Morning, officer. There a problem?"

"Sir, are you authorized to park here?"

"Picking up a client for Evetta Sanger. The attorney?"

Her nose wrinkled at the name: *nice job* you *got*. "Do you have ID?"

"Sure." Producing in order, his license then the letter.

She did the usual up-down, then two more, the last good-measure slow. "Are those prescription sunglasses, Mr. Sage?"

The man pretended ignorance, then snapped to it, impressed. "Right, the photo." Pulling his dark glasses down to reveal his eyes. "Contacts since that was taken."

She scanned it once more and shrugged, handed the license and letter back as if they were tainted.

He smiled. "Everything in order?"

"So far as it goes. One more blow struck for freedom and the American way."

"Ma'am?" he asked.

"I said this Hong character's all yours."

She was turning away when he said, "Officer, I nearly forgot to give you a card. Special rates for law enforcement personnel."

Contempt superimposed on amusement, she said, "Another time. And you might consider running this thing through a carwash with the windows down when you're through. Either that or upgrade your clientele."

"I know what you're saying, officer," the man said, stuffing the documents back in his coat, watching her cross the street and reenter the building. "I surely do."

Calm and control.

Control and calm.

He was tapping the wheel to "Get Back," the Beatles rooftop anthem, when the employee's door opened and three men in black stepped out. The tallest clearly was Dao Hong despite his *Gargoyle* sunglasses: pockmarked face and a walk straight from a rap video. The other two, also wearing shades, assumed positions to his left and right, hands under their unstructured jackets, eyes casing the street like Secret Service. The left one spotted the Range Rover and pointed, steered them that way.

The man waiting opened the driver's-side rear, hand on the lever and a respectful pose as the two guards and Hong blocked traffic. When they'd crossed, the closest bodyguard frisked him, nodded to the other that he was clean, followed Hong into the back, while the other got in front and started checking him out.

"I would be Carson Sage," the man said, bouncing a look off the mirror. "Welcome to freedom, Mr. Hong."

"You got our guns?" Hong said in heavily accented English.

"I'm sorry, but nobody said anything about—"

"*Bitch,*" Hong fumed to curses from the other two. "I *told* those people—" Calming himself after a stage break, but still pissed: "You know where the party for us is?"

"Yes, sir." Snugging his driving gloves and buckling up.

"And I said I wanted a limo. So where is it?"

"Ms. Sanger thought a limousine would attract too much attention. She thought her car would be less likely to—"

"Fuck that," Hong cut him off. "You got a phone?"

"No sir, it's with her. But she did want you to have this with her compliments." Reaching across the guard, he opened the glove compartment, where he'd stowed the plastic bag with three pipes, gold directional lighter, premium-grade Maui.

"Well, now," Hong said, brightening to break the seal, inhaling from the bag to nods from the other two. "This more like it."

The man started the engine, levered into gear. "Sir, did you happen to see the media expecting you outside the main door?"

Dao Hong met his eyes. "Now how would I manage that, Car-son?" Mangling the name and bringing giggles. "You think they put TVs in the elevator?" More laughter.

"Would you like me to circle the block for a look?"

"Bunch of whores talking to a bunch of motherfucking other whores? I seen enough of that inside. Just do your job, *Carson.* And don't be looking back here so much." Hong slapped five with the front bodyguard while the one in back fired the pipes, the Range Rover filling with the sweet smell of the Maui.

The man cracked his window, gave the pedal a nudge.

"No extra charge for second-hand smoke," Hong said as they pulled away and headed down the prearranged route, all three busting up at that. Hong adding, "And get some fucking *bad* on, not this old-fart trash. NWA, Snoop...hell, anybody."

Scanning for it, the man tried to fathom why, of all the gangsters to emulate, this latest bunch was determined to sound like Niggas With Attitude.

❂

They were through the level part of Market, past Castro and gaining elevation, the city spread out below, when Hong said to him, "The fuck is this? I thought you knew where you going?"

"I do at that, Mr. Hong." Maxed out with the rap they'd been blaring; turning it down so he could at least hear.

"Then why we up Twin Peaks?" The Maui having an effect on Dao Hong's speech, two pipes in and a good deal more bantering in Vietnamese. Jailhouse braggadocio, female exploits, couple of references to the Po Sang, Hong cutting it off before much was said. But at his comment, both bodyguards were paying closer attention.

The man said, "I'm not supposed to say. Your associates made it clear it was to be a surprise."

"What goddamn surprise?"

"If you insist, sir, it's the limousine." Swinging right off Portola, last wisps of fog trailing the Marina; Golden Gate coming into view as he wound through Twin Peaks Park: from up there the city clean and shining, the air bay rum on the skin.

"Your guns," he added. "And champagne. Arriving in style is how they put it."

"Well, fuck, why didn't you say so?"

"Please, Mr. Hong, my job. They warned me not to spoil it. Almost there." Rounding a curve, he spotted his marker tree, the limo tucked in where he'd left it: *his* heist from earlier, *his* plant, *his* measure of control, *his* insurance policy against unanticipated encounters. Difficult to make out the extended white Lincoln angled down off the road, but it was there.

"You looking better by the minute, *Carson*," Dao Hong said to nods from the other two. "So what's the plan?"

With a smile, the man said, "We transfer, I drive you to the party, everyone has a good time. Especially the women." Pulling into the space created by the limo's angle.

"Why up here?" the guard in front said.

"Sir, I believe they were reluctant to leave a $200,000 limousine on city streets. Certain elements, you know."

"No shit. No other driver?"

"My question as well," he said. "A matter of trust, fewer being better in this case." Reaching into his pocket for the set of keys from the envelope. Holding them up so they all could see. "Shall we, gentlemen?"

He opened his door.

"*Gentlemen...*" Dao Hong said, drawing out the pronunciation. "You okay, Carson. You party with us, get yourself some black poon. No going back after black."

Smiling at their druggy laughter, the driver deactivated the limo's alarm, let them into the cavernous interior to stroke the leather, work the vanity lamps, high-five each other. "Champagne coming up," he said, reaching into the refrigerator where he'd stashed the .22 semi with the numbers filed and the mag loads that darted like bees inside a skull.

And there it was, in his gloved hand. Two hits per guard: head shots that dropped them where they sat and jerked Dao Hong upright, eyes wide at the pops. Locking with the other button as Hong snapped to what was up and made a move for the far door, the man firing a round through Hong's right biceps to get his attention.

"It's like this," he said without a trace of Carson Sage now. "I say a name, you tell me about him. Who and where. We clear on that?"

Blood seeped from around Hong's fingers, mouth and features frozen as the fog cleared. Fear competed with surprise, then pain.

"Excuse me?" the man said, expelling second-hand Maui from his lungs, maybe half a buzz on from all he'd inhaled. "Nod if I'm getting through."

"*Motherfuck*. Who are you?"

"Not Carson Sage, you can bet."

Hong's face was ashen, the words gritted. "Whoever you are, you a dead man."

"It wouldn't be the first time."

"All right, I pay you." Forced. "How much you want?"

"Sorry, but that's not how it works," the driver who was not Carson Sage explained. "Luc Tran Tien is the name I want, got it? I thought so. And lose the Gargoyles, Dao, they just make you look pinched."

31

TWO-THIRTY, three hours into dissecting the investigative report, Wil banged the pages into the corner and leaned back in his chair. Rubbing the headache that had come with them, he got up and washed down Tylenol with the tea he'd been nursing, cold now. He turned on the TV; after a surf through the daytime dreck, eight-point report type still jittering, he remoted it off, got up, and went out on the deck.

The ocean was the color of bronze, the light dirty from a chaparral fire that had broken out beyond the mountains, the hot valley side: rare when a summer went by without wildfires. Usually, however, they flared up in September-October. This one meant a long season. The smoke had formed a cloud that filtered the sun and turned the normally white valley thunderheads yellow-brown, the fire likely to grow before it retreated.

From the rise and breadth, it was burning someplace inaccessible.

Wil could hear the deep drone of the tankers running fire-retardant drops—teaspoons to put out a pyre, about the way he felt with his own situation. But he didn't even have a teaspoon.

What he *needed* was a teaspoon.

He gave Luc, Wen and Jimmy, Mia and Vinh Tien another half-hour of thought—what he had going (nothing: that again) and what he had to lose (not far off)—then went inside to clean up and make a phone call.

"What happened, you run out of steam on your own?" Inez Lorenz said after he'd called the number she'd given him and she'd returned it ten minutes later.

"Guess I just missed your partner," Wil answered.

"Mac grows on you, all right."

"From all I've seen of you, I half-figured you'd gone home."

"Oh, we've been around," she said. "You finally get smart?"

"Too late for that, I'm afraid."

"Then I'll hazard a wild guess—you'd like us to come by."

"Better yet, I'll come to you," he said.

"You know better than that."

Wil thought a moment. "Are you familiar with Carpinteria, the world's safest beach at the end of Linden? Says so on the sign?"

"I imagine we can find it."

There was a pause while she held her hand over the phone and talked to someone, presumably Maccafee, then she was back on.

"Four o'clock," she said. "There or square."

Thirty minutes after hanging up, Wil cruised Linden, past the Coffee Grinder, The Palms with its namesake Washingtonias lining the sidewalk, shops and food places becoming increasingly beachy as he neared the water. Crossing the last intersection before the turnaround, he saw the Buick, saw their heads crane toward him as he pulled in opposite her open window.

"Don't get up," he said.

"We were just betting on whether or not you were going to show. Mac won this time." She scanned the Bonneville's interior. "Where's your partner?"

"Afternoon nap. He gets crabby otherwise, apt to maul intruders."

She glanced at him and half-smiled. "Sounds like mine."

"Funny, Inez," Wil heard Maccafee say as they got out and he locked the Buick.

"And hello to you, too, Special Agent Maccafee."

Maccafee threw him a nod. Looking hot, he had on a windbreaker that pooched over creased jeans and black loafers while Lorenz wore cotton slacks, a Madras shirt, what looked to be Easy Spirits: Kari's favorite, the buck casuals.

"Lifestyle's rubbing off, I see," Wil said. Figuring they'd drawn straws to determine who came armed and he'd lost that one. "Now if you could just lose the shoes."

"Thanks, but no thanks."

"Probably right," Wil told him. "Might have to chase someone."

Lorenz looked at Wil, then at Maccafee. As Wil slipped out of his Teva sandals and left them by a rock, she unlaced hers and did the same. "Well?" she said to Maccafee.

"I look like the barefoot boy to you, Inez?"

"Not with those on."

"*Hell,*" he let out as Wil and Lorenz strode through the kids and families onto a broad stretch of cool hardpack. White feet drawing even with theirs after shedding the loafers and rolling up his cuffs.

"About the other day, your boy," Maccafee said when the beachgoers had thinned. Lorenz looking away as a director might after calling "action," not wanting to spook an actor's soliloquy.

"Devin," Wil said. "His name was Devin."

"What I'm trying to say is, it must have been rough."

Nothing to add, so he didn't as Lorenz flashed Maccafee a *finish it* look and kept walking.

"Look, I'm trying to do right here," Maccafee struggled. "How about some slack?"

"It's the job," Wil said. "Makes you crazy sometimes."

"The job, right. We're square, then?"

Wishing it were longer, Wil let a beat pass. "Can't dance," he said. "Why not?"

Lorenz cleared her throat. "Some fire going over the hill."

From the beach the extent of the pall was dramatic, a towering cloud flattening east-west at the top, mountains and sky as if viewed through shooting glasses. As one air tanker cleared the ridge toward re-watering, another droned over it.

"Has to be over a hundred on that side," Wil said as they cleared an area with teenagers romping; excited screams and shouts as the waves rolled in or one got splashed. "I don't envy the guys fighting it, and I know some."

"Speaking of a fight," Lorenz segued, "are you ready to join one?"

"I suppose that depends on the terms."

"You know damn well—"

"*Tom...please.*"

"I just want to know which part didn't he understand, Inez."

Wil watched a plane disappear in the haze, took a breath and plunged. "What was Jimmy doing for you that got him killed?"

"As in when did you stop beating your wife," she said. "That's the deal here?"

He said, "I help you, you help me. Sound familiar?"

"It's hard to see you holding the cards," Lorenz said.

"Ever consider that might cut both ways?"

Maccafee laughed derisively. "Based on what?"

Wil said, "A friend at the Sheriff's is close to the investigation. Seems they have no knowledge Wen and her mother were illegal or that you threatened them with deportation. Which says to me that you excluded the county from briefings you must have had or you wouldn't be operating here." He paused for effect. "Not what you might call a model of interagency cooperation, would you say?"

No reaction from either.

"Don't hesitate to correct me if I'm wrong here."

They'd left almost everyone behind now. Maccafee hurled a piece of driftwood into a wave, looked at Lorenz. "We won't," he said. "While you clarify for us what your client's daughter does out at Luc's in the wee hours."

And so much for his theory that the ATF had gone home.

So much for Mia being under their radar.

Shit, shit, shit.

"What?" Maccafee said. "No smart-ass comeback?"

Fallback: the thought they needed him as badly as he hoped, the reason they were here at all. Wil said, "Mia Tien stays out of this or I'm nowhere near it."

"You dictating to us," Maccafee said. "I love it. Your call, Inez, but I think you know what I'd tell him."

Lorenz stopped walking, dug her toes in the sand. They were almost to the point where the rocks began: pair of seals poking up to look shoreward before diving again, water resembling brown glass as the sky continued to darken from the smoke. She stooped to pick up a flat stone, which she skimmed toward the oil rigs, the islands beyond. Without looking at either of them, she said, "That truce didn't last long, did it? Anybody else thinking Mexican standoff?"

32

"IT AMOUNTS TO NOTHING," Wil said, "money Luc's paying her to help with expenses." This after they'd tentatively agreed to a compromise: past and future relevancies for their looking the other way on the girl, provided she was clean.

"That's what she told you, huh?" Maccafee said. "Doubtless approved by her old man."

"Check it out with him," Wil said with more chutzpah than he felt hearing his own words to her thrown back at him. "Vinh could ask how you knew. Then there's the matter of her associates, their reaction to one of their own being under surveillance by a federal agency."

"So fucking what?"

"Campus protests hold any meaning for you?"

"All right," Lorenz broke in. "That's enough."

They were at a campground picnic table near where they'd stopped walking. Shouts drifting over from a badminton game, now and then a disc with a kid in pursuit...warm in the yellow sun.

"Speaking of who knew what," Lorenz said, "how did you know Mia Tien was working for her uncle?"

"A little bird."

"Just the kind of thing she'd volunteer," Maccafee said.

"Move on," Lorenz said. "What exactly does she do for him?"

"Exactly what, I don't know," Wil answered. *No problem there.*

Lorenz's lips became a tight line; she rubbed her neck as if it hurt. "I'm not sure we're getting off to a real good start here."

"Sorry, it's the truth."

"Right," Maccafee threw at him. "Inez, you want to tell him what we need, or should I?"

Lorenz brushed sand off her ankles. "Mr. Hardesty, pursuant to our deal, I'm going to ask you for a description of Luc Tien's house. Which means everything you remember: names of staff, visitors who stood out, best guess on the rest. Anything you know about his computer system—"

"Which is nothing," he interrupted.

"Give it a rest. Firsthand or through the girl," she went on. "Write it down and we'll pick it up tomorrow. If you're going out, leave it on your deck under a lounge pad. I also expect written reports on further contact or conversations with those involved, even marginally."

"Gee, that's all?"

"For now," she said.

"My turn, then," Wil started. "What do you know about Jimmy's boat going down?"

She and Maccafee exchanged looks, Lorenz shrugging. "Double bum for the home team. And if you dug up the reports, which I assume you have by now, you know what we know. Mac?"

"About it," he said. "Nothing to indicate foul play. Just shit for luck."

Maybe to questionable. "Anything you have on it I might check out?"

"Whatever we come across is yours," Lorenz said.

Wil read dry well and tried a different tack. "If Luc Tien *is* the head of this budding national crime organization, how does he recruit?"

Maccafee swiped at perspiration. He said, "By convincing the strongest street gangs to join him, helping them exterminate rivals and consolidate their assets. In other words, to run efficiently, perks to those who buy in. But if somehow the poolside treatment fails, he always has his mulcher."

Wil looked at him to see if he was serious. "His what?"

"Paint yourself a picture," Maccafee said, "the unconvinced going in feet first. Feeding time at Miracle-Gro Ranch."

Wil tried—all those plants—and balked. "You're saying you know that for a fact."

The Maccafee smile. "A snitch we know witnessed one before he permanently ceased operations. Answer your question?"

Lorenz said, "These people live for that example crap. But the bottom line is, dumb is not Luc's style. People who underestimate him don't a second time."

"Is that what Jimmy was trying to uncover for you?"

Maccafee fielded it. "We had Jimmy going on a lot of things, actually."

"Things Wen might know about?"

"Could be, Sherlock."

"In other words," Wil said, "anything that would hang his uncle."

Maccafee shrugged.

Wil said, "And how did Jimmy feel about that?"

"How the fuck would I—"

Lorenz cleared her throat. "What Agent Maccafee means is there was something at stake for the young man or he wouldn't have agreed. Right, Mac?"

"Whatever you say. But you notice who's revealing what here, Inez? How I told you it would play out?"

"I'll take a flier on it," Wil said. "Love and witness protection, happily ever after. Provided Jimmy went along."

A beat passed, glances between Lorenz and Maccafee, then she said, "Close enough for government work."

"And was he living up to your expectations?"

"Put it this way," she came back, brushing at a gnat interested in her eyelashes. "The kid was about to when we lost him."

"Inez, this is bullshit."

Wil eyed Maccafee, said to Lorenz, "One more before I go beat on the Tien girl for you. This tong thing that was all over the tube, the shooter they arrested in San Francisco. You see Luc's hand in that?"

Eyes met again and disengaged. "Three guesses, no proof," she answered for them. "As yet."

"Why stop there, Inez?" The big agent fanning his jacket to let in air. "Tell him the rest."

She thought, finally nodded. "All right. Dao Hong, the one they arrested then released, is a Dragon underboss, a *dai low*. Just before we heard from you, we got word he was found dead in a limo with two of his crew. Small caliber head shots. Presumably by a man posing as his lawyer's driver."

Pro hits, Wil thought, fighting a vague sense of unease. "They get a description of the driver?"

"Caucasian, medium build. The cop who checked his credentials outside the Hall of Justice said he reminded her of Steve McQueen, that short hair of his. Beyond that, nothing."

"You hit us, we hit you," Wil qualified.

"Something like that."

Maccafee's eyes shifted to the oil rigs. "If you want my opinion, we ought to just let 'em go at it, save us all the time and money and to hell with the politicians. Lock and load, I say."

"Except it's never them in the crossfire, is it?" she snapped at him. As though the issue were an old one between them.

Maccafee said, "What my partner's referring to, Hardesty, is an L.A. jewelry heist. Two little Korean girls who nearly bought it when—"

"I can explain myself, Agent Maccafee," she said.

"Never said you couldn't, *partner*. I just know you, is all."

"I must have missed it," Wil said, wondering whether he should duck now or later.

Lorenz took a breath. "A little over a week ago these four fucks, Dragons, are set to waste not only the store owner but his wife and daughters. It's that close to happening when a guy appears from nowhere to drop three of them and drag the fourth out with him."

Wil tried picturing it, winding up with the same question. "How'd he come to be there?"

She said, "The jeweler isn't saying, but we think he has Po Sang ties and hit a button. The same four had done other stores in the area."

"Po Sang gets tired of it and brings a guy in," Wil said. "Which might fit for Hong and his cronies."

Lorenz said nothing, brushed ash from her shoulders after a look at Maccafee, who glanced away.

Wil said, "And the fourth Dragon?"

"Haven't found him—and SFPD never heard of an Anglo doing hit work for the tongs," she answered. "Theirs, anyway."

"So now it's Luc's turn at bat."

Maccafee shifted his holster, fanned his jacket. "Considering how our man hates Chinese, it's always his turn."

Again from left field. "Did I come in late again?"

Maccafee's smile seemed broader. "You get close to ol' Luc, be sure and ask him about it. Stems from his getting buggered while apprenticing in Saigon, this fag gangster he worked for and his pals, Chinese. Likely from *their* high regard for the Vietnamese."

Eyeing Lorenz for reaction, Wil caught patient: changeup, fastball, curve. He said, "I'll be sure and bring that up. What about the guy from nowhere?"

"We wouldn't mind talking to him," she said.

"You're thinking he might have done Jimmy?"

Shrug. "We're not ruling it out. That is, unless you have something to add."

Wil thought about it, rejected what was running through his mind as her fingers drummed the table. "Nope," he said. "Sorry."

"Then I suggest you fish on your own time, Mr. Hardesty."

My fish, your catch, he was about to say, but held off as she went on. "Now, to keep things linear, we want the Dragon, you want to know what happened to Jimmy. Is that accurate?"

Nod. "And with his sister out of it, yes."

"Good," she said. "Then we understand each other."

"So," Maccafee said to him with a now-you-see-what-it's-like smirk as they stood to go. "How's that place we saw with the tall palms? The steak any good?"

Wil stayed seated. "That would be up to you since you get to grill it. And tell me, where do ATF agents hang out these days if not in their Buicks?"

"No need to concern yourself about that, Mr. Hardesty," Lorenz said, moving now to cut across the park. "Stay close and we'll be in touch."

"I have no doubt of it," he called after her. Wondering about the fragility of this shotgun arrangement as they disappeared around an outbuilding and left him with only drifting ash.

33

FIVE-THIRTY—LATE LUNCH, massage, and a stroll to get his game plan together—the man was ready to make his call.

"Guess who?" he said as the voice answered.

"You're clear, I take it," the voice came back.

"You may." Still thinking of where this score could put him: his own island, scoped out during a recent spell in Bali; paradise on the half-shell, that close. "And yourself?" he asked. Ebullient despite his number-one rule: No presence.

"In place," the voice said. "But it's thoughtful that you ask."

"I'm a thoughtful guy."

"And a different one, in my experience."

That got his attention. "Different how?"

There was a pause. Then, "Your independence, your execution. The limousine, for example, that whole scenario. And your grasp of things. Certainly of what they cost."

"Of their worth, you mean," the man responded. Hard not to enjoy this banter on top of the day he'd had.

There was a sound like a chuckle. "However you say."

Recalling the voice's off-beat comment—*Is that what I am?*—the man tried visualizing its owner, the kind of mental exercise that had kept him sane in the camps. The voice was as napless as glass, but with an edge of cruelty. It reminded him of a guard who'd tormented them and whom he'd killed during the escape. Far too quickly, but rule two: You took what you could in life.

The man said, "You're pleased, then?"

"How could we not be pleased with the Dragon gone to dishonor his ancestors?"

"*A* Dragon, I believe you mean."

The voice paused again. "Explain, please."

"But of course. May I assume you're directing these events from a fair distance?"

"Global intelligence and technology have made the world a state of mind," the voice said. "You of all people should concur."

"True," he said. "If we were talking about me."

"And just what is it that we *are* talking about?" Frost creeping in now, an edge of impatience.

The man smiled: two could play this game. He said, "Specifically, that a dragon's claws grow back."

"A point made early on, I believe."

"So it was, relative to its brain being your target. Or am I mistaken about that?"

A breath expelled; then, "I was assured my information regarding Hong was beyond reproach."

"It was," the man admitted. "As far as it went."

Silence. "I see. And your recommendation?"

The man rubbed an old burn scar that air-conditioning often made sensitive. "That it's time to widen your outlook, my genderless friend. Not to mention your wallet."

34

AFTER WINDSPRINTS WITH MATT TO CLEAR HIS HEAD, Wil worked on his recollections of the Luc Tien visit until nearly six—nine pages of notes and he was ready to chuck the whole thing. Mia, Luc, Lorenz, Maccafee—all of it: Good-bye and good luck.

Nice closure, he thought. *Real future in it.*

Another night in the hills seemed a waste, seeing as how his new associates were on the job and better equipped: probably in some neighbor's rental wing or guest cottage with long-lens visual access. Standard alphabet-agency MO. Which reminded him to pay closer attention the next time he was out there, trust not yet a big part of how he felt about Lorenz and Maccafee. To the contrary, he still wondered what he'd gotten himself into; something beyond warmed-over file info, he hoped. Finally getting around to the paper for the first time in several days, he caught a concert listing and on impulse picked up the phone.

"Wil? What—"

"Spur of the moment, Leese, Ronnie Pruett at the Bowl. Dutch treat, we meet there. What do you say?"

"Who?" Tired-sounding.

"This kid I know from Bakersfield who writes and performs his own country-western. He's touring his first album."

Long breath. "Wil, I just got home."

"Guaranteed to perk you up and support a kid who could use it."

"I don't think so," she said after a beat. "But thanks."

"Might be something to take your mind off..."

"My mind off what?"

"Fill in the blanks, one or all" he said, Frank's comments about her looking frayed still kicking around; plus his own observations.

Silence, then: "Is everyone else you know busy or something?"

"What the hell," he said, thinking he probably deserved it. "Bring Brandon if that's it."

"That's *not* it, and besides, he's got baseball," she said, with more emphasis than was called for. "What time?"

He checked his watch. "An hour. Shouldn't be too crowded on a weeknight."

"Which means the kid isn't exactly Willie Nelson yet."

"So I'm out to pad the house," he admitted. "Leese, you'll like him. Money back if not."

In the pause he could hear squawks from Edward, their white cockatoo she'd wound up with. Just as well, Wil had thought in his funk, though he still missed the bird's affectionate nips, their little exchanges. At length she came up with, "You go, and if I show up, I'm there. It's the best I can do."

He said nothing, to which she finally added, "But I'll probably make it."

The Santa Barbara Bowl was set into a notch that stepped up to the mountains. Ringed by occupants who either loved, tolerated, fought it, or moved, the Bowl's location was the subject of no little debate in a town whose preoccupation was debate. Nobody disputed the experience, though: The Bowl was simply a great outdoor venue on a warm evening. Even one touched, as this one was, by the glow of encroaching flames.

From the night coverage Wil had seen, the Santa Ynez fire was now the kind that had relatives believing the whole state was burning. Arriving early, he'd found a spot five blocks away, walked with the knots of concertgoers to the ticket office. He bought a seat for himself and one for Lisa, scanned a concert poster of Ronnie Pruett as he waited.

Somebody named Iger had taken a dynamite promo shot for the new album, all light and shadow and young-Dwight smolder from under a *Kenworth Diesel* cap Wil recognized as Doc Whitney's, the C-W singer Wil helped clear of murder charges and the kid's father. He was wondering about Bakersfield and Wyoming, Doc and Jenelle, the circumstances that had brought Matt to him, when he heard, "There you are," and turned to see her.

Jeans, white shirt with pearl buttons, latigo boots with stars and moons embossed, a pin in the shape of a lariat.

The essential Japanese-American cowgirl.

"What, no hat?" he said. Smiling as he handed her her ticket and they started up the path.

"Moderation in all things." Smiling back. "Now about this Ronnie Pruett..."

Wil went for the version that spotlit the kid's music, leaving out who died, concluding with, "Remind me to loan you one of Doc's old CDs. Ronnie's the image."

"Which reminds me," she said as they got their tickets torn. "How much do I owe you?"

"It's on the stub. Send me a check when you're—"

But she had the money out already.

He said, "Feeling flush is what I was going to say."

"A deal's a deal," she said. "Your line, if I remember."

He was about to comment on it, money ever an issue between them; instead he took in the scene. They were at the lip of the amphitheater, seating terracing from the stage like sound waves. Sycamore trees lined the flanks; colored spots crisscrossed the stage and riser, the arriving crowd; balconies, decks, and glowing windows punctuated the hillside. An usher directed them to seats on the right side, stage lights picking up the shine in her hair.

"There it goes," she said.

"What's that, Leese?"

"The question I always ask myself: Why don't I do this more often?"

"Reading my mind."

She said, "So what is it *you're* getting away from?"

He thumbnailed Jimmy-Wen for her the way he used to: dots to form an overview, thinking that was part of the frustration, having no one to talk to right now. Not that she'd welcomed it when they were together. In fact, that had been their own tar pit: what he did, how he did it, and for whom.

"Poor Li Tien," she said after hearing it. "You think I should call her? Let her know she's not alone?"

He considered her offer, failed to see a drawback, but said, "Let me feel it out, Leese. And thanks, that's—"

A roar went up as the band hit their marks. Then Ronnie Pruett shouted out a welcome and they tore into a rockabilly Wil recognized from last year but better arranged. Two more and Ronnie introduced the band, then spun them into the new album, Wil amazed at the kid's growth. His old man there, yet getting to it a different way.

"How old is he?" Lisa asked at one point.

"Don't ask: twenty-one."

The kid cooled the band for one about his Okie-migrant granddad and a couple others. Two-and-a-half hours and two encores in, he signed off with *Kern River Girl*. Wil stood to take Lisa around to meet him.

"You go. I'll take a rain check," she said.

He took her hand, noted how cold it was, how washed out she looked under the lights.

"You all right?" he asked.

"Nothing a trip to the ladies room won't help." Lisa starting to move with urgency now, Wil thinking of the lines, people who'd waited, not wanting to leave the music.

She made it as far as a trash can, the filers-out giving her a wide berth as she lost it. Several times more until they sat, Lisa catching her breath, roadies packing up, STAFF-shirted kids patrolling for discards.

"Wil, is it cold, or is it me?"

"It's cool." Benefit of the doubt, feeling her forehead as they stood to go. "You have anything to eat before you came?"

"Late client lunch."

"Anything to make you feel like that?"

"Like what?"

Meaning, of course, *end of subject*.

Over her protestations, he followed her home and into her drive, realizing as he saw her to the door that he'd never actually been inside the restored bungalow she'd purchased. Spanish influence in the arched front window and rounded stucco surfaces, the curving tile roof.

"Nice," he said as she unlocked the door and turned toward him.

"I'd ask you in, but—"

"Another time, I know. There anything I can get you at the store? Mylanta?"

"Nothing I don't have."

"Meaning you've had this awhile," he said.

"Meaning—" the look coming over her face again. *"Shit—"* Turning from him to bolt down the hall.

Wil let himself in, heard a door slam, the muted sound of heaving. Moving to the living room, he scanned for things he recognized, found more he didn't: photos, sketches, Japanese calligraphy in a red bamboo frame. Berber carpet, teak dining set, FM station playing background Debussy: the working woman's security system. He was on the couch, thumbing through a copy of *Islands*, when she appeared in her bathrobe, face the color of bone.

"Thanks for seeing me home," she said.

"What can I do, Leese?"

"Nothing. I can take it from here." Eyes like coals in a snowman.

"Looks being deceiving and all."

"Please, Wil. I'm asking."

"What is it, Leese? The unabridged version."

She let a moment pass, brushed her hair back. Then, "I told you, it's nothing I can't handle."

He said, "You asked earlier, and now I'm asking. What were *you* getting away from tonight?" Kicking himself for not having reciprocated, too caught up in the fun she seemed to be having.

"Who said I was getting away from anything?"

"This is me, remember?"

"Life as a game of Clue, how could I forget?" she said. "No, that's not fair."

"It's a simple question, Leese."

"No it's not."

More silence, then, "Look, you want me to go, I'm gone." Hand on the latch, levering it, when she said something he couldn't make out.

"I'm sorry, I didn't hear you."

"I said, it's not that hard to figure out. If you try."

"No more beating around, Leese. I'm tired, too."

She shook her head as if it were an effort. "Why does it always come to this with us? When did it start?"

"I don't know," he said, ache spreading from the bruise that was the truth of it. "But thanks for coming. At least it was what I needed."

He had the door open, palm against the screen, when she finally came to it, the words almost lost in a Bach fugue on the stereo.

"Wil, I'm pregnant and I'm scared."

35

il, I'm pregnant and I'm scared.

Cold rain blowing through a window left open by mistake, sleeting the room and dousing its fire, leaving only a vacuum.

"It was only a matter of time before you found out."

"How?" he said, incredulous. "I thought the doctors had ruled out...I mean, you—"

"How do I know?" she said. Deep breath: "Do you think I asked for this? That *Brandon's* who I—"

But Wil was holding her now, feeling her shake, how thin she felt despite her robe. And for his part: numbness—reverb from six years ago, doctors declaring her unable to conceive after the beating she'd taken for him. *For him,* their catalyst. Richter-scale 8 in a marriage already crumbling like schist under pressure.

"Does Brandon know?" he finally asked.

"He knows."

Wil led her to the couch, frames of Devin flashing as in a photo album: how old he'd have been this year, what he'd be like at eighteen. "Brandon has his life," she said. "Is that absolutely clear?"

"What do you think?"

"Wil, I'm telling you, I prefer it this way. Brandon has no idea what to do. It's not in him. And it's not your place to judge."

"No? Whose, then?"

"Mine, if anyone's, and I'm through with that." Arms to her chest like a raised shield. "All he ever knew was what I told him, that there was no chance."

"But it turns out there was," he said, hating the way he said it.

"And who knew, Wil, you?" she fired back. "I think you'd better go now."

"Going to tough it out, huh?"

"It's all any of us does."

"So what does your doctor say? That this shit is normal?"

"That's between us, thank you."

"And Brandon?" he said. "You don't think he's earned a share?"

"When you see him weighing in with something, let me know."

They'd gravitated to opposite ends of the couch, walled-off body language and breech-proof expressions; Lisa's color somewhat restored by the heat they'd generated, but still looking drained.

"So what are you going to do?" he asked.

"I don't know yet, but it's my problem and I'll handle it."

"Not something you'll regret, I hope."

She looked at him. *"You'd even say that? To me?"*

"Forget it, Leese," he said. "That's the day talking."

"Goddamnit, listen to me. I have regrets in places I didn't know I had. But they're my regrets, my consequences. Do you get that?" Standing now, starting down the hall before she turned back.

"I appreciate your concern, Wil, but it no longer tips the scales."

"At least let me—"

"Good luck with your case," she said. "Check the latch on your way out, will you? Sometimes it doesn't lock without slamming."

I'm pregnant and I'm scared...

Unable to process anything else, Wil took Matt out for a midnight walk on the beach. Offshore, the oil rigs glittered like cheap baubles, La Conchita and the freeway less so with the late hour. Smoke turning it orange made the moon seem as if it were on fire, while a slack tide gave the appearance of a lake, though its smell was of salt and kelp, of something dead not far off.

Brandon has his life...

The sand was as cold underfoot as the night air against his face. Matt was thrilled to be out after an evening inside, checking everything from wood to a washed-up sneaker. Strolling up now and then to see how his slower charge was faring before romping after a night bird or scuttler, the shadows cast by a passing car.

I'll handle it...

It was as if a cosmic joke were at work, one everyone got but Wil Hardesty. Married with a terrific kid one second, something he could only shake his head at the next. That was the worst, the feeling of powerlessness: no say, no plan, no action step, no chance for two-out-of-three. Only *house wins*, and *who's up for double-downs?*

Wil realized the sand had run out and he was staring at the water, Matt beside him. He knelt, stroked cool muzzle and cool fur, thinking that not everything lately had been a loss. But the thoughts were hollow, without legs, and he sat heavily, his strength gone. Not even fighting it, he wept for himself and Lisa, for his lost son, his lost life.

For what might have been and sure as hell wasn't anymore.

36

NEXT MORNING HE GOT UP LATE, zombied around, reinforcing the downer, tempted to call Lisa for purposes he had to admit were absurdly self-serving. The old standby: Fix it and be done, charge right in there, Hardesty rides again. Then the lapsang kicked in and Wil showered, dressed, and drove to Santa Barbara to brief Vinh and Li Tien on where things stood.

Brief is right, he thought, laying it out for them at one of the food-service tables. Deliberately leaving out mention of Lorenz and Maccafee, of Mia being out at Luc's, let alone where they might intersect. Even deciding to wait until he had a more complete grasp of Jimmy's informant role to spring *that* bit of news.

Which left not a lot.

For a moment after he'd finished, they just sat.

"What does it mean?" Vinh asked finally.

Good question; you want to take that one? "Only that we haven't found the key," he said. "Sooner or later one will surface. Then it's like an ice floe breaking up."

They looked at each other. Li Tien said, "Our daughter tells us that you met with her."

Wil spun his coffee mug slowly. "Yes. We didn't get too far."

"Mia is willful, you saw that," Li said. "Outside of the family, she lets few people in. That is, when she lets *us* in."

Vinh cleared his throat. "By now you must be aware that she blames us—me, that is—for Jimmy."

"She's hurting," Wil told him. "You're a ready target."

"Life spares no one," Vinh said. "We all are hurting."

As if a storm had rolled in, Li Tien welled up, left them at the table. Vinh followed her with his eyes. "If anyone, this has been hardest on my wife."

Wil said, "This may be presumptuous, but my wife—ex-wife, I mean—has offered should Li wish to speak with someone who has been there."

At length, Vinh Tien nodded. "Thank her for us, I will ask. Mia, of course, is another matter."

"So I guessed."

"No." Fingers to his temples. "If we are to continue, you need to know the reason my wife left the table."

Vinh Tien's eyes were those of captured enemy soldiers Wil had seen waiting for interrogation, shutterless windows into war-torn rooms. Wil waited.

"In her wisdom," Vinh began, "our daughter decided she would be better off with my brother. We checked her room this morning and found things gone, a note regarding her decision." He left, came out with a quartered piece of college-rule he unfolded on the table.

Black ink, small neat penmanship: *Gone to live at Luc's. Don't try following me, M.* Wil thinking she might as well have twisted the dagger in her father for the way the subtext bled through: *To do what you couldn't.*

"You see, Mr. Hardesty, I've been waiting for you. Li made me promise on my life."

"Promise what?"

The eyes had assumed another look now, that of the interrogator.

"That I would not go there without you. That I would not kill my brother with these hands. Have you any idea how hard that has been?"

❧

As they approached the house, the Yukons Wil had seen last time were pulling out, heading down Mountain Drive. Through the smoked glass he

176

could make out shapes, if unidentifiable ones, no accurate head count, as he and Vinh pulled up in the Bonneville.

He approached the intercom, said into it, "Hardesty and Vinh Tien to see Luc. He'll know why." Wondering if they were on Lorenz and Maccafee's monitors as well.

He was aware of men lounging under green awnings along the far walls. Beyond the spine of ridgeline, smoke still boiled and spread.

"Mr. Tien's not here," the intercom responded. Tinny and hollow: Robb, most likely.

"He's here," Vinh said from the car. "I can feel him."

"It's important," Wil told the intercom.

"Mr. Tien beside you has the phone number," the intercom said back. "Have him make an appointment."

"Thanks. He's tried that."

"Which might tell him something. You, too, you had half a brain."

Wil was about to say something when Vinh put a hand on his arm. He got out of the car and walked to the gate, stood in front of it. Ramrod straight, fists clenched, looking directly into the camera, the yellow-brown sun. Ash drifting down from the fire they couldn't see.

"Try again," Wil told the intercom. "You never can tell."

"Hit the road, Jack."

"Ask yourself, Robb. You see short-term here?"

"Your problem, friend." Signing off.

After thirty minutes, the perspiration that mottled Vinh's polo shirt had formed a solid wedge. Fifteen more and the shirt was soaked and clinging to his stocky frame; sweat ran from his hair, glistened on his neck and arms. And still he hadn't moved.

Suddenly, with no indication from the intercom, no Robb in the golf cart, no sign from the house, the gate swung open. As if in tribute it stood that way, sun flaring off the tri-colored rock, the garage, the hunkering walls. Wil pressed a water bottle into Vinh Tien's hand; after he'd downed it, they walked the drive, past the gate-house to where Sonny leaned against a support post. Same shorts, polo, and lug-soled Caterpillars. With a long look at Wil, he led them through the tiled breezeway that ran along the south wing.

They passed a scroll-barred window, Wil catching a glimpse of someone approximately Mia's size in silhouette. Then they were beyond it and following Sonny through a doorway-filling gate to a walled patio hung with succulents. Sedum spilled from glazed pots while a mission-style fountain dripped water into a float of yellow blooms encircled by lilies of the Nile.

Sonny removed a two-way from his belt and spoke into it. Within moments Luc Tien was stepping through the glass doors that led onto the flagstone, down slab steps to stand in front of his brother, glares met and returned with interest.

For a second Wil was struck by the contrast: Vinh compact and angle-featured, drenched in sweat; Luc in cream pants and a navy silk overshirt, moccasins without socks, himself contrast to the Luc Tien Wil had seen working his garden. Wil was returning Sonny's gaze when the shouting started in Vietnamese, Mia's name about the only thing he recognized.

As if Vinh Tien were a supporting actor to whom the lead generously gave his moment, Luc merely looked at him. "Brother," he said in English, "you won't be here that long." Snapping his fingers.

Behind the glass there was movement, and Mia appeared: hesitant, as though auditioning for the part of the wanton. Short black skirt over stockinged legs and wrap sandals, black blouse with the buttons undone to her waist, gel-spiked hair where it curled at the ears.

Wil wasn't sure Vinh caught the glaze in her eyes, but the effect on him was the same either way. Mia's glance lit on Wil and flitted past, a drugged-out butterfly.

"Tell him," Luc ordered her. "So I won't have to."

"Go home, Dad," Mia over-enunciated. "I'm here because it's what I want."

Vinh found his voice. "Knowing how I feel about—"

"I'm making money, *Dad*. That's what you care about, isn't it?"

He looked stricken. "Looking like that? Like a—"

"Like a what," she said, "not your little girl anymore? Since when have I *been* a little girl, let alone yours? Go away."

"Mia, Your studies—"

"My studies bore me. Is that plain enough?" Addressing what seemed to be a point over her father's left shoulder.

"Not to me, it isn't. Not to your mother."

"What a fucking soap opera. I'm going back to work."

"No. You're coming home with me." Taking a step toward her that Luc blocked.

Mia's eyes found Wil again. "Is that why you brought *him* with you? To drag me off by the hair?"

Vinh Tien turned to Wil. "Sometimes my adopted country's rules are lost to me," he said. "Can you not do something?"

"Mia," Wil said, "if your uncle has drugged or threatened you or us in any way, say it now. If you want to leave with us, say it now."

"You just don't get it, do you? Why is that?"

"What I get is that you need to put an end to this," he said. "Yes or no?"

"No. If it hasn't been plain enough."

"That's it, then," he said to Vinh Tien.

The man looked as if the only thing holding him up was sheer force of will. "Just look at what he's done to her, my own daughter," he said. "Isn't that proof enough?"

Wil felt for him. "I'm sorry, but no, it isn't. Not here." Hating saying it, wanting to drive his fist into the smirk that had formed on Sonny's face.

"Then what good are we?" Vinh said from someplace far off. *"What good?"*

Luc said, "Listen to him, brother, and learn something." Starting inside after Mia without a look at Vinh. "Sonny, get them out of here before I—"

But Vinh had his brother's arm, had spun Luc into a right hand that staggered him, a follow-up kick that dropped him.

Wil moved, but Sonny was there first, a hook to Vinh's kidney that put him down groaning. Wil was timing a punch to Sonny's neck when a Walther-style semi-automatic came up to within an inch of his nose.

Sonny cocked it. "Who's a hero, friend, you? No, I didn't think so."

"Not now," Wil said, backing off. "Not here."

Sonny lowered it, smirked again, turned his attention to Vinh Tien and Luc Tien beside him, stunned but not quite out of it. Back up at Wil, then: "You might want to get your client out of here before I'm ordered to do something you *really* won't like. *Like right now.*" And, as Wil was helping Vinh up, Mia's face ghostlike in the doorway before vanishing again, "Us next time for sure, though. Be a shame not to."

37

THEY DROVE IN SILENCE, ash blowing off the Bonneville's hood and windshield, blue to the west reminding Wil what color the sky actually was. He accelerated around a backhoe trailing a reflector triangle, down into Montecito Village and through it.

"You okay?" he asked Vinh Tien, who'd straightened in the seat beside him and was staring out the window.

Vinh kept his eyes fixed ahead. Finally he said without inflection, "That the system for dealing with his kind is flawed is not your fault."

"I'm not sure the fault is with the law, Mr. Tien."

His eyes shifted to Wil. "You saw her as I did? The way she looked?"

Wil said, "Which might prove a number of things. One, that she drank or otherwise fortified herself knowing Luc was going to let you in. Two, in defying you, she wanted to prove something to him."

Vinh snorted. "My daughter does not otherwise fortify herself. And defy me for what purpose?"

"So you'd go away. So she could go back to work. Just that simple." At the four-way before the Bird Refuge, Wil let a car pass, took his turn to go. Up ahead, the lagoon shone like wet slate in the umber light. To Vinh's silence, he added, "Mia knows computers the way Jimmy did. She also happens to be the only one of us who can get that close."

Vinh thought about that. "Which puts her in the same danger as my son, you're telling me."

"Not necessarily. Despite what you've told me, I'm inclined to believe your brother about Jimmy."

"I do not believe I'm hearing this."

Wil said, "The old rule about fouling your own nest: If it went bad between them, all Luc had to do was turn him out. Given your history, he'd have known how you'd react. Why inflame matters?"

"You're suggesting my brother had too much to lose to jeopardize it on my son."

"No offense, and not that I like it that Mia is out there. But in danger? I doubt it. That would bring more heat than even Luc could stand." Trying to at least sound encouraging.

They were past the lagoon and the zoo now, into town homes and the start of the hotels. Vinh Tien stared at the line of palms, tall thin soldiers. "How much is he paying you?" he said at length.

"Excuse me?"

"The American standard of value, and you can stop the pretense. Obviously my brother has bettered my offer." The man's tone expressing lifetimes more: advantage Luc, always advantage Luc.

What to say and how to say it? "I understand your anger, Mr. Tien. But you're mistaken."

"I think not. Stop the car."

"Look," Wil said. "If you'll just—"

"Now."

Wil pulled over as far as possible and still drew horns, dirty looks from the bike-laners.

"I am to blame for this," Vinh Tien said, getting out stiffly. "I had no right expecting an outsider to solve my problems. If my adopted country does not understand them, why should you?" He shut the door, his face a mask through the open side window. "Is this clear?"

"I think so," Wil said. "You're firing me."

"It was foolish on my part. That is apparent now."

"And there's nothing I can say that will make a difference..."

Vinh shook it off. "Send me a bill and I will pay it," he said. "But this threat to my family is mine and mine alone."

"I see," Wil said. "And Mia?"

"Good-bye, Mr. Hardesty."

38

L EAVING VINH TIEN ON FOOT, glances back until he'd disappeared from view, Wil risked appearing on a federal wiretap by calling the number Vinh had for Luc. None of his messages to Mia was returned. He called Lisa's work and asked the receptionist when her partner, Bev, would be back from lunch. Returning around three, he heard—with a client. One-thirty now.

He decided to take a chance the meet was at a restaurant where he knew they had a trade deal, tax prep for food, and went there. Scanning, he saw her with a woman who listened closely as Bev made a point. Wil ordered club soda and watched fire coverage in the bar, suppression units retreating as orange-red flames jumped Paradise Road, the temperature not helping. He saw the two women rise and shake hands. As Bev followed the client out the door, he called her name.

"Wil?" All stop: brown hair cut short, large-frame bifocals softening the familiar oval face. Pearl-drop earrings, navy skirt over navy pumps.

"I thought that was you," he said. "You on your way somewhere?"

"Just heading back."

"Late lunch myself. Can I buy you a drink—coffee or something?"

She hesitated, shrugged, waved to the client, who smiled knowingly before walking on. Wil had seated her at his table, ordered for them, when she said, "This isn't a coincidence is it?"

"Suspicious mind. What makes you say that?"

"I know what you do, remember? It does not embrace coincidence."

"Not that well, evidently," he said.

"You were waiting for me." A statement, not a question.

"What can I say?" After their coffees had come and the waiter had left. "I was, actually."

"Lust in your heart, a cheap motel." *Sotto voce*, for his benefit.

"A cheap motel in this town?"

Bev took a sip and made a face. "Okay, end of bullshit. Why *are* we here?"

"Lisa," Wil admitted, stirring half-and-half into his.

"Behind her back..."

"Where sometimes friends do their best work. Or are forced to."

"That remains to be seen, doesn't it?"

"Look, I know she's pregnant," Wil said, after a pause, "Brandon, all that. I just want to know if there's more at stake, because that's the sense I'm getting."

"Getting from her..."

"That's right, getting from her."

"And now her ex wants me to share things with him she maybe doesn't want shared. I don't believe it."

"She's alone," he said. "I'm worried about her."

Bev stirred sweetener into her coffee. "Believe me, alone without Brandon is the best news any of us has had in a while. Lisa's just behind the curve." Sipping and finding it more acceptable. "Love will do that to you."

"She loves this guy?" *As if you had some right to it.*

"Did I say that? It's just that anybody's better than nobody sometimes. And then you wake up."

He let it go.

"All right, look," Bev said. "I don't know why but I'm going to write something in my planner. Then I'm going to the ladies room to catch up on some reading. You never saw it, and you can leave the planner with Charlie behind the bar. Under the circumstances it's the best I can do."

Wil touched her hand. "Thanks, Bev. Any time I can—"

"Maybe you'd better wait to decide."

He sat there as she opened the planner but made no move to write in it. She said, "Who am I kidding? She'll know where it came from the minute she sees your face."

"*It,*" he said, hearing restaurant sounds yield to his pulse.

She drew a breath, let it out. "What I was able to pry out of her over a botched tax return and two boxes of Kleenex. They've done tests," she said. "It's a Down's baby."

Wil felt the room move, a grinding as the walls closed in. From far off, he heard Bev say, "She's been thinking of not having it. Her gynecologist's for it. So am I, if you want the truth. I mean, why make nature's screw-up into a life sentence for both? After all, adoption isn't exactly an option here. And aren't you glad you asked?"

39

ONE SHOT OF MAKER'S MARK: That's all it was going to be, he was sure, something to de-spike the post-Bev zig-zags. It was so apparent, the construct: prodigal Wil (*present and accounted for*); the bar with its rows of amber, clear, and green bottles (*looking at you, kid*); frost on the draft he had Charlie pour to chase it (*ready when you are*). *Here and now, fate decreed*: like the gongs in the Hue temple where Wil had stopped to pray for his lost friends...searching for meaning where there was none and could never be, things nonetheless coming together in the metallic resonance. That which now said *Welcome back*, to a counterpoint of *Nobody beats the house. What in hell were you thinking?*

Wil raised his head, the bourbon's heat conjuring images of the firefall at Yosemite when he was a boy camping out with his father. Anticipation, the long river of sparks, cheers erupting across the Valley as it tumbled down the sheer rock face and burned itself into memory. For the moment, all else fading into background.

"Get you another round?" Charlie asked. Fragrance of the limes he was slicing wafting across the bar.

"Thanks, but no thanks," Wil answered, the fire spreading through his nervous system like a sputtering fuse. "It's way too light in here for what I have in mind."

"You okay?"

"Never better, never worse."

"Just take it easy, all right?"

Wil nodded to him. "A day like today? Any way I can get it."

⊘

At the old haunts, it was as if he'd never left. Some bartenders even remembered him, the frenzied way he used to try to staunch the bleeding after Devin's flatline. Buck's on Haley for a pair of doubles; Milpas Street, then, one haunt shuttered but The Mecca still pouring; last stop, Al's Cove in Carpinteria. Black holes: empty beer bottles placed to mark the way back, each freeway exit bringing the night that much closer to their boozy interiors. Finally a fuck-all sprint along the curve of ocean, and home.

For a while, he sat on his deck kaleidoscoping images: black pajamas merging into dripping jungle, gunfire at river's edge and in the tunnel in front of his house, Lisa's moans giving birth. Sonny's gun in his face, Mia's eyeshadowed glare, spinning oil rigs and headlights.

Upwards, backwards, sideways, down.

Time in a mulcher.

Unable to just sit, Wil leashed a curious Matt and headed for the access tunnel, stumbling distance to the pointside restaurant where a black ex-con named Nelson he'd gotten to know tended bar weeknights. Leaving Matt outside where he could see in, lights shining down on the surge, broken waves boiling around the rocks, Wil leaned on the bar top and ordered a Sunrise, double on the Sauza.

Nelson shied as if he'd just inhaled methane fumes.

Stopped polishing the glass he was holding.

"Vitamin C?" Wil followed up with. "Good for what ails you?"

Nelson regarded him. "You're joshing me, right?"

"Look close. You see josh here?"

"The hell are you doing?" Nelson said with a peek at the dining room. "You don't touch that stuff."

"Guess I fooled you again."

"Smells like you been fooling people all day," Nelson low-keyed.

"So—you going to serve me, or what?" The few remaining diners casting glances in Wil's direction now.

Nelson said, "Not if you got wheels outside, I ain't."

"Wheels nothing. You saying I can't handle it?"

"Look, man," Nelson said, one more try for calm. "Do us both a favor and check the restroom mirror, see how you comin' across to people. Then check your breath. You still want one, I make it. Deal?"

"Here's a better one," Wil lurched at him. "How about I come back there and make it myself, fuck you very much."

"Hey now, don't be doin' that," Nelson said. "I mean it. *Hey!*"

But Wil already had one hand on the Sauza bottle, another on the glass he thought was empty. Slipping on the remains that slopped onto the floor and taking bottles down with him as he flailed for purchase; landing in a welter of glass, Kahlua, peppermint schnapps, peach brandy, and Creme de Menthe. Among the identifiable substances.

"*Shit,*" he said into the freeze.

"About says it all," Nelson threw in.

❷

What saved him from an irate assistant manager ready to have him arrested was his credit card—bar and bottle replacement, comp dinners for the remaining patrons, Nelson vouching that he was a local—and Matt, on whom the manager took pity. Walking back barefoot in the cold surf helped. But the horizon still was tilted and the stars looked like time-lapse photography, that smeared pinwheel effect every time he looked up. What sense still clung to him also insisted that he was being followed. Not followed á lá Maccafee and Lorenz, he told himself, more like eyes—something out of place among the revetment boulders, what moon there was painted over by the smoke, everything in deep shadow.

"Come out, come out, whoever you are," he called at one point, cracking up at his own cleverness. "Get it while it's hot."

Wave-rush over the ringing in his ears.

Star-filter-effect lights on the houses clinging to Mussel Shoals.

Truck-rumble up on the highway.

"*Ha!* Didn't think so." Kicking sand in the direction of whatever-whomever without falling down, still managing to get some in his mouth. Spitting out, "My dog's no lightweight either. Are you, Matty?"

But after Matt's inactivity and with the way his master smelled, the Aussie was in full-dash mode: circling, flushing night birds, fetching drift-wood to drop the stick no closer to Wil than about five feet. At which point Wil ceased caring:

Look where it got you.

Look where all of it got you.

They were at the access tunnel, then home, Matty into the dry food, Wil barely making the head before his stomach decided against driving to Lisa's and having it out with her, whatever that meant, that enough was fucking enough.

40

FROM HIS SPOT IN THE ROCKS, the man watched the dog fetch the stick, bring it back and drop it, Hardesty stumble toward the access tunnel. Giving them a moment, he put his eyes even with the roadway, watched man and dog emerge on the other side, lights come on in the small frame house with the good-sized deck and, after a bit, wink out.

He lit a cigarette, drew in smoke, thought about the frame house, its occupant likely passing or passed out. Easy enough to go in if it weren't for the dog. Interesting development, the dog: next time dog biscuits. And yet, his thing with Hardesty could wait; there was work to be done tonight. With a last drag on the cigarette, he punched in a number on his global phone.

"Ah," the voice said, hearing who it was. "We were beginning to wonder."

"In time, remember?" the man said. "It's not a place you simply walk into."

"You've seen it, then."

"I have, and it's Fort Zinderneuf."

"Ah, yes—*Beau Geste*. But you have a plan."

"I have a plan." Turning his collar against the damp rising in off the water.

"When?"

"That's for me to fathom and you to know when it's in effect. Soon enough, you may assume."

The voice waited, then, "As in tonight?"

"*Westside Story*," the man said, knowing it was a reach, but tossing it out in the name of banter. Inwardly pleased but not surprised when the voice came back with, "*Best Picture, 1961.* Anything else in your bag of tricks?"

"Just make sure the money is, that's all."

There was a cold chuckle, stones in a well. "And you, my friend, keep in mind who has been hired by whom."

The man said, "That wouldn't be a threat, now, would it?"

"My friend, any threat I make won't be open to question."

On principle, the man let a moment pass: *calm and control.* Then, "We'll be in touch."

"One way or another," the voice came back as a truck blew past, raising fine grit that stung the caller's eyes.

41

WIL WOKE TO DIRTY SUN STREAMING IN AROUND THE BLINDS, Matt's nose in his ear, his own stench fogging around him. With difficulty he made it to the bathroom, where he managed to get four aspirin down before tossing them, the next batch staying put until he could tamp them with a leftover English muffin. Coffee was a fumble, but he prevailed and got some down, then showered and dressed, wanting nothing more than a shot of sour mash with an egg in it. Anything to still the trembling gelatin his insides had become.

Plumber's Helper in a glass.

Dishes gone from grease to shine in half the time with Joy.

No more troublesome stains.

How easy it was to forget how genetically altered you felt the next day, how genuinely fucked. Not to mention empty of resolve, worth, and humanity. And yet it had never stopped him before, the days after Devin when every shot was supposed to be his last.

Life after flatline, the end of all pain.

Ten-thirty: He threw up again.

By two, after Alka-Seltzer and microwaved oatmeal, he was together enough to listen to phone messages, the first of which was from four forty-five the day before: Lisa saying, "Bev told me…" *Pause.* "If you'd like to just talk, not at me but *with* me, I'll be home tonight." *Pause, click.*

As much in the pauses as in her tone.

Wil tried returning it, but she was in meetings. All day, the receptionist made it a point to stress: audits. The next message—five o'clock—was from Vinh Tien asking for Wil's hours and expenses. Fish-market sounds in the background, Wil picturing the scene, the office from which he'd made the call. *Click.* A third was from John Pereira—seven p.m., John on his way home—telling him they'd received an incident grid and addendum regarding *Harmony* that he'd have his assistant fax over.

Lost in the shuffle, evidently; as yet, no fax in Wil's machine.

The final call was from Mia, approximately when he was bringing down Nelson's liqueur bottles and kicking sand at the shadows, her voice saying, "My uncle heard my dad fired you. He wants you to know he holds no grudges. For some reason you impressed him, because now he's interested in hiring you himself. Some people outside the gate, is how he explained it, whatever that means. He's entertaining guests during the day, so anytime after seven works." And, as if she were reading from notes: "Look...I'm sorry about this morning. But you see what I mean about my dad? Just out of control." Another pause, then, "I'm sorry. I have to go now."

At the same time Wil heard his fax machine activating in the other room, he heard feet on the stairs, saw Lorenz through the door panes.

Alone, from the look of it.

Outside, the afternoon light had turned an even duller shade, and he could see the buildup of ash where he'd hosed the deck off earlier. He opened the door.

"What happened to you?" she asked when she'd finished eyeing him. "Stick your head in a Vegematic?"

"Nicked myself shaving," he said.

"Your eyeballs, too, from the looks."

"Something on your mind, Lorenz?"

"Sharing, remember? You mind if I come in?"

Wil stepped back to let her enter, sniffing the coffee he'd brewed. Waiting until she'd poured some and was braced against the counter before telling her, "Vinh Tien fired me yesterday. End of story."

"Fired you how come?"

"He felt I was consorting with the wrong crowd. Any idea what he meant by it?"

She ignored the crack. "That what made you get boiled?"

"Did it ever occur to you to *not* stick your nose into other people's business?" Trying a little more coffee before backing off and waiting for the wave to pass.

"I happen to have eyes," she said. "Frankly, you look like something the tide washed in."

"Thanks for the update. Where's your partner?"

"Catching up on things." Reaching down to pet Matt, who'd taken up residence beside her and was looking up expectantly. "So what now?"

"You mean careerwise? Where do I begin? Oh yes: Luc wants to hire me for something that might relate to you. Like maybe you've been made?"

She spent a moment regarding him to see if he was serious. Then, "How about canning the crap, huh? If it's true, that's something that could get us dead."

"Touchy," Wil said. "'Some people outside the gate' is the way it was phrased, and for some odd reason I thought of you. I'll know tonight."

She took a breath, nodded. "All right. Call us when you do, it doesn't matter how late. And Hardesty?..."

"Yeah."

"What did send you off the tracks? And don't say getting fired."

"That, Agent Lorenz, is none of your business."

"Right...whatever."

Swallowing the last of her coffee, she rinsed the mug, set it in the drainer, headed for the door. "Take care of yourself," she said, opening it and looking back at him.

"What, you're cutting me loose, too? How can two days bring such favor?"

Her eyes stayed put. "And sober up while you're at it. Self-pity's a broken crutch."

From somewhere inside his spinning center came, *Okay, you want it, you got it*: He said, "My ex-wife decided that being alone and knocked up by Shoeless Joe Jackson the Body Shop King, maybe aborting it because it's Down's, is preferable to asking for help. And for the record, some people don't know when to quit."

Hesitation, then, "Help from you, that would be?"

"Bingo," he said. "The lady by the door."

"To do what, exactly?"

Wil felt the room start in the opposite direction.

"Let me guess," she said. "You felt betrayed because you love her and thought she still might love you, much as you can't be together. Your son or your work or something."

"Spare me the psych ops, Lorenz, I'm not in the mood," he said, pissed he'd risen to her bait. "Whatever I'm feeling, I'll handle it."

"Sure you will. Funny thing, my dad was like that. He never let anybody in either. It got him killed, and for what—some code of fucking male silence. Try and understand, he'd tell me: You make your way and certain things come with the territory. Give me a break."

"Yeah, well, I'm not real clear on a lot of things lately."

Without looking at him, she said, "Mac doesn't buy it, but I think Jimmy was approached by somebody other than us. Somebody who wanted in on Luc's action. That's assuming you still give a damn."

"I might," he said. "Any idea who?"

"Somebody up the food chain would be the guess." A glance his way. "And you didn't get that from me."

Wil nodded. "Thanks, Lorenz."

"Just watch it tonight, Batman. The last thing I want is you on my tab." Feet on the stairs giving way to diminishing car sounds.

Pereira's fax amounted to a grid of the search area and tighter coordinates of where the dragger had hung up on *Harmony*, plus sheets of notes. But instead of deciphering them, Wil opted to crash until Lisa got off work, to gird himself for *that* encounter. Setting the alarm for five, he drifted off to Lorenz saying, *Somebody other than us. Somebody who wanted in on Luc's action. Somebody...*

At six, showered again but still sweating, eyes awash in de-reddener, he was sitting on Lisa's steps with a six-pack of ginger ale when her Lexus pulled into the drive.

"Ground rules," she said, before even a hello, carrying a filecase and her briefcase into the house as he unlocked it with her key. "I talk, you listen. I ask for input, you talk. We clear on that?"

"It wasn't Bev's fault," Wil said. "It was mine."

"Strike one. No, it was mine for confiding in her, mine for ending up this way. Anything else before I start?"

"You want one of these?" Handing her a Vernor's.

"Thank you." She took the rest into the kitchen, came back with two glasses and ice, kicked off her shoes. "I never meant to get you involved, you know that. It's just that I had to tell someone. I should have known it would get back."

"It wasn't like that," he said. "I waited for Bev. I pressured her."

"There'd have been nothing to pressure *from* her if I hadn't blown it." Cream blouse and skirt under a celadon blazer she took off and set aside, pouring her ginger ale and downing some. Looking more closely at him before reaching out to touch his forehead.

"You're clammy. Are you all right?" Sealing her lips to inhale what remained of his breath freshener, eyes widening as it dawned. Saying, "Oh, no. You didn't go back. Not on top of everything else."

Wil fought the flush, knowing it was a losing battle: that it was wrong-headed to come here of all places so soon after a fall. Wishing he'd seen it before barreling in at flank speed, his specialty.

"I'm here about you, Leese," he tried to cover. "Some way I can be of help, if you'll let me." *To do what, exactly?* flashed: Lorenz's little skewer.

"You see why I didn't want you to know?" Her eyes starting to fill. "Damn, six years down the drain. I don't believe it."

"It caught me off guard, Leese. I blew off some steam. It's not like before. Come on, look at me."

"No, look at *us*," she managed before the storm front closed in. "What the hell happened to us?"

42

IT WAS PAST EIGHT BY THE TIME WIL LEFT LISA'S AND HEADED EAST. Seeing Luc Tien, hearing his proposal, were the last things he felt like doing. What he felt like was Jack Daniels, an ocean's worth, tempered with a Titanic-sized iceberg and flushed down with San Miguel.

Bud, Big Mouth...kerosene, if that was it.

Open wide. Here it comes.

He passed a liquor store and almost pulled over, hands damp on the wheel. He tried the radio, snapped it off after everything reminded him of something else. He opened the window to cool his sweat, took deep breaths. Tapped out after going through the books and pamphlets on Down's syndrome at Lisa's, the ultrasounds and doctor's reports, he simply drove, trying to stay objective, dispassionate in light of the options. Hardly his nature.

At least she'd agreed to keep their dialog going.

Something, anyway.

So now what?

Divider bumps caught him drifting, and he jerked back into his lane, exited 101 toward Sand Painting House. Away from the city, the glow from the Valley fire was even more pronounced. The air was dense with it, driven by a sundowner gusting over and down the canyons, bending the tops of the eucalyptus. Two county fire trucks passed him, honking, and as Wil approached Luc's, he saw the first chilling flames—confirmed by the radio reports he'd tuned in again—flaring from the ridgetop and falling back.

Picturing Luc's guests getting a taste of local color they hadn't bargained for, he rounded the final bend to lit walls and gate, saguaro and ocotillo, the house. And something else: blackened chaparral.

Shit…

Smoke still rose from the surrounding burn; here and there a stump glowed red. As he got out of the car, an older-model Wagoneer with wood-grain siding pulled up and a woman about seventy with three collies in back let the window down part way.

"Doubt you'll find anybody inside," she said, the dogs jostling to get a nose out the window. "I watched the fire crews run 'em out, big gray gas-guzzlers plus a white something-or-other, a truck. That's my place back there."

The Yukons. "Any sign of a small red car?"

"Not that I recall."

"Can you tell me what happened?"

"Brush fire," she said. "Spark from over the hill must have started it. Smoke like you wouldn't believe."

"When?" Wil shouted into a gust.

"Couple of hours ago," she shouted back. "I'm surprised they let you in."

"Thanks."

"Don't mention it, I was here for the Coyote fire." Putting it in gear, the dogs still restless, torn whether to bark at him. "My daughter in Lompoc's got a spare bedroom. Do it up, I told her. What's to save, right? You *are* following me out…."

"Couple minutes, tops."

"Good luck, then. I don't want to read about you."

As she swept around the bend, Wil walked to the gate, found it open to about shoulder width: nobody around, no security people, three of the four garage bays open. On instinct, he retrieved the Mustang .380 from the Bonneville, slipped it into the small of his back. A Mercedes station wagon passed the gate honking, mom and dad in front, excited kid faces staring out the back. Off to friends in town, Wil guessed, people to share the evacuation with, everybody talking at once. After they'd driven on, he slipped through and up the drive, past the dramatically lit cacti, night sentinels with halting arms.

He checked the garage, found Mia's Honda in the fourth bay, its engine cold, still no sign of anyone. Buzzy throb from the night bombers running water to the ridge, no sound from the house or pool area.

He thought about that:

Everyone gone? *Not likely.*

Gate ajar? *Less so.*

Figuring anyone left would have made him from the monitors and intercepted him, Wil slipped a round into the Mustang, approached the front door and tried it. It was open but unbudging, obstructed beyond about an inch. Moving to a window where he could get an angle on it, he saw why. The houseman who'd brought them limeade was sitting up against it, blood where his neck had been.

Wil perimetered the house, checked the pool area.

The filter still hummed; refracted blue light spangled off the low walls. Smoke lazed from the barbecue pit to mingle with brush fire and chlorine smells. And still there was no one. Up on the ridge, the flames snapped to with greater urgency, headlights converging through the haze being blown from that direction.

At cop readiness, he eased through the glass doors and into the sitting area where he'd first talked to Luc; up and past the dining room and den with the deep-set window through which he'd glimpsed Mia watching him; past the water dolls and old-looking framed weavings, spotlit niches, thin metal aspen leaves wired to faux branches.

The houseman was between a trio of urns where the entryway took a bend to the right and the front door. Wil checked the wound to his throat, checked that the man was indeed dead, listened for sounds.

Nothing at first, his own breathing.

Television, then...maybe a radio.

Moving down the wing, he sensed it came from a smaller room off a larger den with partly shut doors, hall light revealing a table and matching chairs inside: a meeting room. He picked the den because of the flicker and the sounds, TV and computer setup visible from the door.

On the TV screen, a talking head was expounding on tech-sector stocks, while the computer monitor listed telecom firms in order of their valuation—comparison data for the evaluator, Robb, who sat hunched in the chair facing it. Where Robb's neck met his shoulders, the handle of what appeared to be a boning knife stuck out.

Wil tightened his grip on the Mustang and kept going. Bedrooms showed signs of quick departure, a porno channel played silently in a wall unit. The master suite was in similar disarray, bath and spa lined with what looked to be adult toys, a computer setup in a windowless office adjacent to the suite. Against the wall inside the office were two work stations, one lit, its monitor on screen-saver, both stations linked to the computer tower between them.

Later, he told himself.

Luc and Mia.

The conference room.

Back and listening outside it, hearing nothing, he pushed open the doors, brought the track lights up to shining rosewood tabletop, glasses and spent bottles, pencils and pens, coasters and ashtrays that spoke of a meeting interrupted and hurriedly left. But what caught his attention was beyond the cluttered surface.

The far wall, a darkened floor-to-near-ceiling aquarium.

Water coursed quietly through its pump and filtration system, the room's own white noise. From where he stood, Wil could just make out rock ledges, kelp, water plants, temples, bridges. And something else he didn't quite believe until he located the tank's slider light and brought it up, the aquarium glowing to pinkish life.

For a moment he just stood there.

Staring...

Luc Tien floated upright between the kelp and a ledge, a stunned expression on his face. As he did, hair rising toward an intake jet and the red, green, and indigo dragon on his upper chest seeming to rage at them, the tank's larger residents tore at his entrails while smaller fish darted in to feast on the shreds. The entrails they so fancied had been released by the slash starting at Luc's groin and ending at his sternum. Indeed, as Wil tore his eyes away, forced his attention around the room, he saw one whole corner of it was a red-black lake.

Retreating to the dolls' fountain, where he took deep breaths, Wil fought the urge to cop a bottle of Luc's whiskey and down it, let other people deal with this fucking house of horrors. Instead, he went back to the main computer room. He was moving through a maze of access codes and getting nowhere when he heard it: a single faint bump, as much vibration as sound.

Silence, then.

Wil snapped off the Mustang's safety, turned off the room lights and, to monitor glow, eased over to the louvered closet doors. Listened, but heard nothing. Two minutes by his sweep hand, ready to give it up and move on, he picked up from inside a nearly inaudible release of breath.

Ten seconds...thirty.

Turning on the closet light, he pulled back the left-hand door and dropped into a shooter's crouch, scanned side-to-side, up-down...down: there among the silk shirts, jackets, shoes, and monogrammed robes, far in the back.

He'd nearly missed her.

Wild-eyed and in the black blouse from earlier, breathing in gasps, knees under her and ready to spring, Mia Tien aimed a wicked-looking shortsword at the death she knew had come for her.

43

FRANK LIN CHAIN-SMOKED as an army of detectives, crime-scene and coroner techs, Sheriff's brass and deputies came and went. Media vans—even one that had made the five-and-a-half-hour drive from San Francisco—hunkered beyond the walls for the occasional crumb of information from the officer standing by the gatehouse and conversing with the medical examiner. Generators pulsed, cast pools of thin light that bled into one another.

"What a goddamn mess," Lin said to the man beside him.

Wil didn't reply. Up the ridge it looked as if the firefighters, with the aid of the dying sundowner and the water bombers, had driven back the flames. Just after three in the morning, stars shone in the unsmoked quadrants of sky, others more dully through the veil. The air felt markedly cooler with the hot wind's retreat.

"Yanez wants a briefing at nine," Lin told him. "I promised him you'd be there."

"His master's voice," Wil said, not caring how it sounded after three hours of waiting until the homicide detectives were ready to question him, two-and-a-half more until they'd finished, another hour standing by until Lin intercepted him on his way out.

Lin exhaled. "Not quite. Yanez wanted me to run you in."

Not bothering to ask how Yanez thought he'd make that stick, Wil just said, "Sorry, Frank."

"You're entitled. You also look like shit, anybody tell you that?"

"Take a number. What are you going to do with her?"

"The Tien girl? Hang onto her till it's determined," Lin said. "Other than that the sword came from a drawer and she'd been in the shower and heard nothing, she hasn't exactly peeled back the curtain."

Wil pictured her terror as he'd talked her out of Luc's closet, pictured her sitting slumped and silent in her smeared makeup, the shortsword still in her lap, eyes lost in her cigarette smoke as he phoned it in. "She clarify what she was doing for Luc?" he asked.

"Don't ask me questions you know I can't answer."

"Try careers for five hundred, hostessing and light computer work. Entries most likely, a foot in the door. She heard noises and hid. It saved her life. She's telling you what she knows."

"Thanks for that. I'll be sure to pass it on."

"You know what I mean, Frank."

Lin flicked ash, drew on his cigarette. "And whoever did this just let her alone, didn't even search for her with her car still in the garage. That tell you anything?"

Foil and parry. "Beyond whoever did it set the brush fire as a distraction?"

"Beyond that, yes," Lin came back.

Wil said, "If you're trying to get me to say whoever it was knew she was in there and gave her a pass, that's a crock. Far more like they didn't know or figured she'd gone with the rest or got interrupted."

"But it does come to mind, you'll admit."

Shifting on feet past complaint, Wil said, "When they find out they missed her, she's in deep shit—no matter how much you guys deny she saw anything. Which I assume you will."

"Rudy's decision. Ask him tomorrow."

"You telling me he might not?"

"I'm not saying, period," Lin said, eyeing an activity over Wil's shoulder. "I work for him, remember? The man speaks for himself."

"That's encouraging."

Lin dropped his gaze to Wil. "Excuse me, but I was under the impression you were out of it. Is there something more I should know? Like before I release you."

"You have my statement, Frank."

"I also know you," he said. "What I don't have on it is your gut."

Wil let his eyes scan the ridge, the helicopter traversing it: throp that sent him back to a hot LZ, blinding dust, the smell of his own blood as a medic sweated to stanch it. Thinking out loud, he said, "A team, maybe military or military trained. The houseman died when he answered the door. Robb next, fast, then Luc slow, whoever it was guessing right or sure that Luc wouldn't leave his infrastructure."

Lin eyed him, exhaled smoke.

"You have to do that?" Wil asked. "Why don't you just breathe in?"

"Right. The world's on fire and it's my stogie bothering you."

Wil saw Mia's eyes again. "Anyway, it explains some things."

Lin drew in, turned to exhale. "So could one very strong, very determined individual. Ex-military, perhaps, but good with a knife."

"It might."

"What do you mean *might*?"

Not liking where this was headed, too close to a certain retro conversation on the deck of his house, Wil asked if there'd been any sign of the vehicles the woman in the Wagoneer had spotted leaving.

Lin said, "Her name is Lorraine Argabrite—widow, age seventy-three, the house west of the open area. I've got a man on his way to the daughter's place in Lompoc, APBs out on the Yukons. The white truck's probably the pickup you saw."

"Which says they had a contingency plan."

"Or they were in on it," Lin finished. "Or they may not have heard what happened and they'll come waltzing back in the morning. Pick one."

"With the gate left like that? I wonder," Wil said.

"Wonders never cease, do they?" More smoke.

They watched a coroner's team wheel out a body bag—Robb, from its girth—then open and slam the ambulance doors on it. Down the drive and out the gate to the strobe of flash units.

Wil said, "Have you notified the Tiens yet?"

"In due course. It won't make local TV till tomorrow."

"I'm glad to know you're on top of it." Breeze adding chill to his fatigue. "And where *could* they see her if they just happened to find out tonight?"

Lin looked at him. "That is a complication Lieutenant Yanez and I would not necessarily welcome."

"So noted," Wil said. "Am I free to go now?"

"Don't mess with Yanez, Wil, it's not smart."

"Or you—is that what I'm hearing, Frank?"

Lin stubbed out his smoke. "This client you're so concerned about fired you, right? His daughter says you've been a pain in the ass from day one. Yanez thinks PIs rank with flesh-eating bacteria. Does any of that tell you anything?"

"Yeah," Wil said starting toward the gate, the hunkered media, his car across the road. "There's one born every minute."

❂

Car windows down and a gutted Luc Tien still swimming in his vision, Wil drove home, showered, and drank a half pot of Viennese. Thermosing the rest, he set out for the Tien's, the eastern sky beginning to lighten behind him.

Vinh answered the door, scanned his face, ushered Wil inside. Alert now, as though a courier from some distant front had just awakened him regarding a battle's progress. No preliminaries, Wil's firing or what had led to it; only chairs at the kitchen table, the single question, "Where is our daughter?"

"Mia is safe," Wil said, watching the facial lines soften slightly. From the hall, he heard a sound, and Li Tien joined them, blue robe with a heron in the pattern. Black hair streaked with gray framing anxious eyes, a face that looked as if it hadn't slept in days, senses anticipating a car in the drive, a key in the lock.

As she poured water into a kettle, put black tea into a blue-glazed pot, Wil went through it for them. Occasionally the two exchanged glances, and at one point as Wil was describing the aquarium room, Li put her hand on her husband's. Beyond a long breath, a shake of the head, Vinh was a soldier processing casualties and counterthrusts.

"Have you eaten?" he asked when Wil had finished.

"No," Wil said.

"Li will make you something while I ready myself."

The kettle screamed and Li tended to it; Wil caught the stove clock: seven-ten. "I'm due at the Sheriff's at nine," he said as she put toast on, got out butter and cherry preserves. "I doubt they'll release Mia until later." *If then*, he wanted to say, but held off, at this point sure of nothing.

"They can do that?" Vinh asked.

"Where it's justified."

"She is a suspect to them?"

"She may know things they have to find out."

He nodded. "Then that is where I will be." He muttered something in Vietnamese that Wil didn't catch, Li sighing and nodding. Then, "After what passed between us yesterday, you honor us by coming here. I will not forget that."

"They'll be sending someone to talk to you," Wil said. "Your relationship with Luc in greater detail, where you were yesterday evening, why Mia left home—things of that nature. Just so you know."

For a moment, Vinh Tien's sight turned inward, no telling what he saw from his expression. Then he turned and left the room.

44

T HEY REACHED THE SHERIFF'S BUILDING at twenty to the hour, Wil's eyes rusted traps ready to spring shut. As Frank Lin ushered him into his office, he glanced beyond Wil to where Vinh Tien sat, hands in his lap and looking straight ahead, as if trying to stare a beast back into its cage.

"You declined to take my advice, I see," Lin said from across a metal desk, the shadows under his eyes matching Wil's. Outside a smallish window Wil could see the hills rising toward the mountains still wreathed in burn haze, a closed Highway 154 lost in brown, a seagull soaring toward the dump that lay a canyon over.

"No idea what came over me," he said, stifling a yawn.

Lin said, "At least you're predictable. And it's your turn in the bunker."

The door to Rudy Yanez's office was open. Entering behind Lin, Wil saw a wood desk with facing chairs; photos of horse-and-rider events, Rudy front and center; Fiesta shots, Rudy's Arabian mount and silver-trimmed pommel; Rudy receiving an award; a family portrait—a plumpish Latina and three adolescent boys in descending stages of baby fat. On the desk was a miniature-saddle pen set, lariat name plaque, copper ashtray, and, as if just out of its box, a computer terminal.

No Lieutenant Rudolfo Yanez.

That is, until twelve minutes after.

As he entered, Wil made him for mid-fifties: still-black hair, lines that contributed rather than detracted, eyes that spoke of prizes not lost to distractions. In his nonfolder hand he held a mug, wide at the bottom and rimmed with gold. He toed the door shut, let Frank Lin bring him up to date on some details—the Argabrite woman's statement, two of the three Yukons found stripped and printless in L.A.—while his eyes appraised Wil.

"So," he said when Lin finished. "Are you what you're cracked up to be?"

Wil returned the stare. "Which of us is, Lieutenant?"

"That would be me." Thumbing through Wil's statement from the folder. "And you happened to be out there why?"

Rubbing his eyes, Wil took a breath and went through it yet again— the invitation to come after seven because of guests Luc was expecting, Wil's delay in getting there, all of it.

Yanez let a moment pass in thought. "You have any idea who the guests were?"

"None."

"Try again," Yanez said. "Harder this time."

"Okay. None at all."

The cop locked and unlocked his fingers. "You honest-to-God expect me to believe that his guests weren't at least a part of the reason he asked you there? That you didn't suspect as much?"

"You have my statement, Lieutenant. Believing it is up to you."

"So it is," Yanez said. "And speaking of the deceased wanting you to work for him, do you always change sides that readily?"

"Seldom, and usually not then," Wil said.

"I see. You were just curious."

"I was hoping to learn what happened to Jimmy Tien. I still am."

Yanez clipped off a hangnail, blew it out of the clippers. "On your own dime, of course."

"Your own dime is what it comes down to sometimes."

"Luc being so forthcoming on your previous visits and all."

"Tell me, Lieutenant. Did you stick behind that desk by giving up when it got tight?"

Yanez's expression changed not at all. "Mr. Hardesty, you'd be well served to understand something here. I ask, you answer—get it? Different topic, now: Why the holdup at your ex-wife's?"

"That would be a personal matter." Aware of Frank pinning him with a look, of him avoiding it. "Nothing to do with this."

Yanez tugged an earlobe. "And your relationship with the brother?"

Resigned to it, Wil set up the Vinh Tien hire, ending as he had so many times last night with his being fired.

The dark eyes were unblinking "Yet you ignored Detective Lin's request and actually brought Mr. Tien here with you."

"Save gas, save a tree," Wil said. "However it goes."

"I hate clever, Mr. Hardesty. Clever boys wish they weren't around me."

"It was a long night, Lieutenant. And I'm far from clever."

Yanez cracked a knuckle, drummed the folder. "The fight between the brothers, who pulled the trigger on it?"

"Luc provoked his brother verbally. Vinh lost it."

"First his son, then his daughter, then his temper."

"Something like that."

Yanez rechecked a sheet. "And the bodyguard, the one with the blade in his neck—he took Vinh out after Vinh dropped his brother?"

"Different guard. Robb took the knife. Sonny's the one who took Vinh out."

"I see," he said. "And then Vinh fired you?"

"On our trip back to town, yes."

"Kind of abrupt, in light of things, wouldn't you say?" Sipping from the gold-rimmed mug.

"All in a day's work, Lieutenant."

"But it made you angry, didn't it?" Yanez baited him. "Mad enough to get wasted."

Wil drew a breath, let it out slow. "I'll say it again. That was for personal reasons."

"Well, don't hesitate on my account."

"It's why they're called personal, Lieutenant."

Yanez turned to the window, gazed out it, swiveled around. "Try this scenario," he said. "You lost your job and blamed it on Luc. You lost your head when he wouldn't give you the time of day. So you torched the field and squared it, except for the girl because you figured she'd taken off with the others." He smiled, *mano á mano* in confidence. "A guy like yourself, vigilante type—come on, I can smell it on you. You went there for payback, eyeball to eyeball. None of that long-range shit for a stud like you."

"Looks like it's been a long day here, too."

"They're all long here. That's because of clever boys like you."

Thinking of Maccafee's similar appraisal, second thoughts as to why he hadn't given up Lorenz and the big agent—mainly his suspicion that Lorenz knew more about Jimmy and not wanting to cut that off—Wil shook his head. "And I can't believe you see this as a productive use of your time."

Yanez was about to fire back when he turned toward a knock, a head poking in. Wil recognizing one of the homicide detectives from last night. The detective held up a file, crossed the room and handed it over; when he'd left, Yanez studied the contents, handed them to Frank Lin, who read them, glanced at Wil, then at the photo wall.

Yanez ran a forefinger along his lip and smiled. "You mention a good use of my time, Mr. Hardesty, how's this? While we were talking, the detectives who took your statement were serving warrants, both at your client's home and place of business. Care to know what they found?"

Feeling the elevator drop, that bottomless lurch, Wil said nothing.

Yanez said, "Try a set of knives that match the one found in Robb Huong's neck, one knife missing from the set. Then a very intriguing box of photos and memorabilia linking your man to a military not our own. Unfortunately for those of us on the other side, one noted for its stealth and cunning."

Enjoying it, Wil could see as he went on.

"Add to that both his kids falling prey to the brother, a hatred as old as Cain, a guy who guts fish all day," the points ticked off on his fingers. "And what do we have?"

Free fall, bottom of the shaft.

"Tell me," Yanez added with a note of triumph, "what does it say on your business cards? Will work for blinders? Looks like Detective Lin had it right about that independent streak of yours, you going there before we did." Regarding Lin and nodding, back at Wil, then shoving out his chair. "Follow me, please."

With a glance at Frank, who fell in behind, Wil trailed Yanez to the lobby, Vinh Tien searching the faces as they entered. Settling on Wil's as Yanez stood him up and read him his rights for the murders of Luc Van Tien, Robert Cao Huong, and the houseman, Duy Tan, no middle name.

As Lin cuffed him and a deputy captured it on tape, Vinh Tien's eyes never left Wil's. As though thirty years had fallen away and he was steeling himself for interrogation by focusing on the Judas goat who'd led him to it.

Then Vinh Tien was gone.

Yanez made a move for the doorway; once there he turned and said, "Mr. Hardesty, I'd thank you for not having to run your client to ground, but as you say it's all in a day's work." Smug turning to glitter in the obsidian eyes. "And here I'd only begun to dislike you."

Wil was taking breaths against the Bonneville when Frank Lin came out of the building and scanned the lot. Spotting Wil, he walked over.

"Fucking fire," he said, tracking the ridgeline haze.

Wil ignored him.

Lin said, "I didn't know Yanez was going to do that."

Wil said nothing.

"Did you hear what I—"

"I'm tired," Wil said. "Sell it to somebody who's buying."

"Have it your way. Just don't say you weren't warned."

Wil rubbed the base of his neck. "No way was Vinh Tien heading for the hills or anyplace else. A little matter of his daughter, remember?"

"You can assure us of that..."

"A knife from his gutting rack, a box of incriminating shit when he knew they'd be coming? That sound like stealth and cunning to you?"

"Motive, capability, opportunity," Lin ticked off. "Add it up and what's looking at you?"

"What's looking at me is bullshit."

"Like it or not, it's what's there."

"So's a lot of smoke," Wil said.

"Well, damn," Lin fired back. "Why didn't you just say so and blow it all out?"

"Frank, I saw the man's face when I told him his brother was dead. It was like the life was going out of it."

"The brother he held so dear. Who knew?"

"Love and hate and families, what they're convinced they want until they get it," Wil said. "Hell, I don't have to tell you that."

Lin rested his arm on the Bonneville's roof. Rubbing a spot on the chrome, he said, "You're also hung over and running on empty. And I didn't come out here for this. I came about Lisa. What you said about her in there."

"How do I know what I said. Running on empty, remember?"

"Don't be an ass. Is she all right?"

Wil looked at him through eyes that sought a thousand yards. "Nothing a break or two wouldn't help. On either side of a decision she's having to make."

"Which would be?"

"Sorry," he answered. "Call her yourself."

"How about between friends?"

"Interesting word choice," Wil said. "Now one for you: Is Rudy planning on letting it out about the VC connection?"

Lin eased away from the car. "Three guesses, if you don't know him from in there. And for us, maybe when it's over, huh?"

"They'll tear him up, Frank, you know that. Rudy knows that."

"So long, Wil." Backing up now. "Have a nap, take a load off. Go surfing or something."

"Whatever makes Rudy's case, is that it?" Fighting not to shout.

"He's a cop, I'm a cop," Lin said, turning away. "If that's a big surprise to you, what's been the point?"

45

GLASS SHATTERED IN HIS EAR, or something like it. Wil picked up the phone in a fog, checked his watch through blur: three-twenty…afternoon…four hours asleep. *Shit.*

"Yeah?" he managed.

"It's Frank, two things: One, I'm sorry about this morning, what I was trying to tell you earlier. Two, we're releasing the girl at four, and I thought you might want to be around."

Yawning, eyes fighting the light, Wil said, "What about her car?"

"Techs aren't finished with it yet. Tomorrow or the next day."

"All right, Frank. Thanks."

"You're welcome." A pause, as though deciding, then, "Rudy had his press conference earlier, he and the ADA. You catch any of it?"

Wil squinted open. "What do you think?"

"Websites and radio, TV newsbreaks before their extended coverage. The talk shows are already picking it up." Lin coughed, cleared his throat. "As expected, no free passes for the black-pajama set."

Swell: Plan B, if he had one. "What about Mia?"

"No mention," Lin said. "For now."

Wil swung his feet onto the floor. Holding the portable to his ear, he walked to the front room and peered through the blinds. On the four-lane, a truck airhorned a car whipping around it. Afternoon sun lit the breakers, foam sliding up the beach.

"I appreciate it, Frank," he said. "I mean, letting me know."

"Yeah, I can hear it in your voice."

"In the meantime, how is she?"

There was a pause. "Hard to tell if it's deferred shock or her usual effusive mode around us. Docs cleared her release and Rudy got what he could from her, which wasn't much."

Wil said, "No point clouding the issue with facts, right?"

"No fucking comment."

"Frank, she doesn't *know* much."

"So you keep saying." He hung up.

Wil put on jeans and a shirt he left untucked, then drove the fourteen miles back to the Sheriff's, most of the way behind a Winnebago with stickers on it reading SOMETIMES I WAKE UP GRUMPY. OTHER TIMES I LET HIM SLEEP and WHEN EVERYTHING'S COMING YOUR WAY, YOU'RE IN THE WRONG LANE and, to the right of that, WHEN THE CHIPS ARE DOWN, THE BUFFALO IS EMPTY. Picturing the occupants before timing a break around a white-haired couple in matching ball caps, the man's hands gripping the wheel bus-driver style.

On the road again.

Wil envied them.

He was waiting in the Bonneville, sipping the coffee he'd stopped for, when he saw Mia leave the building. Getting out with Matt, he smiled, raised a hand, met her at the steps.

She was in the same outfit she'd put on at Luc's: white jeans under the black blouse, carbon pullover across her shoulders. Blinking in the light, she looked tired but hanging in, shaking her head when Matt went to her, his hindquarters going nonstop as she dropped to one knee and held him.

"We came to take you home," Wil said.

She rose and went to him. "You know about my dad?"

"Yes, and I'm sorry." Taking her in because she looked as if she needed it.

"It's like being in a nightmare, only you're awake," she said into his chest.

"I know…"

Pulling away, she said, "They called a cab for me. My mom doesn't drive."

"I know that, too. Matt asked me to tell you he brought a Peet's with whipped cream and cinnamon. That and a dog bone."

It brought a smile, or part of one.

He said, "Follow your nose and I'll tell them to lose the cab."

Wil did; then he was in the car and they were heading west at the base of sere foothills, the smudge of brown reduced from yesterday but still casting a tint. "Radio said they knocked the fire back," he said to her quiet. "They're not out of it yet, but a few more days without wind—"

"He told me about arresting my father," she said. "What's-his-name who sat in while they talked to me."

"Lieutenant Yanez."

She nodded, looked vacant.

"Mia, is there anything you remember that might help your dad?"

Headshake. "No, nothing I didn't tell them last night. That I was showering on my break and heard things that must have been my uncle." Adding, "Which was when I hid."

"Anything while you were in the closet?" he asked. "Footsteps?"

"No, but the carpet's thick and I wasn't about to look."

"What about computer keys?"

"You kidding?" she said. "That room's designed to muffle sounds. And my heart was going so loud I thought the closet was coming apart."

"Okay. Keep trying. Maybe something will come."

"Just what I need," she said.

A block went by in silence, then, "Even though I didn't see who did it, it wasn't my father, do you understand that? He couldn't have done what was done. Not to his brother."

Wil eased past a van full of blue soccer jerseys making faces out the window. He said, "But that was what you were afraid of, wasn't it? Him boiling over before you could find out what happened to Jimmy. That's why you made the break…thinking he couldn't do anything to stop you if you were inside the compound."

At first she said nothing. Then, "Can you drive faster, please? I can't imagine what it's been like for my mom."

"Look, Mia, I know I asked you before. But was there anything in the computer that might help with either Jimmy or your dad? Things that Luc was up to?"

"Nothing from the entries I made. They were just numbers."

"Okay."

"Meaning think about it, I know."

They passed flower beds, hedges, and liquidambar trees, split-level homes, an empty school yard with basketball courts. A woman in a straw hat walking a baby carriage and two German shepherds that Matt took an interest in.

"I don't care what he was," Mia said as their turn approached. "Nobody deserves to die like that."

Wil turned on the blinker.

"I'm not safe, am I?" she said, as much to no one as him; hands around the coffee in her lap and staring straight ahead. "Because I was there."

"It's unlikely," he lied. "As long as it doesn't come out that you were."

Dark eyes flicked over to him. "Will it?"

"Not if I can help it," he said, thinking *son-of-a-bitch Yanez*.

46

B Y THE TIME WIL PULLED INTO HIS DRIVE, the mob of waiting TV people had their lights hot, crews ready to roll tape. Among them he
recognized a familiar face: Gail Velarde, the reporter he'd opened
up to in the magazine article Vinh had cross-referenced. In addition to
Velarde and her cameraman, Wil saw vans from the other Central Coast
stations, more from L.A. and San Francisco, a radio pool, several newspapers.

Cain and Abel obviously was a big issue, the element of revenge. Even
bigger, Wil thought, bracing himself, was the Vietnamese angle: thawing
trade relations, culture and politics, money.

Further distilled: *money*.

Fortunately, he'd thought to leave Matt with Mia and the lost-looking
Li, to whom his heart truly went out, Matt lending comfort and distraction, protection amid the fallout. But already Wil missed him, that feeling
of having someone. Matt's look as he explained to him that his duty was
there, on temporary assignment.

Point guard in a full-court rolling press, Gail Velarde met him as he got
out and shut the Bonneville's door. *"Wil, a statement..."*

"Gail. Moving up in the world, I see."

She smiled at the recognition. "Not still mad at me, I hope."

"Nope, only at myself." Blinking into the lights as he edged toward the
stairs and the crews jockeyed into his path.

Ignoring it, she glanced at the 3X5 card in her palm and said, "Since you and I have background, we agreed I'd initiate the questions."

"Always nice to have a plan," he said. "Who did you decide would answer them?"

Gail Velarde's eyes sought the camera's red dot; her voice and expression went anchorwoman. "Private investigator Wil Hardesty found the bodies of Luc Tien and the others last night. Vinh Tien, the arrested man and Luc Tien's brother, was his client. Mr. Hardesty, what was your business there?"

"Let me through, please."

"Can you describe the scene for us?"

"I'm not sure you want to wave that thing in my face," Wil said to a kid holding a microphone on a pole. "The day I've had."

"Tell us about that," a male reporter called from the periphery as flash units went off. "Bringing your client in to be arrested for murder."

"That is inaccurate," he answered. "Vinh Tien went of his own free will."

Gail Velarde—louder, as if to reseize the moment: "Were you aware that Vinh Tien killed Americans as a member of the Viet Cong?"

Way to go, Rudy, true to form, Wil thought as he drew a breath. "And are you aware Vinh Tien is a citizen of this country?"

"Mr. Tien disclosed his Viet Cong ties to you, or you found out?"

"Move, please, Gail. I won't say it again."

"Yet you agreed to represent him for money? You a veteran of that war?"

That war. For money. "War's end," Wil said.

"Mr. Hardesty?" A woman with a radio-station badge holding out a tape recorder. "Lieutenant Yanez indicated you were investigating the death of Vinh Tien's son, possibly at the hands of the brother he's accused of murdering. Can you confirm that?"

"No, I can't."

"Can't or won't?"

Almost to the base of the stairs; kids on bikes, residents out on their porches, some approaching to catch it in progress, maybe get asked on-camera about their neighbor.

From the reporters a voice asked, "What about the rumors of

Vietnamese gang affiliations involving the deceased?"

"How about all of you backing off before someone gets hurt?"

"Is it true that Vinh Tien's daughter was there but was spared? That she was seen leaving in an emergency vehicle?"

"No comment."

"Confirm or deny?"

"All right, deny," he said, tempted to add *emphatically*, but figuring it as tip-off, blood in the water. One foot on the lower rung, the railing cold in his hand.

"But is it true?" Gail Velarde shouted.

"You mean, as if it mattered?" Halfway up the stairs.

"Do you believe Vinh Tien capable of savagely murdering his own brother?"

"Congratulations on finding your true calling, Gail."

But she was merely reloading to ask, "In your opinion, did Vinh Tien kill Luc Tien?"

Wil turned to face her, the pack of them looking up at him. "No," he said, feeling the limb he was out on reach breaking point. "Vinh Tien did not kill his brother."

"You'd stake your reputation on it?"

"What reputation is that?"

Somebody shouted, "Does that mean Vinh Tien is still your client?"

"It means my property starts at the street," Wil said. "Anyone here not get the distinction?"

He turned, went inside, and from his blinds watched them pull back, shoot angles of the house, the deck, and window before returning to their vans. Some taking off then, others starting up with the neighbors, Wil imagining the kind of background they were providing, given his history.

From his rental across from a slide-damaged home thick with weeds, the man with the binoculars watched the vans pull away, the scene settle in. John Sebastian's "Younger Girl" came up and he hummed to it, watched Hardesty leave the house in running shorts and head for the access tunnel. He watched him emerge and start running toward the Rincon then back toward the shoals. Four laps of sprints, two more of cool-down before heading in, the radio easing through "Season of the Witch" and "Like a Rolling Stone."

Stuff that made him feel where not much did anymore.

He watched lights come on inside the house, steam rise from its bathroom window, Hardesty leave the house in jeans, white tee, and windbreaker. *Rebel Without a Cause.*

Almost time.

Giving the Bonneville enough lead to be recognizable, he rolled the rental downhill, chirped its tires hitting speed. He was catching up, easing off at four cars back, when his cell phone sounded.

"Yeah?..."

"Where are you?" the voice asked.

"Watching the sun set," the man said. "You really should see it."

"Meaning you're still in the area."

"Help me here. Is that a question or an answer?"

"An answer, I would imagine. But the question is why?"

"Simple," the man said, feeling familiar heat rise. "My time, my affair."

"Not when they conflict with ours," the voice snapped back. "Especially not then."

"Loose ends." Passing a moving van to keep the distance between himself and the taillights. "Nothing to do with you."

There was a sound resembling a laugh, then the voice: "One never knows about that, does one?"

47

WIL PARKED IN THE DRIVE, brought the box to the door by its edges. His knock was answered by the portal in the big door swinging open.

"Pizzaman," he said. "He delivers."

Lisa shut the portal, pulled back the door, stood looking at him. Worn jeans, paint-splattered sweatshirt with cut-off sleeves. White-tipped brush in one hand.

"Thanks, but no thanks," she said. "Not if it means another go-round."

"Look at me and say that." Balancing the box on his head.

"I'm serious, Wil."

"Just pizza," he said, taking it down. "I promise."

She stepped back to let him in, shut it after him. This time the stereo played familiar country—Ronnie Pruett singing "Oil and Water," one of the songs from the Bowl.

"So I bought the CD," she said defensively. "He's good."

"What'd I tell you?"

She turned it down. "Wil, I watched the news. Do you have any idea what you're doing?"

"Half veggie, half combo," he said. "No ulterior motives, no surprises."

"I meant are you all right?"

"Sure. Why not?"

"Why not happens to be all over the tube," she said.

More or less prepped for it, he said, "Hype is their business, Leese. You know that."

"I know what I saw, Wil."

"So you know what you saw. So do I."

"But you're okay..."

He understood, then. "No booze, if that's where you're headed."

She set the brush across a paint can beside a half-white baseboard, newspapers taped to the floor. She took the pizza into the kitchen, set it on the day table and got out paper plates and napkins, told him there was Vernor's left.

Wil got two, set hers next to the glasses she'd gotten out, cracked his and downed some, the bubbles stinging his nose. "Not interrupting anything, am I?"

"You mean the wilted Fresh Choice behind the Rudy's take-out?"

He smiled, offered her a slice, took one himself.

"Damnit, the Tiens," she said in midbite. "I never got a chance to call."

"It's okay. They're doing okay."

"With him in jail?"

"Sort of okay." Going on to tell her the basics—Vinh Tien's VC connection, the media, the effects it might have, was about to have.

"God, it's like being back in it," she said, shaking her head.

In the living room, Ronnie Pruett hit a shitkicker downbeat.

Wil said, "Leese, if you feel that way I'll go."

"No. It's all right."

"Then what about you?"

"Not much to report," she said. "Less nausea."

"That's good news."

She broke a smile, shook her head again.

"Something funny?" he asked through a bite.

"It struck me that way, us here like this," she said. "I don't know why."

"Laughs R Us."

For a while they ate pizza and drank ginger ale, paint fumes and Ronnie wafting in from the living room. Finally she said, "Ran you out of Dodge, did they?"

"The press? Not really. It's just good to have someplace to go."

Her eyes settled on him. "Even in your mind?"

"Especially there," Wil said.

He was dozing on the couch, Ronnie Pruett low and into a ballad, Lisa on her knees at the baseboards, when his cell phone sounded.

"Hardesty," he answered, feeling more like tossing it in the fireplace.

"It's Inez Lorenz. You asleep or something? I kept getting your machine."

"Sorry. It's been crazy at my place."

"So it looked on the tube. Look, can you come by here?"

"Tonight?" Holding up his watch and squinting to make out nine-thirty.

"No, next Christmas," Lorenz said. "I'm at the Skyway Motel, near the airport. You know it?"

"More or less." Glancing over at Lisa, who looked up at him, her brush angled so as not to drip, then quickly away.

"Room 20," Lorenz added. "Doesn't matter how late. Just come."

"All right," he said. "Give me half an hour."

Dial tone led him back to Lisa, but this time she didn't look up.

48

THE SKYWAY MOTEL was a skip past the airport, a quarter mile from the beach flanking UCSB. Sixties vintage, popular with the charter pilots who ran helicopter shuttles to the oil rigs and with trainees attending the flight schools, it sat across from one of California's premier sewage treatment facilities. Room 20 was set at the end of the line of units facing the road.

Wil pulled in next to Lorenz's blue-gray Buick and knocked.

"Right on time," she said, cracking the door, then letting him in to old smoke and Lysol. Stove and small fridge at one end, make-up alcove and bathroom at the other. Plain bedspread and bureau, chairs and table with an in-use laptop next to a half-empty fifth of Beam.

Window facing the university lights if the drapes had been open.

She wore a working blouse pulled out over pants, flat silver chain, moccasins without socks, a bracelet of twisted silver wire. Color rode her cheeks, or maybe it was the light. The Beretta nine was down at her side.

"Problem with aggressive salespeople?" he said, glancing at it.

"Some are less polite than others," Lorenz came back.

"Tell me about it."

She set the gun on the bureau, clicked the laptop shut, sat down. On the table were a lidded ice bucket and a plastic glass with melting ice. "Drink?" she asked. "I'm having one."

"No, thanks." Wondering how many the one amounted to. "It's back to a day at a time for me."

She poured herself two fingers, nipped one off, leaned back. "My old man drank—like that, I mean—and for Pete's sake, sit down. You rather I stow it?"

"Either way's fine," he said, the waft of it like gasoline.

"Meaning yes." She drained the glass, put the bottle under the table, leaned forward to squint at his eyes. "How long had it been?"

"Six years," he answered, turning from her breath.

"Sorry." Leaning back again. "Hours and days?"

"Nothing so boring as a drunk keeping score."

"But now you've reset the meter."

"With both hands," he said. "What about your dad?"

She half-smiled, dropped it. "My dad lost two families that way, then himself, then me when I tossed him over the side. Not exactly our finest hour."

"I'm sorry to hear it." Whiff of lavender soap as the bourbon smell waned.

"Right," she said. "And what else is new?"

"For some reason I had the feeling you were going to tell me."

Her hand went to the glass that wasn't there, then quickly to the other across her chest. "Some mess out there at Sunnybrook Farm."

"That's what this is about?"

"In part. You have any thoughts on who did it?"

He searched her expression for clues, saw none. "Other than to dispute the prevailing wisdom, no. You?"

Lorenz tightened her lips. "No indication what Luc wanted to talk to you about that might have involved us…"

"None that I found evidence of."

She thought some more. "What about his computers?"

"Mia said they were programmed to dump twenty seconds after anyone without the password tried to enter. She was on a break."

"Backup systems?"

"Nowhere I thought to look," Wil answered. "Evidently Luc did the boots and shut-downs himself."

A prop plane taxied in on the runway, revved, let its engines die. Lorenz rattled the ice in her glass. "The kid was in the house when it happened, wasn't she?"

Wil was about to say no, thought better of it and said nothing.

Lorenz said, "She get a look at who killed him?"

"You think her father would be in jail if she had?"

"Which, of course, begs the question."

Wil rubbed his eyes. "This is why you got me out here?"

Lorenz went to the window, slanted a look through the drapes. Releasing them, she said, "From what I've been able to gather, you made no mention of us to the Sheriff's people. Why not?"

"I've wondered that myself." Letting out a breath.

"Try reaching deep."

"Okay. Because I think you know what happened to Jimmy," he said. "And I think you know it's the key to all this."

"Which means you're still in it."

"For reasons I'm not sure would make sense even to me."

She tapped her nails beside the empty glass, forced her eyes from it. "I'm curious about something. Did you really know your client was VC when you took him on?"

"Thanks for thinking of me," Wil said, rising.

"Sit down, I'm not through. You still could have turned us. Taken your chances and shifted heat off yourself. Why didn't you?"

"Who knows? Maybe I figured it was up to you. That you had something going on that might pay off bigger."

"Professional courtesy," she mimicked. "The broader picture."

He let it stand, said nothing.

Lorenz snorted. "On the other hand, maybe you're just not the forthcoming type."

"I've been told that often enough to think there's some truth to it."

"By women?"

"Cops mainly," he said. "And are you ready to tell me what's no-shit behind Luc Tien? What you're really doing here?"

Her gaze dropped to the glass. "A bad man now off the board. Point is, I just wanted you to know I appreciate what you did. Keeping us out of it."

"And your partner?"

Flicker of something before she answered, a door pulled back before it was yanked shut. "Mac, of course."

"Who happens to be out doing whatever it is he does so well."

Lorenz fixed on him, tried to see in. "Look, we keep up this sparring, you and me, all we're going to have left is raw meat. Which would be a waste and a damn shame, and there, I said it." Flushing darker and shaking her head. "See, I'm not too good at the finer things. Probably because I never had much practice, the places I've lived, military bases and hotspots." She blew a breath, looked away as though weary of exposition. "That doesn't mean my heart wasn't in it."

Wil sat very still. "Are you saying what I think you are?"

"You tell me, hotshot." Still not meeting his eyes.

"Inez, I think you did fine—better than fine. I'm also flattered."

Back to them. "But no dice, huh?"

"It's not just me," he said. "Any man would be."

"*Sure.* Something going on with your ex—is that it?"

"Not what you think," he said. "May I take it from that you're the one who's been following me?"

She gave him a curious look. "Mac was for a while. Not since the world's safest beach, though."

"You're sure of that?"

"Sure as I can be after ordering him off you."

Trying to come up with the tangibles, Wil conjured only ghosts. "There anybody else on the team?" he asked. "A shadow specialist, someone like that?"

"No. Why?"

"Then it's probably my imagination, all that's come up. Look, I'll be in touch. You, too, okay?" He was almost to the door when he heard a metallic rasp, turned to see Lorenz holding out a set of handcuffs. Off-kilter smile on her face, as if the alcohol were propping it up.

She said, "Would these be of help in overpowering that conscience of yours?"

He regarded them, then her.

"Something that's worked before, Inez?"

Shrug. "Once a long time ago. On me, it turned out."

"I'm sorry."

"Me, too. Another time?"

He let it hang there without answering.

"No, I didn't think so," she said. "The postcard from Wisconsin."

Kari's first, the non-rejection one. In the face of her admission about being in his house, Wil decided not to explain, to let his silence say it instead.

"My specialty," she threw in as he was leaving. "Backing the wrong horse."

49

S USPECT IN BROTHER'S SLAYING WAS VIET CONG
INS mum on possible deportation.
PI who found bodies denies client's guilt.
Santa Barbara. *In yet another bizarre development in the slaying of Vietnamese businessman Luc Van Tien, authorities revealed his accused murderer and brother, Vinh Tran Tien, fought American forces as a member of the Viet Cong. While INS officials have been silent on the issue, the man formerly employed by Tien to look into his son's death, private investigator Sean Wilson Hardesty, has not. In a tersely worded statement, the La Conchita resident, himself a Vietnam veteran, denied his client's guilt. However, when asked if he still was working for Tien, presumably to see him freed, Hardesty did not respond. As to the details of Hardesty's admitted knowledge of Vinh Tien's activities in that country, site of America's worst military setback....*

Wil set the pages aside, checked his watch, showered. He put on chinos, navy tee, and the suede sports jacket Lisa gave him one birthday, left the house to sunshine and, for the first time in days, blueing skies. Nodding to the holdover reporters, cameras raised and rolling, he then caught what they were waiting for: his reaction to the note taped to the Bonneville's flattened left front tire. Neat black letters.

We remember our dead
And who put them there.
Brothers in Arms

Wil looked at the cameramen panning from the note to his expression, the waiting reporters. "Anybody see this done?" he asked.

"Before we got here," one answered. "Any comment on it?"

"Yeah. Who's got a tire iron?"

The one he had in the trunk worked fine, but he was still forty minutes late to the Tien's. He was headed up the path, wondering about the white Altima parked at their curb, when a slight Vietnamese man in wirerims and a tan summerweight suit left the house. In crisp English, he introduced himself as Raymond Ky of the L.A.-based Southeast Asian Legal Defense Fund, whose services had been accepted by the Tien family.

"At some point we'll need to talk about your statement," he told Wil. "Assuming you're still sympathetic."

"I'm not going anywhere," he said.

Ky nodded.

Wil tilted his head toward the door. "How's it going inside?"

"The mother is in denial and the daughter's not the most patient person. What exactly is your relationship with them?"

"We're still figuring that out," Wil answered.

Ky eyed him as he might a potential adversary, then softened. Handing over a card as he accepted one of Wil's, he said, "I'll be at the Lemon Tree Motel, then my L.A. office once I get some details resolved. You're the one who told the press he was innocent?"

"Didn't kill his brother, I believe I said."

Ky broke a slight smile. "You ever given thought to law as a second career?"

Watching him leave, Wil knocked and got Matt going crazy through the cracked door. Mia sliding off the chain and holding it open for him, the house smelling of incense.

"There's a shrine in my mother's room," she said, noting him scanning for the incense source. "Big help, huh? Where have you been?" Black shorts and midriff top, black sandals and nails.

"Changing a tire, thanks." Tending to Matt's bouncing all over him. "How's your mom holding up?"

"Take a sniff. You meet our lawyer?"

Wil nodded, rose. "Where'd you find him?"

"We didn't have to," she said. "He found us."

Wil made a mental note to check out Raymond Ky, then took a spot on the couch, Matt against his knee. Casually, he said, "You interested in a fashion tip?"

"What's that?" Wary.

He said, "Like it or not, clothes say things, to the press especially. You might think in those terms."

"Game playing, you mean."

"You're in it, why not be in it to win?"

"Which explains the sports jacket, I suppose."

"What? This old thing?" Throwing in a smile that came back as a question: "There anything else you want from me?"

He was about to ask her what they told Raymond Ky, but she was already moving down the hall, passing Li Tien, who entered in a gray dress. Joined him and Matt to sit watching the bamboo moving in the light beyond the flagstones.

"We thank you for your words," Li Tien said. "On the television."

They sat a moment, then he said, "I did not know they were going to arrest him, Li, or it would have been different. Please know that."

Breeze ruffled the green. "Mia says you were good to her. In that terrible house."

"She put herself there. You have every reason to be proud of her."

"Then you know why she went there?"

He nodded, stroked Matt. "For you, because you couldn't. For her father, even if she doesn't know it. Even if she never knows it."

Li Tien contemplated the herons spilling water into the fish pond, the sound of bees working the water blossoms. In a few minutes Mia came down the hall in a blue shirt, black pants and loafers, enamel academic pendant on a gold chain.

"Better?" she asked him.

"Four aces and a wild card," Wil answered, this time pleased at the smile it drew.

50

THE COUNTY CORRECTIONAL FACILITY was no stranger to Wil, but it was to Li and Mia Tien. Despite the routine nature of the paperwork and the wait during which he checked the Mustang into a locker and got a receipt for it, each sharp new sound sent starts through both women. Finally, their names were called and they followed a correctional officer, a heavyset deputy Wil knew slightly through Frank Lin, to the interview room where Vinh Tien waited in county orange.

When he saw Wil, Vinh's expression revealed nothing, then thawed as his wife and daughter talked softly in Vietnamese, no emotion, no tears from either. Those formed as they rose and turned away, Mia gesturing that they'd wait outside.

Wil sat where they had, dark pupils followed him through the Plexiglas. Finally they blinked and Vinh said, "My wife told me what you said to the press. We are grateful."

"You doing all right?" Wil asked.

"In here? A palace, all things considered."

"Have you anything to tell me?"

The expression was one of contempt. "Why? So you can tell your friends in uniform?"

"No. So I can make your time in here not mean nothing."

Vinh Tien brought his hands together, regarded them as though deciding. Then, "I was at my brother's house—a second time that day. The police know this."

A second time.

Wil just sat there.

"I went to beg him not to do what he was doing to her. To offer him money."

"I see," Wil said. "And what time was that?"

"Three—three-thirty—I don't recall the exact time."

Which meant Yanez had it on tape all along via the system.

Son of a bitch...

"What happened?"

Vinh's face tightened. "He had me thrown out in the road. After telling me she was the best he'd ever had, that he had big plans for her. That in the long run—" pausing to clamp down on it. "In the long run she'd be handing me money in the street, as an empress might a peasant. This while smiling at me."

"Go on."

"I had the knife. From the boning rack at work. Down my back."

Shit, shit, shit. "You're telling me you pulled it on him?"

Vinh glanced at the guard, tapped his teeth with a fist. "Had it been twenty years ago, ten even, there would have been no doubt as to the outcome. As it was, the one who knows martial arts nearly broke my arm while the others laughed."

"Did you tell Raymond Ky this?"

"I did. He told me not to worry."

"What do you think of Raymond Ky so far?"

"When I can afford an opinion, I will render it."

Wil tried another approach. "Luc was having guests, he mentioned it when he tried to hire me. They were in the house when you were there?"

"More in the background," Vinh answered. "But yes."

"Any idea who they were?"

"Laughing faces. I don't remember."

"Nothing you might have overheard?"

The guard approached, held up five fingers, moved off to resume his stance. Lowering his voice, Vinh said, "They were speaking the language. Something that they were expecting: an arrival of some kind."

"Of what?" Wil asked.

"I don't know, but one slapped a girl on the rump as she was leaving. Then they all did it. Luck, or something."

"You heard nothing else?"

"I had other things on my mind."

Wil let it slide, said, "You know the word is out, don't you? About you being Viet Cong?"

Nod. "As we speak."

"Meaning what? You've had threats?"

"If one didn't know better, one might call them that."

"Tell the guards," Wil said. "They'll have you moved."

"And if these things were spoken of in front of a guard?"

Wil ran a hand over his hair, rubbed the back of his scalp.

To the gesture, Vinh said, "I have seen men like this before. They are cowards, unwilling to make a move because of what I am alleged to have done. Weaklings who need the pack."

"Don't underestimate them."

He waved it off as he might a mosquito. "I have a favor to ask. If, at this point, you would consider it."

"What's that?"

"My family," Vinh Tien said. "Whatever you can do to keep them safe, you will find me appreciative."

"That's not a favor," Wil answered. "It's a given."

"You may wish to rethink that."

"Only when a long list of other things comes to pass."

Vinh Tien glanced up as the heavyset guard returned. "My signal to go," he said.

"Have some faith in us," Wil told him, rising also.

The black eyes bored in. "You must understand: Luc was my blood. Even though we were of different fathers, I never wished him dead, merely stopped from what he was doing to my family." Glancing at the guard, then back. "There is something I must know from you. Would you have accepted my brother's money?"

Wil held the eyes. "Would you have put a bullet in me twenty-five years ago?"

They were at the dining table, drapes pulled back, afternoon light slanting in through the curtains, the bamboo now in partial sun.

"How did the media know we were even there?" Mia asked.

"Word gets around," Wil said. "And money."

He could still see the flashes going off, hear the shouted questions regarding the Cong, ones similar to last night's about his knowledge of Vinh's involvement, his denial of Vinh's guilt, comments on the revocation-of-citizenship rumors as they emerged from the facility and made their way to the car. Some reporters even asking if Li Tien were VC as he pulled from the lot.

Mia said, "At least he looked better than I expected."

"Your father is a man," Li answered her in Vietnamese that Wil barely made out. "He has endured worse."

Mia turned to Wil. "Do you think he's in danger in there?"

"It's a controlled environment. I'd say the odds are with him." Knowing she was seeing through it and saying nothing for her mother's sake.

"They were here before you came," Li said in English. "With their trucks and their cameras. Their endless questions."

"You might as well get used to it," Wil told her.

"What more do they want from us?"

"To feed the beast, the press. Part is the way Luc was killed, part is the twenty-fifth anniversary of the fall of Saigon and the extension of trade agreements, the politics."

"So what do we do?" Pouring more tea into their cups, Mia refusing hers.

"We go about our business."

"Which is?" Mia.

"Helping your dad by acting normal," he said. "Not letting this get to us. Beyond that, I have some ideas." And, to her look, "Nothing I won't include you in once they're formed."

Mia's eyes drifted to the dregs in her cup; she looked up at her mother. "Viet Cong, my *God*. I mean, how could he have put us in this position?"

The slap was gunshot unexpected.

For an instant everything froze, then Li Tien was laying into her stunned and openmouthed daughter. Wil was following none of it when the front window exploded inward and a rock the size of a softball grazed the table leg and struck the wall.

Diving, Wil was conscious of Mia's scream and Matt's barking, of Li Tien where he'd sought to shield her with his body, of shouting at Mia to take her mother into the hallway *NOW*, of the Mustang in his hand. Of being at the window then, watching a black pickup, a bare-chested man clinging to its roll bar as the truck squealed through the curve and disappeared.

No way, no chance.

Then, Mia's voice from miles away: "What was that you were saying about normal?"

51

WIL WAS PACKING WHEN HE HEARD THE POP OF GRAVEL, feet on the stair steps. He had the door open as Frank Lin topped the landing.

"Must be nice to be so in demand," Lin said, glancing back at the press contingent, one with a long lens aimed at them.

"Thrill a minute," Wil said.

"Hey, you're pretty good copy these days. Ask Rudy."

"Guys who flatten tires like me."

"Can I come in, or shall we do this for their benefit?" And when Wil gestured him inside, "You planning a trip somewhere?"

Wil thrust his .45 and two clips of hollowpoints he'd wrapped in an old sweatshirt, plus his windbreaker, into the duffel. "And if I were?"

"Might be wise to let us know."

"Us..."

"Me," Lin said. "Remember?"

Wil went through it for him: the smashed window and phone threat that followed, the punk in the black pickup, the vacant eyes of the responding deputy. Li Tien's eyes when she said it reminded her of post-war days before Vinh had been able to send for them.

"I saw the log on it," Lin said. "One of ours will swing by periodically. I will, too, when I can."

"I'll pass it on. Meantime I intend to be out there."

Lin looked out at the ocean, late afternoon sun backlighting the surf. "Rudy was in Nam, too, you know. Twenty-second Airborne. From the stories I've heard, he had a pretty hellish time."

"A lot of guys did," Wil said, continuing to pack. "Anything else?"

"Yeah, as a matter of fact. He'd rather you were more guarded in your comments to the press. That they're helping neither the process nor the family. With which I happen to agree."

Wil put a box of lapsang into a side pocket and zipped it up. "And the videotape, Frank, Tien's second visit? The one you guys forgot to mention?"

Slow exhale. "So you're not in Rudy's loop, Wil. BFD. On camera the guy pulls the knife that winds up in Robb's neck. How would you have handled it?"

"There's a question for you."

Lin turned back to the window, shook his head. "This is like two spikers banging at the net. You think we might call a fucking truce here?"

"Not a bad idea," Wil said. "You can start with the tail you guys have on me."

Lin left the view to face him. "Somebody's tailing you?"

"A pro. Somebody I was thinking might owe Rudy a favor."

"Bullshit. For what reason?"

"I found the bodies, Frank, I had the run of the place. Maybe I'm withholding something from him."

Pause. "Are you?"

"If I were and if it were material, you'd have it." Wil thinking *You're welcome, Lorenz.* Knowing full well who rolled the dice by choosing to keep secret her involvement: not the firmest leg on which he stood. "That said, how long do you think I'd last if I ran everything by Rudy first?"

"Save the act, Wil, I'm not the press. And I'll check around and see if it's one of ours out there."

"All I can ask." Sticking his Dopp kit into the duffel, zipping the main flap, more signal of intent than actual readiness. "And Frank, about your cruising the Tien place? Thanks...them and me."

After Lin left, Wil got out John Pereira's fax regarding *Harmony's* location coordinates. He was thinking of the best way to handle what he had in mind when the phone rang. Expecting another request to put an eager young Bernstein wannabe across from him in confidential circumstances, he let the machine take it and heard, "Pick up if you're there. If not, I'll try the cell phone and the hell with less secure."

"Lorenz?" he answered.

"Flushed you out, did I? Can you come by tonight? I'll be back by eight. It's important."

"Not the best of nights," he said. "How about breakfast tomorrow? On me."

"It's Mac. I still haven't heard from him. He hasn't been by your place has he?"

"No," Wil said, mulling it. "You check his room?"

"I look like Helpless Hattie to you? Of course I checked his room."

"How long?" he asked.

"Since the night you were going out to Luc's."

Going on four days. "And that's unusual for him?"

"Damn right it's unusual. Mac has enemies, people who'd like nothing better than to take him apart. Tell you the truth, I'm worried about him."

"*Enemies,*" he repeated. "Along the lines of our conversation?"

"Places he's been, the things he's seen? What do you think?"

"Who is he, Lorenz? No bullshit, no plastic banana rock and roll."

She hesitated. "Mac is a good agent and an old family friend."

"Just not one used to operating on a tether."

"You'd make a good dentist, you know that? Probe till it bleeds."

"As if you wouldn't," he said. "Any chance Maccafee might have slipped it?"

"You don't know him the way I do, or you wouldn't say that."

The concern in her tone apparent, he said, "No argument from me."

"Forget it," Lorenz said abruptly. "This is obviously a wrong number."

"Hold on a minute, Inez. Maybe later if I—"

But by then she'd hung up.

Carrying it around like a burr, Wil finally found Lorenz's business card and dialed the ATF number in Los Angeles: ten to five by his watch, hoping someone was still there.

Something was: a recording that led him deeper into no-man's land, then recycled his options, none of which applied. Punching out, he dialed the FBI agent he knew from Holly Pfeiffer's kidnap and another case involving murdered vets.

"You've reached the desk of FBI Special Agent Albert Vega. I'm not here right now, but—" Live suddenly, out of breath: "Rosen? Al Vega. Thanks for calling back."

"Who's Rosen?" Wil asked.

Deep breath. "Who's this?"

"Just remember that your mother and I love you very much, Albert."

There was a pause, then Vega saying, "Hardesty? How'd I get so lucky?"

Wil said, "Just wondering if you knew any human beings over at ATF. Preferably of the supervisorial genus."

"I'm due in a meeting. Supervisorial of whom?"

"With syntax like that, you must be Special Agent in Charge by now. At the very least."

"I'd love to chat, Hardesty, but I'm expecting a call."

"Rosen, whoever she is," Wil said.

"*He*, smartass." Pause, the sound of fingers on a keyboard. Then, "Try Marotta, Louis." Spelling it. "Not much for charm, but competent."

"That mean you know him?"

"Heard him speak once after Waco." Vega rattled off a number and an extension. "Tell him I suggested he hang up on you, which is what I'm about to do."

"Al, Al. You always hurt the one you love."

"On second thought," Vega said, "tell him to change his number."

Sorting out his approach, Wil dialed the ATF extension, waited three rings, then heard, "Marotta." New York horseradish on a California roll.

Wil said, "Peter Giannini over at the Wilshire B of A inquiring about an Inez Lorenz who says she works there?"

"You'll need Personnel for that," the voice came back. *Busy.*

"It's about a loan," Wil added. "Won't take a moment."

"A moment more than I have, Mr. Giannini."

"Call me Pete, everybody does," Wil said. "And is that Queens I detect in your accent?"

"Call the office tomorrow, Mr. Giannini."

"We just want to inform her that it's been approved, but we seem to have deleted the information. It's most embarrassing."

"Yes, well, I'll be hanging up now."

"Mr. Marotta, you can't want to see her lose a one-time rate like this. She'll be saving almost four hundred dollars."

Hesitation. Then, "L-O-R-E-N-Z, Santa Monica. But you won't reach her."

Wil let out a breath. "Then I'll have no choice but to recycle her application, Mr. Marotta. Do you see my dilemma here?"

"It's Special Agent Marotta. And I suggest you reconsider since she's on administrative leave."

Bingo—but which meant what? Disciplinary? Investigative? Agency cover for the Luc Tien op? It made sense when you tracked the nature of their contacts with him, but if so, why?

"And this second reference she's listed," Wil went on. "A Thomas Maccafee? Would you happen to know him?"

Long pause. "On second thought, Mr. Giannini, will you hold?"

Fifteen seconds went by, twenty, too much like a tap: Wil broke the connection and sat with it. *Administrative leave.* Opening his laptop, he keyed up a search engine, typed in INEZ LORENZ in quotes and got no hits. He tried THOMAS MACCAFEE, then TOM MACCAFEE, with similar results. Trying another engine, and a third and fourth, he struck out. On a whim, he typed in just the name MACCAFEE and got seventeen— sports figures, musicians, academics, different first names. He was about to head out when he tried the single name LORENZ.

Twenty-four hits, all but the last hit irrelevant.

ABDUCTED AGENT FOUND DEAD IN RAID

Choluteca, Honduras, 1991. U.S. Alcohol, Tobacco and Firearms agents, acting on a tip, found the remains of Special Agent E. Russell Lorenz, abducted during a failed raid on what was thought to be an arms dealer's cache. With the death of Lorenz, the raid now has claimed twelve: a local peace officer, two civilians, three arms traffickers, and six of the forty foreign nationals thought to be awaiting passage to the U.S. who were released from quarters the traffickers set ablaze.

An investigation into the raid's failure has been launched, but a leak inside the agency is believed responsible. Lorenz, a decorated veteran of Vietnam as well as ATF, leaves behind a daughter, Inez Almeria, age 25, currently in Virginia completing her ATF training...

But it was the accompanying photo that kept Wil glued to it: four men in jungle fatigues looking at the ground where several tarps had been laid, one pointing at something or someone out of frame. Three were *Federale* types.

The fourth was Tom Maccafee...

Even with hair, Wil recognized him. Standing slightly behind the others, hand cupped to the cigarette in his mouth, he seemed just to have become aware of the viewfinder fixed on him.

Wil was glad he hadn't been the cameraman.

52

WIL GOT TO THE TIEN'S AFTER SEVEN, but if they minded, it didn't show. On the flip side, both Mia and her mother looked drawn. Dinner was a silent affair, as if the flattened cardboard laid in over the shattered window were a presence in itself. That and the spare answering machine Wil had brought and had Mia program with the Sheriff's emergency number, the machine's alert diode a red throb across the room.

"Raymond Ky came by again," Mia said at one point. "He's made a formal request for my father's isolation."

Wil looked up from Matt, beside him on the floor. "He optimistic about it?"

She shrugged. Li Tien said nothing.

"Have they announced an arraignment date yet?"

"Not that he told me."

Silence.

"I'm going back to classes tomorrow," Mia said, putting down her fork. "Finals aren't far off." And with a glance at him, "We thought it best, Raymond and I."

Raymond and I. "Well, if I had to pick a place, I suppose that would be it."

Li Tien's fork clinked her plate. "I need to say something," she said. "Inside they hurt as we hurt, the ones who threw the rock, who lost friends and family to the war." Her eyes shifted to Mia. "Why do you think your father kept those things in that box, but to remind him?"

No answer.

"Your wife called," she said to Wil. "We talked. It was good of her."

"Ex-wife, Mom," Mia corrected.

Li regarded him. "You are not married to her anymore?"

"No. Not for a number of years."

There was a pause. Then, "Why is that?"

"Mommm!"

Shaking her head, Li rose as did her daughter, Wil trailing with his dishes, setting them in the sink as Mia began rinsing them. Extending her hand to him, Li said, "This has been a long day. Thank you for coming to wait with us."

"You are most welcome." His Vietnamese bringing a tired smile.

After saying he'd take the couch rather than Jimmy's bed, Wil sat brushing Matt and flashing on the Maccafee photo, what it meant in the overall. He made a mental note to try Vega again, the possibility of a service record or agency file. He called the Skyway Motel, room 20, and got no answer: almost nine and Lorenz still out.

Tomorrow for that.

The TV he had on without sound came up on a newsbreak, shots of him, Mia, and Li getting into the Bonneville, reporters mouthing silent questions, a talking head to explain it. He was searching for the remote to regain sound when the break ended, so he clicked it off.

Finished with Matt, he emptied the brush, washed his hands, and lay back, thinking it was nice being in a house with people in it. He felt the gentle rise and fall of Matt's breathing, heard Li Tien say again *Why is that?...Why is that?...Why is that?* until it became an echo rolling through a faraway canyon, then nothing at all.

❷

Next morning, Wil tried Al Vega's number again. Put on hold, he scanned headlines, a front-page photo of himself, Mia, and Li coming out of the jail, the cropping making the closely gathered knot of reporters look like a lynch mob.

PROSECUTORS MAY SEEK DEATH IN BROTHER CASE
Videotape Plus Witness Puts Tien at Scene.
PI Denial As Lawyer Ponders Self-Defense.
Wil cut the line and dialed Raymond Ky's Los Angeles number off his card, connecting on the third ring.

"You seen the papers yet?" he asked.

"Not yours," Ky answered. "What about it?"

Wil read him the subhead, Ky's quotes about the plea.

"Trial balloon," Ky said, "I've notified the family." Sipping from something. "They're on board. As is the Vietnamese community."

"On board what? The *Lusitania*?"

"Mr. Hardesty, there's a reason they've denied our client bond. With what we're facing, self-defense may be the best we can hope for."

"At the risk of sounding like a broken record, what happened to not guilty?"

Ky sighed, the beleaguered but patient attorney gathering himself to explain life's facts. "Mr. Hardesty, I appreciate your efforts, and I know the family does, but you're neither Vietnamese nor a lawyer representing one. I suggest you leave the legal part to us."

Us...

Wil bit down as the lawyer went on.

"You heard the Argabrite woman identified him as having left an hour before the SUVs did? Which gave him time to start the fire then go back in, figuring Luc would have stayed."

"It's bullshit, Ky. No matter how it looks."

"How about letting me be the judge of that?"

"I just hope you know what you're doing."

"Good-bye, Mr. Hardesty."

The Vietnamese community—terrific. Wil dialed Vega again, heard from his secretary the FBI agent was in meetings all day, and left a message: Maccafee's name, a question mark, and his phone number. He was toying with the idea of calling ATF again, but decided Marotta was a burnt bridge. Instead he rummaged the recycling stack, finally found what he was looking for: the newspaper front section from right after his first Lorenz/Maccafee encounter.

August 9. San Francisco.

LOCAL COP DEAD IN CHINATOWN SHOOTOUT
AOCTF Mourns Its Own. Two Attending Funeral Also Die.

Wil scanned: Detective Sergeant Arthur Loh, the dead cop...two reput-ed organized-crime figures attending the Chinatown funeral of old-time tong leader Kan Wan Yee the targets...quotes from Detective Sergeant Terry Leong...

He called information, then the number: Following the inevitable bureaucratic bounce, he asked a male voice answering "Asian Organized Crime Task Force" for Detective Terry Leong, finally getting, "Leong here."

Wil explained who he was and where, his ties to Vinh Tien, and heard, "The Vietnamese the locals made for killing his brother?"

TV—the San Francisco station following the Asian angle. Will said, "Right story, wrong perp, though you'd get some argument from a Sheriff's lieu-tenant down here. I was thinking it might have more to do with your field."

"You have something to say here, or do I make my conference?"

Wil drew a breath. "You lose a man to the Vietnamese who take out the two Po Sang, right?"

"Arthur Loh. Go on."

"Po Sang hires the hitter who reminds your cop outside the Hall of Justice of Steve McQueen. He drops the first hitters. End of story?"

"Is that a question?"

"More the premise," Wil told him. "It's my belief that Luc Tien was behind an attempt to organize his Rising Dragons based on a New York gang's nationwide model. Born to Kill, now defunct."

Pause, then, "And your source for this?"

"A certain government agency."

Intake and exhale, Terry Leong saying, "Mr. Hardesty, let me tell you how it works, if you're not aware. You show me a card from your deck, I may show you one from mine, not the other way around. The fact we're still talking is because of Artie Loh, for whom I had the greatest regard and the highest respect."

"I understand that."

"So, count of one: you have a card to show, or am I back at it?"

"ATF," Wil said. "Agents Lorenz and Maccafee." He spelled out the particulars.

"Neither of whom I know," Leong said after a pause to note it. "And you think Luc Tien might be involved why?"

"Luc has a nice street crime business going, wants to expand in a hurry and sees an opportunity. He orders the Po Sang hit to show them he means business and wants it all."

Wil heard the sound of a cigarette being lit, the exhale from it, then Leong. "Look, let's cut the shit. Po Sang's a paper tiger and has been for years. Gangs like Rising Dragon smell blood and rip off an arm before they realize it's costing them two of their own to ante. These days it's about alliances. Who backs whom."

"Mel Gibson and the warring Scots," Wil offered.

"Somewhere along those lines."

"The Dragons and the Po Sang?"

Dismissive laugh. "About like Serbs and Kosovars lying down together. Unless..."

What the hell, Wil thought, *nothing ventured.* He said, "Unless somebody stronger than either of them were to make both like it?"

This time there was a long pause, muffled background. Then, "Look, I'm late and getting later for this thing. Airport food do anything for you?"

"All depends on the airport," Wil said.

53

SOMEHOW IT WORKED. MOST OF IT, ANYWAY.

Wil just had time to park and buy his ticket, wander outside the red-tiled Santa Barbara Airport terminal. He was looking at his watch, eyeing the Skyway Motel, sun glinting off what looked to be Lorenz's car, when they called the twelve-forty-two and there went the thought of phoning her. As if to make up for it, the flight was smooth enough to shave four minutes off the time. Even the fog was on good behavior, cresting the ridge of coast mountains but advancing no further on Millbrae and South San Francisco, the eons-long construction that was SFO.

He recognized Terry Leong immediately: early-to-mid forties, cop bearing on a taller-than-Frank-Lin build, metal-frame glasses over Chinese-black eyes, sports coat over Dockers and Rockports. Stainless sports watch when his sleeve pulled back in the restaurant booth. Bulge at the right hip.

"First thing we get straight," he said after they'd settled on omelets. "This is not some buddy-buddy deal."

"Nice meeting you, too, Sergeant."

Leong blew out a breath. "You ever been hammered by a civilian review board determined that whatever you say is a cover-up?"

"Not as such," Wil said.

"I thought you might have been ex-cop. Most independents I know are."

Wil drank from water the busboy set down. "Coast Guard Port Security a long time ago. Second tour."

Black eyes met his and blinked. "Two tours, a VC client, people you must have known lost to them. Want to help me out with why?"

"Something to do with lost causes, I imagine."

"Whatever." Terry Leong pulled out a Winston and stuck it in his face, took it out as the waitress brought their food and left. "Let's make this count: We were talking about gangs, networks. Some notion about one stronger than either making them shut up and like it."

"I'm saying it might explain some things."

"Don't let me stop you."

Wil said, "If I'm right, these hits resemble a sports match. Rising Dragon hits Po Sang, Po retaliates. So either they lick their wounds and call it even or Luc Tien is about to fire back when he winds up dead. Nothing as simple as gunfire, either. More like pay attention, here's what happens when you still want trouble." Hungrier than he'd realized, he bore down on the omelet. "But then what do I know?"

Leong rolled the unlit cigarette between his fingers. "And a brother's rage and revenge?"

"True, my version exonerates Vinh Tien," Wil admitted. "But that's because he didn't do it."

"That's convenient for both of you."

"But unconvincing for some."

"Not altogether," Leong said. Shifting the cigarette, he forked in a bite, seemed to decide on something. "Are you up on your triads at all? Those fun-loving crime cartels we Asians are so good at?"

"Red Sun a few years ago."

Nod. "Thailand-based: drugs, cars, hardware—small potatoes by comparison. People are the big thing now, girls they can turn into prostitutes. Fifty to a hundred thou to bring them in, years of servitude for those they don't turn into fish chum." Leong paused. "So the name Under Heaven wouldn't ring a bell?"

"No," Wil said. "Should it?"

"Actually I'd be surprised. We don't even know much about them. Which doesn't mean the feds don't."

"ATF?"

"I'm speculating," he said. "Rumor has it that Under Heaven is a brain-child of the Chinese Army, crime as a way to finance their military buildup. Big money is their blood in the water, and they're heavily armored politically. Only reason I know of them is a Po Sang informant told me they were getting leaned on and that name came up. The plan was to shoehorn the Pos into high tech crime and leave the street stuff to the Viets. Specialize to maximize."

"The Viets meaning Rising Dragon," Wil said.

Leong nodded. "My guy didn't know, and this was before the Dragons hit the Changs and Benny Lum. From what we've gathered, they were trying to rip the Pos off while the Pos were in transition."

"Po Sang being weak for some time, you said."

"Inbreeding. Which always schools up the sharks."

Wil felt loops rounding on each other—and something else that fit: Maccafee saying that Luc hated the Chinese. He said, "So the Pos are a wounded fish both the Dragons and these new guys are after. Which would put them and Luc at cross purposes."

"Under Heaven, and *maybe* is all I'm saying here," Leong said around a bite. "Got it?"

"You still thinking Po Sang hired the McQueen hitter?"

"It's not SOP, but I can see where they'd want somebody from outside. And unless they're getting better under my nose, this guy was way polished for local talent." He focused in. "Why? You know something about it I should know?"

Wil met his gaze, locked in the setting. "Just curious."

"Let's make no mistake here. This guy may have taken out the trash for us, but that's not the way it works. For what he did to Artie, Dao Hong was mine. Now this guy is, and I'll get him. Nobody freelances on my turf—are we clear on that?"

"I think so."

"Deal is, you hear something, you call me. Otherwise, you're in the same cell he is. That clear, too?"

"Crystal."

The waitress brought coffee, eyed the unlit cigarette in Terry Leong's free hand. She looked about to say something when she caught his expression and retreated to a family in Aloha shirts casting about for her.

"Hate to eat and run," Leong said. "I did have a chance to pass your ATF names to a guy I know who's hooked in, though." He stuck the cigarette in his face again but made no move to light it. "Interesting what these things will turn up."

Wil waited as Leong sucked air through the Winston.

"Goddamn pathetic what some people do to each other, isn't it?" he said. "Your Lorenz seems to have authority issues, thought to involve her upward mobility. Maccafee—if it's the right Tom Maccafee, he of the three tours and the Air America stint, meaning CIA—shows up not at all after 1991. Some ATF raid that went south." He slid from the booth, looked back at Wil. "A suspended malcontent and an ex-spook who's been doing who knows what for a decade. That tend to complicate your life, or what?"

54

"FRANK, HEAR ME OUT," Wil said into the pay phone, his other hand cupped to block the terminal noise. "What it means is that somebody besides Vinh Tien had a motive to kill Luc."

"An example to other gangs," Frank Lin said. "To not piss off this whatever-it-is you called it."

"Under Heaven." Over the hollow clatter, the foot shuffle, the unintelligible airline announcements, he could hear office sounds, someone speaking behind Frank.

"Under Heaven," Lin repeated as though thinking out loud. "As in the extent of what they're out after?"

"Who knows with these people, Frank?"

"Hey, why stop there? Rudy digs a dreamer."

Wil checked the time, an hour and fifteen until the flight he'd been able to book left for Santa Barbara. Using the call to start the ball rolling, knowing how far he'd get with Yanez, he'd dialed his hole card.

"Frank, it fits," he said for what had to be the fifth time.

"And for grins, you came by this wisdom how?"

"A gang cop up here named Terry Leong."

Hesitation. "The guy who lost his partner? We talked to him. Right after the media ran with it."

"And?..."

"And nothing," Lin said. "By then we had our man. And local cops, even city ones, aren't plugged in like that. So who else did you get smart from?"

Figuring he'd already told Leong, Wil took a breath and spilled it, no way around it anymore: The ATF connection, Lorenz and Maccafee, his arrangement with them to further the Jimmy angle.

Sorry Lorenz, but there comes a time.

A long moment passed, an expulsion of breath, then Lin: "Are you fucking out of your mind? You hold out on a homicide investigation in which your client is *the* suspect, and you expect the shit not to hit the fan?"

"Sometimes your best call isn't," Wil said. "It happens."

"Not like this, it doesn't. Man, I am not hearing this."

"Open your ears, Frank. I may have screwed up, but you've got the wrong man in jail."

"And Mr. Right is this vague entity imposing its will on the gangs and, in the process, pocketing the globe."

"By halting a gang war that at minimum calls attention to itself," Wil said. "By sending a message to its target: Do not fuck with us."

An older woman who'd just sat down and was fumbling for coins shot him a look as she moved to the opposite side of the phone bank.

"Sorry," he mouthed at her.

"What?" Lin said.

"I said, I'm sorry for my language."

"Playing to an audience, are you? Well, dang me—old Luc had his own set of demons. That's what you're saying here?"

"You got it."

"Maybe. What about Jimmy?"

Wil said, "I'm working on that. You get anything from Luc's computers?"

"No, and we've had people turning them every which way. Hard drive's irretrievable, no backup drive in evidence, no disks. Apparently he used encrypted e-mail for backup. We located the server."

"Anything there?" Knowing the answer before it came.

"This case, you kidding? Luc took the password swimming with him. Server says forget about it, one chance in a mil or something to decode."

Wil let a kid with a boombox pass. "Any indication how long he'd had the account?"

"Server said last December one, paid a year in advance," Lin said.

"Obviously the guy had a Plan B."

Meaning he'd had a Plan A, Wil thought. *Something, anyway.* "Our luck," he said.

Relative silence. "Tell you what: I'm going to verify your Lorenz and Maccafee with our local ATF, then turn it over to you-know-who. At least present it to him that you voluntarily gave up the connection. And you are damned lucky at that."

"I know," Wil said.

"Don't pander," Lin shot back. "With luck he'll be more pissed at the feds. And by the way, Casa Tien? All quiet, even with a new front window to aim at."

"Meaning your patrols are working."

"That's one way to look at it."

"Thanks, Frank," Wil said. "All of it."

"*Nada*. Somebody's got to save you from yourself."

Lights spread out as Wil's turbo-prop circled in off the ocean, touched down, rolled to a stop. He went directly to the Bonneville, paid at the gate, took a right to the motel, pulled in next to Lorenz's Buick, up from two Nissans and an Explorer off by itself. Beyond the tidal creek, he could make out the line of spindly palms that marked the beach. To the right, the amber pinpoints of UCSB.

Old Luc had his own set of demons.

He got out and touched the Buick's hood. Cold: Unless she'd gone for a walk along the bike paths, Lorenz was home. He rapped lightly.

"Lorenz? It's me—Hardesty."

Through thick curtains he could see light, hear sound, the flicker of a TV turned low. Traffic passed; a kid with a backpack and a flashing tail-light cycled toward the bridge and the university. A heron flapped toward the eucalyptus roosts along the strand. He tried the door: locked, too con-spicuous to force, even if he had the tools. He tried the lobby, where a dark-complected young man reading from a geography text looked up as he entered, all breathy sheepishness.

"Ed Lorenz, room 20," he identified himself. "Wife has the key and she's guest-lecturing. I went for a stroll and lost track of time. Left my key in the room."

"What's she teach?" the kid asked.

"Drama. And you could save me a good walk to get it."

The kid tapped a keyboard, looked at his monitor, then up at Wil.

"ID?" Wil asked, fumbling for the ATF card Lorenz had given him, hoping it wouldn't come to that. Prepared to say he didn't drive if the kid wanted a license.

The kid didn't. Outside again, Wil paused at the door, inserted the key. A metro bus passed, the airport loop toward town, and then he was in. To the smell of heat, closed room, and worse.

She was in the chair facing the TV, its picture bathing her in two hosts and a video-framed guest arguing politics. Jerked sideways by the blast from the Beretta still in her hand, her face was white, the temple entry hole patterned with grains of burnt powder. What looked to be chocolate syrup in the light tracked her jaw and neck, spattered the wall, darkened the fabric at which she stared with glazed eyes.

Wil touched her hair, her neck, the line of her jaw.

Son of a bitch...

Son of a BITCH...

As he stood there the political argument raged, then a barrage of commercials, none of which registered, then back to arguing. Same two guys, different framed guest. For a moment he felt like putting a bullet into all three, then like throwing up. Finally, after dialing Frank Lin and telling him, a numbness left him floored against the wall, knees supporting forearms that seemed beyond weight.

After dismissing the kid and the owner who'd come down, some hours later they finished up with Wil, Yanez supervising. Lin finally had reached Marotta, who insisted, as he had earlier, that if Lorenz was running something up their way, he had no knowledge of it. That Maccafee did have a brief record of ATF employment from '88 to '91 but that was it, no contact since, no idea of whereabouts, no forwarding address. Aside from what he'd read, Marotta didn't know Luc Tien at all. Lorenz had been a good but independent-minded agent who'd been taking time to sort out her future with them. Her future, period, it seemed.

"And you believed him?" Wil asked Lin after Yanez threatened to bust Wil on the spot for the withhold, then left the scene to the techs, Lorenz already taken away by ambulance.

"No reason I can see why Marotta would lie." Leaning against his Crown Victoria, a hint of dried things on the offshore breeze.

"Then you buy into it being a suicide."

"That's why we have medical examiners, remember? Everything consistent, nothing to contraindicate. You heard the guy."

"I heard him," Wil said. "No note, no nothing."

"The serious ones don't write notes. Most don't, anyway."

"I'm not talking about most, Frank. She wasn't the type."

"I almost forgot. You'd seen her how many times to qualify?"

Wil let it go, sat there.

"Therapy and antidepressants," Lin went on. "A father fixation that showed up more than once as insubordination, according to Marotta. So there she is, way out there, failed in some self-appointed mission she couldn't even convince her superiors had merit. You need a diagram?"

"She told me she needed to talk, Frank. Maccafee had disappeared and she was worried about him. She said he had enemies. I took that to mean she had, too."

"We have an APB out on Maccafee. He'll turn up."

"Ask Jimmy Hoffa about that."

"Which means what, Wil. That you could have prevented all this?"

"Which means I should at least have—"

"Shut up and listen for a change." Closer to shouting now. "You saw Rudy tonight. All he needed was a reason, and you handed it to him. Your one chance—and I do mean one—is to butt out. Do you see that? Not only are you in over your head, you are genuinely pissing *me* off."

A late bus went by as Wil sat unmoving, its scattered, brightly lit passengers resembling refugees from an Edward Hopper painting. The remaining techs exited the room and sealed it, nodded to Lin, then left. Minutes later, leaving Wil to contemplate the block letters on the tape, the empty runway with its blue and orange lights paralleling the dark line of mountains, Frank Lin did the same.

55

MAROTTA CALLED HIM NEXT MORNING AT HOME and left no doubt whose fault he considered the death of one of his most promising agents, despite her problems. Too burnt to argue with him, Wil asked what had happened to her father, E. Russell Lorenz, in Honduras: the 1991 raid.

Silence. "Not a thing I can think of that concerns you. But then, you could always ask your friend Maccafee when he turns up. Assuming that *was* him, which I doubt."

"I saw the photo, Marotta. I read the article."

"Impressing me not a bit," he said acidly. "And by the way, next time you call here hoping to extract information by pretending to be someone else, your ass is mine. You hearing that?"

"Lorenz was good people, Marotta. She had nothing to prove to me."

"Then I suggest you make her death count for something the next time you decide you're smarter than we are."

"Whatever you say," he said. "A question, though: Have you heard of a Red Chinese triad called Under Heaven?"

Dial tone.

Lin phoned then and, in few words, told him to forget about travel while Rudy contemplated what to do about him. Obstruction being but one option under consideration.

"Come on, Frank," he said. "You know that's a crock."

"It may well be," Lin answered. "But then, I used to think of you as standup. And, yes, you are that close."

After he hung up with Lin, Wil left a message on Lisa's machine, thanking her for the call to Li Tien. Li then told him things were pretty much the same out there, Matt was fine and Mia seemed glad to be back at classes. That with the exception of a particular female television reporter who'd been most insistent, there had been no further incidents.

A particular female reporter...

Taking his coffee out on the deck, he thought of Lorenz, her last call to him. Not quite fear in her voice, but something approximate, her earlier observation that Jimmy might have been approached by heavier players. Who, specifically? When and about what? Luc Tien's guests that last day? Some time before then?

Obviously Luc had a Plan B...

Just not that good a one where he was concerned, Wil thought. Which seemed unlike the man, much as Wil had seen of him—not much, admittedly.

For a while Wil tried losing himself in the sun on the water, fogbank in place where the islands usually crouched behind the oil rigs, gulls wheeling to land on the beach. Line of vehicles parked beachside across the highway.

And *what appeared to be, looked as much like, might possibly be* the gray Explorer from last night parked between two RVs.

Fighting a rising feeling, he scoped it more closely: kids brushing sand off their feet as they sat on its front bumper, sandwiches from an arm inside the lead RV, kids calling down the beach to the Explorer's likely occupants.

Right.

Score another for the standup.

Mentally, he stood down: fat lot of good that had done him or anyone else related to Jimmy Tien. Besides, the day was warm and clear and he was out of it from a long list of standpoints, not simply the media's finally tiring of him and pulling the plug. *Old news.*

Wil turned his telescope on the Rincon, verified what he'd heard over breakfast: that the *chubasco* was at last having an effect on the south swells, some weekdayers already out. What he had in mind regarding Pereira's *Harmony* faxes could wait till later, he told himself. Everything, such as it was, all the scattered and broken pieces, could wait until later. The familiar tremolo call that accompanied his trips out there building in him like the incoming sets, Wil closed up the house and answered it.

@

Wil extracted Southern Cross, the longboard he'd made himself, through its slot in the Bonneville's rear seat. Within minutes, he was in a lineup that included a dozen or so twenty-somethings and two olders he knew in passing—a guy who sold Benz's and an ad agency art director. Out here, the offshore breeze that had been walling up the faces was much more in evidence, wavetops giving the appearance of blowing smoke. With the valley fire close to suppressed, the immediate sky was blue and haze-free, the hills and roadway and eroded bluffs above La Conchita sharp enough to have been cut with a blade.

He waited. Then it was his turn, and he was able to hold his wave all the way from the point to the creek that ran between the houses, the trees and lawns, the fences and eave-high greenery. Geraniums spilling from porch baskets, orange and pink trumpet vine climbing the myoporum bushes, kids ashore frolicking with a yellow Lab.

He'd paddled out again and was waiting, recalling the day much like this when a friend took a bullet meant for him, when he heard a voice behind him.

"Trouble you for a little help here?"

Wil looked back. Directly into the sun.

"Just paid a kid three-fifty for this thing and wondered if I got jammed, that board of yours being so big," the voice said. "Hard to imagine what it's worth."

Wil raised a hand to the glare, saw no wetsuit over deeply tanned chest marred by a thumb-size discoloration above one nipple; flat hard abs, muscular shoulders narrowing to an athletic waist. The speaker wore chinos rolled above the calf—as if he'd just popped in off the road and decided to try out what he'd observing in passing. Dark lens aviator sunglasses masking the squint Wil somehow knew was there.

He heard, "Except you should get your money back from whoever taught you that cutback move."

Wil felt the point, the houses, the very day come down to the face, the voice, the mantle of skin graft he was able to make out on the right shoulder and upper arm. His own throat filling with echoes from a time when Southern Cross was homemade new and the world flat-out belonged to seventeen-year-old Sean Wilson Hardesty and Dennison James Van Zant, the rich kid who opened doors for them both.

That or he kicked them in.

"My God," he said, unbelieving. "Den?"

Barely believing it with the proof looking back at him, the face split by a confirming grin.

"What's up, Mojo?" it said. "Looks like you've seen a ghost."

56

Denny Van Zant rapped Southern Cross with a knuckle and said, "What's it been, a hundred years? I don't believe you're still using this thing."

"Still holds me up," Wil said. "What more?"

"Driving a sixty-six Bonneville wouldn't say anything about you, would it?"

"Try to find one now for what I paid for it."

"Right, half of what it cost you to trick it out. The time warp kid, tell me I'm wrong."

"Change is overrated," Wil said, having to smile.

"And I was part of those summers, too, remember?"

"No shit. That was you?"

Small talk for the long-dammed questions, the flashbacks worn by time, pebbles in a stream. They sat with the windows down, the longboard between them, Denny's arm resting on it. The Explorer was parked alongside, the tri-fin he'd bought on a whim poking out the open rear window. The same bluff where Wil had sat stunned and numb after watching his friend's body pulled from the water six years ago.

It was not an altogether dissimilar feeling, he realized. Denny, back from the dead; no word from him since a note written from the Ensenada hospital where he'd pulled through after being shot by an Australian hit man Wil ultimately survived. This after spending eight years in a VC prison camp following his capture at the Battle of Hue.

Months after the war was over, Denny had busted out in a self-set napalm fireball that nearly burned him alive before going to work as a "disposal specialist" for the same triad Wil mentioned to Terry Leong. Red Sun—the reason, in fact, Wil had known of it. He remembered the note Denny sent two years ago from the hospital, written as Todos Santos broke enticingly in the distance, Denny chafing to get at the forty-footers.

Mojo, it read:

Funny thing about eight years in a Cong prison, you say good-bye to feelings. I did, anyway. Try getting stuck in a cage you wouldn't wish on a contortionist, and the pain's so bad you'd do anything for a bullet in the ear.

Now try it for weeks on end.

You reach a point where you'd as soon kill something as look at it. Surprising what that's worth to some people: They blow away ours, we blow away theirs— regular way of life. Just don't look in the mirror.

Then one day, it's like a nerve coming back. Hardly noticeable at first. A toothache that keeps getting worse.

Three kids under fifteen went with this last deal I nearly did, a family they wanted made an example of. That's when I knew it was over. That and your face popping up when I'd least expect it. My own personal Casper. Weird, huh?

Den

P.S. Friends again? Damn, I hope so.

Rubbing the bullet tissue, Denny said, "You believe this, us I mean? The years and the bullshit? Like it was a dream or something you couldn't break free of."

"Too bad it wasn't," Wil said.

"Tell me about that."

He grinned. "You look good, Den."

"For burned-up and shot, among other things." Tilting the can of Tecate from the six-pack they'd stopped to get him. "Pretty fit yourself. You sure you don't want one of these?"

"Sure as I can be this minute."

"Yeah, I caught a bit of that the other night from the rocks. Some life you lead, in more ways than one."

"Then that was you over my shoulder."

"You made me, huh?" Denny said. "I'm impressed."

"More the shadow than the tail. Mind telling me how?"

He lowered the aviators, winked before resettling them. "Multiple rental cars. A furtive nature, well honed. What can I say?"

"Nobody other than you, then?"

"If there was somebody else, he's better than I am, and I'm the best I know."

They watched a dolphin roll the surface fifty yards out, two more heading west along the shore. Nose-to-tail diesel engines working the coast train track toward Ventura.

"Best at a lot of things, apparently," Wil said.

Denny drained off the Tecate and grinned. "There's the cryptic side of you I love. Remember Huntington Pier? You thinking I'd thrown the surf contest your way, prize money you wanted to buy some beat-up old Harley with? How frigging righteous you got with me?"

"*Did* throw," Wil said. "Obvious to anyone with eyes."

"I must have forgotten that part."

Wil let a beat go by. "What about Inez Lorenz, Den?"

"Who?"

"Skyway Motel, room 20, your Explorer. Same last three plate numbers, anyway."

Denny cracked a new can, shook the foam off his hand. "Pilot error," he said. "What happens when you have to take more than a leak and the guy you're expecting shows up early."

"More to the point, why?" Wil said.

Shrug. "Simple enough. I follow you to the airport, catch you looking that way, figure you might want to see her again when you came back. I had to do something. ATF, I hear somebody say?"

"Don't play me, Den. I'm not in the mood."

"Fair enough." He swigged from the can. "She really kill herself?"

"I don't know. I figured you might."

"Sorry. No gunshots, nobody in while I was there, nobody out."

Wil looked at him and saw nothing but the statement, a residue of smile, blue eyes the color of acetylene.

The smile faded.

"Old Wil, ever the stoic. What did Trina used to call us, the gas and the brakes?"

Trina Van Zant, clear as yesterday: Denny's sister and Wil's first flame—in and out of his life two years ago like a scalpel through heart muscle, the sutures still strained and prone to bleeding. Determined not to get sidetracked, he said, "San Francisco, Twin Peaks, three dead in a limo. A hitter the one witness said resembled Steve McQueen." Swiveling the rearview toward the passenger side so Denny could see himself.

"That your big reach, Mojo?" he said. "Or somebody else's?"

"Just a feeling I had and hoped I was wrong about."

Denny took a breath, lost the shades, angled glances at the mirror. "McQueen, huh? I always thought Redford with more attitude and less hair. Which only goes to show, I guess."

Damnit, Wil thought. *Goddamnit.*

"Then you are back in the life," he said.

"Define life."

"Just what you think it means, Den. Killing for money."

Denny dumped the remaining beer out the window, crushed the can, tossed it in the bag. "Facts-of-life, Wil-boy: no mon, no fun. And I sure wasn't going to the old man for it, such as the crash left him. Which, by the way, almost made me feel sorry for him."

"I'll bet," Wil said.

"Typical Wil, all black and white. You've heard of trying to get clear? Well, this is my chance, my own Bali Hai—beach breaks so perfect you'd think you'd died and gone to heaven. At what cost, you ask? A few shit-bags that tend to call into question any semblance of a divine plan." He thrust the mirror back in place, stayed on Wil. "And do we have to talk about this so goddamn soon? I thought you'd be glad to see me."

"I am, Den," he said. "More than you know."

Denny said, "I mean, who else is left to us? Me and my fucked-up sister; you and that wife you can't seem to let go of." Leaning back in the seat. "Don't sweat it, Trina filled in what I didn't see myself. And she's pretty, by the way, your ex. Japanese, isn't she?"

Wil kept his focus on the horizon.

"What—too distilled for you?" Denny went on. "Well, in case you missed it, Mojo, the secret's out. We're all a baby toe from the third rail."

"Are you about through?" Wil said.

The blue eyes bored into his. "Maybe when you fill me in on why you'd go to work for a VC. And don't pull that look. You expected a free pass from *me*?"

"In a word?" Wil said. "He's a good man who didn't do it."

"Sure he is, like so many I looked up after the war." Denny's whole face lit now. "Guys who swore they weren't the ones who tossed the rats in your cage, stuck your head in the honey bucket. That is, when they weren't employing ingenious little devices to show a guy a good time." He paused for breath. "Care to know what I did to square things?"

Wil said nothing.

"Hell, who would?" Denny added. "At least tell me that with the VC you'd been drinking."

"Tea, as I recall," Wil said.

Denny shook his head as if trying to make sense of something that made none; worse, constituted betrayal. "Wait, I've got it, sure as shit. The guy's kid and grandkid who disappeared off San Miguel, you did it for them, right?"

"And the wife. And the daughter. Innocents, Den."

His face darkened. "Nobody's innocent: nobody. Where I've been, you learn that. They're either doing it to you or thinking about it."

Wil felt his own anger rising. "You do Luc Tien on contract, too? Maybe hang around to watch his brother the VC hang for it?"

"Not a bad plan. I wish I'd thought of it."

"Answer the question."

"You tell me," he said: dead flat. "Is that what you think I did?"

Wil let a breath out to pull it together. "What I think is that apart from some highlight-reel moments we share, I have no idea who showed up here today. Why did you, Den?"

"That's the past for you," he answered. "Always got her makeup on, batting her eyes, and promising more than she delivers."

Unexpectedly, Denny Van Zant smiled, grinned broadly, then laughed: way more Redford than McQueen. "You want to know why this is such a hoot for me?" he said, slapping the longboard, eyes alive at his own humor. "You haven't changed a damn bit."

57

THEY WERE AT WIL'S, the afternoon spent in selective reminiscence. Long-due goop applied to Southern Cross, Denny's sudden-impulse buy rewaxed, Wil's calling John Pereira to see if he could rent the aging Cris-Craft the lawyer had bogged down in restoring.

"When do you want it?" Pereira inquired after taking a muffled question from someone in the office.

"Tomorrow," Wil said. "Early."

"Romantic getaway pumping bilges?"

"Deep sea fishing. Provided the current hasn't dislodged *Harmony* from your coordinates."

"Time on your hands, I take it."

Wil explained, more or less: cursory search, any port in a storm the way things were shaping up. Or rather, not shaping up.

"Key's under the duckboards," Pereira said. "For what it's insured for, I could buy three boats that work. You ever want to invest in one of these things, and I do mean invest, see me first. *Then* see a therapist."

"Full tank and your usual case of Boone's Farm do it?"

Pereira laughed. "You'll need to top off to get out there. And stay on the tube, will you? The wife gets a kick out of saying we know you."

"I'm glad somebody does," Wil said.

"Wait'll you own a boat."

"So where's your dog," Denny asked as Wil hung up. Shirt off and sunning on the deck. Iced tea beside him and his feet up.

Matt, Wil told him. Temporary guard duty at the Tien's.

"Temporary, you say? Just make sure he's in the room when they serve soup. At least the kind they gave us."

"Enough, Den, okay? Give it a rest."

"Resting works for you, does it?" Grinning at him.

"When I let it," Wil said.

"Yeah, sure it does."

Denny cocked an eye at the Rincon and went to the scope, nodded and looked back. "Anybody mention second wind? I mean, it's not Todos out there, but if your goop's cured...assuming it ever will be."

"When will I know?" Wil answered him.

The twilight surf was even better than the morning's: water holding the day's warmth, thinned-out crowd and wind, light bathing the mountains behind them in gold, then apricot, then pink before leaving the field to an already-emergent moon.

Runs were capsule moments of the places recalled while waiting in the lineup: Steamers, Malibu, Trestles, La Jolla—surfer girls and hotdoggers, free-for-alls and e-ticket breaks—each a piece of the jigsaw that was the two of them. As if Nam and what followed had never been: life still sun-warmed Coppertone, drive-ins, Duane Eddy guitar riffs. Each day the first day of summer.

Denny hadn't lost a beat, playing to the crowd gathered to watch them. And afterward, feeling the double-dip in shoulders and legs, they'd driven home with the windows down and the radio up, Wil moving gingerly as he stepped out on deck to the fragrance of searing tri-tip.

"Dawn patrols a thing of the past, huh?" Denny said, turning the meat in a hiss of smoke.

Wil grinned. "Today gaining on yesterday."

"All my troubles seem so far away. Which reminds me, the answer is no."

Wil waited.

"No, I did not do Luc Tien," Denny said.

"But something..."

"Something, yeah. I had a contract to do him."

"From the Po Sang."

Denny glanced out of the smoke. "The Po Sang, huh? Well, well," he said. "The brother made fertilizer out of people who crossed him. To grow his orchids. You do know that?"

"Heard it," Wil said. Then, "Good money, I assume?"

Denny stayed intent on the meat. "I'll ignore that because it's you, Mojo. Bali Hai—that's all it is and ever was. My own special island." Removing the tri-tip from the grill.

Wil finished running the slicing knife across the sharpener, wiped the blade, handed it over. "So what happened?"

"What happened, old friend, is that somebody took out the eight-ball while I was lining up the shot. And if you're asking me to feel anything for these people, you're talking to the wrong guy."

"Maybe." Wil giving him a second. "You familiar with the name Under Heaven?"

"Damn, impress me twice," Denny said, back to slicing the meat onto plates with the green salad Wil had made. Slabs of polenta bread he'd cut apart.

"Terry Leong mentioned it."

"Ah yes, him. The gang cop who wants to thank me for stepping on the bug that did his partner."

"Leong's no joke, Den, don't make that mistake. He thinks Under Heaven might be muscling the Pos. And I thought you didn't take sides anymore."

By now the oil rigs were lit up, a line resembling party ships in the channel. Cars had their headlights on, their rush sounding like the surf sliding in beyond the roadway. Smoke still leaked from the vents in the barbecue lid.

"Reality check," Denny said at length. "I do the people nobody misses and everybody's better off without. I do it because some things stuck to me over there that might not have to the other guy and because I need the money other people are willing to pay. Who these people are is beyond the fact. I don't want to know, and you especially don't want to know."

"Small town PI not ready for prime time. That it?"

Smile. "How modest, our Mojo. But I know about you from Trina, remember? How you canceled John Pomphrey's subway pass that night on the roof?"

"Straight on and him calling the shot."

Denny grinned, the cat with the canary: "One of a number of candidates, if the article I read was accurate. And you haven't exactly been invisible the last few days. Good dinner, by the way."

"All of which amounts to what, Den? That what you do is okay and should be with me? Because it isn't, if you need to hear that."

The grin disappeared. "Aren't we kind of far down the road for the approval bit?"

"Guess that depends on the road."

"Wil, Wil...where did I get you?" Taking a hit on the Tecate he'd cracked. "You want to talk morality plays, we can do that. But 'wrong' hasn't cut ice with me for a lot of years and for a lot of reasons. Besides, I didn't come here for that."

"Maybe it's time you told me why you did."

"No kidding. You'll shut up and listen if I do?"

"While we're young, if that works." What might come of this deeper cut falling away like a first-stage booster.

"I was never young," Denny said. "You just never noticed."

"I noticed," Wil said, matching him. "And I'm still here."

"All right, then. Your guy Tien offing his brother the way he did was fine with the people I'm in with. Saved them a lot of trouble and money. Uh-uh, don't interrupt, I know where you stand here. Long story short, I was going to pop in on you to establish an alibi if it came to that." He drew from the beer can, set it down. "Not that it would have or I didn't want to see you. It's just that business had to come first. Anyway, it's not often I lose a job, so I decided to violate my own rule and hang around. See who stole my money and if I could reason with them."

By now his face was largely in shadow.

"Then you begin generating all this ink about your guy not doing it despite the evidence, blah-blah. Made some people nervous, people who give other people calls late at night." He folded his hands under his chin. "You catching my drift here?"

"Sorry," Wil said. "You're going to have to spell it out for me."

Denny dipped a last piece of bread in the juices and ate it. "It's like this: Keep banging the garbage cans and somebody's going to come out and make the noise go away. Now do you get it?"

"I think so: the somebody meaning the best they've got," Wil said. "Who could get close enough to put a .22 magnum in my ear."

"Fair assumption, m'man."

Holding Denny's eyes, he said, "Not the same somebody who spared a kid who refused to kill two little girls in a jewelry store? Who took the heat off his family once for a murder he didn't commit and one of them did? Not that somebody?"

A different look passed between them.

Night traffic on the highway.

Denny's smile was tired, frayed at the edges. He tapped the beer can on his teeth, shook his head. "You ever think maybe life's too fucked to get worked up over?" Pause. "No, I didn't think so, not you, not our Wil. What time you say you were going out in the morning?"

58

WIL CAME AWAKE to something that became the creak of footsteps, his clock radio reading three. He swung over the edge of the bed, eased down the hall to the living room, and saw him.

Bent over in Skivvies, Denny had a hand against the window frame, the vertical blinds slanting moonlight onto his sweat-bathed face and chest. His breath came hard, as if just in from a run. Turning to Wil with a little smile of apology, he said, "Sorry, Mojo. They still wake me up, napalm and night sweats. Hope I didn't mess up your couch."

"What is it, Den? Malaria?"

"Not exactly." Wiping at the sweat with his forearm. "I managed to dodge that one."

"Not everyone did. Count your blessings."

"Yeah. Unless you figure the war was never more than bullshit to begin with." His gaze returning to the window.

"Tell that to the guys on the wall," Wil said.

"I did." As though run through a sound processor. "They were strangely quiet about it."

For a moment they stood in the slanting light. Then Wil said, "It's over, Den, we lost. And Vinh Tien didn't kill his brother."

"Who?" Blinking as though coming awake. "Oh, yeah—your misunderstood VC."

"So what is it, Den? Straight out."

Denny's eyes swung to his, and for those seconds it was like looking into the kid Denny once had been. The kid whose adopted father packed him off to Nam then washed his hands of him when he was declared missing in action. The kid who'd made it out with hell itself after him.

As though having debated the point and lost, he said, "Agent orange, they suspect, all that hacking and jacking around in it. Poetic, huh? After all the other shit we waded through, turns out it was our own."

Wil had the feeling a wind had reached inside the house.

"What are you talking about?" he said.

Denny hesitated, then, "A form of lymphoma." Running a hand across his face, wiping it on his shorts. "Slow but steady. Turned up in the tests they did when I was recovering in Baja. Welcome to the bonus round, huh?"

Damnit. Wil's first reaction. *Goddamn it.*

He said, "Any chance they might have blown it?" The wind inside *him* now.

"Nice try. Docs up here said the same thing."

...all to hell...

"Which means what exactly?"

"Nine months," Denny said, "maybe a year. No small part of the Bali thing is an herbalist who's been working miracles down there. Need I say, he's more optimistic."

...and gone.

"Jesus, Den, I don't know what to say. There anything I can do to help?"

Totally inadequate sounding. Still, Denny didn't seem to notice, just swung his gaze back to the window, surf booming in the relative quiet, the diminishing *skree* of a night bird skimming the house.

Then, without inflection, he said, "Actually, there is. Pay attention when I tell you these Under Heaven fucks are not the ones you want to mess with."

59

NEXT MORNING THEY WERE AT COFFEE BY FIVE-THIRTY, the harbor by six, packing half and half'd Sumatra in double cups, something to tilt the balance. But morning had at least in part delivered on its promise to banish dark thoughts, the coffee was strong and restorative, and Wil had a plan.

Such as phase one amounted to.

"So tell me again," he said, breaking the silence since they'd stepped aboard Pereira's old Cris-Craft: *Mr. Lucky*, a peeling forty-something-footer with flashes of his restoration efforts. "You're going out with me why?" Sunrise gilding the harbor's masts and hulls, walkways and somnambulant water, the seawall and its flags.

Denny gulped coffee and looked at him. Stained khakis and a cut-off gray sweatshirt, worn running shoes and black-rubber sports Casio. As if the harbor were home.

"Not that I'm not glad for the company," Wil added, lifting the duckboard and finding the key, cranking the engine in a burble of blue exhaust until it caught. "Long as you don't decide I'm banging on any garbage cans."

"Serious shit, Wil—to add perspective."

"What I'm saying is you don't have to do this."

Denny said, "Two years ago, you did things for me nobody had ever done." Activating the instruments that needed it—built-ins and add-on

GPS, depth sensor, and radio grouping. "I wake up with that."

"Done for your mom as much as you," Wil said.

"Now you tell me."

"The point is, you don't owe me anything."

"Thanks," Denny said, busying himself with the radio. "I believe I'll just tag along."

"To report on me for somebody?"

The grin. "*Tag,*" he said. "As in hang. Spend time."

"Meaning you might not shoot me today?"

Denny looked at him, McQueen double-crossed with Redford. "No guarantees, you don't shut the fuck up."

"You always had a way with words."

While Denny loosed the lines, Wil stowed his bag containing windbreaker, backup long-sleeve tee and jeans, the sweatshirt-wrapped .45. He double-checked the gear he'd brought: dive fins and wetsuit with hood; BC vest and tank; regulator, weight belt, and dive knife; pry-bar and torch...vague on the last time he'd been down for anything other than lobster. Deeper, at least, than fifty feet or so. He dug out the faxed coordinates, entered them in the global positioning system as Denny eased *Mr. Lucky* from her slip and into the main channel. Past the sand bar and the wharf and a flight of pelicans skimming low, past the entrance buoys and out.

"Okay, Dad," Denny said. "How long till we're there?"

"Three hours, plus or minus. Depends on *Mr. Lucky.*"

"And you expect to find what?"

"Whatever's down there," Wil said.

Denny angled a look. "And that's your big plan..."

"The hope being that it's enough," he said. "That maybe she'll talk to me."

"Damn, Mojo. No wonder you command the press you do."

They were up to speed now, a steady fourteen knots, *Mr. Lucky* blessed with neither big engines nor new. Yet the day was cooperative, bracing and clear save for the fog still largely obliterating the four island profiles, the bluffed coastline and mountains receding as they angled west: glassine water, wind as yet no factor. They passed kelp beds, dolphin pods, cormorants, gulls working a seal carcass, a swirl of something the size of a station wagon.

Forty minutes passed. Knowing he'd have to be sharp for the dive, Wil went below to stretch out. But his mind was like a tape that wouldn't shut off: Denny and all the suddenness and soul searching, the thought of losing someone as valued as the someone you'd only dreamed of finding again—balanced by the trust you placed in him unobserved in a lifetime of years. Then there was Lisa and what was happening with her, the Tiens and Under Heaven, the very real possibility that he'd made their list. If not yet, likely by setting in motion what he had in mind.

He had the sensation of crossing a chasm on a wire, then he was out. That is, until he was shaken awake in what seemed no time, Denny saying, "Up and at 'em. I've been gridding with the bottom finder."

Wil came upright up to the faint barking of sea lions, wave slap, the brine-sharp smell of kelp. "And?" he said.

Denny's smile broadened. "Every picture tells a story."

Wil watched *Mr. Lucky's* hull and trailing anchor line recede.

A school of sardines flashed and veered away, colors began shading toward the greens and blacks that came with depth. While not actually cold after the initial shock, the water was anything but warm against his wetsuit. It was, however, unclouded, permitting the light to filter down with him, even though the sun he'd left was tempered by the fog drifting out from San Miguel.

Forty feet, sixty...eighty, Wil equalizing the pressure in his ears. A hundred...hundred-ten, his bubbles changing from rumble to the pressure-affected chiming sound they made as the reel defined itself.

Getting his bearings, he picked a direction and tracked it. Lobster antennae waved from hidey holes, sea growth undulated around black urchins, giant starfish, anemones the size of wrestler's necks. Rockfish, calico, and cabezon took note; a horned shark the length of his arm regarded him, then flashed off. Smaller anemones patterned a rusted-out ship's locker too big to be from *Harmony*.

And then, there it was—off to his right, a discordant note among the spine of ledges trailing seaweed and the sheer drops. *H-rm-ny* through the algae that softened her profile and stern, telltaled off her broken rigging and antenna mast. Oddly affecting to view through green half-light the object of so much speculation and heartbreak, the haunting in an otherwise placid dream.

Wil checked his watch: better-than-hoped-for time.

He kicked toward her. As the photographs had partly shown, she'd lodged between massive boulders, the closest plunging into blackness. Largely upright, her bow was pitched thirty degrees to the reef. At intervals, thin strings of bubbles rose...as if she were reaching out to the world of air and light and color, even though it was no longer visible. Strands of orange netting still fouled her deck gear.

For a moment Wil hung suspended: scanning, willing her to reveal what had brought her to this. Nothing. He swam around it, searching for things the investigators might have missed: bullet holes, evidence of fire, ramming, boarding hooks, anything out of place. But apart from the split in her stern, the reef jutting from it, *Harmony* was silent on the points. The way she'd settled, broken rigging and mast, the loss of her windshield—all said wave action.

Wil activated his torch, shone it into chaos. Strewn debris, wormholed charts and upended books, a hooded sweatshirt trailing a sleeve. Looking closer at a sprung cabinet, he saw a bull eel's head poking from it, jaws parted to reveal needle teeth.

As two lingcod darted out, Wil went in.

Pockets of air silvered in the light. He touched one, watched the bubbles scatter, then set about. Silted instruments, two-way radio, and cassette boombox; empty bulkhead mount that presumably held the lost tracking device; Mr. Coffee minus its container; small reefer ajar with the contents long gone; interior lockers with reminders of another world.

Spotting a semi-reflective surface bonded to a closed drop-lid, he opened the lid and found waterlogged cassettes, disintegrating tackle box, package of cough drops, rusting can of 3-In-One oil, lead fishing weights, clipped-together screwdriver set, scattered small tools, a ruptured metal flashlight.

Wil closed the drop-lid, brushed a glove across the plaque; clean again, it read *Harmony. 1989. For Island Seafoods.* Prying the lid off its hinges, he stowed it in the mesh bag lashed to his belt. He was about to leave when he shone his torch on the larger sprung cabinet, the eel's head tracking his movements. Something beneath the eel reflected back, the corner of...something. He checked his watch again: sixteen minutes of the twenty-two allotted, the chill already getting to him.

He nosed the long-handled flash closer.

Closer...

As the eel struck at it, Wil slipped in the bar and, with its hook, extracted a CD-case bottom. No lid or disk, just the clear plastic base and black inset hub. Teeth marks along one edge.

He flashed the deep interior; beyond eel, he saw nothing else. Dragging the base beyond the eel's reach, he put it in the bag, then propelled himself through the windowless opening. With a look back at *Harmony*, at whatever Jimmy and Wen's hopes had been that day, Wil followed his bubbles to the shimmering plane of surface.

60

THEY WERE MIDWAY BACK, San Miguel an indistinguishable line of fog, late sun shadowing the swells and the approaching coastline. As *Mr. Lucky's* engines pulsed, Wil went over in his mind what *Harmony* had tried to tell him—no marks, no alarm-bell indications of foul play, the eel-chewed CD base—until Denny appeared beside him, yawning.

"Boats and sun," he said. "Somebody ought to bottle it."

"There's coffee, if you want some," Wil told him.

"What do you think got me up?" Helping himself, and after blowing on it and another yawn: "So—you going to tell me what all this gets down to?"

"I'm still deciding," Wil said.

"On the meaning or whether to tell me?"

"Both."

Brief smile. "Can't say I blame you on the one. I'm not sure I'd trust me, either."

Wil skirted intersecting swells, the line resembling a monster backbone. "What about Lorenz?" he said. "You have any idea who killed her?"

"Me?" Denny sipped coffee. "I thought we'd been through this."

"She and her partner were into something involving Luc Tien. Something freelance."

"Which would be?..."

Wil shook his head. "I'm not sure yet."

Denny picked up the CD base lying next to the drop-lid Wil had pried off. Turning it in his hands, he said, "So right away you thought of your old friend who bags trash for money making the kill. Divide and conquer."

"Did you hear me say that, Den?"

"You didn't have to, it's written all over your face."

Wil kept his eyes on the water, the churn known as Potato Patch receding on the right.

Slipping on his sunglasses, Denny said, "Last call on this, she wasn't my type. Besides, not being sure who Lorenz was beyond somebody dealing with you, maybe sleeping with you, why would I?"

It made sense, Wil had to admit; yet it provided no closure. He said, "You happen to see her with her partner at all? Maccafee?"

"Big guy going bald, mostly muscle?"

"That's him."

"Once. Where is he in all this?"

Wil angled off a larger swell, reset his line of sight. "Inez hadn't seen him in days. She was concerned about him. She said he had enemies."

"Sounds like she did, too."

"Then you don't believe she killed herself."

"The hell do I know?" he said. "You tell me."

"No," Wil said. "I don't. Worried maybe, scared a little, but not suicidal."

Denny finished his coffee in a gulp. "All right: agreed, for what it's worth. Which likely means we're both wrong." Eyes hidden behind the dark lenses. "And which leaves us where, exactly?"

"Us?..."

"Like I said, Mojo, whoever did Luc has my money. I want it. Now, assuming your VC didn't do it, which pains me to even consider, look at how the thing was crafted to snare him. Which tells me whoever it was is smart *and* good. *And Pilgrim, you might be needing this Winchester of mine.*" Denny lapsing into *Stagecoach* John Wayne.

Long pause. "I don't know, Den. I'll have to think about it."

"Yeah? When does a pair not beat a high card?"

"Just...when it doesn't."

"Won't fit the template, that it? Too much water under the dam?"

Wil let it ride.

"Too bad," Denny said. "For a lot of reasons."

Wil swung wide of a fishing boat on a crossing vector, *Mr. Lucky's* pulse filling the cabin, Denny adding, "Reason one, the big one: You know damn well I could have done you just by leaving you out there. Yet you went down anyway. And do you really think I'd have come clean about what I do if I were going for the bull's-eye?"

"Friends versus money," Wil said after a pause.

"Not friends, bud, *friend*. Except when he's being a righteous prick."

"So why would a CD be aboard at all when there wasn't a player?" Wil said over the music.

"Just the AM-FM and cassette, you're sure of that." Denny leaning toward him to hear.

They were in a restaurant overlooking the harbor. Faces still lit by the day, sailboat masts moving to a music of their own, high clouds and contrails pink with the setting sun. Dinner crowd starting to join the early birds and raise the volume level in the bar.

"I'm sure," Wil said.

"Portable CD player carried by one of them? Washed overboard?"

Wil thought. "That would depend on if it's a music CD in the first place. There's another box I want to check it against. If I'm right, they both came from Luc's —before he went to the encrypted e-mail system for backup last December."

"Right after *Harmony* went down."

"You got it."

The hostess touched his arm, motioned that their balcony table was ready. She led them out to it, left them with menus and their drinks. Ignoring both, Denny asked, "So what's one have to do with the other?"

"The box I have belonged to Jimmy's girlfriend," Wil said. "She or maybe Jimmy used it to store her poetry: overkill for a disk of that capacity, but it's what was around." Taking a hit of his club soda.

"And Jimmy would have had access."

Wil nodded. "According to Mia, computer work was among the things he did for Luc. She also told me Wen was working there when Jimmy met her. It would have been normal for Luc to let them use his CD burner, the same one he used to back up his financial and business data. Lorenz mentioned that angle."

"Was there a burner among the gear when you found Luc?"

"No, and I've thought about that," Wil said. "Enough to see a possible explanation."

"Door number one: It became obsolete and he pitched it."

"Not obsolete, I think. Compromised."

"How? Jimmy?"

Wil set the chewed disk case down between them. "Longshot time: Lorenz and Maccafee were leveraging Jimmy for information on Rising Dragon. Lorenz told me she believed somebody else had gotten to the kid: a step up the food chain is how she put it. But if she knew who it was, she didn't say."

"Hard to see Po Sang," Denny said after a gulp. "They'd be a horizontal step, or one down a rung."

"What I was thinking, too." Popping in an oyster cracker, looking off at the lights coming on, the pink fading off the peaks. "Terry Leong said the San Francisco cops turned an informant. An entity was coming at this guy's people with a plan to reconfigure the Po's into high tech and white collar. Street crime and muscle would go to the Dragons. The name he caught was Under Heaven."

Denny crunched ice. "Them at the top, of course. Which would mean Po *and* Dragon heads rolling, those who didn't take to being reconfigured."

Wil said, "I don't know about the Pos, but my guess is Under Heaven offered Luc a *capo* or whatever and got stiffed. Luc had his own designs on the Pos, and from what Lorenz told me, he hated Chinese of any stripe. Plus, the whole scam would have been his to begin with, only with the Dragons running the show." Washing down another cracker. "Smart, except for one thing."

"Jimmy. Under Heaven offering him the Dragons. Under *them*."

Wil nodded. "Big step up, but a bigger price for it. Sell out his uncle, keep Lorenz and Maccafee at bay thinking they still owned him."

"Lot of balls in the air for a kid that age."

"Yeah," Wil said. "Too many."

Denny turned his Beck's bottle, watched the rings it left. "So why San Miguel?"

Wil shrugged. "My guess? Farthest out of the islands, federal turf, nothing there to speak of. Ideal for a mothership to run cargos in, Jimmy to pick them up and make the payoffs."

The waitress came: pen poised, apologetic, an expectant look.

"Sea bass," Wil told her. "The chalk board?"

"Two," Denny said when she turned to him. "Fries and salads."

After writing it down, and with a long look at Denny, she moved on. Wil grinned. "Not every day she sees a movie star," he said.

"Whoever the hell she thinks it is." No grin. "So, Plan A: Jimmy copies Luc's files onto the disk, heads out to hand it over. After which, Under Heaven takes down Luc and installs Jimmy—with his help."

"That would be my guess," Wil said.

"You think they ever got the disk?"

Wil fingered the teeth marks on the CD base. "No. Luc wouldn't have lasted this long if Under Heaven had it."

"So far okay. Possible to verify any of it?"

"You mean after finding Luc's killer and proving somebody other than my client did him? I'm vague there, enough to ask Wen's mother some more questions."

"You've been to see her, then."

"When I first started," Wil said, sipping his club. "I just didn't know what questions to ask."

"Wild guess." Finishing his Beck's. "There was a little problem communicating."

"You could say that. A neighbor told me Jimmy and Wen looked scared."

"There's an understatement: Under Heaven and the ATF, Luc and the whole family thing. Not to mention how big a bastard he was by himself. Who wouldn't be scared?"

"And yet Vinh said the kid loved his uncle," Wil said, giving it a beat. "It's why he went to Luc's and stayed."

Denny leaned forward. "Meaning Jimmy might have had second

thoughts about turning him? That's what you're saying?"

"For sure? No. We may never know."

"But lacking evidence, it makes sense."

Wil said, "I guess what I'm saying is this…" Reaching into his windbreaker and pulling out the CD Amber had given him: the one Kenny turned up in Jimmy and Wen's old couch, the one Mia ID'd as coming from Luc's. The one with Wen's sad lines on it:

And so I call to you,
My guardian heart
Land of the white water bud, the jade black earth
The burning tallow moon.

Wil lifted the lid, released the plastic hinges and disk and handed the base to Denny. He watched Denny's look go from curious to intent, watched Denny flip it over and compare it to the eel-chewed base on the table, both having tiny crowns stamped into their lower right corners. He watched Denny run a thumb over each, lean back, meet his eyes.

Finally say, "You're full of surprises, aren't you?"

"I wouldn't say that," Wil came back. "Just wanted to see if you wound up at the same place I did."

"Nice. Remind me not to double down any bets with you."

Finally Wil's grin broke, the one he was holding in. "You're just lucky I let you sleep out there."

61

D FNNY OFF TO SEE WHAT HE COULD EXTRACT FROM WEN'S MOTHER in her language, Wil drove next morning to see Li Tien. To share what he'd learned and what it might mean for Vinh.

He could hear Matt barking at the window. Then Li was letting him in and Matt was total wag as Wil bent to him, led him out to the patio, gave him Milk-Bones he'd brought, Li Tien appearing then with tea service. Over blue-glaze cups she told him Mia was at school, they'd been to see Vinh, who looked as if he were losing weight. He showed her the dedication plaque he'd pried off *Harmony*'s dash and, for a long moment, she said nothing. Then the cloud came, and she waved it off and went inside.

Out of respect, Wil took Matt for a walk along the lake near the house, Matt running ahead, circling, dashing off again after making sure Wil was following. When they returned, Li Tien was back in her patio chair, the plaque in her hands, the patio smelling of newly-cut grass and ornamental garlic, wet stones splashed by water from the entwined cranes.

"He was a fine boy, Jimmy, smart and clever," she said when he'd gone through it or tried to, not sure how much was sinking in about the two CD cases. "Always he was making his sister laugh."

Wil slipped the cases back into his pocket. He said, "I have a question about your future daughter-in-law. Did you welcome her?"

Li Tien paused. "How does any mother feel? At first, I did not: Wen was so different than our hopes for Jimmy. But with the baby, what could

I say? Later, I came to like her. Jimmy said she loved poetry, that she knew the *ca dao* folk poems and sang them for him."

They sat silent a moment.

"She was working on her own poems, he told us, but we never offered to sit for them. Such is our loss."

"Did Jimmy tell you where she came from, and how?"

"Despite our curiosity, we talked little of those things."

"What about Wen's mother?"

Li sat as though framing the thought. Then, "She came here with Wen, we knew that much. But I never felt Nguyen Diem was honest with us. She distrusted us, I believe."

"Any particular reason?"

"We were Vietnamese, she was part Chinese," Li said. "As in our homeland, it was enough to divide us."

"So you never learned the circumstances of their arrival?"

"Only that to get here she gave up all of what her husband left her, and still it wasn't enough. Certainly she had no money beyond what Jimmy and Wen could provide. No skills to speak of."

Wil said, "Have you heard from her since last year?"

"No. Nothing."

Curled at her feet, Matt gave a little sigh. The bamboo rustled in a breeze. The phone rang. Li rose, and in a moment she was back with their portable, handing it to Wil.

"Hardesty," he answered, raising the antenna.

"Figured you might be there," Frank Lin's voice said. "Can you talk?"

"Depends...what's up?"

"I'm at the jail," Lin said. "I've been trying to raise that shyster lawyer of theirs, the activist? No luck."

"Raymond Ky? What for?"

There was a pause; then, from Lin, "Just what we needed, three of our finest trapped Vinh Tien in the shower. He whaled on one, but the others beat the crap out of him. He's in the hospital. Possible skull fracture, among other things."

Matt stirred again. Li looked at him. The herons dripped water. A gust momentarily tossed the bamboo.

"Wil? You there?"

"On the patio having tea, thank you."

The line was quiet. Then, "You going to tell her or should I?"

He was in a private room with a uniformed deputy outside when Li and Wil entered, Frank Lin having volunteered to have Mia picked up and transported there. Vinh's face was chalk, his eyes closed, the sockets swollen. His nose was packed with bloody cotton, and stitches ran from behind one ear into a shaved area on his scalp. Another cut running eyebrow to forehead had a bandage over it. A tube ran solution to a vein while a nurse transferred his vital signs onto a clipboard. In one motion Li took the chair beside the bed, took his hand in hers.

Vinh's eyes opened briefly, then closed; as the nurse left, a young doctor hustled in with a manila file folder. "I'm sorry," he told them. "But I really must insist."

"Doctor?" Wil said, motioning him aside.

"What is it?..."

"I go, Mrs. Tien stays. Non-negotiable."

"This man has sustained severe trauma—you do get that?"

"Understood. Thank you."

Outside the blinds, traffic pulsed through an intersection; morning sun glinted off cars moving on the recently reopened San Marcos Pass.

The doctor said, "I know you. You're the one who's been on television."

"Unfortunately."

He clutched the file to his chest. "For your information, my uncle died in that godforsaken war. And I intend to take this up with my superiors."

When the door had shut, Vinh raised his other hand a few inches. "Hang on," Wil said, taking it. "We're getting close."

He was in the waiting room when Frank Lin entered with Mia. "Where is he, where's my dad?" she said, face flushed, eyes searching before coming back. "I have to see him."

"He's with your mom," Wil told her.

"And he's going be all right?..."

"They have every reason to think so," Lin said.

She turned on him. "What the fuck does that mean?"

"That he's strong and resilient, that a doctor will be updating us soon. He's in good hands."

She said, "He was in your jail, your custody. How could you let this happen to him?"

"We're looking into it, believe me."

"*You're looking into it.* How pathetic is that?" A shade this side of losing it. "Get away from me and my family."

"Mia," Wil said, "I have some—"

"Nothing, as usual. Why don't you go play beach volleyball? At least be useful."

"Maybe you should sit down, Mia."

"The big whoop hero, hoping I'd fall all over him from the time he showed up at our house. Derek was right. You are an asshole."

"How about we all sit down," Wil said. "I'll get some tea."

"Tea should do it, all right. *Leave me alone!*" Then, as if the valve in the pressure cooker had blown itself out, "Haven't you done enough already?"

For a moment, they just looked at each other. Then she looked away and he and Lin left for the parking lot.

Getting into his black-and-white, Lin said, "Much as I hate it, she has a point about the jail. If I find out my guys turned their backs, it'll be the last time they do something like that."

Wil said, "Ever wonder where they hide the crystal balls when you need one?"

"Only about every two minutes."

Lin started the engine, gunned out of the lot.

62

WIL WASN'T DUE TO MEET DENNY UNTIL THREE, so he stopped at Peet's, then drove to Lisa's office. She was in a meeting, the receptionist said, due out, but no guarantees. He left a message, then went down to the courtyard, took a seat in the shade of the metal umbrella. He was sipping coffee and listening to the fountain when he heard her footsteps and, "Hey, sailor, what brings you downtown?" Faded navy skirt and loose lavender top, pin in the shape of a hand he'd bought her at the Museum of Art gift shop—a whimsical expressive enameled thing that always seemed to elicit comments.

"Coffeeman," he said, handing her hers. "He delivers."

"You any relation to Pizzaman?"

"Fewer anchovies."

She took a sip from it. "Thanks. Sorry to keep you waiting out here. A very long audit."

"How you feeling?"

She shrugged. "My appetite's better, I think."

"Anything we should infer from that?"

"Look, I appreciate it, I do. But—"

"Get a life?"

"You already have a life."

He sipped coffee.

"Wil, having this baby at my age isn't a decision you just make."

"It isn't what I meant, either."

"Sorry, it's been a swell day so far." Pause. "Want to know what Brandon said when I finally pinned him down? Two words going out the door: *Whatever* and *Babe*."

Wil counted down from ten, chased it with coffee.

"Reassuring, huh?" she added. "At least I know where *you* stand."

"That's what I came to clarify, Leese. If you'll hear me out."

She looked at him, started to speak.

"No—wait," he said. "If you decide having it isn't for you, I'll back you up. If you decide in favor, we'll make it work. Period and somehow. You wouldn't be going it alone."

For a long moment she was silent, hands clasped under her chin. Then she said, "Another man's child."

"Your child, my commitment. So stated."

"To what purpose, Wil? Some dream you want to reinsert yourself into? Because it doesn't work that way. And if you're thinking it's your duty somehow, don't."

"All right. But how *does* it work, Leese? By turning away from a friend who wants to help?"

Time passed, the fountain filling the gap, sun backlighting the spray. She ran a hand through her hair.

"It wouldn't be Devin back, Wil. Nowhere close."

"I'm aware of that."

"Are you?" she asked. "Really?"

"The past is the past, Leese. It won't *come* back."

"This from you…"

"This from me."

"And what would this arrangement look like?"

"Days on, days off," he said. "I don't know. We'd have to talk about it. Hell, we did it once."

"We're not the same two people, Wil, not in miles or years. What about Kari Thayer?"

"This is bigger."

"What? You two have a falling out or something?"

His fingers drummed the table.

She said, "I should be getting back. Thanks for the coffee and the try, Wil."

"Wait, Leese. Bigger meaning that if Kari and I were or weren't, this would come before."

"All right," she said, "let's call it that. What if it meant laying off what you were doing? Your work?"

The still-molten core of it.

"Could be I need another yardstick."

"Could be?" she said. "I know you, remember?"

"And I know you. If that's what it took, yes."

Her eyes searched his face. "Don't take this wrong, but you haven't been drinking, have you?"

"Nope. Six days and counting. Meetings, if it comes to it."

For a while they just sat, the city's hum neither distant nor near. Finally she said, "How's the Tien thing progressing? Still a mess?"

"Coming to a head," he answered. "One way or the other."

"*Illigitimi non carburundum*: Don't let the bastards grind you. You're too good not to make it work."

"Nice thing to say, Leese. Thanks."

"I never had a quarrel with *how* you did anything, Wil, just with *what* you did. And I'll think about what you said. I promise."

They stood to get back, Lisa to the third floor northeast, Wil to map out the rest with Denny.

She said, "Thanks for thinking about it."

"It's going to be all right, Leese."

"Wil?" Pausing as he turned back. "Whatever it is you're into, be careful, will you?"

"Whatever it is I am, I'll do that."

63

THE QUEEN OF THE MISSIONS sat midway up the rise beginning to get serious about the Santa Ynez mountains. Its pink towers awaited the Angelus, its facade another snap of the camera. Yet on weekdays, the mission and grounds were largely empty, the inner gardens a sanctuary of *copa de oro* and agave, the occasional brown-robed padre tending to duties or shorts-clad tourist consulting the self-guided tour.

Wil pulled into a parking space off the fountain and was casting for Denny's Explorer, spotting it finally in the far lot, when his phone sounded.

"And where are we today, pray tell?" FBI Special Agent Al Vega.

"Close, but no cigar," Wil answered him. "You get wind of the brouhaha up here involving ATF? Or not, according to them?"

"Anywhere you are is a brouhaha," Vega said, and before Wil could respond, "That name you left with my secretary, Maccafee? Since we'd already nailed our quota of bad guys, I went ahead and ran him."

Wil watched a man lining up a picture of his wife and two children on the mission steps. "Ex-CIA," he said to Vega. "Three tours in Nam, Air America, Golden Triangle. The full monte."

There was a pause. "Somebody at the next urinal just happen to lean over and whisper in your ear?"

"A gang cop named Leong I met in San Francisco. Quite a mover."

Vega said, "Then yes to all the above. But what struck me was why our ATF friends booted him. Such as I could glean from their meager notes on it."

"That's why you get the big bucks, Al."

"Apparently your guy was taking money from not just both sides but anyone who had it. Downright embarrassing. Even some question he might have gotten his partner killed."

The family hustled back to their car and drove away. Next up, the wharf: wife and kids with town and mountains.

"The partner being one E. Russell Lorenz."

"You going to tell me you know what the E stands for, too?"

"Email. All sorts of them now."

"Emmett, wiseass. Not that it went anywhere. Nobody wanted to look bad."

"With Maccafee gone before they could nail him."

"If he wasn't offered the option first to avoid a stink," Vega said. And after a muffled *Be there in five*, "Anything else you need from your government? Wash your car Saturday?"

"Thanks, Al. And if it breaks the way I hope, you'll be hearing from me."

"Yeah, I was afraid of that," he said before hanging up.

Wil skirted the fountain, up the steps to the gift shop and museum. Purchasing a ticket for the tour, he walked through the spartan-living-quarters exhibits and out to the garden, where a couple strolled, a brown-robed acolyte worked a flowerbed. No Denny.

Wil poked his head into the restored church with its decorated beams and familiar smell of incense, stations-of-the-cross and sanctuary lamp, and saw him. He was by a statue of the Virgin, votive candles flickering in their red glass containers at her feet.

Crossing to that side, Wil slid into the pew beside him.

"You think Father Serra would approve?" Denny whispered. "Under the circumstances, I mean?"

"Any and all," Wil whispered back.

"Spoken like a true altar boy. If memory serves."

"It does. Go outside and talk?"

"I suppose it's more appropriate."

Wil slid out his side, looked back. "After you, my son."

"Just so the door doesn't land on me."

They exited, found a bench shaded by pepper trees near the old grave-yard with its skull and crossbones above the gate. Oleander and trumpet vine cresting the adobe wall.

"All right, here's the deal," Denny said. "The girl's mother wasn't there. Neither was the other woman you described. Just two old people and some kids running them ragged around a sandpile. Even in the language, they knew nothing."

"Damn."

"Not quite. Cruising around, I think I saw the blonde who dropped the CD on you. Miss Sun and Fun on the triplex balcony?"

"Amber. Your basic struggling student."

"Struggling to keep her top on," Denny allowed. "Is it me, or are girls different than when we were in school? What's the word I'm looking for?..."

"Earlier blooming might work."

"Hardly seems fair, does it?"

One of the Franciscans passed in a ball cap reading *Mission Santa Barbara*. After they'd exchanged nods and he'd left via the gate, Wil said, "Den, are you sure about throwing in on this? Leong isn't letting any moss grow looking for you. He was clear on that."

"Covered ground. Any idea how you want to play it from here?"

Wil looked up into the feathery pale green. "Before anything, we need to alert whoever's still around that we have what they want."

"Oh, they're around," Denny said. "Waiting to see how this thing with your guy Tien shakes out. Or if anybody happens to stumble onto Luc's code word. The feds, for instance."

"My thought, too. What they want is the disk. Or what we make them think is the disk."

Denny leaned forward. "Fill me in about that." Tapping his fingers as if in prayer. "Luc's hard drive can't be accessed why?"

"His erasure system," Wil said. "My friend at the Sheriff's said it was unsalvageable."

Nod, Denny's eyes drifting to the skull and crossbones. "Something else I'm not too sure about, Mojo."

"That being?"

"That being the reason you're still in it."

Wil blew a breath. "I'd thought it was clear. One, I need to prove somebody other than Vinh killed his brother. Two, I need to find out what happened to Jimmy and Wen."

"I didn't mean *what*, I get that," Denny said. "I mean given who you're playing games with, *why*."

"Not this again," Wil said.

"How valuable would I be if I didn't at least try?"

"Leave it at a promise I made."

"Ah. Save the client or die trying."

Wil watched the birds darting in the oleander. "It's what I do, Den. In a sense it's what I am. Depending on who you talk to, it may be all I am."

"I take it back," Denny said, shaking his head. "Save the client *and* die trying."

64

THEY SETTLED ON DENNY'S LEAVING to take care of business at a north county gun dealer's, Wil calling the television station where Gail Velarde now worked. After numerous rings, he was about to punch off and take his chances driving there, when she picked up.

"Velarde." Short, sharp, reporterish.

"Gail, it's Wil Hardesty."

"The recollection's vague," she said. "Who?"

"I need a favor," he told her. "A message I need delivered."

"Giving back to the community. Why didn't I think of that?"

"Vinh Tien's life may turn on it. The whole case."

There was a pause. From the Mission, the sloping of Spanish-style homes, trees, and streets, Wil could see the harbor masts, the now fogless islands with their etched canyons.

She said, "And you thought to do this how?"

"I don't know, an interview format, you asking the questions. Though we won't reference an item I'll be holding, the message will come through well enough."

"I get it," she said. "Subliminal, except to whoever it is."

Wil took stock, tried another tack. "Look, Gail, I know you're busy. But if this works, you'll have an exclusive."

"An exclusive, my," she said. Then, "Hardesty, you're so yesterday you don't even know it yet. I'd explain to you who uses whom in the news business, but I haven't the time." Adding before the line went to dial tone, "Try the newspaper. It's amazing the things you find in the personals."

Wil snapped the phone back onto his belt, sat there until it passed. Allowing she might have a point, even though it wasn't what she meant, he drove to the newspaper. By paying extra, he was able to secure three spots in the next edition and through the week, the message composed on the way:

FOUND:

On fishing trip. CD in mint condition. Crowning achievement for lucky buyer. Awaiting harmonic convergence @ ————.

To bypass the usual nutso calls, he listed his fax number and signed it *Jimmy*, handed it to the girl along with his credit card. He then went by the hospital, where he was told that although Vinh Tien was improved, he was seeing no visitors that day, doctor's orders.

Wil drove west to the Tiens, took Matt for a run, went home to wait.

He was in the supermarket checkout line when his phone rang: forty-eight hours of status quo later, Denny taking his shift at the fax machine. Looking apologetically at the checker and the woman in a pink top and matching nails behind him rolling her eyes, Wil punched in.

"Damned if it didn't work," Denny came on. "You decent?"

"Getting groceries," Wil answered. "Go."

"Okay. It reads, *Jimmy: Imperative we acquire lost item. Fax phone number to above, 4 p.m. today, so we may confirm. Serious Buyer.* Hot damn, huh?"

Wil glanced at his watch: three-twenty. Depending on traffic, enough time to get home for the call.

Denny added, "I have a confession, though. It came an hour ago. Figured I had the time, so I faxed the phone number back then called transmission places in the directory, thinking the fax might have come from one."

"Any hits?" Wil said as the woman in pink nudged him with her basket to pay attention. He nodded at her, threw in a smile.

The woman did not smile. Rather, she pointed at the checker, who was waiting with his total, the distraction almost causing him to lose the phone as he shouldered it to his ear, going for his wallet. Long enough to hear, "You still with me? How close are you to downtown?"

65

THE FAX LOCATION WAS AN OFFICE SERVICE PLACE: young men and women bustling around in chinos and blue oxford shirts as the copy machines hummed and collated and customers waited as though mesmerized. Those, that is, not glued to the rental computers.

Wil checked his watch: three-fifty-six. Spotting the phones a glass door this side of the rear entrance and the beamed-over breezeway, he found a copy machine he pretended to use. At four sharp, Tom Maccafee in khaki pants and light gray windbreaker entered via the rear. Glancing around he pulled a taped OUT OF ORDER sign off the phone nearest the door, crumpled it into his pocket, and picked up the receiver. Wil watched him dial his number, then face the wall and the door.

Denny must have picked up at his end because Maccafee was getting set to talk when Wil moved in close enough to press the Mustang into the man's kidney unobserved.

"Reach out and touch someone," he said.

The broad shoulders stiffened, eased. Maccafee said, "That supposed to scare me, Hardesty? In here?" Eyes still on the exit, phone to his ear.

"I'll take that," Wil said, reaching for it. "While you think about all you're going to tell me."

Maccafee handed it to him. "Would you believe I was halfway expecting you?"

"Sorry, but it's the other half I'm interested in." Then, into the receiver, "We're in place here."

"Ditto," Denny said into Wil's ear.

"How very military," Maccafee observed. "Who's that on the other end? Your dog?"

"What's up is this," Wil said. "You and I are going to leave by those doors and stroll out to where I'm parked. Then we're going to swap war stories while we wait for my dog to show up and drive us someplace more conducive to conversation."

"You didn't actually think I'd come alone, did you?"

Wil nudged the gun tighter. "If you mean Lorenz, who was afraid something had happened to you because you had enemies, she's dead."

"Ah yes, poor Inez. No, that's not who I meant. And are you really this dense?"

"Looks that way," Wil said. "Move, please."

"And if I don't?"

"Feds don't like people impersonating them, Maccafee, especially ones who get their agents killed." Then, into the receiver, "We're leaving to the car."

"So I heard," Denny came back. "You okay till then?"

"I think our man's more willing to take his chances with us than with the Justice Department." Turning to Maccafee. "That right?"

"Maybe neither."

"The door," Wil said with a gesture toward it.

"Speaking of thresholds," Maccafee said. "It might be useful to think about the one you're crossing."

"I keep hearing that, but here I am. Move."

"Not after I show you what's still drying in my pocket."

Knowing it was bluff and yet not, what would go wrong if it could, Wil said into the receiver, "It's probably nothing, but hold a minute." Then to Maccafee, "Thumb and index finger, nothing sudden or it's over." Feeling the bottom drop as Maccafee held up what he'd fished out of his windbreaker.

Son of a bitch.

"Change of plans," he said into the phone. "I'll have to explain later."

"Trouble?"

"Polaroid. Not good." Backing off the Colt.

"All right," Denny said. "Calm and control. We'll get our at-bats, but not if you play the hero. Hear me?"

"I'm hanging up now."

Feeling as if he were cutting a lifeline to the surface, he replaced the receiver, Maccafee turning to face him.

"You reset the safety on that thing?" he asked, and to Wil's nod, "Good, then it's my turn. Outside and to your left, the breezeway."

Wil complied and, with Maccafee behind him, saw an Asian man in glasses beside a planting of banana trees. He saw the walk devoid of customers, caught Maccafee's nod, then a blur of motion where the Asian man had been.

Hot white haze.

Red tile.

From far off: "Whoever your dog is, Hardesty, you're both out of your league. Now where's the disk?" Down on all fours, mouth open for the slightest air.

"Not here," he managed to gasp. "No place you'd find."

"Debatable another time," Maccafee said. "How's the disk still readable?"

"Sealed with tape. I checked."

"And saw on it what? Now, please."

"Numbers. Other stuff." Spitting drool.

Maccafee squatted and smiled. "You know, my friend could take you out and nobody'd notice, he's *that* good. And if you had residual doubts about me, think Inez."

"Fuck you," Wil spat. "Get you nowhere."

"I just hope you have proof that you were down there and this isn't some trick."

"Dedication plaque. Pried it off."

"More. What else?"

"Crown mark. Lower right base."

The smile broke Maccafee's face. "Then I guess we'll be in touch, won't we? And in the interest of not wasting any more time with dogs, I'll take your cell phone number."

Wil gave it to him; Maccafee wrote it down. Rising, he gestured to the Asian man.

Wil sensed the kick coming; still it felt delivered by a mule. For long moments he lay knees-up in a ball. Finally, he got to his feet and hunched toward the Bonneville, customers using the lot looking through him or away while the Polaroid of Mia Tien gagged and bound to a chair, eyes imploring and hair plastered to her forehead, burned a hole upward of his screaming ribs.

✆

Li Tien finished wrapping his ribs with strips torn from a sheet, taped it, and set the roll down, having noticed the injury as Matt leaped against him in welcome. Matt, sensing something major was wrong, now lay quietly beside her.

"She is my life," Li said, her voice barely audible, already having rejected the idea of adding Mia to Vinh's list of problems. "As Jimmy was his father's."

"For what it's worth, I can't see them hurting her," Wil said for her benefit, Li's bearing reminding him of wired-together rebar as he put his shirt back on. "They took her to exchange for what they want."

"And what they want is on the disk?"

"What they *think* is on it or they wouldn't have risked taking her," he said. "Which doesn't mean they won't carry out their threat."

Li's voice went further strained. "To harm her if we involve the sheriff…"

Wil tried his range of motion, the pain in his side at least mitigated. "In the end we'll have to, but yes. It depends on where they'll want to make the exchange."

She regarded him with dull eyes, river stones. "My daughter for this disk that is not real."

"In essence, yes," he said. "They have too much invested not to try." Wishing he felt as much confidence as ache.

Li Tien lowered her hand to Matt, her eyes not leaving Wil's. She said, "So if you cooperate with them, give them what they think they want, this will work?"

Wil felt the throb start in his left temple. "I can only hope, Li"

66

Eight-forty, trees and unlit roofs fading against a not-yet-starred sky. Lisa pulled into her drive and Wil met her at the porch.

"I thought that was your car," she said to him. Then, seeing his face, "I was at dinner with some people. What is it? Something bad?"

"Bad enough," he said. "I know how this may sound so soon after our talk, but I need a favor. A big one, Leese, not lightly asked."

"All right. You want to come in?"

"Thanks, but what I need probably means going back to the office."

He could see the fatigue, maybe some wine there, a little sag creep in when he said it. He saw her take a breath.

"Wil, I have to ask. Does this involve hurting anybody? Because I won't have it in my life. Not after all that's happened. Not after all that went into this."

"The opposite, Leese. If it works as I'm hoping."

"You can assure me of that?"

"Much as I can and be straight with you."

"I see," she said with a tired familiarity. "And how straight were you this morning? Or was that all part of the softening-up process? Turning on the charm until the ex-wifey melts."

Wil said nothing. Neither could he meet her gaze.

She said, "Tell me that this whatever-it-is wasn't at least on your mind this morning."

Door's open, he thought. *Save something while you're at it.*

Finally: "I can't do that, Leese. Because straight-up, it was."

"Well, at least you're honest about it. Goodnight, Wil."

He could feel it slipping away: them; the future; Mia and Vinh and Li; himself, in any definition of his choosing. He said, "Leese, I don't know how I can make it plainer. What I'm asking now has nothing to do with earlier. That's why I didn't bring it up, it wasn't the time. Plus I wasn't a hundred percent sure I'd need it."

"And now you are sure?"

"That's right."

"And tomorrow's not okay..."

"No," he answered her. "Tomorrow is decidedly not okay."

She broke it off, searched her bag for her keys, found them. Then said, "For some unknown reason I believe you. But I can't take any more standing in these shoes." Heading for the front door. "You can explain what you need while I change."

Lisa ran him out at midnight, promising the disk before office hours if he'd just *leave*, that he was bigtime getting on her nerves. He'd checked in with Denny and was headed home, sweating a call from Maccafee before the disk was ready, when his phone sounded.

Damnit. Not this soon.

"Yeah," Wil finally picked up.

"What did you think?" Maccafee said. "That I'd go away?"

"Before I agree to anything, Maccafee, I want proof she's alive."

"Hell, I was even going to suggest it," he said. "You want to make sure we're men of our word. Hang on a second."

Wil heard the receiver muffled, then, *"Hardesty?"* The ragged edge in her voice going right through him.

"I'm here, Mia, right here," he said. "I'm working on it."

"They told me my dad was dying, that my mom was at the hospital and I had to come when they said. They did something to my car."

Wil gripped the wheel. "Your dad's okay. And it isn't you they want, it's me, something I have. It's going to be all right."

"Hardesty? I'm sorry for what I said. I was wrong—about you and everything. Because I was mad, I—"

"*Shhh*, it's okay," he told her. "Just hang in. They love it when you're scared."

"You'll tell my mom that I'm—"

At the slap, her sharp cry, Wil nearly sideswiped a flatbed. Horn and swerve, the truck driver shaking his head in the oncoming lights as he sped off.

"*Mia?*"

"That was just a love tap to convince you we're serious," Maccafee's voice came on. "Nowhere near what we could do to liven up a long night."

Red-black-red. "Yours is coming, Maccafee. Count on it."

"Finally we're in agreement on something," the man said. "Now—you know West Camino Cielo off San Marcos Pass? The shooting range where the pavement ends?"

Time... "It's been awhile," Wil said. "I think so."

"Sure you do," Maccafee went on. "Shotgun side on the right, four miles in. Five a.m., as in hours from now. And Hardesty? I'll have people with phones along the way. Anybody with you and she's dead twenty minutes before you pull up. A long twenty, plus I'll be gone. *Comprende?*"

Wil racked his memory for the trap-and-skeet layout, managed only that the road leading to it was narrow and old and that the shotgun side was just off the ridge. The side overlooking the Valley rather than the ocean.

"I'll be there," he said.

"Good," Maccafee signed off. "Rise and shine."

67

"SMART," DENNY WAS SAYING. "Anyone hearing shots thinks it's just some early-bird member popping off." Black jeans and sweat-shirt; index finger on the broken yellow line running along the Santa Ynez range until it met solid road at the 3,000-foot level. "This a back way in there?"

Just off the phone with Lisa, Wil said, "Rutted dirt and rocks, more fire trail than anything." He'd had to tell Lisa they'd need the disk sooner than expected, that he'd be by at four to pick it up and to do as much as she could by then. And afterward, he hadn't wanted to hang up.

"The Explorer has four-wheel drive." Denny, working the action on the Mossberg pump he'd scored at the north county gun dealer's.

"You're talking twenty miles, Den—winding, exposed road, no speed. Sometimes there's a chain across it for no apparent reason."

"And? I've got a bolt cutter in the bag."

Wil gulped coffee he'd made them to stay alert. "With what time we have left and not knowing where they are, it's too much of a gamble. Better to go in off San Marcos, park near one of the bottom houses like it's yours and walk in."

"Your turf. If that's what it takes." Loading red double-aught shells into the Mossberg. "What about you?"

"Lisa's at four, the Pass by four-thirty. On site at five."

Denny swore. "No sooner than that?"

"The longer she has, the more authentic she can make the numbers look. It's not perfect, but it's worth it."

Denny set the safety, returned the shotgun to its nylon bag. "Meaning you actually believe your ex-wife's old client spreadsheets are going to fool these guys?"

"With luck," Wil said, "depends on who's scanning it." Thumbing .45s into the second of his spare clips, already having loaded .380 rounds into the Mustang's spares. "Maccafee's waited this long, it has to be the key to something for him. The exchange will be rushed and the sheets doctored to look real. As long as they don't look too closely."

"Said he, thinking like a Vietnamese gangster."

"Speak now, you got something to say," Wil said, more tired than annoyed. "Well?…"

"It's not the plan that worries me, Mojo." Chambering a .40 round into his black-finish semi-auto. Slipping it holstered into the bag and verifying two a.m. on his watch. "You mentioned there's a pistol and rifle range before you come to the skeet area?"

"On the left," Wil said. "Up a drive with a gate."

Denny said, "I'll check that, too. They might bivouac there. Can't have reinforcements crashing your party. And the way your guy Maccafee promised he'd be gone if you brought in the law smells like a slick to me."

Wil set his last clip on the table. "A helicopter's what I thought, too, but listen to me: There's still time to come to your senses on this."

"Just wave at your taillights, huh? And the girl?"

"The smart money says bail, Den. You know it does."

Denny paused from a hit of coffee and grinned. "Smart hasn't happened to either of us yet, why figure on now? Besides, I'd only sweat up a storm trying to sleep. And about the rest of your plan, are you going in with a wire?"

Wil shook his head. "Even if I had a wire, they'd find it. Same with a pocket recorder." And at Denny's glance at the loaded clips, the .45, and the Mustang: "They're to give them something to be concerned about. It'd look wrong if I came in light. Re the other, I have an idea I'm working on. Unless you know of a high-tech eavesdropping store that's open at this hour."

"Not with this deadline." Denny put a pair of night-vision glasses in the nylon bag, zipped it closed, settled the bag on his shoulder. "Good to go," he said. "I'll be as close as you need."

"You have to know what it means, Den."

"Damn straight," he said, "another dawn patrol where I keep your ass from grief." Turning at the door to add, "Which I intend to kick roundly if you don't watch it yourself."

Lisa was hunched over her computer. As Wil popped his head into the office, she looked up, fatigue evident in the monitor's glow. That and frustration.

She said. "If I only had two more hours..."

"You and me both," he answered her.

She drained the Diet Coke she had going. "Still not going to tell me why it's so important to have this now?"

"It's not my call, Leese. Over and out."

"Which means what, the world ends?" she flared. "Never mind, I don't want to know. Five minutes, okay?"

"Five minutes," he said. "Mind if I use the phone?"

She waved it off, returned to her spreadsheets. Wil entered the office next to hers, Bev's from the family photos. Facing the empty street outside, he punched up a line, dialed Frank Lin's number, got a tired female voice.

"Wil Hardesty, Andrea. Sorry for the hour, but I need Frank. It's important."

Murmurs, then Lin: "Four in the goddamned morning? You never heard of tomorrow?"

"Frank, it is tomorrow. And listen to me: I'm about to trade something for Mia Tien. Maybe some information that'll help clear her old man."

Pause. "Somebody has the girl?"

"That's right," Wil said. "Somebody who'll kill her if they smell you coming. Somebody I believe when they tell me that."

"All right, slow it down. I'm getting there."

"Here's the deal: If it goes bad, the guy you want is Maccafee, maybe in a chopper. He killed Lorenz. If you listen, I might be able to find out why. You might even be able to memo it."

"Memo what? A wire?"

"Not a wire, Frank, a phone call. Open line, that's why I'm calling you now," Wil said. "Pick it up when I call back, but don't talk into it. You might get us killed."

"Us..."

"Myself and Mia Tien. Are you getting this?"

"What's the trade?" Lin asked.

"Spreadsheets I'm hoping they'll think came from Luc's backup files. Records they missed when he crashed his system. Since you'll hear it mentioned, a CD."

There was a pause, then, "Spreadsheets...I fucking don't believe it. Lisa's in on this, isn't she?"

"No."

"Bullshit," Lin said. "Put her on, I want to talk to her."

"The phone, Frank. A little less than an hour."

"Don't be stupid, Wil. In an hour I can have people around you. *Armed* people."

"And who knows, we might even make it out...assuming you can get Rudy to go along," he said. "The call, Frank. And pray it works."

He was hanging up when he turned and saw Lisa in the doorway. For a long moment she looked at him without speaking, eyes shining in the hall overheads. Then she handed him the disk, stepped back into her own office without speaking, and shut the door.

68

T HE TWO-LANE THAT WOVE UP SAN MARCOS PASS and down the valley
side had until the late 1800s been a stagecoach route. Bandits with
Navy Colts and sawed-off double-barrel 12-gauges had waited in
its hollows and around its bends, beneath the ledges along its rutted
grades. Now they waited with cell phones, Wil thought, his headlights
rounding on the occasional turnout and passing lane, construction sites
and traffic cones awaiting the return of Cal Trans.

With the road largely free of traffic, he was able to make out eucalyptus giving way to oak and toyon and, through a curving slice of uptilted
sediment, ridgetop pines silhouetted like the parapets on a castle. The
chaparral rose with him—ceonothus and chamise, yuccas looking like
armless scarecrows—the asphalt switching back as Maccafee's imagined
eyes relayed his approach.

He wondered who else waited up there.

With luck, Denny.

Wil thought about the ex-ghost reappearing in his life, the feeling that
just maybe life decided you deserved another crack at it. But like this? At
five minutes to midnight? Their times together flashed: the boys of summer hellbent after outlaw surf mystique and the perfect break. Their lives
as men, then, how each had formed up along an invisible line. Of where
the line really was, and if it didn't meander at times.

He thought about the cancer eating its way through his friend.

Of the healer in Bali.

Of luck in general.

Then he was at his turn, into it and winding though the few houses tucked into Camino Cielo's base. Crossing a creek, Wil thought he glimpsed Den's Explorer angled in near a roofline, the oaks and bay trees as overarching as any tunnel. Here, the road was old and cracked, wide enough for two cars if one yielded. Through the mother of all hairpins, then past a grass-fringed drop-off, a row of mailboxes for the houses below the ridgeline.

By mile two, they were behind him.

He passed shed-sized boulders, outcroppings against the blue-gray dawn. Promontories offered glimpses of far-below lights and dark ocean, the islands as if outlined with a drafting pen. Just visible on the other side, the San Rafael Range and wilderness backcountry disguised desolate, parched, triple-digit heat. Hiker rescues and thunderheads, flash floods that could carry a camper van miles downstream or bury it to the windows in mud.

The road was rougher now, increasingly pocked and fissured. Half a mile ahead and on the right, Wil could see the roof of an outbuilding he knew was on the shotgun range. Four minutes till five. He punched up Frank's number on his speed dial; for a tense moment the call didn't go through. He dialed again, and a third time.

"Wil?"

Jesus God. "Fingers crossed, Frank. Almost there."

"Listen and hear, Wil. Wherever you are, it is not the OK Corral."

"So we hope. Just don't wander off."

Pocketing the phone, he passed the left-side road leading to the pistol and rifle range, then eased off beside a gray Yukon with smoked windows. The area beyond the gate was graded, relatively treeless, and overlooked the valley side. Seventy yards in, the cinder-block structure stood shut tight and backed by a low wall. Past it the competition areas were gridded out in concrete walkways: wood fence and an open-roofed shelter; two launching bunkers, low and dug-in; straw target backings against a berm on the left.

Pines on the hill behind it.

Silent...shadowed...empty...

Wil got out to chill air laced with blackened manzanita, no one around. Then the Asian man who'd nearly broken his ribs rose from cover, gestured with the machine pistol he now held for Wil to step through the gate's open frame. Wil did and the man followed, pointed beyond the cinder blocks to the fence and shelter, shoved Wil ahead.

They reached the shelter, around and out of sight of the gate and road. At which point Sonny stepped out with a pistol, then Maccafee in his gray slacks and nylon shell. In one fist Maccafee held the other end of a length of dog chain wrapped around Mia Tien's neck. In his other, which rested casually on her shoulder, he held a matte-finish military knife. Mia's wrists were duct-taped in front of her, her ankles in a short loop of it, a strip across her mouth. Her eyes were red with fatigue and tension, wide with something resembling relief at seeing Wil. Looking into them, he could feel his furnace thump to life, his blood course faster, a buzzing behind his eyes.

He took her hands in his, felt the chill in them.

"Did they hurt you?"

She shrugged, shook her head.

"Overall, you're okay."

Nod.

"It's going to be all right, Mia. A little longer and you're out of it." Behind her in the growing light he could see the shards of countless blown-up sporting clays like a field of orange wildflowers fanning out to the rim.

"Well?" Maccafee said to Sonny. "You going to greet our man or just stand there?"

As Machine Pistol backed up a step, Sonny waisted his own pistol and bent to the task. First he found the .45 in Wil's shoulder rig, then the tape around his ribs, grinning as he got a wince in reaction. Then down to the ankle gun—unholstering it and depositing both handguns in the rusting drum beside signs reading PLEASE PICK UP HULLS and THINK GUN SAFETY.

Pants pockets, then the ones in Wil's windbreaker: Pausing there, Sonny came out with the CD Lisa had worked on taped to Harmony's locker plaque in one hand, Wil's phone in the other. Holding up the CD and plaque, he looked at Maccafee as Wil felt time stop. Then, as quickly as it came, the moment passed. Switching the knife to his leash hand,

Maccafee extended his right for the articles, slipped the phone into his own jacket as Sonny waved a wand scanner over Wil's front and back and down each arm.

"He's clean," Sonny said. "No wires."

But Maccafee was fixed on the CD and case, checking for the backside crown mark after untaping it from the plaque he tossed aside. As though marveling it was there, he turned the case in his hands.

"All for this, fucking hard to believe," he said, holding it out for Sonny to take back. "Okay. Run it up and let's have a look. Not that we don't trust Mr. Hardesty."

Sonny reached into a gear bag behind him and came out with a laptop; turning it on and waiting a moment, he activated the CD drawer and backed in the disk. For a longer moment, he tapped keys, scrutinized the screen as Wil let eyes roam casually for signs of Denny.

He saw none.

"The hell is this shit?" Sonny glancing up.

"It's a Vietnamese poem," Wil said, angling a look. Catching Mia's eyes widen and swing his way, just as quickly slide off. "Jimmy's girlfriend wrote poetry. He must have left it on as a decoy, because the spreadsheets come after."

Sonny looked at Maccafee, who shrugged, Sonny returning to the keyboard to skip over, pause, then nod.

"Here," he said to Maccafee. "Grids and numbers."

"What we're looking for?"

Sonny scrolled, stopped again. "Can't tell. Before her, Luc never let anyone but Jimmy in the loop. But it looks like it."

Maccafee reached up and yanked the tape off Mia's mouth, Mia recoiling, gasping at the sudden pain. He forced her eyes down to the screen. "Lie and it's over, Missy," he said. "Here and now, and I *will* know: This is what you worked on?"

She took a long look, then in a hoarse voice, "Not worked on, entered, and not these specifically. The ones I did came later."

Good girl, Wil thought, not even a glance in his direction.

"What about the format?" Maccafee asked her.

"Yes. Now can I have some water?"

"All you want in a few minutes." Checking his watch.

"What about my father?"

"Ah, him," Maccafee said. "Can you say lethal injection?"

Mia's eyes widened and she was about to respond when Wil said, "We have a deal." A message for her in its sharpness: *Not now.* "Her for the disk, remember?"

Maccafee snorted. "Don't you hate when that happens. Or did you really think you were going to cross me and make it out the other side?"

"Straight trade," Wil said. "That was the deal."

The snort became a laugh, Sonny joining in. Then, "You two ever tried bungi jumping from a helicopter? That feeling of freedom without the annoying cord and harness?"

"Bag it, Mia, let it go," Wil said. Forcing his eyes from the mask her face had become. "He's about played out and he knows it."

Maccafee nodded to Sonny and the big man drove a fist into Wil's ribs. Curled against the fire and knives, the roaring in his throat that had replaced air, Wil saw Maccafee reverse his grip on the knife and under-hand it to Machine Pistol, who caught it easily.

"He'll drop as good cold as warm," he heard Maccafee say. "Do it."

Sonny grinned, stepped back to give him room, Maccafee jerking Mia that way. Machine Pistol set his gun on the numbered concrete walk and advanced a step. As he flipped the knife without looking at it, anticipation on his face resembling hunger, Wil caught movement from the shadow side of the bunker.

Suddenly the air blew apart and Machine Pistol was hurled backward as if by a cable. His body arched, flattened, arched again and lay there, one clawed hand scrabbling the ground.

For a moment nothing moved. Not even slow motion.

Then Sonny's pistol was out from behind his back and he was firing, driving Denny, who'd had to hesitate because of Mia and his angle in front of her, down behind the dug-in bunker. Sonny's rounds raised dirt and trap shards, ricocheted off the concrete, sang in the air. Wil lunged for the machine pistol, raised it, and as Sonny noticed and swung toward him, triggered a burst that sent the big man crashing off the wood fence and onto his face.

That quickly, it was over. Except Maccafee had his Beretta out and pressed under Mia's ear, his other arm crooked around her neck.

"Lose it or she dies," he said to Wil.

"Then what?" Wil said. "I drop you?"

"Everybody just stays calm until my ride comes."

Wil steadied on the machine-pistol grip. He said, "You have one chance of getting out of here with what you came for, and it doesn't involve her. We both know that."

"I don't think so."

"My word, Maccafee. She lives, you still win."

"Then who in hell would that be?" Squinting as Denny walked toward him; his jaw dropping as it dawned.

"Son of a bitch..."

"He's right, Mac, it's not in the cards," Denny said to him. "Neither are your two up at the pistol range."

"Well, fuck *me*," Maccafee said. Shaking his head in disbelief. "I heard the Australian got you...what's-his-name."

"Funny thing about that. Wil here got the Australian."

"Hold it, just hold it." Wil to Denny. "The whole time, you knew this meltdown?"

"It's a small fraternity," Denny said. Then to Maccafee, "Here's how this thing plays, Mac. Drop it and turn her loose, tell my man what he wants to know, you walk with the disk. Settle up with me another time."

"And if now suits me better?"

Shrug. "I dust you and hope I miss the girl. Either way, you wind up dead."

Maccafee glanced at Wil. "What about him?"

"Unlike me, he won't risk hitting her." Then, "Sorry, Mojo. Drop the piece and walk from it."

Running odds on the outcome and not liking them, Wil held on as Denny beaded the shotgun on Maccafee, hence Mia.

"Ain't asking, bro," Denny said. "Do it."

Whoever it was that Wil had known, knew, thought he knew, had disappeared. Eyes, body language, expression, voice. Or had that Denny Van Zant ever existed?

Wil set down the machine pistol and eased away from it.

"Now you, Mac, count of three. One...two..."

Maccafee backed off the hammer, regripped and grounded the Beretta.

Smiling, he turned Mia loose. "Your party," he said as Wil cut the tape off her hands and ankles with the K-Bar. "Enjoy the next few minutes. They're you're last."

69

"You all right?" Wil asked Mia when he'd straightened up.

"I think so," she said, massaging her neck with both hands. "God, I hardly know anymore. Who *is* that?"

"No one," Denny answered for him. "Now you, girl: The disk still in that laptop?"

Surprised, Mia just nodded.

"Good," he said. "Set it out there ten yards, the whole thing. *Move.*"

She did, walked back to stand by Wil. Denny said to him, "Go ahead and ask your questions. You don't like the answers, I blow it up."

Maccafee said, "The fuck are you doing? The deal was the disk and I walk."

"New deal," Denny said. "*Your* page, *your* book. Now or never, Mojo."

But Wil already was into it: a patchwork of fact, deduction, and guesswork. Saying to Maccafee, "You killed Luc because Under Heaven wanted the Dragons and said they'd cut you in if you delivered his records. Right or wrong?"

"That what you think I work for, some cut?" Maccafee sneered. "Try it as the *man.*"

Denny fired and a plume of dirt and shards rained down on the laptop.

"Goddamnit, *right. Yes.*"

Wil said, "You made Inez look like a suicide because she was going to turn you in. She was vulnerable at ATF and you got wind of it and used her."

"My ass," Maccafee said, and as Denny aimed again, *"All right!"*

A few more minutes, Wil thought. *Stay with us, Inez...*

He said, "More: She gave you legitimacy, protective coloration. You took her in by convincing her it was Luc's people who killed her father. That she could help bag Luc and save her career by getting Luc to admit it. But it was you who set up Russell Lorenz, wasn't it?"

"So what?" Maccafee said. "The sucker was going soft on me. Russ had been waking up with the zips we'd done over there sitting on his bed. Haunting him. He was going to ruin our side deals. That what you want to hear? And talk to me about loyalty and the feds in the same breath, I dare you."

Wil said, "Was Inez there when you killed Luc?"

"Miss Gung Ho? That's a laugh. Sonny cleared the crowd out for me. All but Robb and a gardener, or whoever that was. Not what you'd exactly call a match."

Mia cocked her head, then they all heard it: the distant throp of helicopter rotors. Maccafee was smiling now.

"Sorry kids. Hate to say it, but you're about done here."

Denny fired again, gouging closer to the laptop. He said, "Last chance before it's junk and you're running from them faster than we are."

"Fuck you. Put that thing down and we'll see who's better."

But Wil could see the sweat on Maccafee's face. "Jimmy," he said to him. "All of it."

The big man glanced toward the throp, swore, blew a breath. "Hardly matters, does it? Finally I had the kid turned by offering him Luc, all of that, the show under me. Then, *bam*, he gets a yen and turns back. Shame about it, too, the fucker was so sharp. Last November that was, before Inez."

Wil glanced at Mia, focused now on Maccafee. He said, "And the stuff about turning him because of Wen's status—that was for Lorenz?"

"Good old Inez," Maccafee said. "She tell you we were lovers once? God she did love it at fifteen. Fresh out of the box and under her old man's nose." A smile, as if seeing it again. "When I found her this time, I told her I was running down Russ's killer. She swallowed it with a spoon, even lent me his old badge. For her it was the chance to get back in the game, all the time thinking she had *me* on a string. Anyway, after Luc suspected the kid had taken off with his data, he really tightened down. Not even Sonny got close."

Wil pictured Lorenz holding out the handcuffs, saying to him, *"Once a long time ago. On me, it turned out."*

Fifteen she'd been… The cost of going along, let alone losing everything to her father's killer in the supposed search for him.

Wil clamped down on it, restarted. "Jimmy was headed to San Miguel to hand you the disk. What happened?"

Shrug. "Who knows? Cold feet, blood thicker than water, who cares? All I know is this storm comes out of nowhere, wind you wouldn't believe. And it's obvious the kid's thinking twice about it because he's headed back around even before it hits. So I cut him off, put a man aboard with a tow line. I couldn't have him bolting on us. But we didn't allow enough slack or something because next thing you know we're angling up this wave that flips his boat like it's a damn bait plug."

Seeing it, *Harmony* a trolled lure on a too-short line, Wil said, "What about Jimmy and Wen?"

The rotor sounds growing louder.

"What about them?" Maccafee shot back. "The girl's out in the water, they both are, and he's trying to keep her afloat, big as she is. Next one rolls them all under—my man, the boat—us with it if we hadn't cut the line. As it was, we barely made it back."

"Makes you wonder, doesn't it?" Denny said.

"Best speak for yourself," Maccafee shot back.

"Say I buy it," Wil said. "Why the island in the first place?"

"Why not? The idea's what got me in to begin with. National Park with sheltered landing spots, nobody much around, you could bring in anything and pick it up later. Besides, I liked the symmetry: fuck the government the way they fucked me," he said. "As far as Luc's cargo went, Jimmy would ferry it ashore in his old man's boats. That make you happy now?"

Wil could see the helicopter tracking the ridge on the valley side to stay less visible; he had to raise his voice to be heard: "Tell me one thing: Do you really think they're going to just hand you the Dragons? These people?"

Maccafee smiled. "Ask yourself who the Jap car honchos put in charge when they want American markets on a plate. People who think American, that's who. Money talks and bullshit walks and I deliver. They know that."

"They'll eat you alive," Wil said. "All they want is the disk. You must know that." Shouting now to be heard.

"And nobody's getting any younger, including me." Maccafee yelling back. "So I guess we'll see, won't we?"

The helicopter separated from its background. Wil could see it was an older Huey with the double doors on each side. Painted black, it hovered as if uncertain—a buzzard examining a downed deer for signs of life. Maccafee waved and the Huey settled in the firing field, orange and black shards gusting in its wake.

Three Asians armed with AK-47s stepped out with a fine-featured man in glasses, dark suit and tie, a light topcoat. Flanked by them, he cleared the still-spinning rotors and waited.

"You'll excuse me," Maccafee said. "Risk-reward and all that."

Denny raised the shotgun as he might a gate and held it against his chest. But Maccafee was already walking forward, picking up the laptop and handing it to the man in the suit. They shook hands and, after words and looks, the suited man gestured to the bodies of Sonny and Machine Pistol. Two of the guards shouldered arms, heaved the bodies into the helicopter.

As it lifted off, Wil could see the suited man concentrating on the laptop, Maccafee over his shoulder. He went to the trash drum, retrieved his .45 and the Mustang, Denny following the helicopter with his eyes.

"They'll be picking up those two at the pistol range," Denny said. "You think you can make the rocks over there with the girl?"

"The name is Mia," she said to him.

"What about you?" Wil said, ignoring it.

"Double your field of fire this way."

"Nice try," he said.

"How long do you think it'll take Charles Schwab up there to figure it out? *Go.*"

Mia said to him, "Would you really have shot me?" Seeing his look, then. *"Who are you?"*

"I told you, no one," he said in Vietnamese. "Now are you going to move out, or make me regret this whole thing?"

She'd made the rocks, had lost herself in them, when they heard the rotors grow in volume, saw the helicopter top the pines and head back toward them. They'd taken positions on either side of the cinder-block building, Wil with the machine pistol now as well, when the Huey pulled up about eighty feet overhead.

He could see the suited man gripping a handbar and looking down, the guards, Maccafee cocking a finger his way. Then there was a popping noise and Maccafee's grin was gone and he was in mid-air, rotating slowly as in a gainer, bouncing on the hardpan to lie motionless.

Wil shifted off him, saw the suited man staring down as if to commit him to memory. He saw the man's other hand leave his jacket pocket, saw the man hold the CD case out as if in disdain. Then it was spinning down, catching the light to smash apart not far from where Maccafee lay.

With a final look and a spoken command from the suited man, the helicopter canted forward and was gone, its sounds giving way to birds and the buzz of insects. And something else, the faint wail of sirens.

Denny turned from them. "Looks like I'll have to see you around, Mojo. Way it goes for some of us."

Fixing on him, Wil could see the kid he knew coming back. Partway stuck, but trying...trying. "Just like that," he said. "Bali Hai."

Denny grinned. "Wait'll you check out Uluwatu, the waves lining up. I'll send you directions."

"Good as in the bank," Wil said, feeling the same ache he'd felt watching his friend leave for Vietnam. The catch in his throat as Denny roared off, grinning in his Jeep, dust lifting in the late-afternoon sun, its warmth fading in the steps in front of Wil's Costa Mesa house.

"Just make sure you're there."

"Speaking of which," Denny said, grin fading, the sirens growing less faint. "I'm not sure I'd want that dude in the chopper looking at me like that."

"Maybe. I have a feeling the shit's flowing uphill for a change."

"Now there's a million-dollar thought. Hang on to that one."

For a moment they stood there. Then Wil was clapping him on the back, Denny doing the same.

"Go easy, huh?" Denny said.

"And you, Den." Feeling the heat in his friend. "Beat the bastard."

"Copy that, all right. All the way home."

Denny raised the nylon bag to his shoulder. And with a brief grin and a wave, he too was gone.

70

FOUR MINUTES AFTER DENNY VANISHED down a path only he could see, Frank and two other Sheriff's cruisers plus a green Forest Service truck pulled up at the gate. Wil had a chance to brief Mia, to check Maccafee to determine his phone had not survived either, when a serious-looking Frank confirmed that with a little help from the phone company they'd homed in on his signal.

"You piss me off," he said. "I hope you know that."

"Did you get it?" Wil asked.

"The gist of it. Some we couldn't hear too well, but we're working on it."

"The part about Maccafee killing Luc and Inez?"

"We got that."

"Jimmy?"

"Less so because of the helicopter, but salvageable. The feds should be turning cartwheels."

Something in his expression. Wil said, "You heard from them?"

"Last night, your friend Marotta. Somehow they cracked Luc's e-mail encryption." A wry smile. "Want to know what it was?"

Wil caught a glimpse of Mia drinking from a water bottle one of the deputies had given her, using some on her face and bangs. Seeing the resilience in her, the bamboo bend, he wanted nothing more than to tell her how proud her father and mother would be of her.

"I said—"

"Sorry, Frank. The encryption?"

"If I'm not interrupting here, the code word was 'brother,' the Vietnamese word for it," he said. "You believe that?"

They sat in Rudy Yanez's office: Frank Lin, Wil, an assistant DA named Sanders he knew in passing, Terry Leong, who'd caught an early flight from San Francisco, and a youngish ATF agent Marotta had sent up. Wil had just finished the latest run-through after twice up on the ridge: his involvement, Maccafee's recruiting Inez to take down Luc, killing her when she realized what he'd done out there. The Dragons and Under Heaven, Jimmy and Wen and all of that, the key being the disk and Jimmy's second thoughts about betraying his uncle. This after Lin's enhanced tape.

For a moment there was silence, then Yanez leaned back in his chair, his eyes first on Leong, then on Wil.

He said, "This dark angel the girl said looked like somebody she couldn't peg, an actor maybe. You say he was *not* familiar to you?"

"That's right," Wil said.

"Yet he was to Maccafee."

"They *seemed* to know each other," Wil answered with a glance at Terry Leong, who had a cigarette out and was rolling it in his fingers.

"Any idea how?" Leong asked.

"Paths having crossed, from what I gathered."

"I see," he said. "And this Mojo he kept referring to?"

Wil shrugged. "Slang for magic is all I know. Pretty generic."

Yanez said, "Then how'd he know you had questions for Maccafee?"

"An exchange was the idea behind the meet," Wil answered. "Maccafee knew I wanted information, so *he* must have."

"You said he flew off with them in the chopper," Leong said. "Considering who he wasted, don't you find that odd?"

Wil took his time so as not to appear too facile or deferential. "Maybe not when you think of him as part of Under Heaven's enforcement arm. Bringing Maccafee to heel."

Yanez leaned forward to unwrap a cigar from a pack, sniffing it before setting it in the copper ashtray. He said, "We've drawn up a sketch based on the girl's input. Detective Leong thinks he might fit for their Po Sang hit man. Sooner or later we'll see. Which might leave you, Hardesty, with the impression I think you're the cat's ass." Cold smile. "That would be a mistake. Frankly, most of what I've heard from you I consider deliberate obfuscation. Unfortunately, without Maccafee or your shooter, there's not much I can do about it."

Wil met the stare as the others watched obliquely. "You have my statement and my impressions, Lieutenant. Will that be all?"

Yanez looked at Sanders and Leong, who shrugged.

"For now," he said. "Not to imply for long."

The ATF agent, whose name was Elizabeth Kim and who'd been largely ignored by Yanez, said, "I have a question. Mr. Hardesty, you said you cooperated with Agent Lorenz. Was that by design?"

Wil looked at her. "If you mean did I catch on, no, not until late. Lorenz was real and professional and I liked her. And if she used me because Maccafee was using her, I guess I used them, too."

"Used in what way?"

"Two-way street," he said. "I'd been inside Luc's, they hadn't. I agreed to diagram the house, which helped get Luc killed, nothing Lieutenant Yanez doesn't know. For that she informed me that Jimmy had been pressured by somebody higher up the food chain."

"Higher than the United States government?" she asked.

Not another one, Wil thought. He suddenly felt sympathy for Rudy Yanez, old-school to new tricks the hard way. "Agent Kim," he answered, "Under Heaven may be your province, but even then I think she was having misgivings about Maccafee and a lot of things, including her father and you people. I just didn't put it together soon enough. I'll always regret that."

With nods to law enforcement, Elizabeth Kim said she needed to get on the road to brief Marotta, and the meeting broke up. Outside in the hall, Yanez and Sanders having a last word, Leong having preceded them, Frank Lin said, "Holy Mother. You don't care who you rub the wrong way, do you?"

"Thanks for going along with the call, Frank."

"What the hell, you're welcome. Thanks for not making a federal case of it. How are the ribs?"

"Don't remind me," Wil said.

Pause, a glance out the window. "You do know the DA authorized your client's release preparatory to waiving the charges?"

Wil said, "I didn't catch that. You mind saying it a little louder?"

"You were lucky. You do know *that*?"

"Never mind, I heard," he said. "It's okay with the hospital?"

Lin stopped at the outlet door, cracked the bar, pushed it open. "Turns out he only had a concussion," he said. "Look, give them my regards, will you? Tell them they might have more friends in town than they think."

71

Terry Leong stood by the glass doors, a black nylon briefcase over his shoulder. He was sucking air through the unlit cigarette and looking out into the parking lot.

"Thinking about a career move?" Wil asked as he headed for him.

Leong swung his way. "Waiting for a ride to the airport, actually."

"Come on," Wil said. "I'll run you out there."

In the car, Leong rolled the cigarette between his teeth. "Things move at their own pace down here, don't they?"

Wil grinned. "When's your flight?"

Leong checked his watch. "Seventeen minutes."

"Time to spare."

He was signaling for their overpass when Leong said, "You knew him, didn't you? And don't give me that wide-eyed look. Your dark angel and my Dao Hong shooter, one and the same."

"There some confusion as to what my words meant back there?"

Leong angled the cigarette to the side. "Obviously Yanez had his priorities, my shooter not being among them."

"Sorry, I wouldn't know." Concentrating on avoiding a fat-tired pickup, the kid driving it wrestling with a hamburger.

"For now. But sooner or later, he'll turn up," Leong said. "And I'll keep going until I have him—*that* you do know. And then I'll have you."

Wil shrugged. "As you say, your business."

They could see the airport now, people leaving the gate toward a tax-ied-up 737. As much to get him gone as there in time, Wil sped up.

"That is, unless you wanted to tell me something to make me change my mind," Leong said.

"Detective, I have no idea what that would be."

"Bullcrap—run it on somebody else. Whatever you did on that ridge, at least you flushed the bastards. And you gave me the guy in the topcoat. That counts for something."

Wil made the turn, pulled up at the terminal: Crape myrtle trees blooming pink, tile and bougainvillea, red-vested luggage checkers by the curb. Leong made no move to get out.

"He never went with them, did he?" he said. "In that helicopter."

Wil looked past him. "Your flight, remember?"

"I figure I'll start with your background, see who shakes out. You know how it works."

"Up to you. I'm here."

"Come on, Hardesty, a reason not to," he said. "Something I can take into account."

Wil met his eyes. "I guess you must like chasing down airplanes on tarmacs."

"That's too bad. For a lot of reasons," Leong said. "You'd have liked him, you know. Artie was a good cop and a good man."

He got out and closed the door, was adjusting the briefcase strap when Wil leaned over and rolled down the window, stuck his head through the opening to the smell of spent aircraft fuel.

"Leong? Take it or leave it: You can close the book on it, my word. He's going off to die." Pausing to swallow. "That's fucking all you get. And eight screaming kids are headed for your seat."

72

THEY WERE ON THE PATIO: Li, Mia, Vinh Tien without the bandage and the swelling, discoloration somewhat diminished, the stitches due out shortly. Matt and Wil sat sharing the sunlight and the bamboo, the fountain, the lapsang they'd brewed for him. Stroking Matt's ears, he said to Vinh Tien, "You're looking pretty chipper for a guy who took on the whole county."

Vinh's eyes stayed on the fountain. "Is that what happened? All I feel are bruises."

"Listen to him," Li said. "Already he's been out with Matt, throwing that thing he made us buy."

"Frisbee," Wil clarified. Then to Vinh, "Did they tell you what Luc was using as a code?"

"Our word for brother, yes." Shaking his head. "Who would have thought it? Not me."

They sat.

"Some daughter you have there," Wil said, nodding to her, half-expecting a comeback. "But I suppose you know that."

Mia touched Vinh's hand, and he regarded her and smiled. "What I keep telling him," she said.

"You show them what you copied off the disk?"

Mia nodded.

"Wen's poems, her gift to us," Vinh said, his words like the splash from a deep well, adding then, "Thank you. And for the plaque that went down with my son."

"More tea?" Li Tien covered for him.

"Rain check, thanks. I just stopped by to say congratulations."

As Li set down the pot, she smiled slightly. "Raymond Ky phoned from Los Angeles. He wants to appear with us at a victory press conference." Something in the way she said it.

"What did you tell him?"

They looked at Vinh, who said, "I told him he was fortunate he was not there when I was released."

"That, I believe," Wil said.

They sat.

"Well, then," Vinh dropped casually. "I suppose you'll be taking Matt with you when you go?"

Wil nodded. "He's my friend and I miss him." Noting the reaction from all three and thinking of a woman he knew at the animal shelter, of calling her on their behalf. "But not for a few days, if that's all right with you."

Nods all around. Li Tien head-gesturing to her husband.

"Ah," Vinh said, picking it up. "I can write your check now?"

"No need this minute. I'll send a statement." Taking the hand that was offered and shaking it.

Vinh Tien said, "Before you go, you must hear something I will say for all of us. We are grateful for what you did. We will never forget." And, with greater emphasis, "*I* will never forget."

A moment passed, a rustle of bamboo, a riff of water in the pond. "In the same spirit," Wil said, "I sometimes wonder if what we need isn't *more* forgetting, rather than less."

Vinh Tien's face darkened. "You say this after all that has happened? After what all of us have been through? What you have been through?"

Wil stood. "What else? You were right about the war, Vinh Tien, what you said about it killing the dead but once and swiftly. That was a gift then and it is a gift now."

73

WIL LEFT THE TIENS, ACHING FOR SLEEP. Instead he stopped for a late lunch at the al fresco grill in the old Cabrillo Pavilion Bathhouse. The building and its 1927 neo-Mediterranean architecture, the blue-and-white striped umbrella shading his table, the sailboats and beachgoers were like an impressionist painting you could lose yourself in.

Or was that find yourself?

He bought two large ginger ales with lemon wedges and ice to go. Taking a chance she might be home before dark, he drove to Lisa's, sat on the steps and watched a neighbor water his lawn, two ten-year-olds clack by on skateboards, a woman thinning out blooms as she cut fresh ones for the table. Things normal people did without thought.

At a quarter to six, her Lexus pulled into the drive and she got out with her briefcase. Burgundy skirt and lighter blouse with pearls, silver antelope pendant he remembered from a trip to Sedona a lifetime ago. She said, "Did I miss your call or something?"

"Nope," he said. Handing her a ginger ale.

Lisa set down the case, joined him on the steps.

"You and ginger ale," she said.

"Hope it's cold. I asked for extra ice."

"You okay?" Holding her glance. "You look a little ragged."

"I had to kill a man this morning. I'm trying to keep my mind off it.

Soon as I figure out how."

"I'm sorry," she said. "Is that why you're here?"

"In part, maybe."

She looked across at the neighbor now dragging the hose around the side of his house. "But you saved her, right? Mia Tien? Bev had the TV on, what's-her-name who did that magazine piece on you. I don't think she likes you very much."

"I'm an acquired taste," he said. "Not to remind you."

"Seriously, are you all right?"

"I came to thank you, Leese. She wouldn't have made it otherwise."

"And you?" After a pause.

"Fair chance of it."

She drank from her straw. The kids walked back up the hill with their boards and had another go at it. Across the street, the woman cutting flowers waved to her and she waved back, let her hand settle on the other in her lap.

She said, "Wil, I've decided something. I've decided there's no future in trying to account for risks every minute of every day. It's no way to live. The only thing you wind up with is your own fear."

On the premise that listening was good, he said nothing.

"I'm going ahead with this baby, if you're still interested. No, even if you're not. I mean, what's an extra chromosome, right?"

"Among friends?" he said. "Nothing, Leese. Nothing at all."

"Meaning you're still in?"

"I'm still in."

"Well…" Deep breath. "So what's next? You want to find some glasses for the ginger ale? Raise a proper toast?"

"The question is, do you?"

She glanced at him. "It'd be a start."

"Hard to ask for more than that," Wil said, getting slowly to his feet. Yet as if by magic the pain in his ribs had abated, the fatigue was gone to a new feeling, a kind of silent rising chord.

"Shall we?" he said, giving her a hand up.

By way of answer, she turned her key in the lock and pushed in the door, which creaked and crept back on its hinges but stayed open.

Burning Moon was printed by Capra Press in May 2003.

Two hundred copies have been numbered
and signed by the author.

Twenty-six copies in slipcases were also lettered and
signed by Richard Barre, Dennis Lehane,
S. J. Rozan, and G M. Ford.

ABOUT CAPRA PRESS

Capra Press was founded in 1969 by the late Noel Young. Among its
authors have been Henry Miller, Ross Macdonald, Margaret Millar,
Edward Abbey, Anais Nin, Raymond Carver, Ray Bradbury,
and Lawrence Durrell. It is in this tradition that we
present the new Capra Press: literary and mystery
fiction, lifestyle and city books. Contact us.
We welcome your comments.

815 De La Vina Street, Santa Barbara, CA 93101
805-892-2722; www.caprapress.com